'A most enjoyable time slip story'

'This was a really enthralling tale - hugely enjoyed it'

'I haven't enjoyed a book so much in years'

'I couldn't put this book down'

'A book to lose yourself in'

'Kept me in suspense all the way through'

KATHLEEN MCGURL lives near the sea in Bournemouth, UK, with her husband and elderly tabby cat. She has two sons who are now grown-up and have left home. She began her writing career creating short stories, and sold dozens to women's magazines in the UK and Australia. Then she got side-tracked onto family history research – which led eventually to writing novels with genealogy themes. She has always been fascinated by the past, and the ways in which the past can influence the present, and enjoys exploring these links in her novels.

When not writing or working at her full-time job in IT, she likes to go out running. She also adores mountains and is never happier than when striding across the Lake District fells, following a route from a Wainwright guidebook.

You can find out more at her website: http://kathleenmcgurl. com/, or follow her on Twitter: @KathMcGurl.

Also by Kathleen McGurl

The Daughters of Red Hill Hall

Kathleen McGurl

ONE PLACE. MANY STORIES

HQ
An imprint of HarperCollins*Publishers* Ltd
1 London Bridge Street
London SE1 9GF

This paperback edition 2020

1
First published in Great Britain by
HQ, an imprint of HarperCollins*Publishers* Ltd 2020

Copyright © Kathleen McGurl 2020

Kathleen McGurl asserts the moral right to be
identified as the author of this work.
A catalogue record for this book is
available from the British Library.

ISBN: 9780008389123

MIX
Paper from
responsible sources
FSC™ C007454

This book is produced from independently certified FSC™ paper
to ensure responsible forest management.

For more information visit: www.harpercollins.co.uk/green

This book is set in 11/15.5 pt. Minion

Printed and bound in Great Britain by
CPI Group (UK) Ltd, Croydon, CR0 4YY

For my husband Ignatius. This is the book you said I should write!

August 1838

The pain was unimaginable. Red-hot blades of it shot through Rebecca's furiously throbbing shoulder, pumping blood across the cellar floor. She lay in agony, groaning, but managed a glance over to where Sarah lay, just a few feet away. The other girl was also bleeding profusely from a shot to her abdomen. The pair of pistols lay discarded on the floor where they had been dropped, their ruby-encrusted stocks glittering in the candlelight.

Rebecca felt strangely detached from the scene. She watched as blood from her shoulder flowed across the floor to meet with the pool that spread from Sarah's skirts. Their life forces mingled and combined, indistinguishable from each other. It was fitting, she thought, that two women who'd been so close in life should be together as they died. For she was certain they would both die from their wounds. It was better that way. They couldn't both live. Not after all that had happened between them, after all the hurt they had caused each other.

Sarah moaned in pain, and her eyes flickered open. Rebecca stared at her across the cellar and a wave of compassion flooded through her. She reached out a hand towards her one-time best friend and adopted sister, causing her pain level to escalate yet further. She watched as with a huge effort Sarah shifted her position and reached out too, until their fingers touched. One last heave and Rebecca was able to entwine her fingers with Sarah's. She felt a weak squeeze in return, telling her the gesture was appreciated. Sarah groaned and sighed, and Rebecca watched as her adored sister's eyes closed. Only then did she allow her own eyes to close as she slipped into blissful, pain-free darkness.

***

Spencer, the butler, had heard something. He'd been putting away the glassware used at dinner when he heard the explosion. It sounded like a shot, or rather two shots, coming almost simultaneously. He hurried along the servants' corridor in search of the source of the noise, and spotted the door to the cellars standing open. It should have been locked shut – they kept a valuable store of wines down there. Spencer snatched up an oil lamp, rushed down the cellar steps and made his way through the labyrinth of rooms and tunnels that made up the cellars of Red Hill Hall. 'Hello? Is anyone there?' he called, his voice sounding shaky and nervous even to himself. Another door was standing open – the one that led to the coal store. From there a flight of steps led to the grounds of the hall. Someone could have come in – and then escaped – by that route.

At last, in an empty room beyond the wine cellar, Spencer found the source of the noise. He gasped as he angled the lamp-light onto the two mounds on the floor and recognised them as Miss Rebecca and Miss Sarah. His adored Sarah – that wonderful, vivacious girl who could light up a room with her smile. Their fingers were linked together, as though they'd been holding hands when they were shot, perhaps trying to save each other.

'Oh my word, girls, what has happened?' he muttered as he approached. His foot kicked something, and looking round he saw one of the old master's duelling pistols. The other one lay close by as well. He cursed himself for not keeping the pistols under lock and key. Someone had clearly got in, probably via the coal store, stolen them from where they were kept in a cupboard in the first cellar, and shot the two beautiful young ladies, whose whole lives had been ahead of them. But why had the girls been in the cellar? He shook his head. Now was not the time to ponder such things. He knelt down in the pool of still-warm blood and checked for signs of life. One of them had no pulse. There was nothing he could do for her. But the other was breathing and had a faint, if erratic, pulse. If he acted quickly, maybe, just maybe, she could be saved

CHAPTER 1

April 2015

Not another fossil. Fossils were so darned boring. Gemma sighed as she pulled what must be at least the thirtieth ammonite today from the dusty box. She loved her job at Bridhampton's little museum, cataloguing their extensive archive, but really, she had seen enough fossils to last her a lifetime. It was inevitable, she supposed, being so close to the Jurassic Coast in Dorset they were bound to have plenty of dinosaur bones and ancient marine creatures in the collection. But fossils did nothing for her. She preferred more recent history and human stories.

'Cup of tea for my hard worker?' Roger, the museum curator and her boss, put his balding head around the door.

Gemma nodded. 'I'd love one, thanks.' Poor Roger. He was practically another fossil. Well, that was unfair – he was probably only about ten years older than her – but he acted as though he was from the nineteenth century. Or before. She grinned to herself as she measured the ammonite and typed its details into the computer catalogue. He was old-school, that was for sure, but he was also the nicest boss she'd ever had. After leaving university with a history degree and no idea what she wanted to do with her life, she'd had a number of jobs in quick succession until two years ago she'd struck lucky here at the museum in her home town of Bridhampton.

By the time Roger returned with her tea, Gemma had finished cataloguing the contents of the box and was packing it up again to return it to its shelf in the museum basement.

Roger put the tea on the desk beside her, and moved some papers off a chair so he could sit down. 'Anything interesting in that one?'

'Half a dozen ammonites. One's nearly a foot across. Weighs a ton.' She closed the lid of the box and taped it up before Roger could start poking around in it. He did have a habit of wanting to pull things out and examine them, making the whole job take so much longer.

'Oh well. Maybe we should use them in a Jurassic Coast display. What do you think?'

Gemma stopped herself from pulling a face. 'We could, I suppose, but then the museum at Lyme Regis covers that so much better. Everyone goes there because of the Mary Anning connection. I think we should stick to other topics – human stories and Victorian themes.' So much more interesting, she almost added.

'You're probably right.' He smiled at her, and heaved the sealed box off the table. 'I'll fetch you the next one, then, to get started on once you've had your break.'

He looked quite sweet when he smiled, Gemma thought, as she watched him go through the door that led to the basement stairs. She resolved to be nicer to him in future. Poor bloke was probably lonely. He lived alone with only a cat called Michael for company. Who on earth calls their cat Michael, she thought, not for the first time.

Roger returned a few moments later bearing another cardboard box, this one festooned with cobwebs. He dumped it on the table and brushed the dust from his pullover. That was another thing. Who, these days, wore a hand-knitted jumper over a shirt and tie? Maybe she should have a gentle word with him about his fashion sense. If he ever wanted to get himself a girlfriend he'd need to first get himself a new wardrobe.

'Here you are, then,' he said. 'Hope there's something more exciting in that one. It was from aisle four, shelf three, if you want to make a note.'

'Thanks.' She jotted down the location code on her notepad, and slit open the tape across the top of the box, as Roger left her to return to the museum front desk. It was a Wednesday – their quietest day. Term time but no school parties booked, so they weren't expecting many visitors beyond a few pensioners who were generally more interested in the tea and cakes they served in the museum café.

Tea finished, she pulled the next box towards her and opened it up. Inside was a crumpled-up piece of fabric – dark green cotton. She held it up – it was a shirt, smelling musty and dating from the 1970s if the collar was anything to go by. The label said *St Michael*. Great. A Marks and Spencer original, of no value whatsoever. Why on earth was it in this box? She threw it into her box of rubbish. It was amazing how much rubbish she had come across – usually screwed-up paper and sweet wrappers chucked into the boxes of artefacts. She looked in the box again. There was a layer of yellowed newspaper, which she pulled out and inspected. *The Times*, from January 1972. That tied in with the date of the shirt, then. It probably indicated the last time this box had been opened. She threw that into the discard pile as well.

Finally, at the bottom of the container, was a wooden box. It measured about two feet by one, and was four or five inches deep. It appeared to be made of mahogany, and was inset with an elaborate parquetry design. This looked more promising! She slipped on a pair of thin cotton gloves and lifted it out of the cardboard box. Clearing a space, she laid it on the table, and investigated its fastening. There was a brass hook and loop clasp, but thankfully no lock. She opened it up and gasped.

'Wow. Just, wow.' She looked around to see if Roger was in earshot, but he'd left the back rooms. Should she call him or wait and show him when he came back? He tended to pop into the back room every hour or so to see how she was getting on. She looked back at the contents of the box. No, this was too good to wait – he needed to see this now. She left the room and went through to the front of the museum to call him.

He came trotting after her. 'I take it that box had something better than ammonites in it, then?'

'Oh yes. Take a look.' She indicated the box, and he gasped too.

'Duelling pistols. And what an elaborate pair! Take one out – you've got gloves on.'

She carefully extracted one from its moulded place in the box. It was a beautiful item. 'Gorgeous! Look at that silver work, and are those rubies on the handle?'

'It's called the stock, not the handle,' Roger said. 'Yes, I'd say mahogany trimmed with silver, and set with rubies. I'll have to have a closer look with a magnifying glass to be certain of the materials. A very fine piece.' He looked at the case. 'And we have the pair, plus the ramrod, and that little flask there was probably used to hold the gunpowder.'

'Yikes, hope there's none in it now!' Gemma squealed in mock horror.

Roger smiled indulgently and slipped on a pair of cotton gloves. He took the little flask out of the case and opened it. 'Empty. We're all right. I would guess those other slots in the case would have held the shot, probably lead. And maybe a cleaning brush. But how wonderful to have the pair, in such a lovely case! I think we'll have to get these out on display.'

'Do you think they were ever used in a duel?' Gemma asked. It was a sobering thought – she might be holding a gun that had killed someone.

'Who knows? They look very decorative. They could have been commissioned and bought just for show. Duelling pistols were often owned as a kind of status symbol. It's unusual to have jewels in the stocks like this. And see the inside of the case's lid?'

Gemma looked. It was beautifully painted with a scene showing two eighteenth-century gentlemen engaging in a duel, standing stiffly, their pistols pointed at each other, tricorn hats and flared coats giving a hint as to the era. To one side of the picture was a spreading oak tree, and two other men stood, holding the reins of black and bay horses. It certainly looked as though the case was designed to sit open, with the interior on display. Gemma found herself hoping that the pistols had never been used in anger.

'Well, I'll leave you to add that to the catalogue,' Roger said, as he stood up and pulled off his gloves. 'Don't put them away afterwards though – leave them on my desk. I'd like to take a closer look after we've closed for the day.'

'Sure, will do.' Gemma grinned at Roger as he left, then turned her attention back to the case. She lifted out the other pistol and the ramrod, and started making notes about the case first. As she turned it over she noticed a yellowing label stuck to the base of it. There was writing on it, in a spidery hand: *Bequeathed by Mrs A. Maitland, 1923. These pistols were the ones used in the infamous shooting at Red Hill Hall.*

Gemma felt a shiver run down her spine as she read the words. An 'infamous shooting'! – but not so infamous it was still remembered in 2015. Red Hill Hall – that rang a bell. She racked her brains trying to think where else she'd heard that place name recently. And then it came to her. Her boyfriend Ben's sister Anna was getting married soon, and the invitations had arrived in the post a couple of days ago. The wedding and reception were to be held at Red Hill Hall. It was a country house hotel about five miles out of town.

Who'd been shot, when, and why? She had an overwhelming urge to research everything she could find about the shooting. If it was described as 'infamous' by whoever wrote the label on the bottom of the pistol case, then it must have been covered by newspapers of the time – whenever that was. She turned to the museum's computer, opened up a Google search page and started typing 'shooting at Red Hill Hall'. But before she could press the Enter key Roger came back.

'Gemma, could you take over at the front desk, please? The café's short of milk and I told Jean I'd pop up to the Co-op to get some. Won't be long.'

'Sure. Coming.' She shut the laptop's lid and left the back room, locking the door behind her so that no visitors would be tempted to wander in. The research would have to wait until later.

As it turned out, she did not get a chance to return to the back office that day. A coach party arrived and she was kept busy at the desk and in the small souvenir shop until closing time. All afternoon thoughts of the pistols ran through her head. Had someone been killed in this shooting? She supposed so – otherwise why would it have been described as infamous?

'Roger, have you seen what's on the underside of the pistols' case?' she asked, as they tidied the little museum shop after closing time.

He hadn't, so she told him. His eyes lit up. 'Well, I haven't heard of this shooting but it certainly sounds like something worth investigating. Feel free to do it here; perhaps start searching online tomorrow?'

'I was hoping you'd say that,' she said, grinning at him. Something to look forward to at work tomorrow – infinitely better than measuring and describing endless ammonites for the catalogue!

***

'You look lovely tonight,' said Ben, kissing her as he stood to greet her in the Men At Arms pub, just a little way up the high street from the museum. It was her favourite pub – dark and cosy, old and full of character. 'We've bought a bottle of Sauvignon. Nat chose it. Hope that's all right for you?'

'Fine, thanks. Hi, Nat,' said Gemma. Actually she was more in the mood for a pint of bitter but as Natalie had got there first it seemed reasonable for her to choose the wine. Ben was so easy-going he'd drink anything. They were sitting at a table in a snug, its walls covered with dark wood panelling and hung with prints of Victorian country houses. She pulled an upholstered stool from under the table and sat down.

'Cheers, then,' said Nat, pouring her a glass and handing it over.

'Cheers!' Gemma clinked her glass against the other two and sighed happily. It was one of her favourite times of the week – being out for the night with her boyfriend and her best mate, the two people she loved best in the world. The three of them were inseparable, and had been ever since she and Ben had got together. Actually, she and Nat had been practically joined at the hip since school days.

'Gemma, did you get Anna and Jake's wedding invitation?' Ben asked her.

'I did. Can't wait! It's not till June though, is it?'

'Nineteenth. I got one too. We'll have to go shopping for new frocks,' Nat said, with a wink at Gemma. 'You'll need something really smart. You can't wear your usual tatty jeans and a fleece to a wedding, you know.'

'Cheeky! Of course I'll get something nice.' Gemma gave Nat a playful punch on the arm. Anna, she hoped, would one day be her sister-in-law, if only Ben would get around to popping the question. And if he didn't, well, next year was a leap year, so she'd do it herself. They'd been together seven years. It was time to make an honest man of him.

She suddenly remembered the wedding venue. 'Hey, Ben, have you ever been to Red Hill Hall?'

'Where?' He looked blank.

'Where Anna's getting married, you dolt.'

He looked sheepish. 'Oh yes, of course. No, never been there. Have you, Nat?'

'No. It's only just reopened under new management, hasn't it? I think it was closed for years before then. I had a look at the website. Looks like a gorgeous setting for a wedding – all sweeping staircases and high-ceilinged ballrooms.' Nat winked at Ben.

'We'll have fun there, won't we – playing at lord and lady of the manor. Gemma, you could be my paid companion.'

'Aw, why can't I be the lady and you the companion?' Gemma pouted.

Nat laughed. 'You'll need a *very* expensive dress if you want to upstage me, my dear. I intend buying something really fabulous. I'll look amazing. *Amazing*, darling!' She fluttered her eyelashes at Ben, who grinned and blew her a kiss, but caught hold of Gemma's hand under the table and gave it a squeeze.

Gemma smiled. Nat liked to play the prima donna and Ben would play along. It was part of their group dynamics. She had no doubt that Nat would look fantastic, and no doubt better than she would herself. Nat was a beautician, currently working at a salon at the far end of town. She'd had many jobs over the years, never staying at any of them for very long. She'd only started at the salon a few weeks ago. Gemma hoped she would stick at it a bit longer than she had at the others. Poor Nat. She'd always struggled finding a job she liked. Before Gemma started working at the museum the two of them had often gone out drinking together to drown their sorrows about their rubbish, dead-end jobs. There was no better person than Nat when you needed a sympathetic ear. She always understood better than anyone else, because she'd been through it all herself.

'Anyway, the hall sounds lovely,' Gemma said. 'I'll definitely take a look at their website. I came across something at the museum today, relating to Red Hill Hall. Bit of a coincidence, having had the wedding invitation this week as well.'

Ben looked at her with interest. 'What did you find?'

'More fossils?' Nat rolled her eyes.

'Guns. Well, duelling pistols. Apparently they were used in

a shooting at the hall.' Gemma picked up the half-empty bottle and topped up everyone's glasses.

'Oh my God. Don't tell Anna that – she'd have a fit if she thought someone had been murdered at her wedding venue.' Ben took a sip of his wine.

'Duelling pistols? So was there, like, a duel there? Does a duel count as murder?' Nat looked as though she wanted all the juicy details.

'Well I don't know yet, whether it was a duel or even if anyone died. I came across the pistols – very ornate ones – in their case, and there was a note saying something about an infamous shooting. Tomorrow's job is to research it and try to find out what happened.'

'Wow. Your job is so much more interesting than mine. Most excitement I get is to work out lifeguard rotas and arrange five-a-side tournaments for school kids.' Ben's job was manager of a sports centre. He shook his head and laughed.

'I don't know. I'd rather do what you do than faff around with dusty relics all day like Gemma does.' Nat flashed him a look. 'I reckon my new job's the best one though. All day playing with make-up and doing people's nails – like being a little kid at your mum's make-up drawer. I love it. Well, I would love it, if only Bitchface Boss wasn't always on my case.'

Gemma smiled but didn't say anything. How she and Nat were such close friends was a mystery. If she was honest, they didn't really have a lot in common, other than their shared memories of course. Nat liked gossip mags, reality shows and loud, modern nightclubs. Gemma preferred historical novels, costume dramas and quiet, ancient pubs. And she'd been with Ben for seven years whereas Nat'd had a string of boyfriends, none of them lasting more than a month or two. Still, ever since starting secondary school at the age of eleven they'd been best friends. They'd been put next to each other in maths class, and Gemma had whispered the answer to a question when the teacher put Nat on the spot. In return Nat had picked Gemma first for a netball team, and the two had become inseparable. Over the years they'd each spent time doing what the other one liked, and somehow their friendship had worked and indeed, had deepened. She would do anything for Nat, and knew Nat would do anything for her as well. Opposites attract – that was as true for friendships as it was for romance – and she and Nat were a great example of that rule.

'Hey, I know!' Nat turned to Gemma, her eyes shining. Gemma knew that look. It meant Nat had hatched a plan, and it was probably something Gemma wouldn't feel completely comfortable with. 'Why don't I do your hair and make-up for Anna's wedding? As the girlfriend of the bride's brother you're quite an important guest, you know. You'll have to look stunning, but not so stunning you upstage the bride of course. I could put your hair up, in some sophisticated up-do, and shape your cheekbones, even out your skin tone, accentuate your eyes. Oh there's so much I could do to improve your looks, Gemma! Do say yes!'

Gemma squirmed. Nat knew how she felt about too much make-up. She was happy wearing her usual subtle bit of mascara and lip gloss but anything else made her feel deeply uncomfortable. As well as making her skin feel itchy. She remembered how they'd experimented with make-up in their early teens, including going through a short-lived Goth phase of deep purple lipstick and heavy black eyeliner. Perhaps that was what had put her off make-up. 'Well, maybe my hair, but I'm not sure I'd want it up...'

'I love your hair left loose and long.' Ben kissed the side of her head and she smiled at him gratefully.

'Oh, well, if you don't want me to, I won't bother. Your loss.' Nat drained her glass and smiled at Gemma. 'More wine? It's your round.'

CHAPTER 2

May 1830

Rebecca couldn't remember a time when Sarah hadn't been there. All her life, all ten years of it so far, Sarah had been at her side, her best friend, her confidante, her playmate and her partner in crime. Today was no exception.

'Look at the sun shining!' Sarah said after breakfast, when the two girls were supposed to be going upstairs to the schoolroom for their daily lessons with the governess, Miss Albarn. 'It'd be wrong not to go out and enjoy it. Who cares about French, drawing and grammar? Rebecca, we must go outside and have a run around the gardens. Come on!' She caught hold of Rebecca's arm and tugged.

'But Miss Albarn will be waiting for us. We can't, Sarah!' Rebecca was halfway up the stairs, and almost overbalanced as she tried to pull her arm free from Sarah's grip.

'Miss Albarn can wait. It's the first sunny day for months and there's a blackbird's nest I want to show you. Come on!'

As usual, Sarah won the battle and Rebecca followed her outside, through the kitchen garden and into the park beyond. In a hedgerow that marked the perimeter of Rebecca's father's estate, there was indeed a blackbird's nest. The tiny, naked baby birds cheeped loudly, their beaks open wide in expectation of food.

'What do they eat?' Rebecca asked. Sarah was almost a year older than her, and as far as Rebecca was concerned, she was the font of all knowledge. Miss Albarn was all very well for piano and drawing lessons, but if you wanted to know something about the real world, Sarah was the person to ask.

'Beetles,' Sarah said, with conviction. 'If we found some, we could drop them in their mouths.'

'Where would we find beetles?'

'There are woodlice in the stables. Those will do.'

Rebecca stared at her friend. 'How can we carry woodlice all the way back here? In our hands? Ugh!'

'We can take the birds there.' Sarah reached into the hedge and grasped the nest with both hands. As she pulled it free it fell apart, and the baby birds tumbled into the depths of the hedge.

Rebecca felt a pang of sorrow for the tiny, helpless creatures. 'You've broken their home. What will their parents think when they come back?'

'Serve them right for leaving their babies alone. Pah! They've fallen right down now. I can't reach them.' Sarah flung the remains of the nest on the ground and started running off across the park. 'Come on. Let's find something else to do. Race you to the climbing tree!'

Rebecca peered into the hedge and whispered an apology to the little birds, then gathered up her skirts and began running after Sarah. They weren't allowed to climb the climbing tree – ever since Sarah had fallen and had only been saved from broken bones by her skirts catching in the lower branches and tearing. Sarah's mother, the housekeeper at Red Hill Hall, had been furious. Rebecca had stood with her head bowed while Mrs Cooper shouted at Sarah. Mrs Cooper had been cross with her too – Rebecca could tell, but she'd not dared to shout at the daughter of her employer. There were some advantages to being the child of the master of Red Hill Hall, Rebecca had learned. Sarah, as the daughter of the housekeeper, had some perks – she shared a governess with Rebecca and had the run of the house and garden – but she was never allowed to forget that she was of a lower class.

Sarah was already at the climbing tree. It was a large overgrown flowering cherry in full bloom. Sarah jumped up to catch hold of one of the lower branches and hung off it, shaking blossom confetti all over both of them. Rebecca laughed and spun around, her arms outstretched and her face tilted upwards. 'It's raining petals!' She grabbed a whole blossom that had been shaken loose and tucked it in her hair. 'I'm Titania, Queen of the Fairies!'

'You are no such thing, Miss Rebecca. You are a naughty girl who has skipped her lessons for the morning. As are you, Miss Sarah. Now brush yourselves off, and come indoors, the both of you. I shall have to mention this to Mr Winton.'

Rebecca looked at Miss Albarn in alarm. They'd been having so much fun. Why did the governess have to come and spoil it all? She pouted, and began brushing the petals from her clothes.

Sarah let go of the branch and landed with a thump on the lawn. 'Sorry, Miss Albarn. We were on our way but Rebecca wanted to come and play in the tree as it is so beautiful when it is in full bloom. I wondered if perhaps we could make some watercolour sketches of it this afternoon? That's if you haven't already planned a lesson, of course.' She dropped a pretty curtsey, eliciting a smile from the governess.

Rebecca watched in dismay. It wasn't the first time she'd gone along with something Sarah had suggested, and ended up in trouble for it. And why had Sarah said it was her idea to play in the tree? It wasn't fair. But she knew that if Sarah shouldered the blame, she'd be punished. She'd probably be made to stand in the corner of the schoolroom all day, or perhaps miss her supper. Whereas apart from the few stern words Miss Albarn had already voiced, Rebecca would receive no further admonishment. Another advantage of being the daughter of the master. Still, it hurt to always be the one to take the blame. Miss Albarn must think she was such a bad girl. And she wasn't sure how much of it went back to her father and mother.

'We might come and sketch the tree, Miss Sarah. Or we might not. For now, we are going inside to read some poetry. With your poor mother taken so poorly, one would have thought the two of you would have more decorum than to be running around the park.'

'Miss Albarn, whose mother is poorly?' asked Rebecca. Oh please don't let it be hers, she thought, though the idea of Mrs Cooper being sick was not a good one either. Sometimes Mrs Cooper felt more like a mother to her than her own mother, who was often too busy to take much notice of her.

'Sarah's. Poor Mrs Cooper. It's come on so suddenly, this time.' Miss Albarn dabbed at her eye with a handkerchief.

'Is it Mama's chest again?' Sarah asked.

'Yes, the poor dear. She can barely catch her breath. Mr Winton has sent for the doctor. She'll be all right I'm sure, but in the meantime, we must not let her ailment distract us from our lessons. How am I going to make young ladies of you both if you insist on missing lessons and running off around the park like wild village children? Now come along, quickly.' Miss Albarn tucked her handkerchief up her sleeve and marched across the lawn towards the house, the hem of her grey gown dragging cherry blossom in her wake.

***

For the next week the girls were not allowed to leave the house. Mrs Cooper was seriously unwell and it seemed the entire focus of the household was on caring for her. The butler, Spencer, had to take over many of Mrs Cooper's responsibilities, delegating as much as he could to the cook and upper housemaids. Dr Millbank was an almost constant presence in the house, and two nurses had been employed to tend to Mrs Cooper day and night. Sarah was allowed to visit her mother once a day, for a few minutes only, for fear of tiring her too much. On these occasions Rebecca lurked in the doorway of the sickroom and watched with tears in her eyes as Sarah sat at her mother's side, clutching her hand and imploring her not to die, while the nurse hushed her and dabbed at Mrs Cooper's forehead with a cool, damp cloth. Rebecca couldn't help but imagine how awful it would be if it was her own mother lying sick and fading.

Rebecca's own parents walked about the house with grim expressions. Her father was a frequent visitor to the sickroom and had insisted that no expense be spared if it would help Mrs Cooper recover.

On the tenth day of Mrs Cooper's illness, the girls were in the schoolroom with Miss Albarn, trying but failing to concentrate on French verbs, when a housemaid tapped at the door.

'Excuse me, Miss Albarn, but the doctor said I should fetch

Miss Sarah to see her mother right away.' Her face looked drawn, and Sarah immediately leapt to her feet, her hand clasped to her mouth.

Miss Albarn scowled. 'This is most irregular. Sarah usually visits her mother after tea. Why must she go now in the middle of our lessons?'

'Excuse me, miss, but I don't know. All I know is Mr Winton agreed and said Sarah must indeed come at once.' The maid gave a small curtsey and held the door open. Sarah rushed through, followed by the housemaid. Rebecca hesitated for a moment then made up her mind. It was more important to be with her friend right now, than learning about the past perfect tense. She glanced at Miss Albarn, shrugged an apology and ran off, ignoring the governess's protests.

Mrs Cooper had been put in one of the main bedrooms on the first floor. It was easier, Mr Winton had said, to nurse her there than in her usual apartment in the servants' wing, where Sarah also slept. Rebecca ran down to the first floor and along the corridor to the sickroom. There was a crowd of people in the room and in the corridor, all speaking in hushed tones, their faces worn and worried. All the upper servants were there, and Spencer, his eyes sad and tired, was trying to keep them calm. Rebecca pushed through them to the door, but was held back by the butler.

'Miss Rebecca, I'm afraid I don't think it is wise for you to go in,' he said, gently. Rebecca liked Spencer. He was a kind and capable man, who had helped defeat Napoleon at the Battle of Waterloo, fighting alongside her father. He'd been the Wintons' butler ever since he'd retired from the army. He and Mrs Cooper had managed the house for as long as she could remember. There was a time when she'd thought they were married to each other, until Sarah laughed at her and told her they were not.

She pulled away from him. 'But Sarah's my friend – she's like my sister. She'll need me if something awful happens.'

'She will indeed, and you are a kind lass for recognising that. But right now her poor mother, poor dear Isobel, is in her final moments, and Sarah needs to say a quiet goodbye. You may watch from the doorway but I cannot allow you to enter the room.' Spencer led her through to the door of the room, which stood ajar, but he kept a hold of her shoulder.

Inside the darkened room, Rebecca could just make out Mrs Cooper's form under mounds of bedclothes. At her head stood one of the nurses, who was constantly dabbing at her brow with a cloth. Dr Millbank and Rebecca's father stood at the foot of the bed in silence, their hands clasped behind their backs. But it was Sarah who drew Rebecca's eye. She had climbed onto the bed beside her mother, and had tucked her head onto her mother's shoulder, draping her arm across her chest. She was whispering something in her mother's ear, but Rebecca could not hear what she said. As she watched, Mrs Cooper weakly raised a hand and laid it on her daughter's face. Sarah turned her head to kiss her mother's palm, and Rebecca could just see the glint of tears running down her face.

The room was silent, apart from the harsh but feeble sound of Mrs Cooper's breathing. Rebecca could not take her eyes off her friend. How she longed to go over and place a comforting hand on Sarah's shoulder. If only there was something she could do, or something she could say. It was too awful to have to watch your own mother die. But Spencer still had hold of her although she could feel his hand shaking, and with her father in the room she dared not disobey. She could only stand and watch.

How long she and everyone else stood there she could not say, but she gradually became aware that the harsh breathing was growing ever quieter. Mrs Cooper's hand slipped off Sarah's face. Sarah gave a little cry and clasped her mother's hand. The doctor took a step forward and placed his fingers on the housekeeper's other wrist. He stood for a moment, then shook his head sadly. Sarah seemed not to have noticed his approach for she did not move at all. Spencer, still holding Rebecca's shoulder, gave a stifled sob, and she looked at him in surprise. The butler was usually so calm. It was odd for him to show any emotion.

She watched as her father approached the bed. He put his hand on Sarah's shoulder. 'Come, child. Leave her. There is nothing more you can do. Let her rest in peace now.'

'Nooooo!' Sarah wailed as she realised what he meant. 'No! It cannot be! Mama!' She threw herself across her mother's body and curled into a ball, as though she was a small child being cradled on its mother's lap. Rebecca's heart broke for her friend. She could not imagine being left motherless. And Sarah did not have a father – at least not one anyone knew about. Her mother had always said that Sarah's father had 'gone away'. Sarah was now an orphan.

'Come, child,' said Mr Winton, again. 'It's time to leave.' He looked over to the doorway and beckoned to Spencer, who let go of Rebecca and went in. Spencer bent over and scooped Sarah into his arms, and carried her out of the room. Sarah was clinging to him tightly.

She tried to go after him but her father pulled her back. 'Spencer will look after her. He will send for you when the time is right for you to see her. Go and find your mother now, and tell her Mrs Cooper has passed away. I shall be downstairs shortly.'

Rebecca glanced inside the sickroom once more, and saw the doctor raising a bed sheet up over Mrs Cooper's face. Mr Winton gently pulled the door closed, then spoke to the gathered servants. 'It is over. Return to your duties, everyone.'

The servants began to disperse, many of them wiping their eyes. Mrs Cooper had been a popular member of staff, firm but fair. Rebecca set off to the morning room in search of her mother. She wondered whether her parents would employ a new housekeeper. She supposed they would have to, but she couldn't imagine anyone else running the household. And what would become of Sarah?

Mrs Winton was in the morning room, sitting by the window on a green silk chaise longue, with a piece of embroidery in her hands. She listened quietly as Rebecca told her what had happened, then she carefully put away her stitching before pulling Rebecca to her in a brief embrace.

'Oh, child. I am sorry you had to witness Mrs Cooper's passing. But perhaps it is for the best that she is gone. She will suffer no more. And the child Sarah, where is she now?'

'Spencer carried her away. I don't know where. Mama, I would like to go and see her and try to comfort her. May I?'

'Of course. In good time. Sit here with me until your father comes. We will keep each other company in the meantime.'

Rebecca sat on the chaise beside her mother, feeling very grown-up to be asked to keep her mother company. Normally she spent just half an hour before tea in her parents' presence, answering questions on what she had been learning with Miss Albarn. Sometimes Sarah was with her on these visits, and other times Rebecca was alone. She glanced at the clock on the mantelpiece. It was just after eleven. Miss Albarn would be wanting to start on another lesson.

'Mama, I am worried that Miss Albarn will wonder where we are. She did not come down when the maid came to fetch Sarah.'

'Don't worry, child. I will send someone to tell her. Lessons are cancelled for today.' Mrs Winton stood, and crossed the room to tug on the bell-pull by the fireplace.

***

It seemed hours before Rebecca's father joined them, but he entered the room just before the clock struck a quarter past the hour. Rebecca stood and curtseyed when he entered the room but he seemed not to notice her there. He flung himself down in a chair opposite his wife and wiped a hand across his brow. 'You have heard the news, Charlotte?'

'I have. Where is Sarah?'

'Resting. The doctor has given her something to help her sleep. She is very distraught, as you might imagine.'

Mrs Winton sighed. 'I fear for what will become of her, the poor mite. It is not her fault she had the misfortune to be born out of wedlock. And now she is all alone in this world at such a tender age.'

Mr Winton stared at her. 'She is not alone. She has us. And of course she has Spencer. She will remain here, under our care, as she has been all her life. There is no question about it. What would you have me do – throw her out?'

'No, no, of course not. She is welcome to stay. It will look odd, though. While her mother was working here it made sense for us to house her and educate her, as a playmate for Rebecca. But to keep her here on her own, after a suitable mourning period of course, well, that would look odd, wouldn't it? We have never publicly acknowledged that Spencer is, well, you know.' Mrs Winton raised her eyebrows at her husband.

Rebecca kept quiet. Both parents seemed to have forgotten she was there. What had they not publicly acknowledged about Spencer? She had no idea what her mother meant by it looking odd if Sarah continued to live with them, but all she could think of was that Sarah *must* stay! They'd grown up together. They were like sisters. Sarah meant everything to her, and a life without Sarah at her side was not one Rebecca cared to contemplate. But she instinctively knew that nothing she could say right now would influence events. All she could do was watch and listen.

Papa was cross. 'Charlotte, there is nothing to discuss here. We cannot throw out a motherless child. Sarah must stay under our roof. Spencer, of course, adores her. He saved my life at Waterloo. The least I can do to repay him is to continue to provide a home for Sarah. Besides, Rebecca would be heartbroken if she were to go. The girls can continue to share a governess, and when they are older Sarah can remain as Rebecca's companion, until such time as she marries or leaves us of her own accord. As we've discussed before it is my wish that Rebecca marry the de Witt boy, Charles, when she grows up.' Rebecca put a hand over her mouth to stop herself from reacting to this. She had met Charles de Witt on a couple of occasions when the de Witts had visited the Winton estate, or vice versa. The boy was the son of her father's oldest friend and was several years older than herself. She had paid him very little attention. So her father intended her to marry him when she was older? That was interesting, and a little bit frightening.

Mama nodded, but didn't look sure.

Mr Winton continued speaking. 'So, Sarah stays with us. Agreed, Charlotte?' Mr Winton stood and towered over Mama as he spoke. Rebecca had seen him do this before to signal the end of a discussion. There was never any point trying to argue further.

Mama looked up at him. 'Yes, of course my dear, whatever you say.' But her lips were firmly pressed together, in a gesture Rebecca knew meant she didn't agree but would not argue any further.

Papa nodded and left the room. Rebecca waited a moment and then followed him out. She ran to Sarah's room in the housekeeper's apartment, and found her friend lying tucked up in bed, asleep. Spencer must have put her there. She sat beside her and stroked a stray lock of hair from her face, considering all that she had heard. Was Sarah perhaps not an orphan after all, and Spencer was her father? She tucked the secret away inside her head.

'One good thing has come of this, Sarah,' she whispered. 'You are to be my sister. Papa said so. I will be married to Charles de Witt, and you are to be my companion. You will stay with me for the rest of my life, Sarah. Isn't that truly wonderful?'

CHAPTER 3

April 2015

'So did you find out anything more about those duelling pistols today?' Ben asked, as he paid the bill. Gemma and Ben had eaten out in their favourite Italian bistro, as was their habit on a Friday night.

Gemma pushed back her chair and slipped on her leather jacket. 'I made a start. There's a sketchy history of Red Hill Hall on the hotel's website, but it's only a couple of paragraphs and doesn't mention a shooting.'

'Did you try googling "Red Hill Hall" and "duel" together?' Ben held the door open for her and they walked out into the mild spring evening.

'I did, yes. I know how to do this research lark, you know!' Gemma laughed. 'Couldn't find anything about it.'

'Aw, shame. Erm, shall we walk the long way back to yours? Via the park?' Ben shuffled his feet as he spoke and seemed unwilling to catch Gemma's eye. She wondered why he wanted to go that way round. It was certainly a lot further. Usually they went straight back to her flat, drank a glass of wine and spent the night together if neither of them was working on the Saturday.

Although very often one or both of them would be working – that was the trouble with jobs in public services like museums and sports centres.

'OK then, if you like,' she said, and linked her arm through his. It was certainly a pleasant enough evening for a night-time stroll.

'So, is that it? If nothing comes up on Google about the infamous shooting does that mean you won't be able to find out any more about it?' Ben asked.

'Not at all. Next step is to search the newspaper archives. Thankfully a lot of old newspapers have been digitised and are available to search online. You need a subscription though, and the museum doesn't have one. So I need to talk to Roger on Monday, and see if he'll agree to fund one. If he doesn't, I'll probably buy a month's subscription myself and research it from home.'

'Do you think he'll agree? Better if you can do this during work hours, isn't it?'

Gemma laughed. 'Better for me, definitely! The more time I spend on this the less time I have to spend on boring fossils. Yes, I think he'll probably go for it. He seems as interested as I am in finding out the background to these pistols.'

They turned away from the street and into the park. An inviting path meandered through well-kept flower beds, and the scent of early roses filled the air. Ben led the way, and Gemma realised they were heading towards 'their' bench. It was where they had sat for an hour or more on the night they first met. Gemma remembered it so clearly. She and Nat had been sharing a bottle of wine in the pub, when Ben and some of his colleagues from the sports centre came in and sat at the next table. Nat had been chatted up by a hunky lifeguard, and had left early with him, leaving Gemma feeling stranded amongst people she didn't know. She'd ended up talking to Ben, and when he'd offered to walk her home she leapt at the chance.

On that occasion it was Gemma who'd led him the long way home, just so she could spend a bit more time with him. They'd sat on this bench in the rose garden at the edge of the park and talked for hours under the moonlight. It wasn't until the early hours that they decided they ought to go home. By the time Ben left Gemma at the door to her flat, kissing her deeply as they said goodbye, she'd fallen well and truly in love with him.

At the bench, Ben stopped. 'Shall we sit down for a moment? Remember the night we met and sat here talking for hours?'

'I'll never forget it,' Gemma said, snuggling up to him. It was a cool, clear night, with a crescent moon casting just enough light to see by. But Ben pushed her gently away.

'I, erm, there's something I want to say, Gem.' Once again he was looking shifty. Gemma wondered what he was holding back. Surely he didn't want to call time on their relationship? They were good together, they never argued, they made a perfect couple – all their friends said so. Nat always said they were made for each other. And he wouldn't have chosen to come here, to this bench with so many memories, to finish with her, would he?

He clasped her hands on her lap. 'Gem, darling, it's been six years...'

'Seven,' she interrupted.

'Seven? OK then, seven years. Gem, they've been the best years of my life. But, it's not enough for me any more.'

Oh God, he was going to say he didn't want their relationship to be exclusive, wasn't he? Gemma felt a pang of dread course through her.

Suddenly he dropped to his knees in front of her. 'Gemma, darling, will you marry me?'

'Marry you?'

'Yes, you know, I mean, like, put rings on each other's fingers, walk up the aisle of a church together, all that stuff. Live together. Have kids. Grow old together. The works.' He looked up at her, his deep brown eyes beseeching her to say yes. Relief flooded through her like a tsunami. Well of course she was going to say yes! She'd been making up her mind to propose to *him*, next leap year, hadn't she?

She slipped off the bench to kneel in front of him, and put her hands on his shoulders. 'Darling Ben. Of course I would be absolutely delighted to marry you! I've been hoping you'd ask me for the last six years!'

'And now I have! Oh wow, you said yes! Really? You'll marry me? Wahey!' He pulled her to her feet and enveloped her in a huge hug. Gemma couldn't help herself – she began bouncing up and down with joy and Ben joined in, his arms still wrapped tightly around her, the two of them jumping up and down together, squealing with laughter.

A late-night dog walker passed by, staring at them. 'We're getting married, we're getting married!' Gemma squealed. The dog walker grinned and gave them the thumbs up. When he was out of sight, Ben pulled Gemma still closer and kissed her, deep and lingering.

'Mmm,' said Gemma. 'You are the best, and soon you will be mine.' She sighed happily. 'I can't wait to tell Nat that we're engaged! And Mum and Dad, and your parents! And Anna and Jake!'

She skipped, clinging on to Ben's arm and stopping every

few steps for another kiss, all the way back to her flat, which occupied the top floor of a converted Victorian terraced house. A sweet elderly gent named Alan lived downstairs, and it was all Gemma could do to stop herself from banging on his door to tell him she'd got engaged. But it was too late in the evening, and Alan would be tucked up in bed by now.

***

When to tell Nat was Gemma's first thought the following morning. She wasn't working but sadly Ben was, so although he'd spent the night at her flat he'd had to get up early to go to work. Gemma got up at the same time, then spent a couple of hours mooching around the flat, waiting until it was a decent enough time to call Nat on a Saturday morning. She knew her friend loved her weekend lie-ins, followed by long bubble-filled baths. She waited till nine-thirty then couldn't stand to wait a moment longer.

The sound of gentle splashing warned her she'd called too soon and Nat was still in the bath, hopefully gripping the phone tightly so she didn't drop it in the water.

'Nat, hey, good morning!'

'Hey, Gemma. Bit early, isn't it?'

'Sorry. I was just desperate to talk to you. You'll never guess...'

'We're meeting up later, aren't we? To start the hunt for outfits for Anna and Jake's wedding. We'll be talking all day, Gemma.' Nat sounded weary. Possibly hung-over.

'Yes, sorry. Did you have a heavy night?'

There was a huge sigh and the sound of gentle splashing, as though Nat had shifted position in the bath, before she answered.

'Yeah. Met a hot bloke in a nightclub, tried to pull him, but he went off with another fella in the end, who was equally hot. So I drowned my sorrows in vodka.'

'Oh, Nat. You don't half pick 'em.' Gemma suppressed a giggle. That was the trouble with the phone – if they were together in a coffee shop or something she'd be able to judge whether to laugh or not by Nat's body language. But on the phone she didn't dare. If Nat was still feeling fragile and rejected she wouldn't appreciate Gemma having a laugh at her expense.

'I do, don't I?' Nat replied, and Gemma was relieved to hear a note of humour in her voice. 'Thing is, Gemma, I need to find a bloke. My invitation from Anna and Jake was for "Natalie plus one". I need to find that plus one. It's bad enough they had to write that on the invite – I *hate* being the single friend everyone's trying to pair off – but it'll be even worse if I end up going to the wedding on my own. I need a man and I need one now – one who'll last at least till after the wedding. Come clubbing with me, Gem? Then if you pull and I don't, you can shove him in my direction.'

Gemma couldn't help herself but laugh this time. The idea of her pulling a bloke when Nat couldn't was crazy. And the last time she'd been clubbing was years ago. In fact she couldn't remember if she'd been at all since she got together with Ben. Before then, she and Nat had gone to nightclubs every couple of weeks – when it was Nat's turn to choose the night out. When it was Gemma's turn they'd usually spent the evening chatting in the Men At Arms.

'Well, it's all very fine for you to laugh, Gem. You've got Ben; you're all smugly coupled up. But a bit of sympathy wouldn't go amiss. I'm getting on. I'll be thirty soon – and no boyfriend.'

'Ah, Nat. Thirty's no age. I'll be thirty before you in any case. And you'll find the right person eventually. I know you will.'

Gemma mentally ran through her male friends, trying to think if any were single and worth introducing to Nat. But she could only think of shy, sweet Roger, and Nat would have him for breakfast.

'Yeah, right. When I'm old and shrivelled. Anyway, what did you ring me for? We're still meeting at twelve in the usual café, aren't we? You're not going to let me down are you?'

'No, still on to meet you there.' Gemma grimaced. After the way this conversation had gone so far, how could she tell Nat she and Ben had got engaged? But if she didn't say anything now, Nat would be furious that she hadn't told her at the earliest opportunity. She was kicking herself for having made the phone call. But if she had waited to meet Nat to tell her, she'd have been in trouble for not phoning. Talk about being between a rock and a hard place.

She took a deep breath. 'Right, the thing I couldn't wait to tell you about is that, well, Ben popped the question last night and I accepted.' There. It was out.

There was silence at the other end. 'You still there, Nat? I'm over the moon – been longing for him to propose for the last six years! And finally – squeee! – he has!'

'Erm, wow, yeah, that's great. Really pleased for you, mate. So, erm, see you later, right? Fuck.'

Gemma was left staring at her phone. Nat had hung up. She wondered whether she'd heard that last word properly. It really hadn't been the kind of reaction to her news she'd expected from Nat. Well, she'd timed her call wrongly, and it seemed Nat'd had a disastrous night out, so maybe it was all because of that. When they met later in town she was sure Nat would be delighted for her. She hoped so – otherwise, well, otherwise she had no idea what was going on.

40

CHAPTER 4

November 1834

'I am so bored,' Sarah grumbled. 'I wish something would happen. Anything. Or at least if it stopped raining we could go out riding.'

Rebecca gazed out of the window. They were each sitting on a window seat in their old schoolroom, on the second floor of Red Hill Hall. Their governess Miss Albarn had been dismissed a couple of months previously – now that they had both turned fifteen the girls were deemed to have learned all that she could teach them. They now used the old schoolroom as a kind of sitting room. Rebecca didn't mind the rain as much as Sarah. Sarah always seemed to become stressed and fretful if she had to stay indoors, whereas Rebecca was quite happy to sit with a book or in front of the piano, for hours on end. In fact a rainy day was sometimes a good thing, as it meant they were expected to stay quietly indoors and Sarah could not drag her outside on some crazy scheme.

Last week, against her better judgement, she'd allowed Sarah to persuade her to ride their ponies out of the estate, through the woods and across farmland. They weren't supposed to leave the estate without a groom accompanying them, but Sarah had insisted, and had said she would go alone if Rebecca didn't go with her. Rebecca had had no choice. She'd followed Sarah galloping across the fields, but her pony had shied at a jump and she'd fallen. She was still bruised.

'I don't know that I shall ever want to go riding again, after last time,' Rebecca said.

'Spoilsport. Who will I go out riding with, then? If only the grooms were more handsome, I shouldn't mind having them as companions. If only they were more like that handsome farm labourer, Jed Arthur. He smiled at me last time. And winked. I believe he thinks I am beautiful.' She paced around the room and sighed, dramatically. 'Oh, being cooped up in here is so tedious. If only there was something to do.'

With Sarah in this mood Rebecca realised she would not progress with reading her novel. She stood, and held out her hand. 'Come on, then. Let's go and find something to do.' Although Sarah's plans sometimes went wrong, as Rebecca's bruised shoulder could testify, Rebecca knew that her life would be far more boring without Sarah around. She loved Sarah for the excitement she brought to what would otherwise be too quiet a life.

They went downstairs, and visited the kitchens where Cook gave them each a finger of shortbread before making it clear to them that they were in the way. When they were younger they'd been allowed to linger in the kitchen, sitting by the fire toasting bread or marshmallows, but now they were supposed to behave like ladies, and ladies shouldn't be in the kitchens.

'What now?' said Rebecca, as she followed Sarah out of the kitchen and back into the main hallway of the house. Sarah stopped in front of a glass-fronted cabinet, which stood opposite the foot of the stairs. It housed two ceremonial swords and a mahogany display case containing a pair of pistols.

'Those.' Sarah pointed to the pistols. 'Papa brought them home last week. I should like a closer look at them.'

Rebecca frowned. Sarah had recently taken to referring to Mr Winton as 'Papa'. But he wasn't Sarah's Papa, he was hers. Sarah had no Papa – at least not one that was acknowledged. While Rebecca loved having Sarah as a constant companion, almost a sister, and she loved her dearly, she did not want to share her parents with her. It was very sad when Sarah's mama had died, but that was years ago, and Sarah should think herself lucky that Mr and Mrs Winton had continued to care for her all this time. Rebecca knew it was just so that she, Rebecca, had a suitable playmate, and that when Rebecca married Sarah would become her paid companion. She didn't want to think about that, though. She couldn't imagine being Sarah's employer, instead of her sister.

'The cabinet is locked,' Rebecca said.

'Let's ask Spencer. I want to know how to use them.' Sarah turned with a toss of her hair and a swish of her skirts, and strode off in search of the butler. Rebecca scurried along after her. It may be a rainy stay-indoors kind of day but it seemed Sarah was still able to concoct wicked plans that could get them into trouble. Not with Spencer – Sarah seemed able to do no wrong as far as he was concerned – but with Papa or Mama, if either of them discovered what they were up to.

Spencer was in his little office in the servants' wing. He was filling in some figures in the household's accounts book. He looked up with a scowl when Sarah pushed open the door, but his expression quickly changed to one of fond indulgence when he saw who it was.

'Well now, Miss Sarah, what brings you here?' The butler twisted round in his chair and smiled broadly at the girls. He was middle-aged, greying, kind but firm with the servants. He'd worked for the Wintons for as long as Rebecca could remember.

Sarah flashed him a bright smile. 'We were wondering whether you might show us Papa's new duelling pistols. The ones in the display cabinet. They are so pretty, set with those rubies. We would so like to take a closer look at them.'

'Well, I'm not too sure whether Mr Winton would allow that...' Spencer rubbed his hand across his eyes.

'Oh please, Spencer, dear! Just for a minute. Papa doesn't need to ever know. He's still away in London, isn't he? And Mrs Winton is closeted away in her private sitting room. She won't come out till dinner time. She never does. Please, Spencer?' Sarah had clasped her hands in front of her, and was bouncing up and down in front of him like an overexcited child. Rebecca watched, in awe of the way Sarah seemed able to manipulate him into doing whatever she wanted to do. She remembered the secret her parents had let slip after Mrs Cooper had died, and once again wondered whether Sarah knew the truth.

'Well...'

'Please?'

'Very well. We will take them out and you shall look at them. But only for a moment, mind, Miss Sarah.' Spencer fixed her with a look that was supposed to be stern, but that wasn't at all. Rebecca couldn't help but let out a giggle.

'I suppose you want to see them too, Miss Rebecca?'

'Yes please, if it isn't too much bother,' she replied.

'Don't be silly, Rebecca. It's never too much trouble for Spencer, doing something for us. He'd do anything for us. He loves us, don't you, Spencer?'

'That I do, Miss Sarah.' He got to his feet with a weary sigh and crossed the office to his key-board, where he selected a bunch of small keys. 'Come along, then.'

Sarah gave a small skip of excitement as she followed the butler back through to the main hallway. Rebecca trailed behind, keeping a watch in case someone came along and saw them. Although it would only matter if Mama saw them, and as Sarah had said, she was unlikely to leave her room until dinner time.

Spencer unlocked the cabinet and reverentially took out the mahogany box. 'Mr Winton bought this as a display piece,' he said. 'In the last century, owning a set of duelling pistols was a kind of gentleman's status symbol. I don't think they have ever been fired. The pistols and their case are really just a decorative item.'

'But *could* they be fired?' Sarah asked.

'Certainly. They are fully functioning pistols. Let's take them somewhere we can lay them out and I'll show you all the pieces.' Spencer led the way back towards the servants' wing, and into the servants' dining hall. It was deserted. He closed the door behind them and laid the box on the table. He seemed almost as excited as Sarah was by the thought of taking them out of the box. Rebecca watched as he removed first the two pistols, then a rod, a brush, a flask and a small box, and some other items. He checked the mechanism of one pistol then handed it to Sarah to hold, before doing the same with the other, which he handed to Rebecca.

'They're unloaded, so they're perfectly safe,' he said. Nevertheless she felt her heart pound as she turned the pistol over in her hands. This was a weapon capable of killing a man at a distance. It was heavy, and felt unbalanced, as though it would be an effort to hold it pointing straight. The dark wooden stock was set with engraved silver plates and studded with rubies, and the mechanism was made of shiny brass.

'What are all these other things?' Sarah asked, indicating the items Spencer had removed from the box.

'The ramrod, cleaning brush, shot, and the gunpowder,' he replied, indicating each item. 'And tools for maintaining the pistols.'

'Real gunpowder?' Rebecca gasped.

Spencer opened the flask. 'Yes, there is some in there. The set is complete, in readiness for a duel. The two pistols would be primed and loaded by the duellists' seconds, men who'd been chosen to ensure the duel was carried out fairly. The gentlemen would then take a pistol each, stand back to back and take an agreed number of paces away from each other before turning and firing. The paces would be counted out loud by the seconds.'

'It's barbaric.' Rebecca felt slightly sick at the idea of two men, men such as her father, wanting to shoot and kill another man just to settle a point of honour. She glanced at Sarah. The other girl's face was flushed, her eyes bright with excitement.

'Can you imagine having two men fight a duel over you, Rebecca? Wouldn't that be the ultimate declaration of love? Suppose, for example, a gentleman fell in love with you, but you are promised to Charles de Witt so he challenged the other man to a duel! Wouldn't that be thrilling? I should simply adore it if men fought to the death over me!'

'Ah no, Miss Sarah. Duels are rarely fought to the death. Often the duellists will purposefully miss their targets. The point is to prove you were prepared to put yourself in danger for the sake of your honour.' Spencer smiled indulgently at the girls.

'But sometimes people would be shot?' asked Rebecca. She put her pistol back into the box.

'Yes, sometimes, and occasionally a duel would result in a death. Thankfully duels are rare nowadays. If a man is killed in a duel then his opponent is deemed guilty of murder and should be tried accordingly. Although I must admit, very often if the duel is considered to have been fought fairly, he will be let off lightly.' Spencer held out his hand to take the second pistol from Sarah, but she did not pass it back.

'I would very much like to learn how to prime it,' she said quietly.

'Sarah! We mustn't load them! It mightn't be safe!' Rebecca was horrified. It was bad enough holding a dangerous weapon but if it was actually loaded... She had heard Papa read out newspaper reports of pistols that had misfired and injured their owners.

'It would be perfectly safe, Miss Rebecca,' Spencer said. 'Duelling pistols are the most reliable flintlocks there are. And I assure you I know how to prime it safely.'

'Have you acted as a second, perhaps, in a duel?' Sarah asked.

'No. But I have not always been a butler. As you know, I was previously in the army. I fought at Waterloo and have a medal to show for it.' Spencer pulled himself upright as though standing to attention in front of a superior officer. 'Therefore I am well acquainted with weapons such as these, although it has been a long time since I handled one.'

'So will you show us?' Sarah pleaded.

Spencer regarded her for a moment, then nodded. 'Very well. You may watch but don't touch anything.' He picked up one of the pistols and twisted the cock on the top, which held the flint. 'There, that is in the half-cocked safety position, which means it can't accidentally fire. Now it is safe for me to prime and load it.'

Next, he opened the little flask and measured out a small amount of gunpowder, which he tipped into the muzzle end of the pistol. He added a ball of lead shot encased in paper from the little box, and pushed the whole lot down the pistol with the ramrod. 'The gun is now loaded but not primed,' he told the girls. 'It is still safe.'

He then opened the flash pan lid on the top of the pistol and tipped a little more gunpowder onto the pan, before closing the lid. 'And now it is primed. But it still cannot fire in this half-cocked position. The cock must be fully back in order for the trigger to work. If fired, the trigger releases the cock, which causes the flint to strike the frizzen – look, this piece here. That causes a spark, which ignites the gunpowder in the flash pan. The flash passes through a hole into the barrel, igniting the main gunpowder and thus discharging the gun.' He looked at the two girls as though to see if they had followed all this.

Rebecca was not sure she understood how the mechanism worked, but she knew she'd seen enough. 'Thank you, Spencer, that was most informative. I think perhaps you ought to unload the weapon now, and we should put it all away.'

'No, Rebecca, don't be a spoilsport. I think we should all go outside and Spencer should fire the gun. It doesn't look as though it is possible to get the shot and all the gunpowder out unless the pistol is actually fired. Isn't that right, Spencer?' Sarah stared at the butler, and Rebecca thought she saw her wink.

'Well, the shot should come out if you tip the gun upside down, and the flash pan is easy enough to empty. But you are right, not all the gunpowder can be extracted from the combustion chamber. I do not think Mr Winton would be very happy if I fired his gun, however.'

'Mr Winton isn't here so won't ever need to know. Come on, Spencer, look, the rain has eased off so we could go outside and fire it? Please? Dearest Spencer, I would so like to see it fired, just once!' Sarah was in full persuasion mode again, Rebecca noted, and it was working. 'And now that it is loaded, you might as well. You can't put it away like this, for that certainly wouldn't be safe.'

Spencer sighed, and then smiled indulgently at her. He put the other pieces back in the box, but kept the loaded pistol out. Handing the box to Sarah to carry, he led the way out of the servants' dining room, along a corridor and out through a side door. This led into the kitchen gardens, which they skirted round and left through a gate, emerging into the wide open parkland. Spencer stopped about twenty yards from a large spreading oak tree. 'I shall discharge the weapon at the tree,' he said.

Rebecca gasped. 'But what if someone gets in the way?'

'Miss Rebecca, look, there is no one in the way now. You and Miss Sarah shall stand behind me, a good distance back. No one can possibly approach without us seeing.' He stood sideways on, raised his arm and pointed the pistol at the tree. With his other hand he cocked it and then fired, before either girl had a chance to say anything more. There was a flash, then an enormous bang, and a shower of bark fragments flew from the tree. A crow flapped frantically away cawing loudly and a pair of pigeons followed, from higher in the tree. Rebecca couldn't stop herself from squealing and clasping her hands over her mouth, while Sarah was jumping up and down clapping her hands. There was a sharp, acrid smell and a puff of smoke rose and dispersed on the breeze.

'There, my ladies. I have defended your honour and fired my pistol. The tree is injured, though not mortally so, but he will not dare cross me again!' Spencer's face was flushed, and

Rebecca realised he'd enjoyed the feeling of holding and firing a pistol again. Perhaps it was the first time since Waterloo, almost twenty years earlier.

'Thank you, dear Spencer! Thank you! What a wonderful loud noise it made. It was simply thrilling!' Sarah flung her arms about the butler to his astonishment.

'Miss Sarah, this is no way to behave! I must remind you I am still holding the pistol and it must now be cleaned and returned to its case. Come along now, and watch this part of the proceedings too. And then I really must return to my duties.' He extricated himself from her embrace and picked up the case that she'd put down on the ground, tutting over the water marks from the wet grass. 'I hope those don't show when it's dry or we shall all be in trouble.'

He set off back to the house, and Rebecca followed him with relief. That was quite enough excitement for one day. She hoped after the pistols were put away Sarah might settle to some quiet reading or embroidery, or some other occupation more suited to young ladies.

CHAPTER 5

April 2015

Gemma was first to arrive at the coffee shop where she and Nat always met, in town, around the corner from the museum. She picked a table near the window from where she would see Nat approaching, and ordered two lattes as usual. She felt strangely nervous. After Nat's reaction to her news on the phone that morning, she wasn't sure how things would be between them. Hopefully it had just been due to her bad timing with the phone call, and Nat's hangover. Nat would breeze into the coffee shop, embrace her in a huge bear hug and squeal with excitement about the engagement. As she sat staring out of the window and stirring her coffee, she convinced herself that was what would happen.

When Nat arrived, perfectly made up and stylishly dressed in a loose silk shirt over jeans, Gemma's first thought was that she'd been right. Nat smiled broadly, kissed Gemma on both cheeks and sat down with her latte.

'Well, Miss Sneaky-Pants, you're finally going to make an honest man of our lovely Ben, are you? You never told me you were planning on getting hitched. Would have been nice if you had mentioned it.' Nat winked, giving the lie to her words, and sipped her latte.

'It was Ben who proposed! It was a surprise – I really wasn't expecting it. And I did tell you, first thing this morning,' Gemma protested. She wasn't a hundred per cent sure whether Nat was upset or not.

'Ha, yes, when I was in the bath and hung-over.'

'I thought if I waited till now to tell you you'd have been upset, so I told you first. Haven't even told Mum and Dad yet. I'll ring them this evening.'

Nat looked pleased to have been told the news before Gemma's parents. 'They'll be *delighted* their baby girl is getting wed. They'll offer to pay for half of it, your mum will turn up in a huge hat and your dad will grin from ear to ear as he gives you away. You have no idea how lucky you are, Gem. God, if it was me, my mother wouldn't care unless it meant free booze for her at the wedding, and my father would say, "That's nice, sweetheart," but of course he wouldn't come, Australia being too far away and a daughter's wedding being not enough of a reason for him to exist for a moment in the same country as Mum, let alone the same church.' Nat shook her head as though in despair at her family. Her tone was jokey but Gemma thought she could detect an undercurrent of seriousness. She had a point. Gemma's family were certainly more conventional than Nat's. As a rebellious teen she'd envied Nat's chaotic home life, but as she'd matured she'd come to properly appreciate her close, supportive parents.

'I'm sure that's not right. Your dad would fly over if you were getting married, and your parents would surely be able to be in the same room for one day.' Gemma was about to say something about limiting the supply of drink to Nat's alcoholic mother, but thought better of it.

'Yeah well. It's not me getting married, is it, so no point discussing it. I'll probably never marry. I'll end up a bitter and twisted old spinster living in a house that smells of cat wee. You'll bring your kids on duty visits, and they'll say, "Oh no, not batty old Aunty Nat," and you'll sit there drinking bitter coffee with me and wondering how soon you can leave. Oh, I can see it now. All our years of friendship will come to nothing once you're all cosily married up.'

Again, although Nat laughed as she made this speech, there was a touch of bitterness underneath her words. Time to change the subject, Gemma thought, though she'd been longing to tell Nat exactly how Ben had proposed and how it'd made her feel, and what her early ideas for a wedding, venue, dress and honeymoon were. But she had the feeling that any more talk of her engagement would just wind Nat up and perhaps it was best left at that. In any case, there was another much more imminent wedding – that of Ben's sister Anna and her fiancé Jake – and the whole point of today's shopping trip was to try to find outfits for that.

Gemma drained the rest of her coffee. 'Well. Shall we get started? It's midday and we've a lot of shops to get round. I'm thinking of a dress and jacket combination. What about you?'

'Not a dress and jacket, that's for sure. I'm not old enough for that kind of outfit. It's what the mother of the bride would pick, along with an oversized hat or a fascinator a foot long. Have you paid the bill?' Nat stood up, slung her bag onto her shoulder and began leaving the café without waiting for an answer.

'Yes, all paid, my treat, don't worry,' Gemma said, at Nat's retreating back. She shook her head. Nat was in a very strange mood today.

***

The shopping trip was a disaster. Nat tried on a hundred outfits but liked nothing. Gemma barely got a chance to try anything on, except for a couple of items Nat picked out for her, which were completely unsuitable and not at all her style. A seventies-print maxi-dress with shoestring shoulder straps, and a pair of wide-leg pink silk trousers with a strapless sparkling silver top. Every time Gemma fingered an item she liked the look of Nat hurried her along to the next shop. If Gemma didn't know Nat better, she'd think she was sabotaging the shopping trip on purpose. It wasn't at all like the hundreds of other shopping trips they'd done together in the past, when they would both try on loads of outfits, giving honest opinions, giggling if something looked awful on, encouraging each other to buy what suited them best. She supposed her friend must be still grumpy about the badly timed phone call this morning. Or still hung-over. Whatever it was, Nat was snippy all day. As in the coffee shop, she'd say something snarky but then smile brightly or wink or laugh. Gemma was perplexed.

After a while she gave up trying to find something to wear to the wedding. She'd shop on her own some other time. She spent the afternoon following Nat around, trying to say the right things about the clothes Nat tried on, and trying not to mention Ben and her engagement, although it was all she could really think about.

Eventually they reached the top end of the High Street. Gemma suppressed a sigh of relief. 'That's that, then. No more shops. We'll have to call it a day, I think. Maybe nearer the time there'll be some new stuff in.'

Nat gazed down a narrow side street. 'We haven't tried *La Belle Femme* yet. She pointed at a boutique tucked into one of the historic old buildings along the street.

'Bit pricey for us, isn't it?' Gemma had only looked in the

window once or twice before but had seen enough to know it was out of her league. And she was pretty sure Nat earned a lot less than she did.

'Speak for yourself. I'll spend what I like on clothing, and I'd have thought you would too, as it's your future sister-in-law's wedding. I quite fancy that dress in the window.' Nat pointed at a skimpy dress, the skirt of which was embroidered with a peacock feather design, the top half encrusted with sequins. It did not look cheap. She pushed open the door, which rang a bell somewhere in the back of the shop, and Gemma had no choice but to follow her in.

There were very few clothes rails in the shop. A shabby-chic leather sofa took up most of the space in the middle of the room, and a few dresses were artfully arranged on hooks on the wall. The lighting was... subtle, if Gemma was being kind. Dim if she was being truthful.

A woman wearing far too much make-up, dressed in a neat black dress and heavy gold jewellery emerged from the back room. Although she quickly put on an expression of polite helpfulness, Gemma had noticed her previous expression when she'd seen who was in the shop. Clearly she and Nat weren't the right sort of customers. Her instinct was to spend about thirty seconds looking at the items on show and then leave. She glanced at Nat, who apparently had other ideas.

Nat was fingering a black silk dress with an asymmetric hem and feathers around the neckline. Not machine washable then, Gemma thought.

'I'd like to try this on, please,' Nat said to the sales assistant. 'And the peacock dress in the window, while I'm at it.'

'Certainly. This way, please,' said the assistant, leading them into a small changing area at the back of the shop. Half the cubicle was taken up with a huge rubber plant. 'Wait here while I fetch the garments.'

'Classy place,' Nat said, when the woman had gone.

'What price are those frocks?' Gemma whispered.

'Dunno. Don't care, either!' Nat pulled a leaf off the plant and used it to fan her face.

'But can you afford them?'

'Course not. But it'll be fun trying them on. You try them too. That black one would look great on you, with your blonde hair.'

'Oh, no. I wouldn't feel comfortable doing that if I've no intention of...' Gemma broke off speaking as the sales assistant returned, with the two dresses each on padded hangers and covered with plastic. The assistant glared at her, then hung the dresses on a hook beside the rubber plant.

'I'll fetch a chair for your friend,' she said, while Nat began stripping off.

'Oh, no, please don't trouble yourself,' Gemma said, but the sales assistant only glared at her again and brought an uncomfortable-looking gilt-backed chair from behind the sales counter. Gemma perched on it. It was as uncomfortable as it looked.

Nat had the black dress on. 'What do you think?' She twirled around, admiring herself in the mirror.

'Not with those shoes,' Gemma said. Nat was still wearing her red Converse trainers.

'Obviously. Well, this one's nothing special. I'll try the other.'

The peacock dress looked good on Nat, Gemma had to admit. It fitted her perfectly, showed off her lovely legs and curvy waist, and her long black hair was stunning against the glittery top half. 'Wow. That's just amazing on you, Nat. Show me the price tag?'

Nat twisted so that Gemma could peer at the label hanging from the zip at the back. 'There's no price on it.'

'I guess, if you have to ask…' Nat rolled her eyes dramatically and peeled the dress off. Gemma had a fit of the giggles at Nat's eye-roll, and Nat soon joined in. This was more like it, Gemma thought. The whole shopping trip should have been a girlie giggle, rather than all the snide comments and snippiness. Perhaps Nat's hangover had finally worn off. It was good to end the day on a high note.

'What's the verdict, ladies?' asked the sales assistant when they exited the changing room.

'I don't like the black one on me. The peacock is nice, but aren't peacock feathers supposed to be bad luck? I'm not sure I could wear it, for that reason. Something awful might happen to me. I'd be constantly fearing for my safety.' Nat breezed out of the shop. Gemma hurried after her, one hand clamped over her mouth to hold back the laughter that threatened to erupt. The shopping trip had certainly ended on a high.

***

That evening, Gemma rang her parents to tell them of her engagement. They were as delighted as she'd expected they'd be. Her mother immediately started planning the guest list while her father jokingly grumbled that he supposed he'd have to buy a new suit, even though he'd just retired.

Later, Ben came round to Gemma's flat for a meal. She'd offered to cook fajitas for him. Their first meal together as an engaged couple! She sang along to Ed Sheeran's *Thinking Out Loud* as she chopped onions and peppers. Perhaps they should have that song as the first dance at their wedding? It was so romantic; it was definitely one of her favourites. She'd ask Ben later what he thought. He'd probably agree. Dear old Ben, he was generally happy to go along with what other people wanted. Gemma knew already that the wedding preparations would be largely up to her to decide upon. Although no doubt her mum would want to get involved.

She had the tiny table in her kitchen set, the food chopped and ready to quickly cook, and a bottle of wine open when her flat doorbell rang. Why didn't Ben use his key? She'd given him one years ago. As she went to let him in she wondered why they'd never moved in together. They'd idly discussed it on a few occasions, but neither of their flats was really big enough for two people with many years of accumulated possessions. They'd both have had to sell up and buy something bigger together. Well, now they were going to get married they'd have to do that anyway. Gemma would miss her cosy little flat but was sure that she could make a house she shared with Ben just as comfortable and cosy.

'Hey, gorgeous!' Ben leaned over and kissed her as she opened the door. 'My fiancée, no less! Mrs McArthur to be. Looking good, girl!'

'Come on in, *Mr Rowling*,' Gemma said, giggling.

'That's a bit progressive! I don't mind if you don't take my name but not sure I'd take yours. Well, something smells good.' Ben shrugged off his leather jacket and hung it on a coat hook.

Gemma handed him a glass of wine. 'Shiraz all right for you?'

'Anything, darling, you know me. So, how did the girlie shopping trip go today? Did you get your outfit for Anna's wedding sorted?'

Gemma grimaced. 'No. I'll have to look again some other

time. Nat tried on loads of stuff but I don't think she's made up her mind what she wants.'

'Did you tell her our news? Bet she was delighted, wasn't she?' Ben grinned at her expectantly. She chewed her lip as she decided how to answer him.

'Well. Yes, she was pleased for us.'

'You don't sound too sure of that. What did she say?'

Gemma shook her head. 'She didn't say much. That was the funny thing about her reaction. She just didn't seem to want to talk about it or to let me tell her anything much about it. She didn't even want to know how you proposed.' Gemma brushed away a stray tear that had come unbidden to her eye. 'It's not the reaction I was expecting from my best mate.'

'Aw, Gem.' Ben moved over to her and wrapped his arms around her. 'Don't be upset. Perhaps she was having an off day.'

'She was hung-over. She tried to pull a bloke who turned out to be gay last night.'

'Oops!' Ben gave a snort of laughter. 'That is so like her.'

'But even so, no matter how bad she felt, she could have at least said congratulations, couldn't she? She wasn't feeling so bad she couldn't manage an afternoon trailing round the shops.' The more Gemma thought about it, the more bitter she felt. Why hadn't Nat hugged her and squealed and been excited for her? She would have, if their positions were reversed.

'Very odd behaviour,' Ben agreed. 'Wonder what's up with her?'

'No idea.' Gemma shrugged and went back into the kitchen to get on with the cooking. Ben followed her in, bringing his wine. 'Frankly, Ben, it pissed me off. I mean, it's the biggest and best thing that's ever happened to me, after meeting you in the first place of course, so for her to just ignore me when I tell her we're getting married is really hurtful.' Gemma threw the vegetables she'd chopped earlier into the frying pan where they sizzled and spat violently.

'I'm sure she didn't mean to hurt you. Is that pan too hot?' Ben reached over her and turned the gas down a little.

He had a point. Gemma realised she'd spattered oil all over her favourite T-shirt. 'Bugger, look at me.'

'I wonder if she's jealous,' Ben said. 'Perhaps you laid it on a bit thick and came across too smug. Some single people hate couples just because they're not part of one.'

'I didn't get the chance to lay it on too thick!' Gemma retorted. 'I mean, I barely had chance to say anything about it, apart from that you'd proposed and I'd said yes. She just didn't want to know.' She flung the chopped chicken into the pan along with the vegetables. It wasn't sizzling enough now, so she turned the heat up again.

Ben held his hands up in submission. 'Hey, I know you wouldn't have rubbed it in. Maybe she'll be all right with it next time you see her or talk to her – when she's had chance to think about it a little. She'll be as excited as you are, I bet.' He caught Gemma's eye. 'You *are* still excited about it, aren't you? Not having second thoughts?'

She laid down the wooden spoon she'd been stirring the fajita mix with, and put her arms around his neck. 'Course I'm still excited. Nothing I want more than to get married to you, silly.' She stretched up and kissed him, long and lingering. His hands ran up and down her back, pulling her close. She felt as though she was where she belonged. In his arms, safe and secure, where nothing else mattered.

A sudden deafening beeping caused them to separate. 'Argh,

the smoke detector!' Gemma said, grabbing a tea towel and flicking it frantically under the detector.

Ben turned the gas down, put the extractor on, and opened the kitchen window. 'Thought you had the pan too hot,' he said.

'I've ruined it,' Gemma said, feeling close to tears. Her first attempt at cooking for her new fiancé and she'd managed to smoke out the flat. And she was usually so super careful about the oven and hob, checking several times that the gas was off before leaving the flat, for example. Now she couldn't even cook a simple stir-fry. What a failure she was.

'No, it's fine – look.' Ben was stirring the mix. 'My fault. I got carried away there, snogging you. So, actually, it *is* your fault after all for being so flipping irresistible. You go and sit down and I'll finish this off. And no more worrying about what Nat does or doesn't think about our engagement. All right?'

CHAPTER 6

June 1837

'I don't feel old enough to marry,' said Rebecca. She looked at Sarah. 'Do you?'

'Who said anything about getting married?' Sarah put down her stitching. It was, Rebecca noticed, quite poorly executed. She glanced at her own handiwork – the stitches neat and tidy, the back of the embroidery almost as good as the front. Sarah just didn't have the patience to sit and sew. Her threads were tangled, the material puckered where she'd pulled it too tight, and there were grubby fingermarks on one corner of the sampler.

'We're eighteen now. You're almost nineteen. Mama and Papa will soon be wanting us married and settled. That's why we're going to all those balls, of course. Although those are really for your benefit as I am already promised to Charles de Witt.' Rebecca smiled at her adopted sister.

Sarah rolled her eyes. 'I know all that, silly. And I know you seem happy to go along with Papa's plans to marry you off to that oaf, Charles. But I don't want to get married. I'd rather stay single and independent. For a few years at least. Maybe when I'm twenty-five or so I'll marry but why rush into it?'

'Twenty-five – why, you'll be an old maid by then! I think a girl should be married by the time she turns twenty. I hope I will be. Charles de Witt has recently returned from his travels on the continent, and has taken a house in Bridhampton. He is to come to dine with us tonight, to renew our acquaintance. I confess, I am a little nervous about seeing him again – it must be six years since we last met. I was just a child. I hope he is *not* an "oaf" as you put it, as he is supposed to become my husband.' Rebecca gazed at Sarah, whose hair was fairer, eyes bluer and figure shapelier, than her own. 'He'll probably prefer you, in any case. You are by far the prettier of the two of us.'

'Nonsense! You have the sweeter nature.' Sarah flashed her a smile. 'In any case, I shall not be interested in him. I told you, I do not wish to marry for some years. I'd rather be free, to flirt a little with whomever I choose. Like, for example, Jed Arthur.'

Rebecca glanced at her in shock. It was not the first time she had mentioned that name. Jed lived in one of the cottages on the estate. He was but a farmhand. A handsome one, admittedly, but a labourer nonetheless, and not someone Sarah ought to be encouraging.

'Sarah, it is not ladylike to flirt with farmhands. Surely you know that,' she admonished. She received only a dismissive shrug in reply.

The girls were sitting on the window seats of their second floor sitting room, the old schoolroom. Sarah gazed out of the window for a moment before speaking again. 'Papa's plan for me is that when you marry, I will go with you as your paid companion. You know that. And my plan is to save all my earnings so that I have a small fortune of my own. With money, a woman can be free to do whatever she wants. She does not need to marry. And my only chance of having money is for you to marry and me to become a member of your staff. So I wish that Charles turns out to be personable, and that you and he live happily ever after.'

Rebecca laughed. 'I too hope for that, as long as there's a happy ever after for you as well, dear sister.'

What would Charles be like? Rebecca hadn't seen him for years, and this would be the first time they'd met since she was grown and of marriageable age. She felt strangely nervous at the prospect of meeting the man who was intended to become her husband. While she knew that her father would not force her to marry Charles if she found him truly detestable, she did so want to please her parents. The happiest outcome of the evening would be if she found Charles to be an appealing sort of person, and if the feeling was mutual. She resolved to take extra care with her appearance when she dressed for dinner that night. She would wear her pale green gown. She'd been told it suited her best.

***

At the dinner party Rebecca found herself placed beside Charles. Sarah was sitting opposite, between Mr and Mrs Winton. It was pretty clear that the older folk wanted Charles and Rebecca to have a chance to get to know each other. Rebecca's mother sent many an encouraging smile at her across the table.

As the soup was served, Rebecca stole a sideways glance at Charles. He was certainly pleasant enough to look at, now that he was a man, more so than she would have guessed from her sketchy memories of having met him as a child. His hair was dark, his nose straight, his eyes a warm brown. He was reserved yet polite, and when he smiled his face lit up. He looked, Rebecca thought, like a kind and thoughtful man. She smiled to herself, wondering what his first impressions of her were.

'Rebecca, dear,' Mama said, breaking into her reverie. 'I do hope you will play the piano for us later this evening.'

Charles turned towards her and smiled. 'I should like to hear you play, Miss Winton. There is nothing I enjoy more than sitting by the fireside listening to an accomplished young lady playing the piano.'

Rebecca blushed. 'Oh, I would not call myself accomplished. Competent, perhaps, but no more.'

'Rubbish, Rebecca,' said her father. 'You are a very fine pianist. Your piano tutor told us so. And the Lord knows you practise enough.'

'I enjoy playing, that is true.' Rebecca wished the conversation could move away from her abilities. She glanced at Sarah hoping her friend might help steer the company onto another topic. But Sarah was scowling across the table at her. Rebecca frowned. Earlier she had said she was not interested in Charles, and would be happy if things worked out between him and Rebecca. But now she seemed quite put out that all his attention so far had been on Rebecca.

Rebecca turned back to Charles who was regarding her with a smile on his face.

'So you will play for us later?' he asked.

'Yes, of course. I only hope you are not disappointed.'

'I could not possibly be disappointed by you. I am looking forward to it immensely.'

'Do you ride, Mr de Witt?' Sarah interrupted them.

'I do, yes. Do you, Miss Cooper?' Charles answered. Rebecca felt a mixture of relief that her musical abilities were no longer the topic of conversation, and annoyance that Charles's attention was now focused on Sarah.

'As often as I can,' Sarah said. 'In fact, if the day is fine tomorrow, I think I shall go riding. I shall try to persuade Rebecca to come too. Perhaps you might ride over and accompany us?'

'That sounds like a delightful plan,' Charles answered. 'I shall certainly ride over here tomorrow morning.' He smiled across the table at Sarah, who wore a faintly triumphant look.

Rebecca no longer went riding, and Sarah knew it. Ever since she'd been thrown from her pony a few years ago, on one of Sarah's ill-advised escapades where they'd galloped across the parkland and her pony had refused to jump a hedge, Rebecca had been put off riding. She would not be persuaded to go out. Why was Sarah doing this? It was as though she was trying to win Charles for herself despite all that she had said earlier. Perhaps she liked the look of him after all.

'What do you make of our new queen?' Charles asked Rebecca. 'I think she is about your age. Imagine becoming Queen of England at just eighteen! What a weight she has to bear on such young shoulders.'

'I should hate to be in her shoes,' Rebecca replied. 'So much will be expected of her. She will not have a moment's peace to enjoy her life. Everything she does will be reported in the newspapers.'

'But she is rich and gets to live in a palace and do whatever she wants,' said Sarah.

Charles smiled indulgently. 'I think what Miss Winton is suggesting is that Queen Victoria won't be able to do just what she wants. She will be expected to perform her duties and be an example to the whole country. She'll be expected to marry soon, and her choice of husband will be critical.'

'She's queen – she can choose anyone she wants to marry,' Sarah replied.

Charles shook his head. 'Not at all, Miss Cooper. Her choice of husband will be closely scrutinised and will have to be approved by her advisers. He will need to be someone of suitable status, perhaps a foreign prince.'

'What if she chooses not to marry?' Sarah asked. Her tone was flirtatious. 'After all, Good Queen Bess never married, so an unmarried queen is not unprecedented.'

'Perhaps she will find someone suitable who meets with her advisers' approval and whom she loves,' Rebecca said. She did hope so. It felt a bit like her own situation – being expected to marry but wanting to love the person her parents had chosen for her. She stole another sideways glance at Charles, then blushed when she realised he was looking at her.

'I hope she does,' he said, quietly. 'No one should be forced to marry someone for whom they don't care.'

***

After dinner, when the party had retired to the drawing room, the call went out once again for Rebecca to provide some music. She nervously settled herself at the piano, and looked to Sarah to stand at her side and turn the pages of her music. But Sarah was across the room, deep in conversation with Charles, their heads close as they chuckled together over some private joke. Rebecca noticed her mother frown as she saw them together. This was clearly not part of the plan.

In the end Spencer was called upon to act as page-turner. As Rebecca played a selection of Bach arias she lost herself in the music. When she finally finished playing, she glanced up to find Charles gazing at her from across the room, an expression of deep admiration on his face. Sarah, beside him, looked distinctly unhappy.

***

The next day dawned bright and clear, and Sarah shook Rebecca awake early.

'Hurry up! Charles will be here soon. Remember we promised to go riding with him?'

Rebecca groaned and hauled herself into a sitting position. 'You did. I don't ride any more, as well you know.'

'But I can't go with him on my own. It wouldn't be proper, if just he and I went riding. If we both go, that is more acceptable. Besides, you are supposed to be getting to know him, aren't you? What better opportunity than trotting gently through the woods together, side by side, chatting about this and that? I shall follow behind as your chaperone, and I promise I will not get in the way, nor encourage you to gallop.' She smiled to herself. 'Though I may have a gallop myself across the open parkland. I doubt I shall be able to resist.'

Rebecca sighed. 'Sarah, I have not ridden since Bluebell threw me. I do not intend going riding again. You know my preferred pursuits are quieter, less strenuous and indoors. I don't understand why you torment me like this.'

Sarah sniffed. 'I am only trying to help progress your budding romance. If you don't want to go, then I shall have to go alone with him after all. We mustn't disappoint him, as he is expecting to go riding. When we return perhaps you could delight him with your musical skills again, or show him your embroidery. I am sure he would enjoy *that*.' She left the room, letting the door bang closed behind her.

Rebecca was left bemused. Why was Sarah acting like this? They had always been so close. It broke her heart when Sarah treated her badly. She shook her head. Perhaps she was being too sensitive. She decided to keep out of the way until Sarah and Charles returned from their ride, and to spend some time with him afterwards. He had been invited to lunch with them, so there was plenty of time. She rang the bell for her maid Tilly, and asked for breakfast to be brought up to her in her room. She sent Tilly away with a message: 'When Mr de Witt arrives, please ask Spencer to tell him I am indisposed for riding but will gladly meet him later for lunch.'

A little while after breakfast, she stood at her bedroom window and watched Charles and Sarah ride across the parkland behind the hall. They looked good together – Sarah's dramatic red riding habit looked stunning against the grey mare she was riding, and Charles's green coat contrasted well with his black mount. They appeared to be laughing together at something, as they cantered over the grasslands. Rebecca lost sight of them as they approached the woods at the far side of the park. She turned away from the window. Perhaps Sarah would be a better match for Charles than herself? He'd appreciated her piano-playing last night, and they had discovered a similar taste in literature, but if he wanted an adventurous, lively wife then Sarah would be better for him than she would. If only she hadn't liked him so much, or if her parents had not planned for her to marry him, she would gladly have stepped aside and made way for Sarah.

But she *did* like Charles, and she did not want to let him go without a fight.

Rebecca was reading in the library when the riders returned. There was some commotion in the entrance hall, so she put down her book and rushed out to see what was happening.

Charles was standing in the hallway, being relieved of his mud-encrusted green coat by Spencer. 'Sir, I shall have this cleaned for you, and perhaps you can borrow something of Mr Winton's to wear on your ride home this afternoon.'

'Thank you. I fear it is quite ruined. Ah, Miss Winton! We missed you on our ride, did we not, Miss Cooper?' said Charles.

'Oh, please, Charles, do call me Sarah. Let's not be quite so formal with each other. I am so sorry about your fall, truly I am.'

'Whatever happened?' Rebecca asked, torn between wanting to reproach Sarah for being so informal, and concern for Charles who was walking stiffly across the hall, rubbing at his shoulder.

'It was nothing,' said Charles, taking a seat on a hall chair.

Rebecca crossed the hall to kneel before him. 'You are hurt? Should Spencer send someone to fetch the doctor?'

'Not at all. It is just a bruise.' He smiled at her, and Rebecca felt her heart leap. His smile was warm and made his eyes light up. Was it only for her, or did he use that smile for everyone?

'Poor Charles,' Sarah said, coming to kneel beside Rebecca. 'His horse took fright as we went through the woods. I tried to help but am afraid I could not manage to catch the reins of his horse before it threw him.' She suppressed a giggle. 'Oh, do excuse me, but it was rather funny, you see, he landed right on the muddiest part of the path. A foot to either left or right and his coat would not have suffered as much.'

'But I think my shoulder would have suffered more. The soft

mud at least cushioned my fall.' Charles was unsmiling as he answered Sarah.

'Come, Mr de Witt. Let's sit in the drawing room. It is not long till lunch, but I shall ring for refreshments for you immediately.' Rebecca stood up. Instinctively she held out a hand to pull Charles to his feet, but retracted it before he could take it. She wasn't sure now whether he was courting her or Sarah.

***

Mrs Winton joined them at lunch. Mr Winton was in town on business. Sarah told the story of Charles's fall, once again. Rebecca flinched at her sister's undisguised glee at the poor man's misfortune. Mrs Winton seemed not to approve either, glaring at Sarah from her place at the head of the table. She insisted on providing a carriage to take Charles home, rather than allow him to ride with his injured shoulder.

After lunch, when Charles had left, Rebecca and Sarah were making their way upstairs to their sitting room, when Mrs Winton called them back and bade them sit a few minutes in the drawing room with her.

'Charles has grown into a very pleasant young man, has he not?' she asked, addressing her question to Rebecca.

She blushed. 'Yes. I like him very much, Mama.'

'I like him also,' Sarah said. There was a touch of defiance in her voice. It worried Rebecca. What Sarah wanted, Sarah generally got, by one means or another.

'You, my girl, are to stay clear of him. He is promised to Rebecca. We have had an understanding with the de Witts for many years, that when Charles and Rebecca were grown, if they liked each other they should be encouraged to marry.' Rebecca watched as Mama wagged her finger at Sarah as though she was a misbehaving child, and Sarah set her jaw. 'Do you understand?'

'Yes, Mama,' Sarah said.

'I am not your mama. Do not forget your place in this household, Sarah. My husband has indulged you for too long. As has Spencer. You will not steal Rebecca's suitor from her. I hope I have made myself clear.'

Sarah raised her chin and stared straight ahead. 'Yes, Mrs Winton. Perfectly clear.'

Mrs Winton stood then. 'I am going upstairs to my room now. I shall see you both at dinner.'

Sarah followed her up, but Rebecca decided to return to the book she had been reading in the library. She felt she needed a break from Sarah's company for the rest of the afternoon. It was the first time she could remember feeling like that about her adopted sister. Was this part of growing up – growing apart from the person you thought you loved most in all the world? No. It was just a phase. Meeting Charles had disturbed their equilibrium. They would regain it once the excitement had subsided and it was clear which of them he preferred. And if he really did prefer Sarah, even though she did like him, she would step aside. Somehow she would persuade her parents it was the right thing to do. There would be other suitors in time. She picked up her book and settled in a chair near the window.

Screams and a clatter from the hallway sent her running out of the library again almost immediately. Spencer had come running too, along with a couple of maids. Rebecca first noticed Sarah, standing on the gallery at the top of the stairs, leaning over the rails. There was momentarily an odd expression on her face, and then she screamed, one hand clutched over her mouth, the other holding on to the railings. And then Rebecca saw what she was screaming about. Partly hidden by Spencer who was kneeling on the floor, was her mother, lying in a crumpled heap at the foot of the stairs.

'Send for the doctor, immediately!' Spencer shouted at one of the maids, who went running off at once.

'Mama!' Rebecca ran across the hall and threw herself down beside her mother. Her body was twisted, legs bent at unnatural angles, and her face was deathly white.

'Oh, Mama!' Sarah came running down the stairs too, and sat beside Rebecca. 'She tripped on the stairs! I tried so hard to catch her, but I couldn't!'

'Make way, Miss Winton and Miss Cooper. Let me examine her.' Spencer gently pushed the girls aside and leaned over Mrs Winton, his fingers feeling for the pulse at her neck.

Rebecca watched, her mouth open with shock and tears cascading down her cheeks as he sat back on his heels and shook his head sadly. 'I'm so sorry, girls,' he said. 'I believe she has broken her neck. There is nothing that can be done for her.'

'Mama! No! No, it can't be!' Rebecca flung herself across her mother's body and wept. She was vaguely aware of a weight on top of her – Sarah, also sobbing loudly. She reached for Sarah's hand and clutched it tightly, and drew strength from feeling Sarah squeeze her hand in return. Despite their earlier differences, they would need to help each other through this terrible tragedy. Her mother, dead, from a broken neck! How could that have happened? One moment she was there, admonishing Sarah for flirting with Charles, and the next she was gone. So sudden, so terrible, so shocking. Nothing would ever be the same again.

CHAPTER 7

April 2015

Gemma hadn't planned on telling Roger that she'd become engaged first thing on Monday morning but she couldn't help herself; it just slipped out before she'd even hung up her jacket or switched on her laptop.

Roger looked vaguely surprised by her announcement. 'Wow, erm, well done, Gemma, I mean, congratulations. Yes, congratulations, that's the word. Splendid news.' He nodded at her, and swallowed hard making his Adam's apple bob up and down. 'Would you like a coffee?'

She smiled at him. It was typical of Roger to be not quite sure how to react to her news. But at least he'd said congratulations, which was more than her best friend had done. 'Yes, please, Roger. Then if it's OK with you, I want to start researching the shooting at Red Hill Hall that those duelling pistols were apparently used in. Can I buy a month's subscription to the newspaper archive website on the museum's account?'

'Of course. I'm as fascinated as you are by this. Let me know if you find anything interesting.' He coughed and shuffled his feet for a moment. 'Right then. I'll fetch that coffee. I really am pleased for you about the engagement. Yes, delighted.'

Gemma grinned and shook her head as he left the back room. Dear old Roger. Socially awkward but such a lovely person to work for. She started up her laptop and set to work on the research.

By the time Roger returned with the coffee, she'd set up the newspaper archive subscription, run a search on 'Red Hill Hall' and 'duel', and had already found and downloaded her first article. It was from what appeared to be a popular gossip magazine. She scanned it quickly, her eyes widening as she took in its contents.

'Roger, listen to this.' She began reading.

'*The Curse of Red Hill Hall? If any Esteemed Readers of this publication are invited to stay at Red Hill Hall in the county of Dorset, they should perhaps consider their response carefully, for the place appears to be cursed. First the lady of the house took a tumble down the stairs and broke her neck, though one must ask whether she was perhaps pushed; then the gentleman of the house died suddenly of a broken heart, though again one wonders whether he was perhaps poisoned; and in the most recent tragedy the two daughters of Red Hill Hall were found in a cellar, mortally wounded. A pair of duelling pistols was found, both discharged, at the scene. The hunt is on for the murderer who apparently escaped by means of the door to the coal cellar. It occurs to your Author that our Esteemed Readers are unlikely to be furnished with an invitation to stay at Red Hill Hall, for there would appear to be no one left there to act as host or hostess. What will become of the house and estate your Author does not know, but should such information be forthcoming he will of course share it in a future edition of this magazine.*'

Gemma looked up from her reading. 'Wow. The whole family

seems to have died in suspicious circumstances. The place was cursed indeed!'

Roger laughed. 'What publication was that?'

'*County Tall Tales*. Hmm. Sounds a bit like a red top.'

'The clue's in the name. Tall tales, indeed. But nevertheless, there could be some truth buried under all the sensationalism. Keep looking, would be my advice, and hopefully some more reliable papers will have covered those events. What date's on the magazine?'

Gemma peered at her computer screen. 'August 1838.'

Roger nodded. 'Compulsory registration of deaths began in 1837. So if all those tragedies were recent when that was written, you might be able to find the death certificates. You'll need the names of the deceased, of course. Which hopefully you'll find in some other articles. At least you have a rough timeframe now for the shooting – summer of 1838 or a little before. No telling how up to date this rag would have been with its news. Well, you've got your coffee now. I need to open up out front. Good luck!'

Gemma took a sip of her coffee, created a folder on the laptop and saved the article she'd found, before going back to her search results on the newspaper archive website. By playing around with search terms and setting the date range as April to October 1838 she soon found a number of reports of the shooting. She saved each article and jotted down the main facts as she found them. It had happened in August 1838, and the two victims were Rebecca Winton and Sarah Cooper. In some articles they were described as sisters, despite the different surnames, and in others Rebecca was referred to as Miss Winton, and Sarah as a servant. None of the reports was clear as to exactly which, if either, died. Some newspapers reported that both girls died, while others reported they were just badly injured, or that only one had died. The one thing they were all agreed upon is that the perpetrator had escaped, leaving the pistols dropped beside the wounded girls, and that he was still at large. The public was invited to come forward with any information they might have about the murderer, although no reward was offered.

Gemma felt more and more intrigued by the story. She had to know exactly who had died, and what the girls' relationship to each other was. And was the perpetrator ever caught? She jotted down a list of questions to follow up. If she could discover the whole story, she could make a laminated poster to display alongside the pistols in the museum. It was the sort of exhibit that went down well, especially with school groups who loved anything a bit gory.

Roger returned to check on progress. 'You can look for death registrations under those two names,' he said. 'And search for newspaper articles for the following twelve months to see if anyone was caught. Might also be worth having a look at the 1841 census to see who lived in Red Hill Hall then – after the shooting of course, but if that gossip magazine article is correct and the master and mistress of the house had also died, it'd be interesting to see what happened to the estate.'

Gemma noted all this down. Clearly there was more than a day's work here! 'Was there an earlier census? So we could find out who lived in the hall before the shooting?'

Roger shook his head. 'No, the 1841 census was the first complete census in England. But if it was an important country house, there could be some other records somewhere. It'd just be a case of tracking them down. Not sure I can justify you doing all the work on museum time, however. I wonder what became of the hall itself, whether it's still in existence or not?'

'Oh, I can answer that,' Gemma said, smiling. 'It's now a country house hotel. I'm going there in June – Ben's sister is getting married there.'

'Ah, right! Could be worth getting in touch and finding out if they have any archived papers stored away somewhere. Probably not if it's a hotel but you never know. Do what you can online first. And if there's any chance of you cataloguing a few more boxes of fossils in between the research, I'd be ever so grateful.' Roger flashed her a goofy grin and patted her shoulder as he left.

Gemma left the museum that evening in a fabulous mood. She'd enjoyed the research, and even the next couple of boxes of artefacts she'd opened had contained interesting items rather than boring old fossils (a set of Victorian postage scales and a collection of gorgeous Edwardian evening bags). All day, every now and again, she'd remembered that she was now engaged to Ben, and that had given her a little fizz of excitement. As she skipped down the museum steps she checked her watch. Ben should be home by now, and on a whim she decided to go round to his flat rather than straight home to hers. She popped into a supermarket on the way and bought a bottle of Prosecco and some chocolates. Why not celebrate their new status again?

A few minutes later she was knocking on the door of Ben's flat. She really ought to get a key from him. Or better still, and surely sooner rather than later, they should sell both flats and buy a house together. One with a garden, and a spare bedroom or two. Maybe they'd have children in a few years' time. They'd need space to expand into. She was completely lost in her daydreams when she realised that she was still standing there, outside the door to Ben's flat, and no one had answered. She rang the bell again, and rechecked her watch. He definitely wasn't on a late shift today. He should be home. She pulled out her phone and dialled his mobile. There was no answer, so she left a voicemail, then, frowning, walked home to her own flat and stuffed the Prosecco and chocolates in the fridge. They'd do for another day.

Gemma ate a lonely dinner, and tried Ben's phone a couple more times, but it went straight to voicemail. Then she tried Nat's. She was in need of some company now; maybe Nat could come round and share the Prosecco. But Nat's phone also went to voicemail. What was the point of having a mobile phone if you didn't leave it switched on? Gemma felt oddly annoyed with Ben. While they'd never lived in each other's pockets, now that they were engaged she felt she ought to be able to contact him at any time, or at least know where he was and why he couldn't answer the phone. She'd have to talk to him about this. She decided to have a soak in the bath with a good book – always her favourite way to unwind. She'd hoped to be able to tell him all she'd found out about Red Hill Hall.

Half an hour later, submerged in bubbles up to her chin and with her Kindle in a resealable food bag to protect it from splashes, Gemma was just beginning to lose herself in the latest Barbara Erskine novel when her phone rang. She hauled herself out of the bath, cursing, and wrapped a towel round her to go and answer it.

'Hey, Gemma. Just returning your call.' Ben sounded weary.

'Where've you been? I called round earlier and have been phoning you all evening but your phone was switched off after the first call.'

'Sorry, love, it ran out of charge. I'm home now. Did you need me for something? What's happened? Are you OK?'

'Nothing's happened. I was just hoping to spend a bit of time with you this evening. Just, you know, to celebrate our engage-ment. Again.' Gemma tried desperately not to sound as though she was whinging or bitter. She didn't see herself as the possessive type – even when they were married she wanted to think they'd be able to do their own thing, lead their own lives, without always having to answer to the other. Except – she did want to know where he'd been.

'Ah. Sorry. Actually I wondered where you were. Poor Nat, eh?'

Gemma frowned. 'Nat? What do you mean, poor Nat?'

'Haven't you spoken to her?'

'No, what's up?'

'She's ill. I mean, really poorly, the poor thing. She could hardly get out of bed today. Flu, or something. I thought she said she'd phoned you and asked you to pick up some medicines and drop them round in your lunch hour?'

'No, she didn't call. Oh, poor Nat.'

'She swore she had. Then when you didn't call her back or text her, she called me and asked me to get them. So I did, after work. Stayed at hers for a while making sure she was all right.' Ben paused. 'You sure you didn't get a phone call from her?'

'I think I'd remember. I'll call her in a minute, see how she is.' Gemma felt irritated that Ben didn't seem to believe she hadn't heard from Nat.

'Erm, I wouldn't if I were you. She was going to try to sleep. And, well, she's a bit pissed off at you for not responding to her cry for help.'

'Cry for help?'

'Her words.'

'I told you, I didn't get a call from her. How was I supposed to know she needed me?'

'Hey, calm down. I'm just the messenger. Anyway, she's got what she needs now, and I changed her sheets and put a bottle of water by her bed. If I ever want a new career I'd make an excellent nurse, though I say it myself. Maybe you should pop round tomorrow after work? I can do Wednesday. We could take it in turns until she's better. Must be shit for her not having a flatmate or boyfriend or relative nearby to look after her. She says her mum doesn't care and wouldn't lift a finger to help her. At least she's got us.'

'Yes.' Gemma couldn't think of anything else to say. Why was Nat so convinced she'd called her? Perhaps she was so ill she'd been hallucinating. That was a worrying thought. Poor Nat.

'Well, love, I'm pretty knackered now and haven't eaten yet. I'm going to call for a takeaway then get an early night. If you see Nat tomorrow, let me know how she is. And if there's anything more I can do.'

'Sounds like she'll phone you if she needs you, in any case.' That just slipped out. Gemma hadn't meant to say anything so snippy.

'Yes, I suppose she will. Right then, goodnight, love. See you soon.'

'Night.' She hung up, and shivered. Realising she was still wet, wrapped in her towel, she went back into the steamy bathroom and climbed into the bath. She lay there for another twenty minutes until the water had cooled, pondering the conversation with Ben. Maybe she should phone Nat after all, and apologise for – for what? There was definitely no message from Nat on her phone, either voicemail or text. So how was she supposed to know Nat was ill? And once Ben had found out, why didn't he ring her to say he was going round? Gemma would have dropped everything to go and help her friend; he must know that. Presumably he hadn't called because his phone had been out of charge. But he could have used Nat's phone, when he got there.

The interrupted bath had not had its usual calming effect on her. She climbed out, dried off and got into a pair of warm pyjamas. What a rubbish evening this had turned out to be! But she shouldn't think like that. Poor Nat. Maybe her odd behaviour at the weekend had been because she was already sickening with this bug. Gemma got into bed, promising herself she'd pop round to Nat's in her lunch hour tomorrow. She'd do whatever she could for her. And she'd go again after work. Nat was a good friend. She remembered a time, many years ago now, when the boyfriend before Ben had dumped her. She'd phoned Nat in tears; Nat had cancelled her own date and come rushing round bearing a bottle of wine and a DVD, to help take Gemma's mind off her woes. They'd ended up having a fabulous, giggly girlie evening. It was the sort of thing Nat always did – put her friendship with Gemma first. 'You'll be around when the blokes are all long gone,' she'd said. 'So I'll always put you ahead of them, in your hour of need, any time.' The least Gemma could do was put Nat first when she was ill, to pay her back for all her support in the past.

CHAPTER 8

March 1838

Rebecca was still in mourning for her mother, nine months after her tragic accident. The household had been much subdued ever since it had happened, although Charles, who had leased a house in nearby Bridhampton, was a frequent visitor and did what he could to lift their spirits whenever he was there. He would go riding with Sarah, sit and discuss books and poetry with Rebecca, or try to engage Mr Winton in talk of business or politics. It was Papa who needed the distraction most, Rebecca thought. He had shrunk into himself since the death of his wife. He had lost weight, had a grey pallor to his skin and was seemingly uninterested in his estate and investments. Poor Papa. Mama's loss had hit him so hard.

It had been a long cold winter, but today was the first day that there was a hint of spring in the air. Rebecca put down her stitching and gazed out of the window of the old schoolroom where she still liked to sit. Weak sunlight shone through the still-bare branches of the magnolia and flowering cherry trees. It was the kind of day that made her want to go outside and be a part of it, not just an indoor observer.

Charles was due to call on them today. He would probably want to go out riding with Sarah, to make the most of the glorious weather. Rebecca sighed. A pity, because she would be pleased to have his company today. She decided to suggest a walk; perhaps if she caught him before Sarah did, he'd agree to come out with her. Were they competing for his attention? She didn't like to think of it in that way. The unofficial agreement, that Charles would eventually marry her, Rebecca, was still in place, although her father had not mentioned it since Mama had died. Sarah was still insisting that she would be happy for Rebecca if she were to wed Charles, but sometimes Rebecca doubted her sincerity.

At last, the distant jangle of a bell announced a visitor. Rebecca checked the mantelpiece clock and was sure it would be Charles. She threw aside her stitching, patted her hair and smoothed her gown, then rushed downstairs to greet him. He was standing in the hallway, still in his cloak and hat despite Spencer hovering nearby waiting to take them from him. Sarah, unfortunately, had reached him first. Where had she been lurking? In the library, perhaps, so she could pounce on him as soon as he arrived and suggest going riding. As Rebecca approached she realised that was exactly what Sarah was doing.

'It's a beautiful day. Oh please, Charles, don't waste it indoors. Let's go for a gallop, feel the wind in our hair and the sun on our faces!' Sarah was clinging on to his arm, trying to pull him across the hallway towards the corridor that led to the stable yard. She had dressed, Rebecca noted, in her new riding habit, her golden hair providing a fine contrast with its bright scarlet hue.

'It is indeed a beautiful day, but I must decline your offer, my dear Sarah. Ah, here she is.' Charles shook Sarah from his arm and bowed as Rebecca approached. 'Rebecca! Good morning. How are you today?'

'Very well, thank you. Shall I ring for some coffee for you?'

'Thank you, no. If you are willing, I would rather like to walk in the grounds with you. There is something I should like to discuss.' The last sentence was said quietly, as though Charles did not want Sarah, who still stood nearby, to hear.

Rebecca glanced at her. She had heard, and was glaring at them both. So Charles had brushed Sarah off in favour of her, Rebecca, then? That was unusual. He was usually too polite to risk offending either of them. She smiled up at him. 'Yes, I should love to go for a walk. Let me just run upstairs and change my shoes and fetch a shawl.'

'I shall wait for you on the terrace,' he said, with a smile, and he strode away across the hall.

Rebecca ran upstairs towards her room. On the turn of the stairs she glanced down to see Sarah still standing there, staring up at her. She looked furious. She had obviously planned to intercept Charles and go riding with him. It was the first time he'd turned her down. Rebecca felt a little rush of guilty triumph at the knowledge Charles had this time very definitely chosen *her* over Sarah.

***

Minutes later Rebecca joined Charles on the terrace, and they set off through the formal gardens at the back of the hall, and towards the small lake fringed by weeping willows, which was Rebecca's favourite part of the estate. Charles offered his arm and Rebecca took it, enjoying the warmth and strength of it under her hand. They talked of this and that, commenting on the buds just appearing on the trees, the mildness of the day for the time of year, the beauty of the swathe of daffodils under a spreading oak. Finally they reached the lakeside, where Charles pulled out a handkerchief to wipe down a white-painted wrought-iron bench. 'Shall we rest a while?'

Rebecca sat, and gazed across the lake. 'It is so beautiful here.'

'It is indeed,' he replied. She realised he was looking not at the view but at her. 'Rebecca, you are more beautiful than the scene before us. I wonder – I know our parents had a long understanding that we should wed, but...'

She sighed and looked away. Here it was. He was about to declare his feelings for Sarah over her. She knew it. 'Charles, it is all right. I do not hold you to that agreement. If you prefer another, then you must act on your feelings. My father will understand.'

He looked shocked. 'No, my dear Rebecca, you misunderstand. Perhaps I am not expressing myself very clearly. What I wish to say is that regardless of whether our parents had an agreement, I would at this moment be wooing you anyway. I have developed deep feelings for you. I hope, and pray, that they are reciprocated in some way? If they are not then of course I will release you, but maybe, if you could contemplate a future as my wife, then...'

Rebecca stared at him. His deep brown eyes were wide and pleading with her to let him know her feelings. He cared for her! He wanted her! She wanted to throw her arms around his neck and kiss him in response to his words, but that was not quite the ladylike thing to do. She blushed deeply as she answered him. 'Dear Charles, I should be delighted to be your wife. I know our parents, especially my mother, God rest her soul, always desired it, but more than that I too have grown to care for you over these last months. I think I should be very happy as your wife.'

'Oh, Rebecca!' Charles took her hands in his and leaned forward to claim a kiss – brief but soft and satisfying. Rebecca felt herself melt into his arms, and instinctively knew she belonged there.

'We must go back to the house, and tell everyone our news! My father, and Sarah...' Even as she said it, she felt her heart sink. What would Sarah think? What would she do? Despite Sarah's insistence that she would be happy if Rebecca married Charles, it was obvious she had come to hope she could claim Charles for herself. Well, it was not to be. Charles had chosen, and proposed, and Rebecca had accepted.

'Let's keep it to ourselves, just for an hour or two,' said Charles, with a smile. 'We have not yet finished our walk. Come, let's do a circuit of the lake.' He held out his hand and Rebecca took it, skipping happily alongside her fiancé. Her fiancé!

They followed the path that led along the banks of the lake, looping around its western end. A small wooden footbridge crossed the stream, which flowed out of the end of the lake. As they threaded their way through the willows towards the bridge Rebecca spotted a flash of red – it was Sarah's gown. She was crossing the bridge, then running up the hill away from the lake. Rebecca caught Charles's arm. 'Wait. I just glimpsed Sarah. Why is she running?'

Charles stepped forward and raised his hand to shield his eyes from the glare of the sun. 'She's gone up the hill. There's someone else up there. A man.'

'A man?' Rebecca gasped. 'Who?'

'I can't tell. I can only see an outline. They're talking, standing close.'

Rebecca followed his pointing finger and saw them. As she watched, Sarah placed her hands on the other figure's shoulders, reached up and either whispered in his ear or kissed him – they were too far away to tell.

'She seems to know him well, whoever he is,' said Charles. 'Come, we should continue our walk. Unless you fear she is in some danger and I should go to her aid?'

Rebecca was still staring up the hill. Something about the way the man held himself was familiar. Yes, it was that farm labourer Sarah had sometimes spoken of, the one she admired. Jed Arthur.

'She's in no danger,' she replied. 'Except perhaps from herself.'

Charles glanced at her but said nothing. She took his arm and they turned about, walking back the way they had come. Well, Rebecca thought, no need to fear Sarah's reaction on learning of her engagement. Sarah was clearly keeping her own secrets. There was still her father to tell. He would, she was sure, be delighted.

***

'Splendid news, absolutely splendid!' Mr Winton clapped his hands together in delight. 'We shall open a bottle of the best wine for dinner this evening. And you, sir, or soon I may say "son", will join us, will you not? In fact, stay. I shall have a guest room made up for you.'

Charles nodded. 'I should be delighted. It will mean I may spend more hours in the presence of my beloved fiancée.'

Rebecca smiled happily up at him. They had gone straight to Papa's study when they returned from their walk and found him absorbed in his accounts, but he hadn't in the least minded being interrupted when he heard their news. 'It is what Mama wanted, is it not, Papa?'

'Yes, she very much hoped for this to come to pass.' Papa beamed at them both. 'Ah, is that Sarah I hear? Call her in. She too must hear our happy news!'

Charles went out to the hallway to summon Sarah. Rebecca bit her lip. What would her adopted sister's reaction be to the news? An image of Sarah reaching up to kiss Jed Arthur crossed her mind. What was Sarah doing? Should she tell Papa?

'Rebecca, you are happy with this union, are you not? Please don't enter into it merely to please me, or for the sake of your dear mother's memory. I want only what is best for you. You do understand that, don't you?' Papa crossed the room and took hold of her hands.

Rebecca realised she must have been looking concerned as she thought of Sarah. She smiled and hugged Papa. 'Of course I understand it. Be assured, dear father, that I agreed to marry Charles because I love him with all my heart, and I believe that he loves me too.'

Papa smiled broadly, relief flooding across his face. 'I am pleased to hear that. It means I will be able to go to my grave in the knowledge that you are in a secure and happy marriage. Charles has a large fortune so you will be well provided for, even if my own fortune is split between you and Sarah.'

'But Papa, you are not going to your grave yet; please don't speak so!'

'Not yet, my dear, but it will happen one day. And you must...' He broke off as the door to the study opened and Sarah entered, followed by Charles.

'Charles says you have some news I must hear,' Sarah said, looking from Rebecca to Papa.

Rebecca stared at her feet. Who should be the one to tell Sarah?

She supposed she ought to, being closest to her, but felt herself unable to find the right words. Charles crossed the room and stood at her side, placing an arm around her shoulder. Rebecca glanced up at Sarah. Charles's gesture had told her everything. As Papa began to speak – 'We have wonderful news! Rebecca is to be married to Charles!' – Sarah glared at Rebecca as though she had done her a grievous wrong.

Rebecca opened her mouth to speak but Sarah got in first, quickly rearranging her expression into one of delight. 'Why, that is, erm, wonderful news, dear sister. I hope you will both be very happy. Don't forget, I shall always be with you, as your companion, for as long as you will deign to have me at your side. Now please, excuse me, for I am tired from my walk and must rest a while before dinner.' She turned and left the room.

'Ahem. I would have thought she might have shown more enthusiasm for your match. Perhaps she'll be more excited for you at dinner time. I'm sure she's delighted. You two have always been so close. Well then. I suppose I must return to the more mundane matters of the estate accounts. Off you two youngsters go and I shall see you both at dinner.' Papa returned to his desk and waved a genial hand at them.

'What do you think is wrong with Sarah?' Charles asked, as they left the study and went into the drawing room.

Rebecca wondered how to answer. Sarah was jealous, that was obvious, but if she told Charles that, might he wonder if he could have picked Sarah instead? Despite what he had said when he proposed, she still felt that possibly he might deep down prefer Sarah.

'I don't know. I wonder if her mood has anything to do with that farmhand we saw her with? I think she is keeping secrets from Papa and me.' She watched Charles frown and shake his head slightly. Good. If she could turn him against Sarah she would feel more secure. For the first time in her life she wished that there was no Sarah to share everything with. She wanted Charles for herself.

CHAPTER 9

May 2015

Gemma left work a few minutes early with Roger's permission. She needed time to pop to the supermarket and pick up a few things. Ben was coming round that evening. She'd hoped they might have a night out, perhaps to their favourite bistro, but he'd said he would rather come round to her flat as there were things they needed to discuss. She guessed he wanted to get started on setting a date and finding a wedding venue, Gemma thought, as she walked up the main street, away from the museum and towards the supermarket.

It was a bright, sunny evening. If she had a garden she'd have suggested they sit outside this evening. Something for the 'must-have' list for the house they'd buy together. She'd already given their wedding and future together plenty of thought, and had written several lists on her laptop at home. She'd also bought a few bridal magazines. It was time they talked about all this together. If they wanted to get married next summer they'd need to find a venue quickly. The summer months always got booked up a year or more ahead.

She whizzed around the supermarket collecting the ingredients for a dish of spaghetti with chilli, prawns and courgettes. It was an old favourite, took minutes to prepare, and always had Ben exclaiming what a great cook she was. As an afterthought she threw in a bottle of Prosecco. It may be over a month since Ben had proposed but she still felt like celebrating their engagement at every possible opportunity.

She still hadn't properly celebrated it with Nat, however. At first she'd put that down to Nat's illness – a bad bout of flu that had her off work for a fortnight. Then even when Nat was better she claimed she couldn't drink and was too weak to go out much. Gemma had held off, assuming that once Nat was back to full fitness and ready to go out to the pub again, they'd get the chance to drink to her engagement together. It just hadn't happened yet. She'd barely seen Nat – when Nat had been ill she hadn't seemed to want Gemma there, and then once she was back at work, their days off had rarely coincided. That was the problem with having customer-facing jobs – the hours were rarely nine-to-five or Monday to Friday. It was sometimes hard enough finding days to spend with Ben.

With the shopping bought she hurried home and got every-thing prepared, the table set and the sitting room tidied before the time Ben was due. She grinned. She was turning into a proper little housewife. Her mother would be proud. Well, as long as Ben didn't expect this every night once they were living together. Unless he did it at least fifty per cent of the time…

The doorbell rang at precisely the moment she was expecting Ben. Just like him to be on time and not to use the key she'd given him. She let him in and reached up for a kiss.

'Erm, I brought you these,' said Ben, gently pushing her away, and producing a bouquet of spray carnations from behind his back. Not the most imaginative of flowers but a lovely gesture. Gemma was touched. He'd only bought ever her flowers on her birthday before.

'Lovely! How sweet of you – what's the occasion?' She felt a sudden panic – was it exactly a month since they'd got engaged? If so, she should have remembered, and got something for him… Did people celebrate their one-month engagement anniversaries? What was the etiquette? There ought to be a handbook for newly engaged couples.

'No occasion. Just, well, I just felt like buying them for you. Shall I put them in water?' He stepped around her and into the kitchen.

'Sure, thanks. There's a vase in that cupboard. You bought them simply because you love me, right? Looking forward to plenty more, if that's the case!' Gemma skipped happily after him and wrapped her arms around him from behind.

'Erm, yes. I suppose.' Ben pulled himself out of her grasp and filled the vase with water. He pushed past her to take them into the sitting room, and placed them on the middle of the coffee table. 'Is it OK if I put them here?'

'Yes, lovely. Right, I'll open the Prosecco and get cooking then.' Gemma reached into a cupboard for a couple of champagne glasses.

'Not for me, tonight, thanks.' Ben held up a hand.

'What? No alcohol?'

'Not in the mood. Sorry.' He took off his jacket, sat down on the sofa, picked up a magazine that lay beside him, and began flicking through its pages. It was the free county magazine that had plopped through the letter box a few days before. Gemma knew he'd have received the same one at his flat. She realised he hadn't yet made eye contact with her this evening. Something was wrong.

She sat down beside him. 'What's going on, Ben? You seem kind of distracted.'

At last he raised his head and looked at her for a brief moment. There was confusion and sadness in his eyes. 'Gem, we need to talk. There's stuff we need to sort out.'

'Talk? Yes, we do. Do you mean about the wedding?'

'Yes, about that.' He was still flicking over the pages in the Dorset magazine.

'I've started on a list of possible venues. I don't think we should set our hearts on a date until we've decided on a venue and checked its availability. OK with you if we do it that way round?' She was gabbling, she knew, but that look of confusion in his eyes had scared her.

'Gem, it's not about the venue. We don't need to be rushing into finding a place or setting a date, or any of that.'

'But Ben, we've been together seven years so I thought there'd be no point having a long engagement. Can't we get married next summer? Or even before – how do you feel about a winter or spring wedding?' She gave a little laugh, which sounded nervous even to herself. 'I really don't mind. Or actually, maybe I do mind, and the sooner the better, hey, gorgeous?' She moved towards him to kiss him, but he leaned back away from her.

'Ben? What's wrong?'

He didn't answer immediately, but stood up and moved to sit in her favourite armchair, the one she used to curl up in to read or watch TV when she was on her own. He was looking down at the floor. 'Shit, Gemma. I don't know how to say this. But Nat said I had to talk to you. She said it's not fair to let it go on any longer.'

'What's not fair? What can't go on?' Gemma felt as though a band of cold steel had clamped itself around her gut.

'Our engagement. We need to call it a day. It's not fair. On you.' Ben let out a huge sigh, and raised his eyes to hers. They were huge and brown and full of sadness.

'What do you mean, not fair on me?' Gemma was full of foreboding. Surely Ben wasn't cheating on her, was he?

'I'm releasing you, Gemma, from your promise.'

'Releasing? That sounds a bit Victorian. I don't want to be released. I want to marry you, Ben!' She stood and paced around the sitting room.

'I pushed you into it. You weren't ready. We'll call it off for now, and see how things go, and maybe… in time…'

'I was ready! I *am* ready!' She was screaming now. How could he be doing this to her? She'd been so happy knowing they were finally going to get married. Suddenly she felt as though she barely knew him at all. Seven years they'd been together. Seven years! She should have insisted they move in together. He must be seeing someone else. 'Is there someone else?'

'No. There's no one else. I just don't think now's the right time…'

He sounded so lame. He didn't really have a reason for breaking things off. Gemma recalled that he'd mentioned Nat at the start of this conversation. Surely he wasn't cheating on her with her best friend? The thought made her feel sick. 'Why did you mention Nat?'

'Nat?'

'At the start of this conversation. You said Nat had said you must talk to me. What's that all about?'

'Nat's been a good friend. She's been advising me.'

'When?'

'When she was sick. I was round there a lot, remember, helping to look after her. We got talking. She advised me.'

'You're having an affair with her?' Gemma whispered. If that were true, it would be unbearable, the worst thing that could happen…

'No! Not at all! Oh God, don't think that for one minute!' Ben's eyes were wide, and she believed him, with a rush of relief. 'We were talking, that's all, and she knows you so well and we discussed my proposal and your acceptance in detail. That's all. And Gemma, we really shouldn't marry just because we've been together so long and people expect us to. There has to be more to it than that. Otherwise we'd just be doing it for form's sake. Not because we *really* wanted to. I get that you have reservations and feel pressurised. I don't want you to feel like that. So I think we need to call it off, have a bit of a break, and then if we really can't live without each other we can try again, properly – move in together, make commitments and everything. Or we might find we're happier apart. It's been so long. Can you even remember being single?' He gave a hollow laugh but his eyes were blank.

Gemma realised her mouth had dropped open. He was making no sense. First he said it wasn't the right time, then he said they'd only got engaged because it was expected of them. Suddenly she realised what he was really trying to say. He'd got cold feet.

She shook her head sadly. Better to let him go, in a dignified manner, than rant and rage at him, although her instincts were telling her to shout and throw things. 'If that's how you feel, then I suppose you are right. We should call it off.' Breaks my heart to do so, she wanted to add, but stopped herself. She pressed her lips together and stood up, picking up his jacket to hand to him. 'I suppose you should just go, now. What the fuck did you bring me flowers for, if you knew you were going to ditch me?'

'I don't know. Kind of an apology in advance.' He took the jacket from her and shrugged it on.

'It didn't work. Well. See you around, then.' She opened the door and waited for him to leave.

He paused as he passed her, and looked as though he was about to say something more. There was hurt in his eyes. Hurt! He'd dumped her, not the other way round! She held his gaze, hardening her expression, until he sighed and went on his way.

She closed the door behind him, counted slowly to ten to be sure he was downstairs, out the door and out of earshot and then let out a huge roar of frustration, disappointment and pain. She grabbed the flowers and stuffed them into the kitchen bin, screaming. 'Apologise with flowers for breaking my heart? You git, Ben. You absolute bloody GIT!'

***

Gemma looked at the half-prepared dinner ingredients. The last thing she felt like doing now was cooking or eating. She considered the still-unopened Prosecco. If she opened that she'd be in danger of finishing the bottle. How sad was that, drinking alone? She realised she needed to be with someone who understood and could help her through this. Whenever she'd had any kind of stress in the past she'd turned to Ben, and if not Ben, to Nat. So in this case, it would have to be Nat. Thank goodness the misunderstanding about Nat's illness was all in the past. She went to the bathroom and splashed cold water on her face, then grabbed a jacket and her bag, and left her flat to drive the short distance across town to Nat's tiny rented flat, remembering the evening when Nat had cheered her up after being dumped years before. Somehow she felt that even Nat wouldn't be able to work the same magic this time. This was far more serious. But she needed her. She wanted too, to find out what Nat had said to Ben, when they'd discussed the engagement.

As she rang Nat's doorbell she took a deep breath. She didn't want to blub all over her friend but knew it was pretty likely that was exactly what she would do.

Nat answered the door quickly, and looked surprised to see Gemma there.

'Can I come in? Need a friend,' Gemma said, and felt her eyes well up with tears. So much for not blubbing.

'Course you can, Gem. What's happened? Need wine?'

Gemma nodded and followed Nat inside. 'Ben's dumped me.'

'Whaaaat? Jesus, you DO need wine. Give me two seconds.' Nat disappeared into the kitchen while Gemma went into the tiny living room and slumped on the sofa, her head lolling over one armrest and her feet over the other.

Nat was back within a minute with two glasses and an open bottle of Pinot Grigio. 'It's not cold, I'm afraid. Didn't expect you. Now come on, tell all.'

Gemma told her the full story, while Nat sat on the floor beside her and poured the wine. She struggled as she tried to explain Ben's reasoning, and realised she simply didn't understand it herself. He'd made absolutely no sense. 'He said he'd spoken to you about this, and that you'd given him some advice. What did he say? What did you tell him?'

Nat took a long swig of her wine before answering. 'Yes, he came round here a few times when I was ill, and we talked. He, well, he seemed unsure about your engagement, as if he thought he'd done the wrong thing by proposing. He seemed scared and uncertain so I tried to get him to open up about his worries. I don't think I actually, I mean, I didn't exactly advise him to actually do anything. I probably said he should talk to you sooner rather than later, if, well, if there was anything wrong.' She took another gulp of wine. 'And it looks like he did. God, I'm sorry if I've messed things up at all.'

Gemma shook her head. 'No, you haven't. I mean, if he was sure about us getting married then nothing you could have said would make him change his mind. So he must have had his doubts.' She sat upright and drank some wine. 'You probably helped. Would be worse if he'd let things go on and we'd planned the wedding and everything, and then he dumped me.'

Nat leaned forward and hugged her. 'So glad you're not blaming me. I'd do anything for you, you know that.'

'You're my best mate, Nat. I know you've got my best interests at heart, always.' Gemma smiled. After being dumped by Ben it was such a comfort to know Nat had her back at all times. She'd always been at her best in a crisis. It was your girlfriends who were always there for you, who you could really rely on, and Nat had always been the very best. What would she do without her?

CHAPTER 10

June 1838

Rebecca put down her stitching and smiled to herself. She'd been so happy since Charles had proposed. She loved to just sit quietly for a few moments every now and again, imagining her future as Mrs Charles de Witt, mistress of the de Witt county seat in Leicestershire, with a half dozen children playing at her feet, handsome boys who'd look like their father, and girls in pretty white dresses with ribbons in their hair. In these fantasies somehow Spencer would now be her butler, having left her father's employ, although she knew he would never do this. She'd picture a summer's afternoon, sitting on the lawn while the children played happily and Spencer served them tea.

Where was Sarah in this fantasy? Rebecca sighed as she realised that once again, she'd written Sarah out of her imagined future. If they were to follow her parents' wishes, Sarah was to move with her when she married and become her paid companion. But as she spent more and more time with Charles, Rebecca realised she had less time for Sarah, and no longer felt as though she needed her. It was as if, she thought, she was growing out of her childhood friend, as one grows out of a favourite doll. That was something she had never thought would happen. But increasingly, if she entered a room Sarah would leave it, or if she saw Sarah there, she'd turn around and go elsewhere. They met at dinner, and exchanged polite conversation in Papa's company, but that was the extent of their interaction in recent weeks.

Papa had apparently not noticed. He would still refer to their great friendship, talk about Sarah as being Rebecca's sister, and smile happily whenever he saw the two of them together.

At the thought of Papa, Rebecca's forehead creased in a frown. She was worried about him. She'd noticed him clutch at his chest, gasp for breath and redden on a few occasions. He would always shake off anyone who expressed concern. 'I'm perfectly well, thank you very much. Just let me have a bit of space and air and I shall be fine,' he'd say. And indeed, he would recover quickly and go about his business. Once, Spencer had been in the vicinity when Papa had one of his attacks, and he had looked very concerned, talking about bed rest and sending for the doctor, and cutting down on after-dinner port for the sake of his health. Papa had, of course, shrugged all this off and had admonished Spencer for fussing. 'Like an old woman, you are, Spencer. Leave me alone!'

But it did seem as though Papa himself might be quietly worried about his health, Rebecca thought. He'd been spending a lot of time in his study, sorting paperwork, and his solicitor Mr Neville, a short, beady-eyed man, had visited on several occasions. Rebecca had the idea they'd been preparing Papa's will. And Papa appeared increasingly keen for Rebecca and Charles to marry as soon as possible. 'Wed, settle, install Sarah, and I will be at peace knowing you are both happy,' he'd said, more than once.

Rebecca was happy to get married quickly too, but Charles had not so far talked about setting a date. She had hinted at how lovely a summer wedding would be, but he had not picked up on it. Ah well, they were young, and there was plenty of time. No need to rush things. She was perfectly happy as she was, and if theirs was to be a long engagement, then it would be a long and happy one.

Charles wasn't due to visit today, and indeed the weather was poor for the time of year – there had been squally showers and gusty winds all morning – so it was with surprise that Rebecca heard his voice in the hallway. She quickly put away her sewing project, patted her hair and smoothed her skirts, and went out to greet him.

As she left the drawing room she stopped abruptly. Charles was at the other side of the hallway, near the entrance to the passageway that led to the kitchens and other servants' areas. He'd clearly come in from that way, and was shaking rain from his hat. Sarah was with him. She was wearing her scarlet riding habit, and was also damp and flushed. They had obviously been out riding.

Rebecca stepped back into the shadows of the doorway. What did Sarah mean by going out riding with *her* fiancé? Why hadn't Charles said he would visit today? They were standing close, and talking. Rebecca strained her ears to hear what they were saying, but could not make it out. She watched as Sarah laid a hand on Charles's arm and stretched up to mutter something in his ear. Whatever she said must have been amusing for Charles threw back his head and laughed aloud. Sarah looked triumphant at having entertained him. Rebecca had the awful, terrible feeling they were laughing at her expense. Why should she think that? Why was she hiding away here, and not walking across the hall to greet her fiancé? She shook her head to pull herself together, straightened her shoulders and stepped forward.

'Why, Charles, what a surprise! I did not know you were to

call on us today. Isn't it a wonderful surprise, Sarah?' She smiled brightly at both of them.

'Rebecca! My dear, I was out riding, and had not intended calling today, for the weather is not such that we could go for a walk together. But I came across Sarah, also out on her horse, and we completed our ride together. Despite the rain and the wind, or perhaps because of it, it was a thrilling jaunt, was it not, Sarah?' Charles turned to Sarah for confirmation. She was scowling at Rebecca but rearranged her face into a smile for Charles.

'It was, indeed. Such a pity you don't ride, Rebecca. You miss out on so much. Doesn't she, Charles? Do you think you will ever persuade her? I suppose if you cannot, then you can always come riding with me. I shall *never* say no to you.' She smiled flirtatiously and then headed for the staircase. 'Excuse me. I must change out of these wet things.'

Rebecca watched her leave and then turned back to Charles. 'Don't ask her to ride with you again, please, Charles. I don't like to think of the two of you out without me.'

'My dear, I did not ask her. Not on this occasion, in any case. I came across her, on the road just outside Bridhampton. We chatted for a few minutes then as it began to rain, she suggested we gallop back here together.' He sighed, and took her hand. 'Why do you not like to think of us riding together? Your fiancé and your sister – is it not a good thing that we are friends?'

'She is not my sister,' Rebecca retorted. 'She is the daughter of our one-time housekeeper. That is all. My father continued to give her a home after her mother died out of the goodness of his heart. Sometimes I wish he had not done so.'

'Rebecca! That is harsh. Where else would she have gone? Would you have had her go to the workhouse? I only referred to her as your sister because that is how you yourself described her in the past, when I first met you. I don't know what has caused this cooling of your relationship with her but I sincerely hope it can be reversed. If there is anything I can do to help reconcile the two of you, then of course I will do it – you only have to ask.'

'The only thing I ask is that you stop riding with her. If you desire a riding companion then there are always grooms in our stables who need to exercise Papa's horses. Go with one of them.'

'I can't ask your father's servants to ride with me. They are busy with other duties. You must excuse me now, Rebecca. It looks as though the rain has eased off. I should go home and change my clothes. I shall call on you tomorrow, if the weather is fine.' He bowed to her and left, by the servants' passageway.

Rebecca was left standing alone in the hallway. She realised he had not actually promised to stop riding with Sarah, at all.

***

As he had promised, Charles returned the next day. Rebecca was pleased that he came to the front door, where he was admitted by Spencer, and shown straight into the drawing room where she had been sitting quietly reading a book of poetry. Sarah, Rebecca knew, had been lurking near the stables, dressed for riding, and hoping to catch him when he arrived and before he came into the house. She smiled. This time things had worked in her favour.

'Charles, how lovely to see you! Spencer, would you arrange for coffee to be brought to us in a little while, please?'

'Of course, Miss Winton.' Spencer bowed as he closed the drawing room doors, leaving them alone.

'It is a lovely day. Perhaps we might go for a stroll after coffee?' Rebecca said. 'Come and sit with me.' She patted the space beside her on the sofa.

'I shall stand, for the moment, Rebecca.' Charles strode over to the window and stood with his back to her, gazing out over the formal gardens.

Rebecca was puzzled. What was wrong with him? Usually he would sit beside her, kiss her hand, chat happily about this and that, and all in all seem both delighted and contented to be in her presence. Today there was a prickliness about him, an unease. As if he had something to say to her and yet didn't know how to say it. She began to feel uneasy herself. 'Does it look as though the sun will stay out?' she said, to fill the silence. 'After yesterday's squalls it is good to have some more settled weather. The garden will have appreciated the rain, I think, though not the wind…'

He turned to face her. 'I'm sorry, what were you saying?'

'Nothing of importance, dear Charles, I was just rambling about the weather and the garden. Such a very English topic of conversation, don't you think?'

He ignored her and turned back to the window. She felt irritated now. What was so interesting out there? She laid her book on a side table and got up to stand beside him, her shoulder leaning gently against his arm. 'What are you looking at with such interest?'

He moved away, crossing the room to stand by the fireplace, although no fire was burning on this warm summer day. With a sigh he began to speak. 'Rebecca, there is something I must say to you. Please, take a seat back where you were. This may well be uncomfortable for both of us.'

She did as he suggested, and looked up at him. He would not meet her eye.

'Rebecca, it is about our engagement.'

He was going to set a date? Her spirits lifted and she smiled. 'I am happy to marry as soon as it can be arranged, Charles. I see no reason to wait, and I know Papa feels the same.'

'The thing is, I don't think we should set a date. Not now. I – oh, this is exceedingly difficult. I think – I am not sure that we should marry after all. There. I have voiced it.'

'Not marry? But why? Have you – have you tired of me?' Rebecca could not believe what she had just heard.

'No, not tired of you, but, well, I simply don't think we made the right decision. I think perhaps we felt pressurised into it, knowing it is what our parents expected and desired. We should not have allowed their wishes to force us into something that isn't right for us. These are *our* lives we are talking about – our futures, and after all, we only get one chance at life. We owe it to ourselves to make the right choices for the right reasons, and give ourselves the best chance of happiness.'

He looked exhausted by the end of this speech. Rebecca was astonished. It took her a moment to formulate a reply. Her first instinct was to contradict him – marrying him felt absolutely to be the right choice, the one that would give her the best chance of happiness, as he'd put it. But if he didn't feel the same way, then the marriage would not work. He would stray, or stay away from her. They'd feel trapped and become cold towards each other. The love she had for him would endure, but it would be a bitter, unrequited love. He had made his feelings clear. She must accept it gracefully. She wanted to shout, rant and rage, but that would make the whole conversation yet more painful.

'If that is what you believe, Charles, then I shall not fight it. If you feel we were pressured into our engagement then of course we should call it off. Papa will be devastated, but he will want what is best for me – whatever will make me happiest.' She felt tears spring to her eyes. Not now. She mustn't cry. It would pain Charles to see her weep. She took a deep breath before continuing. 'I should hate to be trapped in a marriage without love, and if that is what ours would become, then you are right that we should break the engagement now, before it is too late.' She could barely believe what she was saying. With all her heart she wanted to fight to keep him, under any circumstances. But her head told her to let him go, if that is what he wanted.

He fell to his knees in front of her. 'Thank you, dear Rebecca, for making this easy for me. Well, not easy. It was not an easy thing to say, but you understand – you have proved you understand by your response – that it had to be said.' He kissed her hand, but she pulled it away, and he got back to his feet and returned to standing near the window.

Rebecca stood to leave the room – it was too uncomfortable to remain sitting there, in the same room as her ex-fiancé, and besides, she wanted to throw herself on her bed and sob, until she fell into blissful, oblivious sleep. But before she had chance to begin moving towards the door it opened, and Sarah stepped inside. She stopped as soon as she saw Rebecca, and looked from her to Charles and back again. 'What is happening?' she asked.

'A private matter. Nothing that need concern you,' Rebecca snapped.

Charles said nothing. He looked, Rebecca thought, deeply unhappy as he raised his eyes to Sarah's.

'Is your engagement over?' Sarah asked, her question directed at Charles.

He nodded but said nothing. A gleam of triumph crossed

Sarah's face. 'It is for the best, as I counselled you yesterday,' she said.

'You? Counselled Charles to end our engagement?' Rebecca was aghast. Was this all somehow Sarah's doing?

'We spoke about it. He seemed unsure whether the engagement was the right thing to do. I merely said he – anyone – should be absolutely sure before entering into marriage. It is a lifelong commitment, and I believe it should be for love.'

As Sarah uttered those last few words, she looked directly at Charles, who gazed back. Rebecca looked from one to the other. She couldn't decipher Charles's expression but Sarah's was clear enough. Not love, but lust. She wanted Charles for herself. That was clear. Rebecca realised she'd known this for a long time, but had pushed the thought from her mind. Well, it was up to Charles. If he did prefer Sarah, he was welcome to her. She was well rid of both of them. She lifted her chin, and strode out of the room without a backward glance. She would not let either of them see her pain.

Upstairs, she collapsed sobbing on her bed. How would she tell Papa? She resolved not to, not now. He was currently in London, and would hear of the end of the engagement sooner or later. She would not write to him to tell him, but would wait until he returned. She feared it would affect his health. To think only this morning she had been so happy – in love and with her life ahead of her. How quickly things could change!

***

She did not know how long she had been lying there sobbing when there was a tap at the door, and her maid Tilly entered, not waiting for an answer. She stood beside the bed, twisting her apron in her hands.

'Oh, miss, I have heard the news and I am so sorry, for you was very happy with Mr de Witt. I cannot think why he broke things off. Please, miss, if there is anything I can do, anything I can get for you...'

Rebecca pushed herself up to sit at the top of her bed, and Tilly hastened to tuck a pillow behind her back. She brushed away the tears that streamed down her cheeks. 'You are very kind, Tilly. I do not understand either why Charles ended our engagement. But he did, and I must live with it.'

'Pardon me for saying, miss, but he is a fool who will find no better woman in all of England, than you.' Tilly opened a drawer and pulled out a handkerchief, which she passed to Rebecca.

'Thank you.' Rebecca dabbed at her eyes. 'I fear he may have already found a better woman. He enjoys Sarah's company so much. I do wonder – might he transfer his affections to her? It would be hard, but I could bear it, I think, if the two people I love most found happiness together...'

Tilly looked shocked. 'Miss Sarah? Oh, no, miss. I don't think he would want her. Besides, she already has...' She clamped a hand over her mouth.

'Sarah already has – what?' prompted Rebecca.

'I were going to say, miss, but probably shouldn't, but you being the mistress I can't keep no secrets from you...'

'Tilly, please get to the point.'

'Yes miss, sorry miss.' Tilly blushed. 'I were going to say, Miss Sarah already has a sweetheart. 'Tis that Jed Arthur, miss. Word is she goes out to meet him, sometimes on her horse, sometimes walking. He's not her class, but she do seem to like him a lot.'

Rebecca nodded, but said nothing. She recalled how she had seen Sarah with Jed on the day Charles had proposed. So the servants had noticed too, and were gossiping. She should put a stop to that, she supposed, to save Sarah's reputation. But why should she? If Sarah really did like this Jed then she was welcome to him. Rebecca would not stand in her way.

CHAPTER 11

June 2015

Gemma was still struggling to get her head around the fact that Ben had dumped her by the time she went to work the following Monday morning. She'd spent the weekend in her pyjamas, watching old DVDs and eating tins of treacle pudding with custard – the comfort food her mother always gave her if she'd had an upset as a child. Her parents had been horrified when she rang them to tell them the news, and Mum had offered to come to stay and look after her. Gemma had appreciated the offer but turned it down. She wanted to wallow in self-pity for a couple of days. Nat had been round. She was the only person Gemma could bear to see. She'd talked through the break-up a hundred times with Nat, and still could make no sense of it.

But now it was Monday, and time to pull herself together and get back to work. If she threw herself into it it'd take her mind off things. She felt ready for that.

'Morning!' Roger said cheerfully, as she tucked her bag into a locker and opened up her laptop. 'Good weekend?'

'Erm, no. Not really.' She might as well tell him now, straight out. She took a deep breath to try to stop herself blubbing. That wouldn't do. Not in front of the boss, even if the boss was just sweet, geeky Roger. 'I broke up with Ben. Well, he broke up with me, really.'

'What, your engagement is off, now?' Roger's mouth dropped open.

'Yeah. All over.' Gemma felt tears welling up. She stared at the laptop and typed in her password. It took a few goes to get it right.

'Oh. Well, I am, erm, very sorry to hear that.' Roger laid a hand on her shoulder in what she recognised was the best he could do at offering sympathy.

After an awkward moment or two she shrugged slightly to indicate he could remove it. 'It's OK. Well, it's not, it's really not, but what I mean is, I'll be OK. Right then. I'm going to do two boxes, then if you don't mind I'd like to dig around to try to find out some more about those ruby pistols and the people of Red Hill Hall.'

'Good plan. Well, I'll be out front. We've got a school party coming in this morning and I'll be giving them the usual tour. Christine's on the desk and gift shop.'

He left and she sighed. She'd almost managed to tell someone without crying. Almost. She put her head in her hands.

'Oh, coffee?' Roger was back again.

'Yes, please. Would love one.' She forced herself to lift her head and smile at him.

'Right then. I'll be back, as the Terminator says.' Roger chuckled at his little joke and once more left the room.

Two hours later Gemma had completed cataloguing the contents of two boxes as she'd promised. At last it was time to get back to the mystery of the pistols. She hoped it would take her mind off her woes. She decided to go back to searching the newspaper archives around the possible date of the shooting. She still had a list of questions to resolve. What was the relationship between the two girls who'd been shot? Had either or both of them died? And of course, who had shot them? Was he ever caught? She played around with different search terms and read each article in detail, saving any she didn't already have. She was beginning to build up a fascinating story of events at Red Hill Hall towards the end of the 1830s.

One article mentioned a new name, in passing – a man described as having been a frequent visitor to Red Hill Hall prior to the shooting. His name was Charles de Witt, and it seemed he was the owner of another large house, Carlstone Hall, in the county of Leicestershire, but resident for the time being in Bridhampton. Gemma noted the name, and wondered where in Bridhampton he'd lived. She began searching for more about Carlstone Hall and Charles de Witt. The hall was no longer in existence. A brief mention on a Leicestershire history website said it had been pulled down in the 1920s and a golf course built in its grounds. But the newspaper archive threw up some fascinating details about poor Charles de Witt.

'Good grief, another tragedy!' Gemma muttered to herself as she skim-read through the articles she'd found about Charles. *The County Herald* newspaper had the best report:

Body found in well believed to be that of missing Leicestershire landowner, Charles de Witt. *The partially decomposed body recently hauled from a well on the Red Hill Hall estate has been identified as that of Mr Charles de Witt, of Carlstone Hall, Leicestershire, who had not been seen at his Bridhampton lodgings for over a month. Mr de Witt had been engaged to be married to Miss Rebecca Winton of Red Hill Hall, Dorset. It is unknown how*

he came to be in the well, but it seems likely that he fell into it,
in a tragic accident, as there are apparently no witnesses and no
evidence to the contrary.

So, Mrs Winton had fallen down the stairs, Mr Winton had died 'of a broken heart' according to *County Tall Tales,* then Rebecca Winton's fiancé had met his end by tumbling into a well on the estate, and finally Rebecca herself, along with Sarah Cooper had been shot. Gemma was beginning to believe that *County Tall Tales* was right in saying Red Hill Hall was cursed. There had been far too many accidents in a short space of time. Obviously the shooting was no accident, but what of the other tragedies? Could the same person who shot the girls also have had something to do with Charles's death? Falling into a well seemed very unlikely to be an accident. Perhaps some distant relative would stand to inherit Red Hill Hall, once the Wintons were out of the way. But why also kill Charles? Gemma's mind was buzzing with possibilities. 'I should have been a novelist,' she muttered to herself. 'This would make a fantastic story. What would I call it? *The Suspicions of Gemma Rowling? The Mystery of The Ruby Pistols?*'

'How about *Confessions of a Museum Curator?* How's it going, Gemma?' Roger had snuck up on her.

'Oh, hi, boss. It's going well. Seems the fiancé of one of the girls who was shot with our pistols met a sticky end as well, not long before the shooting.'

'Wow. It was all happening in that neck of the woods, wasn't it? Actually I came to see if you were all right, I mean, after your shock this weekend. Do you need to take any time off or anything? Or if you need to talk to someone… I mean… I'm always, well, there for you, if you want me. Or need me. Or whatever.' He coughed slightly, adjusted his tie and left the room.

Gemma smiled. He really was the sweetest boss to work for. Well, her work had certainly helped take her mind off her problems. But each mention of Red Hill Hall reminded her that next weekend it was Anna and Jake's wedding, and even though she'd split up with Ben she still needed to go. Jake had been her brother's friend, and it was she who'd introduced him to Anna, when they'd all bumped into him in the pub one evening. She couldn't not go, although it would be hard to be there with Ben, and yet not *with* Ben. She wondered whether the seating arrangements had been changed to separate them, or whether she'd have to sit beside him throughout the dinner. That would be too painful for words.

***

The day of the wedding dawned clear and sunny, but with a cool breeze. The perfect weather for getting hitched, Gemma thought, as she looked out of her window that morning. There was bound to be some beautiful vista at Red Hill Hall, which would make an amazing backdrop to the wedding photos. If she and Ben had still been together, she'd have been making notes on whether it was the type of wedding venue she'd have wanted. She sighed. It wasn't to be. No point stressing over it. Today was a day for joyfulness, to celebrate Jake and Anna's wedding. They were a perfect match. Gemma was so happy for them.

She pulled on the turquoise silk dress she'd eventually bought, and put on some make-up. Rare for her to wear any but this was a special occasion. She'd found some flesh-coloured shoes, with just enough heel to look elegant but not so much she couldn't walk, and a patterned wrap to drape around her shoulders if it was cool. Add a small flesh-coloured bag and a long string of fake pearls, and she felt she looked exactly right for a summer wedding. 'Eat your heart out, Ben,' she muttered, as she inspected her appearance in her wardrobe mirror. 'See what you've lost.' She raised her chin defiantly. She would not be beaten. At the last minute before leaving her flat she tucked a small pack of tissues into her bag. Well, everyone cried at weddings, didn't they?

It was about five miles to Red Hill Hall – Gemma drove out of Bridhampton, along the bypass a little way, then followed a network of lanes winding their way amongst the Dorset hills until she found the turn-off to the hall. A gravel drive led between ornate gate posts, each topped with a battered stone lion, past a small lodge and then between two rows of poplar trees up a slight hill towards the hall itself. The grounds were beautiful. Obviously at some point in the past the park had been professionally landscaped. Huge spreading beech trees were dotted around, a stream ran through the lowest point of the park into a small lake ringed by ancient willows, and a pretty little bridge crossed the stream just above the lake, where peacocks strutted, displaying magnificent tail feathers. Gemma tried to imagine Rebecca Winton and her fiancé Charles de Witt strolling arm in arm around the grounds. She found herself hoping they'd had at least a few moments of happiness together before the horrendous events that had ended their lives occurred.

Eventually the drive rounded a bend and Gemma had her first view of the hall itself. It was a magnificent Palladian mansion, built at some point in the mid 1700s. It was made of a pale grey-white stone, possibly local from Purbeck, she thought. There was a grand central doorway, with a columned and ornate portico. On either side of the door were three tall windows, and a row of similar windows at first floor level with smaller ones above that. Signs pointed the way to the car park, which was tucked around the back and side of the hall, beyond a row of low buildings, which had presumably once formed the stables block. She parked her car and made her way over to the house and in through that beautiful doorway.

Inside, the huge hallway housed a receptionist's desk, and signs pointed the way to the various function rooms. Gemma had a single bedroom booked for the night, so she checked in and took her small overnight bag up to her room – on the top floor, and presumably once a servant's room. Its window looked out over the neat Italianate gardens at the back of the house. Back downstairs she followed signs to Anna and Jake's wedding, which was to be held in a modern extension at the side of the house. She felt disappointed it wasn't in one of the old rooms, but supposed none were quite big enough. At least the bar, breakfast restaurant and residents' lounge were in the old parts of the house. She'd get a chance to explore in the morning. For now, guests were beginning to arrive for the wedding and it was time to claim her seat for the ceremony.

Gemma took a deep breath before entering the wedding room. She knew Ben had been asked to be an usher. Sure enough, he was just inside the doorway, handing out the orders of service. Gemma kept to the other side of the entrance and took her order of service from another usher – a friend of Jake's. She was careful not to catch Ben's eye, although she could feel his gaze on her back. It was ridiculous. A few weeks ago they'd been each other's best mate, as well as lovers. And now they couldn't even look at each other. She felt tears prickling and blinked in an attempt to stop them falling, then took a seat on the groom's side of the hall.

She glanced around the room. It had been beautifully decorated, with huge arrangements of white flowers on stands around the edges of the room. The chairs were all covered with white linen covers, tied with silk bows at their backs. Gemma was impressed by the obvious attention to detail. Even the order of service had a narrow white ribbon tying the pages together.

A few minutes later, Nat arrived and sat beside her.

'Hey, girl, looking good!' She fingered Gemma's sleeve. 'Nice dress. Seen Ben?'

'Saw him, yes, but didn't say anything. Wow, your dress!' Nat was wearing the peacock dress she'd tried on in *La Belle Femme* on that ill-fated shopping trip. It seemed another lifetime ago – it was when she and Ben were still together.

'Oh, yeah, well, I pushed the boat out and bought it in the end. Nothing else looked as good on me. Like it?'

Gemma nodded. 'It's gorgeous on you. I said that at the time. But wasn't it really expensive?'

'Erm, it was reduced when I bought it. So not quite as much as I thought. Anyway, shh, here comes the bride!'

Gemma turned to look, as Anna, wearing an elegantly draped off-the-shoulder ivory gown, walked down the aisle with Jake. 'Isn't she supposed to enter with her father?' she whispered to Nat.

'That's a bit old-fashioned. Anna's not some object to be passed from her father to her husband,' Nat scoffed. 'Much nicer this way – they're approaching marriage together.'

'Yes, I suppose so,' Gemma said. If her own wedding had gone ahead she'd assumed she and Ben would have done everything the traditional way. But this was lovely – Anna looked radiant and Jake looked immensely happy. Gemma was so pleased for them, although her heart was breaking at the thought that it would never be her and Ben standing up there, making promises to each other.

The ceremony passed in a haze for Gemma as she concentrated most on not crying. She was grateful to have Nat at her side, squeezing her hand and loaning her strength. Nat was the one person who fully understood how difficult this was for her. She was relieved when finally Anna and Jake were pronounced husband and wife, and kissed each other to a rousing cheer from the guests.

***

Later, Gemma found herself outside on the lawns in front of the hall, with a welcome glass of cold Prosecco, while the photographs were taken. She and Nat stayed to one side, well away from Ben who was hanging around with the other ushers. She'd congratulated the happy couple – Anna had given her an extra squeeze but had wisely made no comment. Jake had hugged her and whispered, 'My new brother-in-law's officially an idiot,' into her ear. She'd somehow managed to avoid shaking hands with Ben and Anna's parents.

The photographer called for all close relatives of the couple, and Gemma turned away as Ben put his hand up and yelled, 'That'll be me, then!' and bounded over to join the group.

'How can he be so cheerful?' she said to Nat.

Nat put an arm around her. 'Aw, he'll be just putting it on for Anna's sake, I'm sure.'

'Or he's just so happy now he's finally free of me,' Gemma replied. 'I can't watch this any more. I'm off to the bar. I'll see you later at the dinner.' Without waiting for an answer she went back inside.

The bar was housed in what had obviously once been the library. One wall was covered with bookcases, but Gemma was vaguely disappointed to see they were all modern paperbacks, probably bought in bulk from charity shops. Opposite this wall was the fireplace. The bar was at one end of the room opposite a bay window, which overlooked the Italian gardens, away from where the photos were being taken. It was a dark room – more suited to a winter's evening than a summer's day – but its sombre colours suited Gemma's mood. She ordered a glass of wine and settled in a battered leather chair to one side of the empty fireplace. There was a stand holding a stock of leaflets on a side table, entitled 'History of Red Hill Hall'. Gemma took one and read it with interest, but it mentioned nothing of the shooting or other tragedies. It was mostly concerned with when the hall had been built, and then what had become of it in the twentieth century, during which it had changed hands several times. The Winton family wasn't mentioned at all.

The last paragraph was the most interesting. It gave the new owner's name – Don Gorman – and mentioned there was a large archive of material to do with the house, that one day, when he had time, he planned to go through. Gemma smiled to herself. Now *there* was a project that had her name written all over it! She pulled out her phone and made a note of Don Gorman's name.

***

Gemma sat next to Nat at the dinner, at a table near the back of the room, far from where Ben sat at the top table with the bride and groom. They were circular tables so Gemma chose a seat with her back to the room. Even so, she was glad when the meal was over. Just the evening party to get through. She was beginning to wonder why she'd come, and why she'd booked a room to stay the night. She could have just come for the ceremony then gone home. Jake and Anna would have understood. Ah well. She was here now, and had already drunk too much to be able to drive home. So she might as well make the most of it. But first she decided to have a bit of a rest. She went up to her room and lay on the bed for an hour.

The disco was held in the same modern extension as the ceremony and reception had been – the chairs and tables now cleared away to the sides and a DJ set up where the altar had been. As Gemma came back downstairs and into the dance hall, the disco was already in full swing. She looked around for Nat. That peacock dress was hard to miss, but it took her a few moments to spot her, on the far side of the room, sitting down with a glass of something in her hand. She was chatting to someone, but Gemma couldn't immediately see who it was as there were dancers in the way. She began making her way across the room but stopped halfway, as Nat leaned forward and put her arms around the person she was talking to, and kissed him, full on the lips.

It was Ben. And he had his hands around her waist, kissing her back, as far as Gemma could make out. She turned on her heel and left the room. She'd seen enough.

CHAPTER 12

June 1838

Papa had not taken the news of Rebecca and Charles's split very well. In fact, Rebecca thought, he could not have taken it worse. As she had stood in front of him in the library, head bowed, telling him that Charles no longer wanted to marry her, Papa had collapsed into a chair clutching at his chest and gasping for breath.

'Papa! I shall fetch Spencer!' She tugged on the bell rope to summon the butler, then rushed to Papa's side, but he batted her away.

'I am all right. Just let me have a bit of air.' He was pulling at his collar to loosen it.

Spencer tapped on the door and entered, then went straight to Mr Winton when he saw what was happening.

'Oh, Spencer, he looks so ill! Should we send for the doctor? I am afraid he has had a shock – I had to give him the bad news that Charles and I will not be marrying, after all...'

'Sorry to hear that, Miss Rebecca. It may be the shock that has brought this on. Sir, I really think we need to send for the doctor now.'

'No need, no need. I shall be all right. Bring me a glass of brandy to revive me, would you?' Papa was beginning to breathe a little easier now and Rebecca was relieved to see the worst of the attack was over.

'Yes, sir.' Spencer crossed the room to where a decanter sat on a small table, and poured a glass of brandy. Rebecca noticed his mouth was set in a thin line, as though he disapproved of using brandy for medicinal purposes. But if it revived Papa then what harm could it do? And as Papa sipped it, his colour did seem to return to normal.

'There now, Rebecca my sweet. You see? I am recovered already. I am very sorry about your engagement. Extremely sorry indeed. Spencer, please send a message to Mr de Witt. I wish to speak with him at his earliest convenience, but do not feel quite well enough to go to Bridhampton, therefore I desire that he should come here.'

'Yes, sir, I'll send one of the grooms over immediately.' Spencer bowed and left the room. Rebecca kissed her father and then followed him out. She did not wish to see Charles when he came to see Papa. She did not wish to see Sarah either. Her own bedroom with its tiny adjoining sitting room was the only safe place to go.

She was still ensconced in her little sitting room, trying but failing to concentrate on reading her book, her mind circling over recent events, when she became aware of noise from downstairs. She put down her book and ran out to the top of the stairs. Sarah was at the foot and called to her.

'Rebecca! Come quickly; it is Papa!' Her face looked stricken.

Rebecca picked up her skirts and raced down the stairs. Spencer was shouting for someone to send for the doctor. The housemaids were running hither and thither across the hallway and Sarah was standing at the door to the library, her hand across her mouth.

'What is it? What has happened?' Rebecca said.

Sarah's only answer was a shake of her head. Rebecca pushed past her and into the library. Papa was slumped in the same chair she had left him in. His head lolled backwards and sideways; his face was a dark grey. She screamed and ran over to him, cradling his head in her arms. 'Papa! Oh, Papa, no!'

'Shh, Miss Winton, shh. Come away. There is nothing you can do for him. I'm so sorry.' Spencer laid his hand on her shoulder and gently pulled her away. She sobbed and threw herself into his arms, where he held her and rocked her as though she was a small child and he was her father. 'Shh, there now,' he whispered to her, over and over, as he led her out of the room and into the drawing room, where he settled her onto a sofa.

Sarah followed them in. Rebecca watched, sobbing, as Sarah sat down on a chair on the opposite side of the room. Despite their recent differences, right now she felt she'd have given anything for a hug from Sarah. If they'd been close like sisters the way they used to be, Sarah would have sat beside her, held her close, let her cry on her shoulder. But it could not be. Rebecca realised she was alone in her grief. No Charles, no Sarah to lean on. Only good, solid Spencer, but he was a servant, not an equal. She was an orphan now. Like Sarah.

'He's gone, isn't he?' Sarah said.

Rebecca looked up at her. Tears were streaming down Sarah's face. She felt a pang of pity for her. 'Yes. He's gone.'

'We're alone, now. No Papa.'

'You have never had a father. It is I who have lost my Papa.'

Sarah looked away, and then back at Rebecca. She opened her mouth as if to say something more, then glanced at Spencer who was still in the room. With a jolt Rebecca remembered what she'd overheard as a child – the secret she'd sworn she would never mention, about Spencer being Sarah's father. Her father had provided for Sarah as repayment for Spencer saving his life at Waterloo. She looked at the butler. He was gazing at Sarah with an expression of sadness and tenderness. Was he really Sarah's father? It didn't matter. All that mattered was that Papa was now dead, and she was left alone in the world.

Spencer's voice broke into her thoughts. 'Miss Winton, if I may suggest, it would be wise to take some refreshment to keep your strength up. The doctor has been sent for, though there is nothing he can do for poor Mr Winton. I will send also for your father's solicitor, Mr Neville. He will help with financial arrangements. With your permission, Miss Winton, I shall also send for Reverend Theobald. We will need to make funeral arrangements, and perhaps he may be able to help comfort you a little.'

***

Five days later, Rebecca was still reeling from the shock of her father's death. He had been buried in the family plot in the local churchyard, alongside her mother. She was glad that part was over. Papa had no relatives except herself, but many of the county gentry had attended the funeral along with the estate tenants, the servants, and Sarah and Charles, of course. As soon as Charles had arrived Sarah had flung herself against him, clinging to his sleeves and sobbing. He had gently prised her off, and approached Rebecca to offer his condolences. He had, she thought, promised to call on her again soon, but she'd been so upset she could not remember for certain. In any case, he had not called, so presumably he'd said it only for politeness' sake.

The funeral had been an ordeal, but Papa was at peace now,

Rebecca kept telling herself. Nothing more could hurt him. And he was reunited with dear Mama. She tried to derive some comfort from the thought of them finding each other, wherever they might now be.

***

Today Mr Neville was expected, to read through Papa's will. It would be but a formality, telling her what she already knew – as her father's sole descendant, and as he had no siblings or cousins, Red Hill Hall would pass to her. She was now a wealthy woman, Spencer had told her. She would be much sought after by eligible bachelors. He had promised to advise her, should she feel she needed it. Rebecca had felt numb. If she couldn't marry Charles she didn't want to marry at all. Perhaps she could simply run the estate herself. It was unheard of, for a young unmarried woman to run an estate the size of Red Hill Hall on her own, but why shouldn't she try? With Spencer, the housekeeper and the estate steward to help, surely she could manage? What would become of Sarah she was not sure. Perhaps somehow she might find a husband. But not Charles – some respectable gentleman from the middle classes. Or she might become a companion to someone else, or a governess. There were plenty of suitable occupations for a well-educated young lady such as Sarah.

When Mr Neville arrived, Spencer showed him into the library and arranged for coffee to be brought in. Rebecca was already waiting, sitting in a chair beside the fire. She gestured to Papa's desk.

'Please, Mr Neville, do sit there if you need to spread out your papers.' It was strange to see someone else sitting at Papa's desk but she knew she must get used to it. Indeed, if she were to run this estate, she herself would need to sit there to manage her affairs.

'Thank you, Miss Winton.' Mr Neville settled himself and pulled some papers out from his leather satchel. 'Now then, where is Miss Cooper?'

'Sarah is in her room, I believe. Why, is she needed here?'

'Yes, she is. There are elements of the will that concern her and I should like her to hear them at first hand. Spencer, would you send for Miss Cooper, please? And then return here yourself, as you also are mentioned in the will.'

Spencer went out to the hallway and had a word with a footman, then returned to the library where he stood near the door, awaiting Sarah's entrance. Rebecca sat in silence. The only sounds were the ticking of the mantelpiece clock and the occasional shuffle of Mr Neville's papers.

At last Sarah arrived. 'I'm needed here, I understand?' she said, looking from Spencer to Mr Neville and back, but avoiding catching Rebecca's eye.

'Apparently so,' Rebecca said, and Sarah took a seat near Papa's desk.

Mr Neville cleared his throat. 'Thank you for attending. As you know we are here today to read the will of the late Mr Winton. I shall read it straight through, and then will summarise the salient points. I should warn you, it is not, perhaps, quite as you might expect. Very well. I shall begin.'

He picked up a sheaf of papers, placed a pair of spectacles on the end of his nose, and once more cleared his throat. It was, Rebecca thought, as though he was putting off the moment when he needed to divulge the contents of the will. What did he mean by it not being what they might expect? She had no idea.

Mr Neville began to speak, his voice droning on in the rambling and unintelligible jargon that was typical of legal documents. Rebecca struggled to make any sense of what he was saying. She thought she had the gist, but then again, what she thought he was saying could not possibly be correct. She must have misunderstood something fundamental. She glanced at Sarah, who looked shocked but triumphant. Spencer too seemed as though he was struggling to comprehend. Mr Neville was now listing a string of minor legacies for the staff of Red Hill Hall. Rebecca could bear it no longer, and interrupted him.

'I am sorry, Mr Neville. Could you please summarise the main points so far, before finishing reading it out? I am not sure I have understood it at all...'

He looked at her with what appeared to be an expression of pity. 'Of course, Miss Winton. Perhaps I should have summarised it first. Very well.' He put down the sheaf of papers he'd been reading from, and picked up another.

'In summary, then, Mr Winton's will, which was made just a few short weeks ago and witnessed by myself and my clerk, says this: On the assumption that Miss Rebecca Winton will marry Mr Charles de Witt, the owner of Carlstone Hall, Mr Winton leaves the Red Hill Hall house and estate to his adopted daughter, Miss Sarah Cooper, in the hope that she will manage it herself until such time as she marries, and thereafter her husband will manage it. Miss Winton receives a legacy of two thousand pounds, which is to be used for her wedding expenses, trousseau and a tour of Europe with her new husband. Mr Spencer receives a legacy of one thousand pounds for his long and faithful service, and in particular recognition of special services rendered. Each of the servants receives...'

'Wait. Red Hill Hall is to be Sarah's?' Rebecca could not believe what she had heard.

Mr Neville looked over his spectacles at her. 'That is correct. As you are to marry Mr de Witt, Mr Winton wanted to keep the two estates separate.'

'But I am not going to marry Mr de Witt! The engagement is off!'

'Ahem. I am indeed sorry to hear that. However, at the time Mr Winton drew up this will, he believed you were to marry. He knew he was unwell and wanted to make sure both you and Miss Cooper would be well provided for. His fear, as he voiced to me several times during the course of our meetings about his will, was that Miss Cooper might find herself penniless and homeless, if Miss Winton did not continue to give her a home, or if Miss Winton died.'

'So he gave her *my* home? Sarah's the daughter of a house-keeper!'

'He loved you both, Miss Winton. Very much. He believed you were very happy at the prospect of marrying Mr de Witt and as Carlstone Hall is a substantially larger estate than this one, you would still be socially superior to Miss Cooper. He had no idea your engagement would not last.' Mr Neville looked at Spencer as though asking for support.

'What can be done? Can I contest the will? It is not what he would have wanted. Had he time to amend it after I told him of the end of my engagement I am sure he would have done so.'

'Rebecca, there's nothing you can do. Papa wanted me to have the house. Not you. It's a shame you and Charles have broken up but he wasn't to know that.' Sarah smirked. 'Listen, Rebecca, I shall not throw you out. You can stay here with me. Perhaps as my paid companion. But *I* shall be the mistress.'

'You! Mistress of this house? Never!' Rebecca stormed out of the library and ran upstairs to her bedroom. She would not stay in the house if Sarah were its mistress. That would be too much to bear. If she could not marry Charles to escape it, she would find some other way. She would go to London, be presented at court, do a season and find a husband in that way. Or perhaps she would not marry – she would find a way to keep herself. She could become a governess perhaps, for a good family. Or a companion – but not Sarah's. Someone else's. In her room she threw herself onto her bed, pulling a cushion onto her face to sob into. How had it come to this? All those possible futures she'd considered suitable for Sarah were now hers to choose from, and didn't seem nearly so attractive. What had Papa done? It was unthinkable! There must be some clause buried in the will that would provide for her should her marriage to Charles not go ahead. Papa would not have left her destitute. He had cared for Sarah, and admirably wanted to provide for her after his death, but not at the expense of his own daughter, surely.

There was a tap at the door. Rebecca did not answer. If it was Sarah – and who else would it be? – she did not want to see her. But the door opened anyway, and Spencer stepped inside.

'Forgive me, Miss Winton, for intruding. I came to see if there was anything I could fetch for you. A drink, perhaps? Something to eat? Or should I send for Tilly? You have had quite a shock.' His voice was sympathetic, but Rebecca thought she could already detect a change in his demeanour. He was already treating her as the second-rate female in the house. It was only a subtle change but it was there. His daughter was now the mistress, which made him, in a sense, now the master.

'Send Sarah to me,' she said. 'There are things we must discuss.'

'I will see if she is available.' Spencer bowed his head slightly, less than he used to, and left the room.

Sarah arrived a few minutes later. 'I have been thinking,' she said, as she walked in. 'I would like this room. It is bigger than mine, and as the mistress of the house I think I should have the superior bedroom. We shall swap. Or you could take one of the rooms on the second floor. Yes, the second floor would suit you very well. Also, Tilly will from now on be *my* lady's maid. You will have to manage without, as I always did.'

Rebecca could not believe her ears. She was to be thrown out of her bedroom, be allocated a room on the servants' floor, and lose Tilly who'd been her maid for five years? 'Sarah, the will is morally wrong. I shall contest it. Papa would never have meant for this to happen. You must see that. Obviously he wanted to ensure we were both well provided for, so I think we should act on the intention rather than the letter of his will. We should share the estate and live here as equals. We can manage it between us. If he had amended the will after Charles and I split up, I am sure that is what he would have done.'

Sarah smiled, but the smile did not reach her eyes. 'I have spoken to Mr Neville. The will is legally binding. We cannot guess what may have been in Papa's mind. We can only go by what was written in the will. The estate, dear sister, is mine. I have said I shall not throw you out. But if you continue to protest about our changed circumstances then I may feel I have no option. So I would suggest you keep quiet and put up with your new, reduced status.' She walked around the room fingering the furniture, the curtains, the upholstery. 'This is a lovely room. I shall enjoy living in it.' She turned suddenly to Rebecca. 'It is, after all, *your turn* to be the poor relation. I have suffered thus for so many years. Only

Papa treated me as equal. Your mother could barely stand the sight of me and you, despite our childhood friendship, have always made sure to treat me as inferior. Now, dear *sister*, it is your turn to be looked down upon.'

'I never treated you as inferior!' Rebecca gasped. 'You were my friend. I loved you as much as I would have loved a sister.'

'I *am* your sister. Papa adopted me, remember? And if you would just think back a little, you will remember how you always insisted I was but the daughter of your housekeeper. You never let me forget that. Well. I will send your maid to you to begin removing your clothes and personal belongings from this room. Spencer has already gathered the servants together to tell them the contents of Papa's will so they will do as I say.' Sarah did not wait for an answer but spun on her heel and left the room, leaving the door wide open.

Rebecca slammed the door closed behind her. How could Sarah do this to her? How could Papa have done this? It wasn't fair. Even if she had married Charles, she should still have inherited Red Hill Hall. She was a Winton, and it had belonged to the Winton family for many generations. It was hers by right. Sarah's parents, Spencer and Mrs Cooper, were nobodies – just servants. Papa had provided for Sarah and treated her as if she was his own daughter, it was true, but only because he felt indebted to Spencer for saving his life at Waterloo. Why had he then left so much to her, and nothing to his own daughter? She shook her head. It was incomprehensible.

CHAPTER 13

July 2015

The morning after the wedding, Gemma woke up in her hotel room with a hangover. She eyed the empty bottle of wine on the dressing table and remembered with a jolt – Nat snogging Ben. She'd purchased the bottle and brought it up to her room to drink herself into oblivion. Groaning, she rolled out of bed and into the shower. Thankfully there were tea-making facilities in her room, and after her shower and a couple of cups of tea she began to feel more human.

She decided to skip breakfast. What if Ben or Nat were there? Her mind went into overdrive. What if they were there *together*? What if they'd spent the night together? How could they? Ben had only dumped her a couple of weeks ago. Surely it was too soon for him to start seeing someone else. And why pick Nat of all people? Nat, her best mate? Gemma wasn't sure what hurt more – the idea of Ben with Nat, or Nat with Ben. It felt like a betrayal by both of them, and she couldn't decide which was worse. Even if they were attracted to each other, perhaps had always felt an attraction, surely because they both still cared about her, Gemma, they'd have resisted each other? For a while, at least, and definitely while at an event when they knew she could have walked in at any time. It hurt so much; it felt like a heavy ball of cold iron in her gut. Right now she felt as though she never wanted to see either of them again.

She threw her belongings into her overnight bag, picked up her car keys and phone, and went down the stairs to the entrance hall. There were several guests from the wedding milling about, but no one she knew well. Thank goodness. She just wanted to get home without having to talk to anyone.

But when she reached her car, she found Nat leaning against it.

'Hi, Gem! You wouldn't mind giving me a lift home, would you? I'd meant to call a taxi but I've no cash left. Fab wedding, wasn't it?' Nat's eyes were bright, with a smudge of yesterday's make-up underneath. She wore jeans and had her peacock feather dress draped over one arm. She looked in better shape than Gemma was, this morning.

'Nat, hi. Yes, I suppose I could give you a lift.' She unlocked the car, threw her bag on the back seat and climbed in. The cheek of the woman. How could she turn up, cool as a cucumber, and ask for a lift home after what she'd done? And why had Gemma agreed? She'd have to say something. Otherwise the Ben-and-Nat kiss would be sitting like an elephant in the car between them all the way home.

'Cheers!' Nat got in the passenger side and fastened her seat belt. 'So, where'd you get to last night? I didn't see you at all after the meal. Was hoping to get pissed and have a bit of fun on the dance floor with you. Some of Jake's mates were hot – we might have pulled!'

That did it. Gemma turned angrily towards Nat. 'For fuck's sake, Nat. It looked to me like you did pull. Last time I saw you, you had your tongue down Ben's throat.'

'Ah. You saw that, did you? Gem, it wasn't what it looked like. Yes, we did kiss, but just the once. He came on strong to me. He'd had a lot to drink, I guess. Listen, Gem, it wasn't me. I pushed him away, as soon as I could, and told him, no, it wasn't fair on you.' Nat held Gemma's gaze as she said this, and put her hand on her arm. 'Gem, you have to believe me. I wouldn't do that to you, would I? I mean, you've broken up, so really he's fair game, but it's too soon. And anyway, I wouldn't, because of you. You mean more to me. Honestly, as far as I'm concerned he's off limits. For a long time yet.'

Gemma considered this. Ben reaching for Nat in a drunken moment, perhaps not realising what he was doing, or who he was doing it with. She tried to remember who had instigated the kiss, but after the wine she'd drunk and from where she'd stood across the room she couldn't be sure what she'd seen. Nat had declared that she considered Ben off limits, at least for the moment. Did that mean after a suitable time had passed she would consider an affair with him? Gemma wasn't sure how she would feel about this. But for now, if Nat was to be believed, there was nothing going on. She realised she had a choice. She'd lost Ben, but she didn't have to lose Nat as well.

'OK,' she said, at last, with a sigh. 'I believe you. You're right – he's not mine any more so I shouldn't care, but I guess I've been secretly hoping he might come to his senses and come back to me. If he was coming on to you, that means he's not likely to.' To her shame she felt tears welling up. 'God, Nat, I miss him so much. It's unbearable.'

'Aw, Gem, come here, my lovely.' Nat reached across to her and enfolded her in a huge girlie hug, while Gemma gave in and cried huge, shuddering sobs on her friend's shoulder.

It was a week or so after the wedding when Gemma's credit card statement arrived. She knew it would be a hefty one as she'd paid for her wedding outfit and the wedding present by credit card, but nothing had prepared her for the four-figure sum at the bottom of the statement. The post had arrived early, before she went to work, and she'd torn open the statement envelope over breakfast.

'What the hell? How can it be that much?' she exclaimed. There must be a mistake. She scanned through the list of charges. There were two or three large ones she didn't recognise. What were they? She'd need to go through the wodge of credit card receipts she'd tucked into a pocket of her handbag. But surely she would have remembered transactions of that size. It wasn't as if she earned so much that she didn't worry about three-figure purchases. Looking at her watch she realised she needed to get going to work. Perhaps over her lunch hour she could check through her statement, and phone the card issuer. It certainly didn't look right. There must be some mistake.

It was a long morning at work. The credit card bill kept playing on her mind. What had she been buying? Between cataloguing a box of Victorian children's toys and some eighteenth-century china plates she tried to remember when she had used her credit card in the last couple of months. OK, so she'd been depressed after Ben dumped her but she hadn't drowned her sorrows in a shopping spree – that wasn't her style. She'd bought herself a few treats but surely they wouldn't have added up to so much?

She decided to have lunch at the museum café, and ordered a slice of quiche and a side salad. As a museum employee she was entitled to a discount in the café. She sat at a small round table in the corner and laid out the credit card statement and her pile of receipts on the seat beside her. She spent her lunch hour alternating between a mouthful of food and ticking off a receipt on the statement. By the time the quiche was finished she had gone through all receipts and there were still three items unchecked on the statement. They added up to over £650.

'What the heck are these?' she muttered.

'Is something wrong, Gemma? Only your lunch hour's up and I wanted to take my break now.' She hadn't noticed Roger approaching. She looked at her watch and realised she'd already gone five minutes over.

'Oh God, sorry. I was a bit distracted there. I'll get straight back to work. Want me to cover the front desk over your break?'

'Yes please. We're short today as Christine is off sick. I'll only take thirty minutes. I know you'll want to get back to your cataloguing. What have you found today – anything interesting?'

'Lead soldiers and a sad-looking wooden dolly. And a huge credit card bill. I'll have to ask you for a raise, Roger.' Gemma tried to laugh but it sounded hollow even to herself.

'What? Is that what you've been poring over?'

'Yes. There are a few things here I don't remember and can't find the receipts for. I know I've been distracted lately but didn't think I was that bad.'

'May I see?'

She handed the statement over to him. It was an uncomfortable feeling allowing her boss to see how much money she was spending. Roger frowned and pointed at the un-ticked items. 'These are the ones you don't have receipts for?'

'Yes.'

'They're for large amounts. Two look like internet shopping. Have you checked for email receipts?'

'I never use my credit card to shop online,' Gemma said. She was beginning to feel scared.

'Hmm. I wonder if you've been the victim of credit card fraud. I think I would get this card stopped as soon as possible,' Roger said. 'Ring them up now. They'll put a block on the card and there'll be no more spending on it.'

'Credit card fraud?'

'Yes, somehow someone has got hold of your card details. Identity theft.'

'Shit. How, though?'

'No idea. Maybe you shopped online on an insecure site, or put credit card details on an insecure email.'

Gemma shook her head. 'As I said, I don't use the card to shop online and I'd never put the details on an email.'

'The third un-ticked transaction is from somewhere called LBF Bridhampton. Sounds like a local place. Hmm. Doesn't ring a bell with me, I'm afraid.' Roger scratched his chin.

'*La Belle Femme*?' Gemma said suddenly.

'Where's that?'

'A dress shop, just off the top end of the High Street.'

'Ah, could be. Are you sure you haven't bought something there?'

'God, no. Have you seen their prices? And their stuff is not really my style.' Even as she said it she remembered browsing in that shop with Nat, who'd tried on several items, including the peacock dress she'd worn at the wedding. The one Nat had said she'd bought in the sale, heavily discounted. But what if... No. Nat wouldn't do that. She wouldn't steal Gemma's credit card details, would she? Surely not?

'What, Gemma? Have you thought of something?' Roger looked concerned. 'I really think you should call the card company now and get a block put on that card. Go to the back office and call them. I can wait a while longer for my lunch.'

'Yes, I think I had better.' Gemma got up and went to the back room. It only took a quick phone call to the number printed on the back of the card, to put a block on it. The card company took the details of the disputed transactions and assured Gemma she would not be liable unless their investigations proved that she had authorised them.

'All sorted?' said Roger as she came back out to cover the front desk and gift shop.

'Well, the card has been stopped, and I won't have to pay. I feel a little sick about this.'

Roger put his hand on her arm. 'It'll be all right. Don't worry. They won't make you pay for the transactions that weren't yours. The one in that shop is odd, though, as it's so local. That kind of points to someone from this town having got hold of your card details. How on earth could that have happened?'

Gemma shrugged but said nothing. It would have been easy for Nat to get her card details. How many times had Nat kept an eye on Gemma's handbag while she went to the loo in a pub, for example? It would have been very easy to take her card out, copy the card number, expiry date and security code down. If a purchase was made over the phone that's all they asked for, no need for a signature. Had Nat copied her details then phoned the shop to buy the peacock dress? And made a couple of online purchases while she was at it?

'Listen, Gemma, if they do hold you responsible for those transactions and you're short of money, then, ahem, don't hesitate to ask me for help. I could, erm, loan you some money if you need it. To pay that bill, I mean. If there's any way I can help you, I will.'

'Oh, Roger, that's so kind of you but I don't think I could borrow money from you. It wouldn't seem right.' How lovely was her boss? Not for the first time Gemma felt a wave of warm feeling wash over her at Roger's kindness.

'Well, from the museum then. Against your next couple of months' salary, if that would make you feel better about it. Just don't leave yourself short. What an awful thing to happen to you.'

'Thank you. I'll bear it in mind. But hopefully I won't have to pay the whole bill.' Gemma smiled weakly at Roger. His face lit up, as it so often did if she smiled at him. He was so sweet.

'Well. I should get my lunch now. You'll be all right here for a bit?'

'Yes. I'll cope with the rush.' She rolled her eyes and he laughed.

'You're right, we're not that busy are we?' There was a total of about half a dozen people in the museum. It was a shame Christine was off, otherwise she could have got on with the Red Hill Hall research. That would have helped take her mind off things again, as it had after Ben had split up with her. Who were Rebecca and Sarah, and how had that man Charles de Witt ended up drowned in a well on the estate?

When he'd left, Gemma set to work tidying the display of postcards. As she worked she thought about the peacock dress. The *La Belle Femme* transaction on her bill was for £350. Was that how much the dress had been when Nat had tried it on? She couldn't remember. Perhaps if she went to the shop and asked the snooty sales assistant – she might remember whether it had been reduced, or whether it had been a purchase over the telephone. It was a horrible thought – to be sneaking around checking up on whether your best friend had done the dirty on you – but Gemma needed to know. The credit card company would probably be asking the same questions anyway. She wondered if Roger would give her an hour off this afternoon to go and investigate. Dare she ask him?

As the afternoon wore on the question tumbled around and around in her head. By mid-afternoon she had convinced herself that there was no way Nat would do such a thing. She was her best friend, her rock. Nat had stood by her through thick and thin. She remembered the time when she'd tried to take a day off work, from a previous job as a waitress, so she could visit her sick grandmother. The café manager had said no, they were too short-staffed. But Nat had walked in, taking a sickie from her own job, saying she could cover the shift, leaving the manager no option but to acquiesce. Nat was like that. Always ready with a practical solution, willing to put herself out for her friend. She wouldn't, couldn't have stolen from Gemma.

Nat must have bought the dress in the sale, as she'd said. It was sheer coincidence that whoever had got hold of Gemma's credit card details had used them to make a purchase at *La Belle Femme*. Coincidence, that was all. When all this had blown over she and Nat would be able to have a laugh about it together. Imagine, I thought you might have charged your dress to my account! she would say to Nat. That's a good idea – why didn't I think of it? Nat would reply, and the two of them would roll around laughing.

The more she thought about it the more she realised she'd been stupid to think for a moment that Nat had used her credit card. What a ridiculous notion that was.

CHAPTER 14

August 1838

It was two months since Papa had died, and Rebecca was still not used to the new order of things at Red Hill Hall. She had reluctantly given up her bedroom to Sarah, realising she had no choice. The servants deferred to Sarah always, and would only do what Rebecca asked after checking with Sarah first. Even Spencer, although in his eyes she could see him wrestle with the conflicting loyalties. Only Tilly remained completely loyal to Rebecca, despite being now officially Sarah's maid.

Sarah had made further changes to the way the household was run. There were new horses in the stables, and extra staff. The sitting room was being redecorated. The dinner hour was now later, to give Sarah more time to ride and then change for dinner afterwards. At least once a week she threw a dinner party for local gentry, but Rebecca had noticed there were no invitations in return, and their guests looked upon her, still wearing black in mourning for her father, with pity. She was sure they whispered, behind their hands, about how it was too soon after Mr Winton's death to be socialising, and wasn't it awful that Miss Cooper was now the mistress of Red Hill Hall, and wasn't she only the housekeeper's daughter after all, and who had her father been in any case? There were rumours, they whispered to each other, that it was the butler, Spencer; no one had ever confirmed this, but why else would old man Winton have kept the girl on after her mother died? Rebecca could see that Sarah would never become fully established as one of the gentry. Perhaps if she married well they would accept her, but people would always remember where she came from and how she had inherited the estate.

One or two of the older women looked sympathetically on Rebecca, and would ask her what she was going to do. How would she find herself a husband with no dowry and no fortune? They supposed she would stay with Miss Cooper as her companion, and wasn't that lovely, as the girls had always been such close friends as they grew up? But what a shame her engagement to Charles de Witt had ended. What a terrible thing for that man to do. And what had become of him in any case, for no one had seen him in the area for some weeks. He had apparently left the area although he hadn't given up his lodgings in Bridhampton – it was believed he had paid his rent up till the end of the summer at least.

Rebecca wondered about this. Where had Charles gone? Despite their break-up, she would have thought he'd have let her and Sarah know if he was returning to Carlstone Hall out of politeness if nothing else. She realised she had not seen him since Papa's funeral. She did not know if he had heard about her change in circumstances, but she assumed he had heard the gossip at least. Maybe he was staying away *because* of her changed situation. Well, he meant nothing to her now. Nothing.

It was around lunchtime that the news that would change

everything arrived. It was Tilly who first alerted her. She came rushing into the library where Rebecca had been quietly reading, without knocking.

'Miss, oh miss, there you are. Come quickly, 'tis terrible!' She was white, her hand held over her mouth.

'What's terrible, Tilly? Please, calm down and tell me what has happened.' Rebecca was seized with dread. Tilly wasn't a girl normally given to hysterics.

'Oh, miss, a body has been found. The water had gone bad and they sent someone down to look and it was a body. A man.' Tilly was shaking.

'A body? Found where?'

'In the well, miss. The old one up near the empty farmhouse. 'Tis rarely used nowadays since the pump was put in at the village. But one or two people still fetch water there to fill troughs for their livestock sometimes.'

'Who is it?'

'They – they don't rightly know. They are not sure.' Tilly looked away when she said this. Rebecca felt that sense of dread again. Tilly knew more than she was letting on.

'Where is the body? Who is investigating?' She may no longer be mistress of Red Hill Hall but Rebecca felt she should take control here.

'He – it – is in the stables block. They brought it here by cart. Doctor Millbank is there, and Constable Barnsworth. He is looking at the body to try to – erm – identify it.'

Rebecca began to cross the room. 'I must go and see if I can help in any way.'

'Oh, no, miss. Please. Stay away.' Tilly caught hold of her arm and tried to pull her back to the sofa.

'But I must. I am, well, I *was*, mistress here. It is my duty. Has Miss Cooper been informed?'

'She is out riding. One of the grooms has taken a horse and gone to search for her. Please, miss, don't go to see the body. It is truly terrible. I believe it has been in the water a long time and – is hardly human any more.'

'If Miss Cooper is not available then I must definitely go. The body has been brought to my, I mean Miss Cooper's, house, so it is most certainly my business.' Rebecca pushed past Tilly and left the room.

She went out to the stables via the servants' corridor. There were a group of men huddled around a rough cart, which contained what looked like a pile of blankets. As she approached, one of the men spotted her and nudged another – Doctor Millbank. He quickly crossed the yard to her.

'Miss Winton, please, do not come any closer. It is not a sight for young ladies. The body has been in the well for some weeks and I'm afraid is somewhat decomposed.'

Rebecca realised she could smell it – a foul, rotting stench that filled her mouth and nose. She put the back of her hand to her mouth. Her intention had been to view the body no matter what was said, but the smell was forcing her back. 'Do you know who it is?' she asked.

'We are not sure, due to the state of the body, but…' The doctor's voice tailed off as he looked back at the cart.

'You have an idea who it is?'

'The grooms here recognise the jacket. It is a fine quality, dark green riding jacket. Quite distinctive. Miss Winton, you will have to hear it sooner or later, and perhaps it is best coming from me. I am so sorry, Miss Winton. We believe the body to be that of Mr Charles de Witt.'

Rebecca felt the words hit her like a punch to the stomach. She gasped and doubled over. Charles had broken off the engagement but she had still loved him. How could it be him in the well, dead and decomposed? Charles, gone for ever, with no hope of ever seeing him again. The pain was unbearable. Please let it be someone else, anyone else, not him!

'Miss Winton, I am so sorry to have had to break such awful news to you. Come inside. I shall call for Spencer to fetch something to revive you. A brandy would do the trick. Come, lean on me.' The doctor took her arm and led her gently back to the house. Spencer was summoned, told the news, and he quickly arranged for her to be put into the drawing room, laid on a chaise with a rug tucked around her.

Rebecca let herself be fussed over. She found she could barely breathe, let alone speak, and the only thought that was running round her head was that Charles was dead. Dead, gone for ever. If only she'd had the chance to see him again. Perhaps persuade him to change his mind. Might he have done so, if he'd known what was in Papa's will? Her head said no – that would have turned him even more against her and perhaps towards Sarah. Her heart said yes – he would have taken pity on her and married her after all, as Papa had wished and expected. And if they had been together, might she have saved him from the well? How had he come to be in it, in any case? Now there was a question that needed answering.

She pushed herself up onto her elbow. Tilly was in the room, attending to her. 'Tilly?'

'Yes, miss?'

'Please, go and ask the doctor or the constable if they know how Mr de Witt came to be in the well. Did he fall in, or was he, perhaps p-pushed?' She stumbled over the last word. The thought of someone wanting to kill Charles was yet more unbearable. But he was unlikely to have fallen in by accident. The third option was that he jumped in himself, but that possibility was even harder to contemplate, for that would imply he was unhappy, miserable enough to want to end it all.

Tilly nodded and left the room. A few minutes later Rebecca heard screaming and sobbing in the hallway. She threw off the rug, heaved herself off the chaise and went to see what was happening. It was Sarah. She was hysterical – though Rebecca had calmed down now she could see that Sarah was in a worse state than she herself had been. Sarah was being restrained by Spencer and the doctor, but was thrashing around and screaming, her face red, her eyes streaming.

'No, no, no! Charles, dead! No!' Sarah wrenched herself free of the men and flung herself to the ground, battering the floor with her fists.

Despite their recent differences Rebecca's heart went out to Sarah. She was taking this even worse than Rebecca had herself. She ran to her one-time friend and knelt beside her, putting a comforting arm around her.

'There now, Sarah. Calm yourself. It's a tragic thing, but we can do nothing about it, and wailing and thrashing won't help at all. Remember your position now, as head of this household.'

'Get off me!' Sarah screamed, pushing Rebecca away. 'It's all your fault! He has thrown himself in the well because of you!'

'Me? No, Sarah, you are mistaken. It is not because of me; it cannot be…' Despite her words, Rebecca had a moment of doubt. Had Charles still cared for her in some way? Could he have killed himself because they had split up, regretting the end of their engagement? No, surely not. He would have come back to her, tried to rekindle their romance, and of course she would have taken him back immediately. No, that was not the reason. If Charles had thrown himself in, it must be for some other reason. Perhaps he had preferred Sarah, as she'd always suspected, and Sarah had spurned him? Which would make it Sarah's fault. She stopped herself blurting this out. She would not throw that kind of accusation around, even if Sarah did.

Spencer and the doctor were still standing nearby. Now was not the time to have this discussion with Sarah. It must wait. She stood up. 'Well, Sarah, if you don't want my comfort then I will leave you alone. But please calm yourself. As the mistress of the household, you should set an example here, and take charge. You must grieve in private, as I will.'

The words seemed to hit home, for Sarah sat up, wiped the back of her sleeve across her eyes, and heaved a huge sigh. She set her lips into a tight line. 'I shall grieve how I see fit, Rebecca. Now then, Dr Millbank, you must show me the body.' She held out a hand and Spencer helped her stand upright.

'Miss Cooper, as I have already explained to Miss Winton, I don't think either of you should view the body, for it is a gruesome sight having been in the water some time...' the doctor began, but Sarah raised a hand to cut him off.

'Nonsense. I am made of sterner stuff than my sister, and I insist on seeing it. I need to make sure...' Sarah broke off and shook her head sharply.

Rebecca frowned. What had Sarah been about to say? Whatever it was, she'd stopped herself.

The doctor was also frowning. But Sarah was striding across the hallway towards the servants' corridor, apparently recovered from her hysterical outburst, and he and Spencer had no choice but to hurry after her. Rebecca followed, but at a distance. She had realised the doctor was right, and if there was no need for her to view the body she should keep away. You can't un-see something once seen, and she had no desire to torment herself with memories of Charles's waterlogged, decomposed body. Better to remember the handsome, charming, lively man he had once been. At this thought a sob rose in her throat and she had to breathe deeply to keep herself from wailing out loud, as Sarah had been doing just a few moments earlier.

She remained standing at the kitchen door, from where she could just see Sarah approach the cart. Spencer stood close beside her as if to catch her should she faint, and the doctor, after a nod from Sarah, lifted back the old blanket that covered the figure on the cart. Rebecca watched as Sarah took a step forward, her hand over her mouth and nose, and looked closely at the corpse. She gasped loudly, then stepped back.

'It is indeed Charles de Witt. I recognise that jacket. He wore it so often when we went out riding. And the shape and size of the man are correct to be him. The hair colour, too. It is most certainly him. Oh, poor, poor Charles. To think he has come to this! Oh, the poor man, to be so thwarted in love he felt he had to take his own life.' At this she turned back towards the house and glared at Rebecca, as if to accuse her once more of being the cause of Charles's demise.

Rebecca turned and left. She would not be drawn into a fight with Sarah now, in front of witnesses. It must be left until later, and done in private. For now she felt the need to lie down, clutch hold of a pillow tightly, and allow herself to cry herself to sleep. And before she slept, to ponder – had there been a look of triumph in Sarah's expression? Something like the expression she'd had when she was standing at the top of the stairs, on the day Rebecca's dear mama had fallen and broken her neck?

CHAPTER 15

July 2015

It was a few weeks now since Ben had ditched her, but Gemma still could not get used to the idea that she was a single woman again. After being part of a couple for so many years she simply couldn't get her head around the idea of being on her own. Nat had taken her out to the Men At Arms once and had tried to persuade her to flirt a little with any likely-looking lads, but Gemma had shaken her head. 'No, mate. It's too early. I'm not over Ben.'

'You'll have to start dating again sometime, you know,' Nat said. 'You can't just sit at home and mope on your own. You're in danger of ending up as an old woman smelling of cat piss.'

'I'm so not!' Gemma said, punching Nat on the arm. She was quiet for a minute, then added: 'I'm more likely to get a dog.'

'See what I mean? You're already planning your non-human companions. Get yourself another man, and quick. Show Ben you're over him, and that he hasn't hurt you.'

But he *has* hurt me, Gemma thought. More than Nat would ever know. She had smiled briefly at Nat and changed the subject.

***

And now, at work, it seemed Nat wasn't the only one trying to persuade her to get back into the dating game. Christine, the part-time member of staff, had spent half her lunch hour perched on the corner of the desk in the back office where Gemma was cataloguing a box full of Roman coins and pottery fragments, chattering on about how it was a good idea to go out with a few different men as soon as a long-term relationship ended. 'So you quickly get over that awful first time out with someone new,' she said. 'When my marriage broke down I found myself a new fellow within a fortnight. It only lasted a short while, mind, but it got me over that fear that no one else would ever find me attractive. And I never looked back, you know. I had a lot of boyfriends, one after the other, and eventually found my lovely Steve. There'll be someone out there for you, Gemma dear, if Ben wasn't the one. Don't you fret about it, but do get yourself out there. You're hardly going to meet anyone eligible in this dusty old museum, are you? There's only poor old Roger, and I don't suppose he's your type, is he, ha ha!'

Gemma smiled politely at this, but shook her head. Christine seemed delighted with her joke. She slid off the desk and patted Gemma on the shoulder. 'Well, that's your agony aunt Christine's advice. I'd better be off back to work now.'

Gemma returned to her cataloguing. The school summer holidays had started, and Bridhampton was full of holidaymakers. The museum tended to be quieter on the sunny days, when everyone was at the nearby beach hunting for fossils, or walking the Jurassic coast path. But on wet days the museum could be very popular, and she would be kept busy out front, on the entrance desk or gift shop. On those days she got very little cataloguing done. Her research into the ruby duelling pistols had taken a bit of a back seat lately, but she hadn't forgotten them, and was desperate to get back to Red Hill Hall and find out if they had any archives.

She'd barely started typing again when Roger interrupted her. He was wearing a particularly fetching pale yellow cotton sweater today, despite the weather being warm. One day she would have to take him out shopping and buy him some decent gear that suited him and wasn't thirty years out of date.

'Sorry, Gemma, don't let me interrupt you,' he said, as he began opening doors and drawers.

'It's all right, you already did,' she said. 'Looking for something? Can I help?'

'Erm, well, some Sellotape. Blu-Tack. Whatever – I need to, erm, stick something up.'

'Second drawer.' Gemma pointed. He was being as odd as ever – it was clear he hadn't actually come in for either tape or Blu-Tack. Why he couldn't just come in and say what it was he wanted to say straight out she would never know.

He was still standing there, reel of Sellotape in hand. She tried to wipe the irritated expression off her face and looked up at him. 'Was there something else?'

'Erm, no, erm, yes. Well, sort of. Not work.'

'I'm listening.'

'So, erm, tonight, would you like to go for a drink after work? I mean, as colleagues. We rarely get to chat much. Thought you might like a visit to the pub, now that you don't get out as much.'

Bless him, Gemma thought. He was so awkward in these situations. He'd more or less suggested she needed to get a life, now that she was on the shelf again. Well, she might as well go out for a drink with him. There were a few work issues she could talk about. It could be a useful meeting. She forced a smile. 'That's a nice idea. Shall we invite Christine as well? Make it a whole-team event?'

'Erm, I think Christine needs to get home early. Her husband Stuart—'

'Steve.'

'Oh, is he called Steve? OK, her husband Steve is taking her out somewhere. Their anniversary I think she said. Wasn't really listening.'

'Aw, that's nice for them. Their anniversary I mean. She didn't mention it when she was in here a while ago. Anyway, yes, I can come. I wanted to talk to you about a few things anyway. See you later.' Gemma smiled at him, and got a blush and a grimace, which was presumably supposed to be a smile, in return. As Roger left the back office, having put the Sellotape back in the drawer, she realised it would be the first time she'd ever seen him outside of work. They'd tried to arrange a Christmas staff meal out last year, but he'd had flu and hadn't made it, and the year before he'd been on holiday with his mum. Gemma could hardly imagine him outside of the museum; he seemed so much a part of it – sweet, but as fusty and old-fashioned as the exhibits.

***

At six o'clock they closed up the museum, tidied the shop and put the takings into the safe. 'I'll do a bank run tomorrow,' Roger said. 'Right then, when you're ready, shall we, erm, go to the Red Lion?'

Not her favourite pub, Gemma thought. Usually populated by old men supping pints of real ale. But it was just across the road from the museum, and had a small garden that might be nice to sit in. It did not serve food in the evenings so was unlikely to be full of holidaymakers. 'Lovely!' she said, brightly. 'I'll just get my bag and jacket.'

As they crossed the road, Roger took hold of her elbow to steer her across. Gemma resisted the temptation to shake him off. He was just trying to be courteous, and behave towards a lady as he thought a gentleman should. It irritated her, but he couldn't help being so old-fashioned. His chivalrous ways worked in her favour once inside the pub, however, as he found her a table, pulled a chair out for her and insisted on buying the first round. 'Gin and tonic for me, please,' she said. A change from the gallons of Prosecco she normally drank with Nat, which didn't seem the right choice for an evening out with the boss.

Roger nodded and smiled as though he approved of her choice, and returned a few minutes later with the drinks. His was a pint of the local brew.

'Well, this is lovely,' said Gemma. 'Cheers!'

'Erm, cheers,' Roger replied, sloshing his beer as he clinked glasses with her. He fell silent as he took a sip, and then seemed unsure how to begin a conversation.

After a minute or two Gemma stepped in with some waffly chat about the museum: the themed displays they might exhibit, the layouts they could consider. 'I'd love to do something on local mysteries and scandals. We could use the duelling pistols' story as the centrepiece. We've got that hoard of Roman coins that was found buried in a medieval pot, and I'm sure somewhere there's a bloodstained nightie that's supposed to have come from a haunted house. It'd go down a treat with school parties. What do you think?'

'Erm, yes, great idea. You can work on that after the summer season is over. But let's not talk work, eh Gemma?' He blushed and took a sip of his beer. 'How are you?'

'Me? I'm fine, Roger.'

'No, I mean, how are you really? It must have been hard since you lost your boyfriend. I want you to know, Gemma –' he reached out across the table and put his hand, which was cold and slightly wet from holding his pint, over hers '– that I'm always here for you. I, erm, care about you, Gemma. As your boss, but also, I hope, as a friend. A true friend.'

Gemma looked in confusion at his hand on hers. He must have taken her expression as one of distaste, for he removed his hand quickly and reddened again.

'Sorry. Erm, well, that's what I wanted to say to you. Why I asked you out tonight. So. Yes, let's talk about this mysteries and scandals exhibition. Sounds like an excellent idea. You can design it. I'll agree to any reasonable suggestion. Yes. Splendid.'

He was waffling again. Gemma smiled indulgently and chatted on about her ideas. Might as well make good use of this time when she had his attention and he seemed willing to agree to her plans. She'd knock up a proposal tomorrow and get his agreement in writing in case he backtracked later. The more she talked through her outline plans the more she felt excited by the idea, even though it had only really come to her this evening. She found herself becoming more and more animated, and realised Roger was sitting back smiling benignly at her. Was she making a fool of herself? No, the idea was a good one. The only fool here was Roger, bless him, with his social awkwardness. It still wasn't entirely clear to her why he'd invited her out this evening.

They had a second drink, also bought by Roger who insisted on it. 'I don't like to see a lady standing at the bar,' he'd said, and Gemma had gritted her teeth.

When the second glass was empty she shrugged on her jacket

and picked up her bag. 'Well, thanks so much, Roger. It's been a lovely evening and I've enjoyed having the chance to talk about my ideas. I'll send you a write-up by the end of tomorrow.'

'You're leaving already?' He looked horrified.

'Well, I'd better not drink any more without eating something. No telling what might happen if I have three gins on an empty stomach, ha ha!'

'I'll walk you home, then.' He got up, and pulled out her chair. Gemma realised she could not say no to him without offending him, even though it was daylight, she only lived ten minutes' walk away and she always walked to and from work alone.

'All right, if you want,' she said.

They walked the short distance more or less in silence. Roger took her elbow when they crossed roads, but otherwise walked beside her, with a careful gap maintained between them. When they bumped shoulders on a narrow part of the pavement he apologised and immediately stepped back to let her go first. Finally they reached Gemma's building, and she stopped outside the door to fumble in her handbag for her key.

'Well, here we are. Thanks once again. I'd invite you in, only the place is a mess and...' She broke off. What was she saying? She didn't want her boss in her flat. She preferred to keep things separate. She was about to apologise some more when suddenly Roger's hands were on her shoulders, his nose was bashing into her cheek and his teeth were clashing against hers. Good grief, he was trying to kiss her! Her mind raced as she worked out how to push him away without hurting his feelings or ruining their working relationship, but at the same time making it very clear that no, this was not what she wanted, not at all.

She pursed her lips together to return the kiss in a chaste

kind of way, as if he'd meant to kiss her cheek and somehow had missed. She put her hands on his upper arms, gave him a short squeeze and then pushed him away. 'Yes, thanks once again. So, right, see you in the museum tomorrow. I'll get that proposal written.' Yes, that was the technique, pretend he'd meant a friendly goodbye hug and peck on the cheek, and remind him they were work colleagues. Anyone would take the hint their advances weren't welcome after that.

Anyone that is, except Roger. He kept hold of her shoulders. 'Gemma, I know it's not long since Ben left you but a lovely girl like you – you shouldn't be on your own. You need a man, and, well, I'd like to be that man. What do you think? We get on so well, we've had a lovely evening…'

Oh shit. She shook her head, trying desperately to keep her expression regretful but firm. 'Roger, you're so sweet, and I like you a lot, but…' Again, any other man would have been able to fill in the rest of the sentence after the 'but'. Roger, however, still looked hopeful so she had to continue, after heaving a huge sigh. 'But I can't consider you in that way. It's far too soon since Ben left me. I'm not ready to date again, and in any case, I'm so sorry, I just don't think you and I would be right together. We work together. We should keep our relationship on a professional level only.'

'Oh. Right. Well, if you change your mind…'

She smiled. 'Then I'll know where to find you. No hard feelings, eh?'

'None at all. Thanks anyway for this evening.' He held out his hand to shake hers. An odd, but typically Roger-ish gesture.

'We should do it again sometime. I mean, to discuss work, new exhibitions and all that. Thank you for the drinks. Goodnight.' Her instinct was to lean in and give him a peck on the cheek but she stopped herself in time, in case it muddled the message too much.

Inside, she flung her bag and jacket down and flopped onto the sofa. Well, that had been a surprising evening! Who'd have thought it?

She reached for her phone and dialled Nat's number even before she realised what she was doing. She needed to share the evening's experiences with someone, and as always, there was no one better than Nat.

Nat answered immediately. Gemma related the events of the evening, exaggerating the awkwardness of the situation at poor Roger's expense. She felt a pang of guilt – he was such a lovely bloke, but she knew she needed the catharsis of laughing about it all. At the other end of the phone Nat was in stitches, gasping for breath as Gemma went on.

'Oh, Gem! But he's so sweet, how *could* you turn him down? Just because he's got hands that feel like dead fish, the dress sense of your dad and the social skills of a duck-billed platypus, doesn't mean you couldn't be deliriously happy with him! Ha ha ha! I can't believe he tried to kiss you! Was it tongues and everything?'

'More like teeth and blubbery lips!' Gemma giggled.

'Ew! Like kissing an Australian blobfish! Remember when you were at uni, and I came to visit, and your flabby flatmate tried to pull me? We called him Mr Blobfish for years after, didn't we?' Nat dissolved once again into peals of laughter. It was infectious, and Gemma couldn't help but join in.

By the time she ended the call, her ribs ached and her spirit soared. The evening hadn't been unpleasant, the awkwardness was brief and she'd brushed Roger off politely and sensitively.

And she'd had a darn good giggle with Nat, reminiscing about the worst dates they'd ever had. It had done her good.

The one thing that was totally confirmed in her mind, after her brief experience of being courted by someone else, was that she wasn't ready to give Ben up completely yet. She was going to try to get him back.

CHAPTER 16

August 1838

Since Charles's body had been found Rebecca had barely slept. Each night she lay tossing and turning and fretting. Her mother had fallen down the stairs and broken her neck, while Sarah stood at the top with that expression Rebecca could still remember so vividly. That expression of triumph, quickly rearranged into shock and grief. Her father died of a heart attack but not before he'd amended his will and left the estate to Sarah. Charles, calling off the engagement and then, when he apparently wouldn't transfer his affections to Sarah, being found drowned in a well. Rebecca had lost her fiancé and her inheritance, all to Sarah – the girl she had loved as a sister throughout her childhood. But now – now she no longer loved her. She hated her. Sarah had taken everything from her. Everything! And now Sarah was threatening to force her to leave Red Hill Hall. Leave the house where she had been born, where she had always lived, and which she should have inherited, to go – where? She was as good as penniless. Rebecca's future was in tatters. There was no hope for her.

She felt threatened by Sarah, she realised. Her future, her fortune and indeed her life felt as though they were in Sarah's hands. She was but a plaything, and Sarah would not care if she were to be broken. A memory flashed into her mind – Sarah, aged ten, tugging a bird's nest containing fledglings out of the hedge, and flinging it down in disgust when it fell apart in her hands. Sarah had no respect for living things. If they ceased to entertain her or be of use to her, or, worse, got in her way, then she would do whatever was needed to be rid of them. Had she shoved Mama down the stairs? Pushed Charles into the well? The more Rebecca thought on it, the more she considered Sarah capable of all these actions.

Now Rebecca herself was presumably superfluous to Sarah's needs. Although the estate was Sarah's, there were still mutterings amongst the staff, reported to her by the loyal Tilly, that Rebecca should have inherited. Possibly they would never accept Sarah as mistress all the while Rebecca was still there. Even if Rebecca went away would they ever fully accept Sarah? Perhaps they would only see her as the true owner and mistress of Red Hill Hall if Rebecca was removed from the estate, in such a way that she could not come back – in other words, if she was dead.

Rebecca shivered. Could she really be in danger of her life, from Sarah, her childhood friend, her adopted sister? It seemed incredible, unbelievable, but yet, she *did* feel threatened. She should take steps to defend herself. To be ready, should Sarah try to harm her in any way.

It was with this dark thought in mind that she went to the hallway, to the display cabinet that housed the duelling pistols her dear Papa had bought. She checked no one was looking, and unlocked the cabinet. The pistols were not there. A couple of old, patterned plates stood on the shelf where the pistol case had been. It was odd. They'd been displayed there since Papa had bought them, several years before. Sarah was making changes everywhere in the house. To where might she have moved the pistols? Rebecca checked the library and drawing room but found no sign of them. Perhaps they were in Sarah's bedchamber, or hidden away somewhere? On a sudden instinct she considered the cellar. It was worth checking.

The steps to the cellar were at the far end of the servants' passage. She made sure Spencer was not watching from the butler's pantry, and made her way down, taking an oil lamp from the passage to light her way. There were several rooms in the cellar, storing wine, coal and sacks of potatoes and flour. One held some built-in cupboards and old, unwanted furniture – mostly broken chairs from the servants' hall. If the pistols were down here, that was where they would be stored.

She was right. The mahogany box was in an unlocked cupboard in the first cellar. She tutted when she found it. Something as valuable as this ought to be kept locked away. She would have a word with Spencer later. With a jolt she realised it wasn't her place to do that any more. The pistols, like almost everything else in the house, belonged to Sarah now, and if Sarah was happy to keep them in such an insecure place then that was up to her.

Well, at least it made it easier for her to do this. She hung the oil lamp from a hook in the ceiling. As she opened the lid of the box she wondered once again how things had come to this: that she was considering arming herself against her childhood friend. She eased open the lid, and gasped. Only one pistol lay within. The other was missing.

Her first thought was that it had been stolen – anyone could have come down here and taken it. Any of the servants, or even outsiders, for there was a second set of steps at the far end of the cellars, leading up to a door that opened into the kitchen garden. That door was often left unlocked, as it was well hidden behind high hedges.

But her second thought was far more chilling. Perhaps Sarah had removed the second pistol. Perhaps Sarah planned to use it against her. With shaking fingers Rebecca checked the other items in the box. Had the other gun been loaded when it was removed? All the other components of the box were in place, but it did look as though they'd been taken out and perhaps rather hurriedly replaced. The ramrod was not quite in its slot. And the flask of gunpowder was half empty. If Sarah had taken the pistol and loaded it – well, then Rebecca must defend herself and do the same. There was no further question in her mind as to what she should do. Her hands trembled as she took out the remaining gun. It needed to be loaded, or it would be useless. She racked her brains to remember what Spencer had shown them, all those years ago. She opened the pot of gunpowder, and poured some down the muzzle, stuffing a cartridge in after it, then pushed it all down with the ramrod. She tipped a little more powder into the flash pan, and closed the frizzen. There. Now it was primed and loaded.

All she would need to do to fire it would be to cock it and pull the trigger. Not that she ever intended firing it. But it would be as well to have everything to hand, so that if Sarah did threaten her, she would be ready. Ready to defend herself, or at least look as though she could, should the need arise. She tucked the pistol into a pocket of her skirt, closed the pistol case lid and cupboard, and began to make her way out of the cellars.

Someone was coming down the steps that led into the cellars from the kitchen garden. Rebecca turned to see who it was, holding her lamp high. She gasped when she realised it was Sarah. Thank goodness Sarah hadn't come a few moments ago, while she was still loading and priming the pistol. Lord knows how she would have explained herself. She remembered with a shudder that she had the *second* pistol, and that it was perfectly possible that Sarah had the first.

'What are you doing down here?' Sarah demanded. Her eyes flashed in the lamplight as she approached.

'Erm, I was looking for something,' Rebecca replied. Why did she even have to answer the question? The house by rights should have been hers, and she could wander around her own home as she pleased without having to explain to anyone.

'It's my cellar,' said Sarah, as though she'd heard Rebecca's thoughts. 'And I want you out of it. In fact, I want you out of the house. You have had long enough since Papa's death to sort out your affairs and find somewhere else to go.'

Rebecca stared at Sarah. 'It's too soon. I have nowhere to go, and no money.'

Sarah laughed harshly. 'Get a job. Live on the streets. Sell your body. What do I care? I just want you gone from here.'

How could she be so unfeeling, so uncaring, after all they had shared in the past? Rebecca appealed to Sarah's better nature. 'But why, Sarah? What has gone wrong between us? We were so close, such good friends, as good as sisters, while we were growing up. Before Papa died, we were the best of friends, were we not?'

'It seemed so, when we were little. But as I grew older I realised that we were never equals. You had everything. Status, family, money, inheritance, fiancé. Everything. And I had nothing. The daughter of the housekeeper, kept on after my mother died as an act of charity. Permitted to attend lessons with you only to keep you company. Expected to stay as your paid companion for the rest of my life. Pah! Not allowed to find a husband and home of my own! How do you think I felt, knowing that was the future I had to look forward to? And you never once let me forget I was your social inferior. Never once!' Sarah's spittle as she shouted the last few words shone in the lamplight.

'I would not have forced you to stay as a companion if you had wanted to go. If I'd married Charles I would not have needed a companion in any case. But you stopped that, didn't you? You wanted him for yourself, and did what you could to turn him away from me.' Sarah was not the only one with grievances. Rebecca had a sudden realisation that this conversation, or rather, argument, was going to be their big showdown. She felt strangely glad of the comforting weight of the pistol in her skirts.

'He had only agreed to marry you out of a sense of duty. He did not want you.' Sarah took a step forward, and her face, lit by the lamp, was distorted and twisted. 'And because he then broke things off, you prevented me from having him, by sending him to his death!'

'I? I had nothing to do with his death!'

'You hounded him. Made him feel guilty for breaking off the engagement. In the end he could not bear what society thought of him for doing that, and threw himself into the well. You're as guilty of his death as if you'd pushed him in yourself.'

'I did not hound him! What a ridiculous notion. I loved him, but when he broke things off I let him go with dignity. I did not even see him again afterwards, except at Papa's funeral.' Rebecca was furious. How dare Sarah accuse her of playing any part in Charles's death? 'And it is not only Charles you took from me, Sarah. You stole my inheritance. The estate should have been left to me, as the only child of Papa. Not you. You are right in that you were never my equal. You are indeed only the daughter of a housekeeper, with an unknown father. This house, these grounds – it should all be mine. Then I would be throwing *you* out, and see how you like that!'

'But Papa left it to me, didn't he?' Sarah said smugly. 'And my father may be unknown to you, but *I* know who he was.'

Rebecca longed to wipe that smug expression from Sarah's face. 'I know who he was as well. Actually, it's common knowledge. Poor Spencer, having a daughter like you.'

'Spencer!' Sarah threw back her head and laughed. 'You think *Spencer* is my father? Well that is what my *real* father wanted people to think, to protect his own reputation. Dear old Spencer went along with it, all these years, out of his sense of duty.'

'So who was your real father then? No one of importance, I'd wager.'

'He was equally as important a man as yours was.' Sarah's eyes flashed in the lamplight.

'How do you know? You never even met him. He abandoned you and your mother.'

'Oh, I met him. Plenty of times, all my life. And he didn't abandon us at all.' Sarah's tone was triumphant.

Rebecca shook her head. What Sarah was implying could not possibly be true. She was making it up. It was just Sarah's little fantasy. She'd always wanted to be a proper part of the family, and Rebecca's true sister rather than just adopted.

'So you see,' Sarah said, 'I am just as eligible as you to inherit this estate. In fact as Papa's firstborn, I have more claim to it than you. But it is all irrelevant anyway. Papa's will clearly left it to *me*.'

'You *made* him leave it to you. You turned Charles away from me. You have taken my love, my fortune and now you are trying to take my father. I hate you, Sarah! I hate you!'

Sarah laughed. 'And I hate you too, dear sister. That's why I want you out of my house. By tomorrow. Go, or I shall have you thrown out, and all your belongings burned.'

Rebecca looked down at her feet and let out a sob. Sarah sounded serious. She had always hoped that she would relent, and allow her to stay on. She had nowhere else to go. She put her hand into her skirt pocket and fingered the jewelled stock of the pistol.

'You will go.' Sarah's voice had taken on a harsher tone.

Rebecca looked up and gasped. Sarah was pointing the other pistol at her, and it was cocked. She pulled out her own pistol, and with her other hand swiftly cocked it. Now it was Sarah's turn to gasp. 'What are you doing with that pistol?'

'Defending myself,' Rebecca said. 'It seems we are evenly matched.'

'The pistols may be even, but the women holding them are not,' Sarah sneered. 'You do not have the courage to fire. You are weak and feeble. My will is so much stronger. If I wanted to kill you I could, so very easily.'

'And you'd be hanged for it. Drop the gun, Sarah. Put yours down and I will put mine down. This is just silly.'

'Silly? I'm serious. Deadly serious. I want you gone, and I don't care how. I won't hang. I'll say someone broke in and shot you and threatened me. They'd never suspect me of shooting you. I'm your *sister*. Your blood sister. Sisters don't kill each other!' Sarah took a step back and raised her gun, taking aim at Rebecca's chest.

'Sarah, no!' Instinctively Rebecca raised her own gun. How had it come to this? They were but yards apart. If either fired they could not miss from this range, and a shot on target would be fatal for sure.

'Why not?' Sarah hissed. 'I can't think of a single reason why *not*.' She brought her left hand up to steady the right, the one holding the pistol.

Rebecca kept her eye on Sarah's fingers. It was hard to see in the dim light. Was she squeezing the trigger? Would she? Would she *really*? Could she? The only thing she was certain of was that if Sarah tightened her fingers on her trigger, then she must match the movement and tighten her own. If Sarah fired, so must she.

CHAPTER 17

August 2015

Gemma had a week off work. She had booked it months ago, back when she was still with Ben, and they had planned to drive down to Devon, camp near Woolacombe on the north Devon coast, and spend their days lazing on the beach or walking the clifftop paths. On her own, however, the prospect didn't seem so appealing. Instead, she had decided to stay home and spend the week (the weather forecast was abysmal) pushing on with her research into the ruby duelling pistols and the events at Red Hill Hall.

She had contacted the owner of the hall, Don Gorman, and asked if she could visit to have a good look around. When she had told him she was from the museum and researching the hall's history he had been very excited. 'Yes, come, and I shall show you around myself. I believe I have something you would be very interested in, and perhaps we can come to some sort of arrangement...'

She had not been sure what he meant by this but his enthusiasm had spurred her on, and on the first of her days off she had driven over to the hall. It was a miserable kind of day – low cloud and drizzly rain – so she was in no danger of wishing she'd gone to the beach instead.

At the reception desk she announced who she was and asked for Don. Immediately a man came through from the little office behind the desk. He was tall with dark hair that had just a few streaks of grey in. His face was open and although not classically good-looking he had a friendly, welcoming smile. She liked him at once.

'Gemma Rowling? Welcome to Red Hill Hall! Is this your first visit?' He came round from behind the reception desk and shook her hand firmly.

'I was here a few weeks ago for a wedding,' she replied. A pang of pain rushed through her as she recalled Ben and Nat dancing and kissing. Well, all that was in the past. She must move on.

'OK, so you'll have seen a bit of the hotel, like the new function rooms. Let me give you the full tour. Or would you rather have a coffee beforehand?'

'Thanks, but no. I can't wait to get going,' she replied.

He grinned, and held open a door to the right of the reception desk. It led to the bar-cum-library, which she remembered from her earlier visit.

'I love this room,' she said, noticing that one bookcase was now filled with leather-bound vintage books, rather than the paperbacks that had been there before.

'It's beautiful, isn't it? I'm gradually collecting suitable books to fill the shelves. It'll cost me a fortune but hey-ho, to my mind it is worth it. One can never have too many books. Perhaps you can have a look through and tell me if I have any valuable ones in amongst that lot? They were all bought as a job lot at a car boot sale.'

She laughed. 'Well I'm no expert on antiquarian books but I'd love to have a browse through them.'

'You're welcome to, whenever you want. Right then, onwards?'

She nodded and followed him back to the entrance hall, then into what had been the drawing room and was now the hotel's dining room. Staff were bustling around, setting the tables ready for lunch. 'Not many original features left here, unfortunately,' he said. 'Just the ceiling cornicing and the fireplace.' It was another magnificent fireplace, like the one in the library but larger. A huge gilt-framed mirror hung over it.

It was hard to get a feel for how the house would have been in the old days from that room. So far, Gemma liked the library best.

The tour continued. Don showed her all the public areas, and a couple of unoccupied bedrooms. Sadly apart from the fireplaces and the library bookcases there were few original features left. The original servants' wing had been remodelled to provide some downstairs bedrooms with disabled access, and a modern kitchen added in an extension at the back of the building. Gemma tried hard to imagine how it would have been around the time of the shooting but it was difficult. She felt vaguely disappointed. Hopefully the archive, which had been mentioned in the existing brief leaflet about the hotel's history, would make up for it.

Finally Don showed her into a small office. 'This was once the butler's pantry, I believe. He'd have stored the silverware in here. These days we use it to hold something much more valuable, to my mind.' He grinned at her as he unlocked a built-in wall cupboard. It was full of cardboard boxes of varying shapes and sizes. 'Our archive. It's a mess, but if you're interested and want to help sort through it all, I am not going to stand in your way. I've done a bit of genealogy research myself – found my ancestors in the census records, that sort of thing – but although I'd dearly love to know what's in this I just don't have the time to go through it myself, plus I wouldn't know where to begin. It was all here when I bought the hotel.'

Gemma gasped as he pulled out a box and opened the top. It was stuffed full of yellowing paper and old, marbled notebooks. She looked inside, then pulled a pair of white cotton gloves from her handbag. She'd brought them from the museum in anticipation of exactly this moment. 'May I?'

'Go ahead.'

She put on the gloves, then carefully took out the topmost piece of paper. It was a letter, dated 1865, and addressed to 'My Dear Charles.' Underneath that was an accounts book from the mid nineteenth century, then a bundle of other letters.

'Wow. There is treasure indeed in these boxes! It'll take a while, but I would love to go through and put it all into some sort of order, and find out more about the history of this place.'

'You're very welcome to have access to this archive whenever you want. You can take over this room, spread out, do whatever you need to. May I ask, why are you so interested in Red Hill Hall? I mean, I'm interested because I bought the place, and because... well, never mind, but what's in it for you?' He looked at her quizzically.

She wondered briefly what he'd been about to say, but answered him anyway. 'Something happened here, in the summer of 1838, and I'm intrigued to find out more about it.' She quickly outlined what she knew so far about the shooting and the other mysterious deaths. 'I'd like to put the pistols on display at the museum, with a board telling the story of how they were used. I've been doing a bit of digging on the internet – newspaper archives and that sort of thing – but I'm hoping there might be some information in amongst these boxes.'

'Wow, so there may have been a double murder here?'

'Single murder. One of the girls survived.'

'And the man in the well?'

'The newspaper reports weren't clear on whether foul play was suspected in that case. He may have fallen or jumped in himself. But as it happened on this estate, who knows, there might be something in this archive.' She fingered the bundle of letters, itching to get going with the work.

'OK, well I had better leave you to it then. Let me know if you find anything really interesting. Can I bring you a coffee?'

She shook her head. 'Not in here, while I have the papers out. I'd hate to spill something on them.'

'Good point. Well, you know where the bar is, in the library. They'll make you one later if you need a break. And if you want me, ask reception to page me if I'm not in the office.' He smiled and raised his eyebrows at her.

'Thanks, will do.'

And finally she was left alone with this treasure trove of material. Talk about a busman's holiday, she thought. Nat would think she was totally crazy. She spent her working days going through dusty archives and had chosen to do more, unpaid, for fun, during her week off.

***

The time passed so quickly. It was only when her stomach began to tell her it was well past lunchtime that she stopped to take stock. She had sorted the contents of the boxes into piles spread across the tables. There were dozens of estate accounts books – both for the internal running of the household and for the income from the farms. Many of the internal accounts books from the 1830s had totals summed and checked each month, and a signature: G. Spencer. Who was he or she, Gemma wondered. Perhaps a housekeeper or a butler or some other senior member of staff. She had noted the name down. The 1841 census, which was the first full census of England and Wales, would include all servants who lived at the hall as well as the 'upstairs' residents. She had yet to check up on this. So much to do!

There were scores of letters as well, which she had attempted to sort into roughly date order, but she had not had chance to read any of them yet. It would pay to be methodical. Sort it all first, read them later.

And then there were some journals and diaries. Those would possibly be the most interesting documents. Again she had stacked them into date order, but keeping those with similar handwriting together. There were certainly some from the 1830s though whether any of them would shed light on the mysterious deaths at the hall remained to be seen.

Don tapped on the door and entered the room just as she was thinking about going in search of lunch. 'How's it going?' he asked.

'Really well. I'm having a quick pass through it all to sort it first, then I'll start reading through the documents tomorrow. There look to be some really interesting items here.'

'Anything to help with your mystery shooting?'

'I don't know yet. I really hope so. There are certainly some documents from around that time so hopefully we'll be in luck. And I should be able to write up a good history of the hall for you, with all this material.'

He smiled. 'That would be marvellous. When you have, I'll get it published. It'll be such a surprise for… But meanwhile, my staff say you have not left this room since you arrived. Come on. I'm taking you for a late lunch. The kitchen can rustle us up some club sandwiches, if that sounds good to you?'

'Perfect!' He held the door open for her and she followed him to the bar. He was tall and trim, with a muscled back showing through his casual shirt. Tasty, she thought, wondering briefly if she'd stand any chance with him. But as soon as that thought crossed her mind it was chased away by a wave of pain from having lost Ben. She was not ready to date anyone else, as the disastrous evening out with Roger had proved.

***

By the time Gemma left Red Hill Hall that evening she had re-boxed all the documents, but now they were sorted by type and date, ready for her to start reading through and making notes. Her back ached from shifting boxes and leaning over the table, but she felt fired up by a successful day's work, and was looking forward to getting back to it the next day. She was thinking about the archive throughout her drive home. What would she find? Would it deepen or resolve the mystery?

Back home she put some pasta on to cook, and treated herself to a glass of wine. She was on holiday, after all, so why not? She was about to sit down to eat when her mobile rang.

'Dad! Hi. How are things?' It was unusual for her dad to call her. It was usually Mum. She felt a sudden pang of worry that perhaps something was wrong with Mum. 'Is everything all right?'

'Yes, love, we're all fine. Are you having a good week off? I'm surprised you didn't go away anywhere, but I suppose with this weather it wouldn't have been much fun.'

'I'm having a great week. I'm doing some research...' She'd been about to outline her work when he interrupted her.

'Sorry, love, there's just something we needed to talk to you about.'

That cold hand of dread clutched at Gemma again. She knew it. One of them had cancer or something awful like that. 'Go on, I'm listening.'

'The thing is, well, it's a bit awkward really, but your friend Natalie wrote us a letter.'

'A letter?'

'Yes. A very strange one. We're not quite sure, your mum and I, what to make of it. In the end I said, well we have to phone Gemma and tell her, and get her side of the story. You're our daughter, after all, so we should believe you over Natalie. If it came to that, I mean – your word against hers.'

'Dad, what are you talking about? What did the letter say?'

'Well now, she said that at the end of last year she loaned you some money, as you were short, and were struggling to buy Christmas presents... Now you must know, love, that we don't care whether or not you buy us a present. It's enough that you come to Christmas dinner...'

'Dad, she didn't loan me any money. I wasn't short. Well, no more than usual.'

'... and she said that you'd promised to pay it back by March at the latest, but despite reminders she was still waiting for it, and you were refusing to see her now. I know that last bit's true – your mum said you must have fallen out as you'd not seen her as much lately.'

'We haven't fallen out,' Gemma protested, but he was right, she had not seen as much of Nat. Not since the wedding. She hadn't told her parents about Nat and Ben kissing, or about the credit card fraud.

'So, listen, we've been talking, your mum and I, and we've said we'll pay your debt to Natalie. I hate to think of my girl owing money. We've got enough in the savings account...'

'Dad, I never borrowed any money from Nat. She's making it up.'

'Making it up? Why on earth would she do that?'

'I don't know, Dad.' Gemma sighed. She honestly had no idea why Nat would do such a thing.

'You're *sure* you don't owe her anything? I mean, could you have forgotten?'

'Dad! I'd remember something like that! I never borrowed a penny off her.'

There was a pause at the other end of the phone. Her dad sighed, and then said decisively, 'OK, I believe you. Because you know, if ever you were short of a bob or two, you can always ask us. We'd not see you go without. But this is all a bit awkward now...'

'Why?'

'Your mum, she went straight off and wrote out a cheque. I said we should talk to you first but she wanted it dealt with.'

'Has she sent it to Nat?'

'I rather think she posted it straight away. Oh dear. We've known Natalie so long, of course. At times she was like a second daughter – always round our house at the weekends. Came on holiday with us a couple of times, didn't she? That time in the caravan in south Wales, and the holiday cottage in Cornwall. You two lived in each other's pockets when you were at school. Oh, love, I can't believe she'd be defrauding us like this. It just seems too incredible for words.'

'The alternative is to think I'm lying now, when I tell you I never lent her money. Who do you believe, Dad?' Gemma struggled to control her voice. Her mind was racing. If Nat was trying to defraud Gemma's parents out of some money, it made it seem more likely that she'd also stolen the credit card details.

'Erm, well of course we don't think you're lying, love. But what should we do? We've posted the cheque already.'

'How much was it for?'

'Five thousand.'

Gemma gasped and almost dropped the phone. 'Five thousand? For a few Christmas presents?'

Dad sounded sheepish now. 'She said you were behind on your mortgage payments as well, and had a large credit card bill. She said the loan was to get you back on top, and that she'd been happy to help, but needed you to start repaying it now before she ran into financial trouble herself. Oh, love, you can see why we decided to pay her back straight away, can't you?'

'Without checking with me first?'

'I thought we should talk to you first. But we knew you were out all day and your mother just wanted to put things straight. You know how she feels about debt.'

'You need to ring your bank and get the cheque stopped, Dad. Right away.'

'That'll cost…'

'Yes, but a lot less than five thousand! Bloody hell. What does she think she's playing at?' The more Gemma thought about it the more furious she became. Nat, trying to defraud her parents out of so much money? She'd been willing to consider that the credit card fraud had not actually been Nat, but not after this. Definitely not after this. It was too much of a coincidence.

'Dad, there's something else you should know. I had a problem with my credit card...'

'So that part's true? That you were in debt?'

'No! Just listen a moment.' Why did he have to jump to conclusions? 'There were some transactions on it last month that were not mine. One was from *La Belle Femme*. And the dress Nat wore to Anna and Jake's wedding came from there. It had cost a bomb, but she said it had been reduced.'

'What are you implying, love?'

'I think she stole my credit card details to pay for it.'

'Oh, but she wouldn't do such a thing, surely?'

Gemma rolled her eyes. Was Dad being deliberately obtuse? 'Just like she wouldn't write to my parents accusing me of failing to repay a loan I'd never had?'

'But why?' Dad asked yet again.

'I have no idea. I don't understand it at all. But I can see I am going to have to confront her and ask her what she's playing at. Meanwhile, please do get that cheque stopped. I'm still waiting to hear from the credit card company who are investigating that purchase in *La Belle Femme* as well as a few others that weren't mine. They've sent me a new card already.'

'All right, I'll phone the bank helpline now. What a mess, eh?' Gemma could imagine him shaking his head sadly and bemusedly.

'Yes. And I'll go and see Nat as soon as possible. That'll be fun, I don't think.'

'Do you want me to come with you, love? Moral support and all that?'

'Aw, Dad, thanks for the offer, but no. I think I'd be better off going on my own. Maybe there's a reasonable explanation.'

'If there isn't, and you're right about the credit card fraud as well, then we should call the police, don't you think? I mean, I know it's Natalie and we've known her since she was a child, but...'

'It'd ruin her, Dad. I know, you're probably right, but I feel as though I want to give her a chance to explain it all first. I'll let you know what happens, all right?'

'All right. Well, love, I'd better get off the phone and get on to the bank. Bye, love.'

'Bye, Dad.'

Gemma hung up. Her pasta had gone cold. She scraped it into the bin, no longer feeling like eating. Why was Nat targeting her like this? What had she ever done to Nat to deserve it? What on earth would she say to her?

CHAPTER 18

August 1838

She was drowning. Underwater in her bath. Water flowed through her veins, filled her lungs and dulled her senses. Yet the bath was soft – not the hard enamelled tin she was used to. The softness of whatever she was lying on, the warmth of whatever covered her, were the first sensations she was aware of. And then came the pain. Unimaginable pain. There was a spiky ball of pain, and she was wrapped tightly around it.

The sensation of drowning lapsed, but the pain remained. She was not in a bath. She was in a bed. People were talking – she could hear a blur of voices behind the incessant buzzing and pounding noises that filled her brain – but what they were saying she could not make out. There was a metallic taste in her mouth. Her lips were dry. She tried to moisten them with her tongue but the small movement just expanded the ball of pain. She moaned aloud.

'I think she's waking up.' Someone said that. She had been asleep, then. Was it morning? Why were people in her room? Why was she drowning in pain?

She forced open her eyes. There was light, and some dark shadows moving around in the light. It hurt, everything hurt, so she closed them again. She wanted to sleep some more so that the pain might stop.

'Give her some laudanum to lessen her pain, if she is able to swallow it,' said the voice.

Something to lessen the pain. Yes. She wanted that. She wanted the pain to go. She forced open her eyes and mouth, and tried to speak. Tried to say yes, give me laudanum, but all that came out was a croak. If indeed the croak came from her.

A cup was brought to her lips, and a hand behind her head, to lift it from the pillow. A wave of pain cascaded over her, but it was necessary to endure so that she could take the painkiller. She sipped the bitter liquid. Some dribbled out of the corner of her mouth. How strange that she could still feel such a delicate sensation, when her entire existence was defined by a mountain of pain.

She tried to remember what had happened to her. A vision of a gloomy cellar came to mind. The cellar, and another person, and in her hand – oh, in her hand she had held a ruby pistol. She had held it, and she had squeezed the trigger, and there had been an enormously loud bang, and then the pain had hit and she had collapsed on the floor. They had both been on the floor.

She realised with horror that they had both pulled the triggers. They must have done it at precisely the same moment. They had shot each other.

Another memory surfaced – of lying in the pain and the blood, and reaching out, and being comforted by the touch of a hand: the hand of her sister.

Her thoughts were swimming in the laudanum now, and the ball of pain was muffled as though the drug had wrapped it in thick wool. She let out a sigh and allowed herself to drift off, to a place where the pain subsided and the memories evaporated like gun smoke on the breeze.

This time it was the pain that she felt first. Centred in her shoulder, but spreading its tentacles into her arms, her neck and her abdomen. She moaned and opened her eyes.

'Hello, miss. It is good to see you awake.' A hand squeezed hers gently. She followed the sound of the voice and saw a young woman in a plain grey dress, with a maid's cap on her head. Tilly.

'Do you want more of the laudanum? It will ease the pain but will send you to sleep. The doctor said you could have it if you wanted it, when you woke again.'

She nodded. The pain was everywhere. She took a draught of the drug, and settled back once more to wait for it to take effect. What of her sister? she wanted to ask, but could not find the words or the strength to voice them.

***

The next time she woke it was better. The pain was there still but it was not submerging her. She could see and feel beyond it. She tried to speak. 'Tilly?'

'Yes, miss?'

'What happened?' Her voice was but a croak.

'I'll fetch Spencer, miss. Better that you hear it from him.' Tilly turned and almost ran from the room.

Tilly returned with Spencer in moments. His face looked drawn and tired. He seemed to have aged twenty years since she last saw him. She realised she had no idea how long she had been lying in the bed. How long since the shooting?

'Spencer, tell me, what happened?'

He sat in the chair by her bedside, where Tilly had been, and took her hand. It was a strange, rather familiar gesture for him to make but she did not pull away. His touch was comforting. 'You were shot in the shoulder. The surgeon has patched things up as best he could. You should make a full recovery, in time, although your right arm might always be a little weaker than it was. Meanwhile you must rest as much as possible.' He took a deep breath before continuing. 'I heard the shots, and came rushing down to the cellar. You were both lying there, in pools of blood. I've been to war, as you know, but this was the worst thing I have ever seen.' He gulped and breathed deeply, as though trying to compose himself. 'Whoever did this got away. The door to the kitchen garden was open. He must have got in and then escaped that way. The constables are out looking for him. He'll be caught, whoever he is.'

'But…' She stopped herself just in time from saying there was no need to look for anyone else in connection with the shooting. She should hear all the other facts first. Especially – what had happened to Sarah? Was she still alive, perhaps being cared for in another room?

'Miss Winton, I am so sorry. Miss Cooper did not survive the attack. She was dead by the time I reached you.' There were tears in Spencer's eyes as he said this. Sarah had always been his favourite.

She turned her face away as she considered the implications of what she'd heard. So Sarah was dead. That made her, Rebecca, a murderer. She could hang for that. But the authorities were assuming that someone else, a man, had shot them both. As long as she kept quiet, no one need know who had pulled either of the triggers.

Sarah, dead. Her lifetime friend, and recent enemy. Did that mean the estate would now be hers again? She, Rebecca, was her father's only living relative, so surely it must pass to her now. As it should have done in the first place. A memory surfaced. Something Sarah had said – that her father hadn't abandoned her... No. She pushed that memory out of her mind. It could not be true. She would not allow it to be true. The old rumour, her belief that Spencer was Sarah's father – that had to be the truth. It had to be. The rest was Sarah's lies.

She would need to speak with Mr Neville as soon as she was well enough. She winced as a wave of pain rushed through her shoulder. It would be some time before she'd be able to get out of bed. Time to think things through, and plan for her future. At least she had a future. Unlike Sarah, or Charles. But what would her future be like, on her own here at Red Hill Hall?

***

The following day Tilly gently woke her from an afternoon nap, with the news that Constable Barnsworth had been waiting for some time, hoping to ask her what she remembered of the shooting. 'Miss, are you well enough to see him now? Spencer will tell him to come back tomorrow if you would prefer it.'

Rebecca shook her head. 'I am well enough.' Might as well get this over with. She had spent her waking hours rehearsing her story, knowing that sooner or later she would be obliged to tell it.

The constable was rotund with copious side-whiskers, and in the warmth of Rebecca's chamber beads of sweat quickly appeared on his forehead. He probably wasn't used to interviewing ladies who lay in their beds, she thought, with a pang of pity for him that she quickly suppressed.

'Erm, Miss Winton, thank you for agreeing to see me today. The magistrates, you see, with it being a murder case, want the evidence gathered as quickly as possible. It's been several days already. And if our man is still on the loose the sooner we can get a description of him from you, the more chance we will have of catching him.' Barnsworth coughed and shuffled his feet, twisting his hat in his hands as he awaited her reply.

'What is it you need to know from me?' she asked.

'Erm, well, if you could tell me what you remember of the shooting. What the man looked like, where he came in, that sort of thing.'

So he had already decided there was definitely another person involved. That was interesting. He wasn't even going to consider any other possibility. Presumably no one thought it possible that young ladies would know how to fire pistols, still less that they would fire at each other. Sisters don't shoot each other, Sarah had said. She barely believed it possible herself. And only Spencer was aware they knew how to load and fire the guns. She hoped he'd have forgotten he'd ever shown them.

'All right, Constable, I shall tell you what I recall, but I am afraid it isn't very much and you will be disappointed.' She fixed him with a firm look, which made him shuffle even more.

'Anything you can tell me will be very helpful, I'm sure, Miss Winton.'

'Very well. I remember going down to the cellar to check on stocks of wine. Sarah, that is, Miss Cooper, had asked me to do so. She came down after me, by the garden steps. We were discussing what stocks to order in.' There would be no way anyone could refute the purpose of their meeting. But in case Sarah had been seen going down to the cellar, it was best to stick to the truth about her route there.

'And then?' prompted the constable. He had moved a little closer in anticipation of what she might reveal.

Rebecca shook her head. 'There was a noise – footsteps, then a huge bang – and then the next thing I knew was waking up here, in this bed, with Tilly tending to me. I am afraid I did not see anyone, and I do not recall anything being said. I only remember that I heard footsteps, and perhaps I was turning to see who it was. The lamplight was very dim.'

'From where did the sound of footsteps come, Miss Winton? I am sorry to press you, but it could be important.'

Rebecca remembered that the assumption was the intruder had come down the garden steps. So let them continue to believe that. 'I cannot be certain, but from the garden steps, I think, following Miss Cooper.'

Barnsworth nodded. 'It is as we believed. The murderer followed Miss Cooper down, and shot you both. He may have already had the pistols loaded and in his possession from an earlier visit. Or he may have taken and loaded them quietly while you were in discussion about the wine. Were you talking for long?'

'A few minutes only. The pistols were not stored in a locked cupboard, more's the pity. Now I wish I had spoken to her about that, and had them moved somewhere more secure. Oh, if only one could go back in time and have events play out differently!' She put the back of her hand to her forehead.

'Please, Miss Winton, do not upset yourself. The door to the garden ought to have been locked, but I suppose it was open because Miss Cooper had come down that way. It is not your fault. No one could have known what might happen.' He coughed and shuffled a little more. 'I shall keep you no longer, Miss Winton, for it is clear you need to rest as much as possible. Thank you for the information. We shall catch this scoundrel, never you fear. We shall catch him and he shall hang. That poor, poor young lady. Ah, I remember how she collapsed with shock when poor Mr de Witt's body was pulled from the well. And just a fortnight later she herself has met with a sticky end. Who'd have imagined such a terrible thing? Ahem. I am sorry. I shall leave you in peace now.' He bowed and finally made his way out of the room.

Rebecca heaved a sigh of relief. He seemed to have accepted her story. She could not, she had realised, give any details whatsoever of the fictitious attacker, in case the authorities arrested some innocent man who fitted her description. Better to plead amnesia. Better by far.

***

Within a week Rebecca was able to get out of bed and spend part of her day sitting wrapped in a shawl in the drawing room, or at her father's old desk in the study. Tilly stayed within calling distance at all times. 'In case you needs anything, miss, or if you feels tired.'

One thing that had become clear was that all the staff seemed devastated by Sarah's death. Spencer, in particular, appeared a broken man, confirming her belief that despite what Sarah had said, Spencer had indeed been her father. She entered the study one day to find him standing by her father's desk, stroking the polished walnut. 'It is so hard to comprehend, Miss Winton,' he'd said, when she'd asked him if anything was the matter. 'First your mother, then your father, God rest his soul, and now dear Miss Cooper. The people I loved best, Miss Winton, along with you, of course, if you don't mind me saying so. All gone. But never forgotten.' He had then pulled himself up straight, bowed to her and left the room, shaking his head sadly.

The whole house seemed subdued. Rebecca had to constantly remind herself to behave in a way befitting a woman who had lost a beloved sister. As her injuries healed that became harder and harder, and once or twice she had found herself being glared at by a maid for smiling. She'd come across groups of servants chattering but they had always stopped talking and gone about their business as soon as they saw her. She had the distinct impression they'd been talking about her, perhaps comparing her with Sarah.

She also wondered whether anyone suspected the truth. Or were they all still convinced there was someone else involved, someone who was still on the run? If anyone ever guessed that they had shot each other, and that therefore she was a murderer, her life would be over. Although at the time, down in the cellar, her only thoughts had been to defend herself if Sarah shot at her, now she realised that to rely on that as a defence would be a very risky strategy. Who would believe her? She needed the authorities to keep looking for that fictitious man. In time they would surely give up and the case would remain forever unsolved. If she was lucky. And meanwhile, she must act the part of the grieving sister. *Adopted* sister, she reminded herself. She refused to believe that what Sarah had implied in the cellar could be true.

Spencer was the only person who might suspect anything else, she realised. He had shown them how to load and fire the pistols. He had been first on the scene, and had seen where the pistols lay in relation to their bodies.

If he thought they'd shot each other, maybe as a duel, he was keeping quiet. At least, for now he was. But for how much longer?

CHAPTER 19

August 2015

Gemma woke the morning after the shocking phone call from Dad with a pounding headache. She had barely slept – she'd tossed and turned all night wondering why Nat would have done such a thing. Accusing her of failing to repay a fictitious loan, and then practically stealing five thousand pounds from her parents – it was incredible. And the credit card fraud had to be Nat's doing as well. Today she had to contact Nat, and confront her about it. The thought made her feel sick. She'd eaten nothing for dinner the previous night, but had somehow managed to polish off most of a bottle of wine. It was supposed to be a drink to celebrate her first day going through the archives at Red Hill Hall, but had ended up being a drink to drown her sorrows. No wonder she had a headache this morning.

She didn't feel like eating breakfast either, but forced herself to eat a bowl of porridge with a strawberry yogurt mixed in. Along with a strong cup of coffee that helped her begin to feel better. She resolved to make her number one priority today the confrontation with Nat. The more she put it off the less she would sleep. And there was a danger her father might go to the police after all, if

Gemma didn't do anything about it first. The research at Red Hill Hall would have to wait.

This was not something that could be tackled by a phone call, so after breakfast she set off in her car to Nat's flat. She wasn't sure what hours Nat was working, but there was a chance Nat wasn't working today, so it seemed sensible to try the flat first. She parked outside, climbed the steps to the communal front door and rang the bell. Her heart was pounding, but she'd rehearsed her speech and had to go through with this.

There was no answer. She tried again, just in case, then retraced her steps and drove to Nat's workplace. Perhaps she'd be able to catch her on a coffee break.

The salon was busy – there were several people having their nails done and two people waiting. The front desk was manned by Jasmine, who Gemma had met once or twice when she'd gone out with Nat's work friends. Jasmine was wearing the longest false eyelashes Gemma had ever seen other than on a pantomime dame.

'Hi, Gemma! What can we do for you? We're busy but I bet we could squeeze you in somewhere.' Jasmine ran a pink and silver talon across the open page of the appointments book.

'I was looking for Nat. Is she working today?'

'Nat? No, erm, hasn't she told you? Haven't seen her for ages. She left, or was sacked or something. I don't know the details – she wouldn't say – but she did go through a phase of turning up late and hung-over every day. I think the boss got fed up of it. Anyway, she's off on holiday this week, she told me. In Tenerife. With her new man, no less!'

Gemma was startled. She had no idea Nat had lost her job. If she'd been fired that might explain her being short of money.

'Ah, no, I didn't know that. Haven't seen her for a few weeks, to be honest. Her new man? Who's that, then? Have you met him?'

'No. She's been very secretive. His name's Ben, apparently. Oh, look I'm going to have to see to these ladies now, sorry, Gemma. See you around, yeah?'

'Yeah, see you.'

Gemma left the salon feeling numb. Nat, on holiday with Ben? Her Ben? How could he? So soon after breaking things off with her! It was one thing to have a drunken snog at his sister's wedding – she could imagine forgiving him for that – but to go away with the woman who was supposed to be her best friend? Just two months after dumping her? The more she thought about it the more her numbness turned to rage.

And as for Nat… she shook her head in sorrow. It was as though Nat was trying to take everything from her. Money, her parents' trust, and now Ben. It was unbelievable. And probably unforgivable, although Gemma did still feel she wanted to give Nat the chance to explain it all.

But if Nat and Ben were away in Tenerife there was no chance of confronting Nat about the letter to her parents, or anything else, until she got back.

She couldn't resist pulling out her phone and sending Ben a text, though. 'Have a nice holiday.' Just so he knew that she knew. She pressed 'send' before she had chance to change her mind.

***

There was nothing more she could do about the 'Nat' problem now, so she returned to her car and drove to Red Hill Hall. Hopefully getting stuck into the research would help take her mind off things. She found herself quietly looking forward to the prospect of seeing Don again. Perhaps they'd have another drink and chat together. She rather liked the idea of that becoming a regular feature of her visits. He was very easy to get on with, not to mention easy on the eye.

Don was in reception when she arrived. Almost as though he'd been waiting for her, she thought, with a smile.

'Gemma! Good to see you. I realised something after you'd gone yesterday.' He came out from behind the reception desk and gave her a peck on the cheek.

'Hi, Don. What was that, then?'

'We missed going to the cellars on the tour. I've not had chance to do anything with them yet, so they're a bit dark and dingy. But didn't you say something about that shooting taking place in the cellars?'

'I did, yes, and in all the excitement about the boxes of papers I completely forgot to ask you about them. Ooh, can we go down now?' Gemma felt a rush of excitement at the thought of seeing the exact location where the mysterious shooting took place.

'We certainly can!' Don produced a couple of torches from his pockets. 'Look – I'm all prepared!'

She laughed. 'Like a Boy Scout. Is there no lighting down there, then?'

'Nothing that works. Some lights were installed before the Second World War but the wiring has never been replaced. It's on my list. I want to store the wine down there, and if I can get it dry enough, I'll store some of the more seasonal stuff there. Hey, you're not afraid of the dark, are you?'

'Of course not! I'm a woman, not a wuss. Lead the way!'

He grinned and set off towards the old servants' corridor, past the room where she'd spent the previous day rooting through the archived papers. At the end of this corridor was a locked door. Don took a heavy iron key from his pocket and unlocked it. The lock was stiff. 'I must get this oiled before anything else,' he muttered, as he shouldered open the door. 'Mind the steps.'

Gemma switched on her torch and followed him down the steep brick steps. Once she was at the bottom she shone her torch around. She was in a smallish room with a low ceiling. There were two doorways leading off it, into deep darkness. A wooden cupboard was built against one wall, its doors hanging off their hinges. Everything was covered in a thick layer of dirt, and the air smelt stale and damp.

The hairs on the back of her neck stood up as she imagined Sarah and Rebecca confronting the murderer down here in the dark. They'd only have had an oil lamp at best, or perhaps just candles to light their way. Was this the room where the girls had been shot, she wondered? She was being fanciful, she knew, but she felt as though she could detect a presence here – the violence of the past perhaps keeping the spirits of the girls trapped here. She shivered and glanced over to the doors on the other side of the cellar. What lay beyond?

As if reading her mind Don crossed towards the left-hand doorway and beckoned her to follow. 'This room was the wine cellar.' He shone his torch around and the remains of wine racks were visible in the gloom. 'But I think I'd use the first room for wine.'

'You'll have staff running up and down those stairs all day. Is that safe?'

'I'd only store surplus stocks down here, and the expensive wines that we don't sell often but that need to be kept in the right environment. The everyday bottles would stay upstairs in easy reach of the dining room.'

'What's through there?' Gemma pointed to another archway in the corner.

'Come and see. Mind, the floor's a bit uneven here.'

She shone her torch downwards and picked her way across the flagstones. The arch led to another cellar, with a vaulted brick ceiling. There was a set of crumbling steps leading up on one side. She felt a jolt of recognition as she realised those must be the steps that led to the kitchen garden, the route by which the killer was supposed to have entered and left. She shone her torch towards the steps. 'Is the door at the top in use?'

'No. On the outside it is completely smothered by ivy. Another job on the list – to cut that right back and rediscover the door.'

'It led to the old kitchen garden, I believe.'

'Which is now just an overgrown area at the back of the house, that I have not yet had a chance to tackle,' Don said. 'It's out of view of the main guest areas so has been low down on the list of priorities. I'd like to rebuild a kitchen garden here. It'd be useful to grow our own herbs and some seasonal veg. If you find any clues amongst those papers as to what it would have looked like, pull them out for me, will you?'

'Sure, will do.'

They retraced their steps back to the first room, then looked through the other doorway leading off. This led into another brick-vaulted cellar, with what looked like a hole in the ceiling.

'The coal cellar,' Don explained. 'Somewhere up above there'll be a trapdoor, and the coal was tipped down the chute to land in a pile in here. There's still a few pieces left around the edges of the space.'

'I wonder in which cellar the girls were found,' Gemma said. 'I don't know why, but I have a feeling it was the first one, where the old cupboard was.' She turned to go back into that room, and shone her torch into the corners of the room. She found herself wondering if there'd be any trace of blood left, but the floor in this room was made of dark red quarry tiles, rather than the paler flagstones in the wine cellar.

'The girls could have come down from the house, and the murderer came in through the garden entrance. He could have been hiding in one of those other cellars and confronted them here,' Don said. 'It's pretty spooky, isn't it, imagining what happened right here, so long ago. When was it, again?'

'1838. Getting on for two hundred years ago.'

'Wow. Well, I don't think I should keep you down here any more, in the gloom, when there's all that lovely paperwork for you to get stuck into. Cup of coffee before you get going?'

'That'd be lovely, thanks.' Gemma followed him up the stairs and back into the servants' passage. She felt relieved to be back in the light, in fresh air. 'Phew. Bit creepy down there, if I'm honest.'

He chuckled. 'Yep, I'd agree with that. I'll get some proper lighting installed before I venture down again. Or at least hang up an inspection lamp on a long lead. Right then, refreshment before we get on with our respective jobs.' He led the way to the library bar and ordered the coffees.

Gemma took a seat in the corner of the bar. It was lovely that Don seemed so keen on her research. She supposed it was natural, since he now owned the hall, but she couldn't help wondering if there was some other reason for his interest, something he wasn't telling her. It didn't matter if there was – she was happy to do the research and write up the history, and he seemed delighted to let her do it. He'd offered to pay her for her time as well. It couldn't be a better arrangement.

She smiled happily to herself and glanced around the bar. There were a few other guests. With a start she realised she recognised a couple sitting at the opposite end of the bar. The woman spotted her at the same time and came over.

'Gemma! Hey, nice to see you. We're here reminiscing about our wedding. Can you believe we've been married two months already?'

'Anna! Wow, two months. Doesn't time fly?' Gemma forced herself to smile. Of course she realised it was two months. Two long months since she'd last seen Ben, when he was snogging Nat. Anna and Jake were looking tanned and relaxed. 'How was your honeymoon?'

'Fantastic. Really good. We were in Corfu. Had a relaxing time on the beach and sipping cocktails all day. It was perfect, wasn't it, Jake?' Anna turned to her new husband who'd come to join them.

'Yes, lovely. What brings you here today?'

'Research. Oh, Don, this is Anna and Jake, my friends. They got married here recently. Anna, Jake, Don's the owner of the hotel.'

Don shook their hands. 'I remember. Mr and Mrs Byatt, isn't it? Welcome back to Red Hill Hall. Gemma, I'll leave you with your friends, then. Come and find me later if you need a break from your research.' He picked up his coffee and left the bar.

'New man?' Anna asked.

'No, of course not!' Gemma was hurt. How could Anna think she'd forget her brother so quickly?

'Sorry, that was crass of me. I apologise. Jake's always saying I need to think before I speak. To be honest, I still can't believe you and Ben aren't together any more. After all those years.' She shook her head sadly.

'Well, he seemed to move on quickly enough, but I can't. Not yet.' Anna had always been a good friend, but it felt weird discussing her love life with Ben's sister.

'What do you mean, moved on? I don't think he has at all. He spends his days moping around. I don't understand why he broke things off if it makes him so sad. I said that to him, as well, but he won't talk to me about it. Has he contacted you at all?'

'No.'

'He's an idiot. You and he were so good together.'

'He obviously didn't think so. And he has moved on. He's on holiday with his new girlfriend this week – if that's not an indication of having moved on I don't know what is.' Gemma tried but failed to keep the bitter tone out of her voice.

Anna looked puzzled. 'Holiday? New girlfriend? What are you talking about?'

'He's in Tenerife. With my one-time best friend Nat.' Gemma felt her eyes welling up as she said this.

'Oh, sweetheart, come here.' Anna reached over the table and put an arm around Gemma's shoulders. 'Look I don't know quite what's going on here, and it's probably none of my business – no, hey, it IS my business. He's my kid brother, and he's stupid. And you – well I'd begun thinking of you as the sister I never had but soon would have, if you know what I mean. Anyway. Ben is most certainly *not* in Tenerife. He's at Mum and Dad's house this week, helping Dad with a bit of decorating. He's moping around, not going out at all, has a face as long as a wet weekend and is driving Mum mad. He's not seeing Nat. Or anyone else. I'd know if he was.'

Gemma frowned at Anna, trying to take all this in. 'But at your wedding, they were snogging. I saw them.'

'I saw that too, and questioned him about it. Just a drunken mistake, he said, and it sounded to me as though Nat practically forced herself on him. She'd had a few too many as well. Don't read anything into it. He hasn't seen her since our wedding as far as I know. Mum doesn't think he's been out at all other than to work. She's been worried about him, but he won't talk to her any more.'

A drunken mistake. At home decorating, not on holiday. Moping around the house. Hadn't seen Nat since the wedding. Nat came on strong to him, not the other way round as Nat had said. Well, given what else Nat had done since then, Gemma could believe Nat had lied. She opened her mouth to say something but felt lost for words.

Anna hugged her again. 'Honestly, Gemma, you have to believe me. Frankly I think he's regretting the break up but doesn't know what to do about it. I have no idea what possessed him to end your engagement. He's a stupid bugger, if you'll pardon the technical term. If you have any feelings for him still, then, well, I wish you and he would talk about it. Maybe you can work something out.'

Gemma blinked away tears. 'I don't know, Anna. He hurt me a lot when he ended things. I'd been so happy, and then suddenly he pulled the rug out from under my feet. It'll take a lot to come back from there.'

Anna nodded. 'Yes, it will. But I'm sure he still loves you, and if you still love him, then it's worth a go, isn't it? There must be some explanation for what he did. He won't tell me, but if you were to talk to him, properly talk, then maybe...'

'Maybe.' Gemma smiled weakly. Perhaps Anna was right. Perhaps she should call Ben and give him a chance to explain himself. Did she want him back? She looked deep inside herself.

Yes, she darned well did want him back! If Anna was right and there was nothing between him and Nat, she wanted an explanation and then a reconciliation. But did she have the courage to be the one to make the first move? It was Ben who'd broken things off. He should be the one to call her and explain, apologise, and beg her to take him back. She'd make him suffer, oh yes, but probably only for a second or two, before she fell into his arms and forgave him.

CHAPTER 20

September 1838

It was three weeks since the 'accident', as Rebecca referred to it privately. Sarah had been buried in the churchyard, beside Mr and Mrs Winton. Rebecca had refused to allow her to be in the same plot, or have her name added to the Wintons' headstone. She had not attended the funeral, pleading too much pain from her shoulder. The household was beginning to run on an even keel again, and Rebecca was able to be up and about for several hours each day. Her wound was recovering well, although she could not lift her right arm above chest height, and the doctor had said that it was quite possible she never would again. But she was alive, and other than that, well, and had much to be grateful for. So said the vicar, Reverend Theobald, at least. She could so easily have died when that ruffian murderer broke in. And then what would have become of the house and the estate and all the people living and working here? It was as well she had survived and now her duty was to the staff. He had given her a long lecture on this, when he came to call after the funeral.

But was the estate even hers? She had yet to meet up with the solicitor, Mr Neville. He had been in London on business and although he had written to her since the accident, sending his condolences on the loss of Sarah and promising to visit as soon as he was able to, he had not confirmed that the estate would actually pass to her. Rebecca felt as though she was in limbo.

Finally, the news she had been waiting for arrived. A letter from Mr Neville, saying he would call the next day to meet with her. Rebecca had risen early and made an effort with her appearance. She'd spent the time since breakfast sitting with a book in the drawing room, awaiting his arrival.

At last there was a tap at the door, and Spencer entered, announcing the arrival of Mr Neville. 'Shall I show him into the library, Miss Winton?'

'Yes please.' Rebecca stood up and straightened her skirts. Her shoulder was aching badly today. Perhaps she had been holding herself too tensely. 'Send in some refreshments in a short while, Spencer.'

'Certainly.' Spencer bowed and stood aside. As she passed him she tried to catch his eye, wondering once more whether he suspected she'd had anything to do with Sarah's death. But he kept his eyes cast downwards.

'Miss Winton, it is a pleasure as always to see you again, though I am deeply sorry about the circumstances. Poor Miss Cooper. What a terrible, tragic event. And I hope you are well recovered now?' Mr Neville bowed as Rebecca entered the library and took a seat near the window, holding her right arm across her chest as always, so as not to pain her shoulder.

'I am not fully recovered, but am well enough,' she answered.

'You have lost your father and friend in such a short space of time. And it is not much more than a year since your dear mother met with her accident. So much loss. Not to mention Mr de Witt, who was of course your fiancé.'

'Yes.' There was an edge to his voice that she didn't like.

Mr Neville looked her squarely in the eye. 'Far too much death for one household. Almost seems too much of a coincidence.'

'I agree, there has been far too much death.' She held his gaze. She had not for one moment thought that Mr Neville of all people might suspect not all the deaths were accidents. But he seemed to be implying that her parents' and Charles's deaths weren't natural. Surely he couldn't think she had anything to do with those events?

'Your mother fell down the stairs. Your fiancé was found drowned in a well shortly after breaking off your engagement. Your father died very suddenly. You were naturally shocked and upset that the estate was left to Sarah and not you, and then within a few weeks Sarah also died, shot by some mysterious man who has not been named or found. It is all very odd, don't you think?'

'Mr Neville, what exactly are you implying?' Facing him head on seemed to be the only way forward.

'I am implying nothing, my dear, only voicing the kind of suspicions that others are sure to have. Indeed, some folk are already questioning what has been happening here.' He brought a sheet of newspaper out of his pocket. ''Tis only a gossip magazine, but you should be aware of what people are saying.'

Rebecca took the paper and scanned the article he pointed to. '"*The Curse of Red Hill Hall*". Oh, for goodness' sake. What is this paper? *County Tall Tales?* They'll print any old rubbish to titillate their readers.'

'Yes, of course, but readers will think there is no smoke without fire, and will wonder if there is any truth in the matter.'

'Mr Neville, you have known me since I was a child. I loved my mother and father immensely and of course I had *nothing* to do with their deaths. My father, as you know, died of a heart attack – an entirely natural death. I – I will admit it, I loved Mr de Witt as well, and although I was heartbroken when he broke off our engagement, that did not drive me to try to end his life. You think I pushed him in the well? What a ridiculous notion!'

'Miss Winton, let me assure you, *I* think nothing of the sort. I only wished to warn you what others may think – indeed, are already thinking and gossiping. I would advise you to do all that you can to advance the search for Miss Cooper's murderer. If it can be proven that her death at least was not at your hands then that will help quash the rumours.'

'So people are thinking that I shot Sarah? And how do they think I came by my own wound?' Rebecca widened her eyes and mustered the most indignant, incredulous tone she could manage. She sent up a silent prayer that he would not guess the truth.

'Self-inflicted, they say, to throw the authorities off the true scent. Ludicrous, of course, but it is as well you are aware of the gossip. I am only sorry I could not get here sooner and advise you earlier, to prevent the rumours taking hold.'

'Ahem, excuse me, Miss Winton, Mr Neville. I have brought coffee.' Spencer entered the room bearing a tray, which he placed on a small table beside the fireplace.

'Thank you. I will pour; you may leave,' Rebecca said. How much had Spencer heard? If he did have suspicions about Sarah's death, there was a danger that they'd be reinforced if he knew other people were also wondering what really happened. Mr Neville was right. Her only hope was for the hunt for the fictitious man to be successful. But how could that be? To be successful, someone would have to be caught or at least named. And that someone would be innocent. She would not be able to stand by and let an innocent man take the blame, would she?

She poured out the coffee in silence and handed Mr Neville a cup. She wished he would get down to the real business of the day, regarding ownership of the estate.

At last he put down his cup and took some papers out of his battered leather bag. 'Very well then, if you are refreshed, we should continue with our business. I am sorry to have been the bearer of the bad news about the gossipmongers but I thought you needed to know. Now then, as to the estate...'

'Yes?'

'There are several considerations. Firstly, did Miss Cooper leave a will? Certainly she did not consult with me regarding this, but possibly she may have employed another solicitor. Her possessions, papers and her room should be searched, in case there is a document I was not a party to. However, as it was such a short time between her inheriting the estate and her death, I would think it unlikely.'

Rebecca stifled a gasp. It had not crossed her mind that Sarah might have drawn up a will. If she had done so, who on earth would she have named as her heir? Whoever it was, it would not be Rebecca – that was for sure.

'Secondly, if we cannot find a will we must assume that Miss Cooper died intestate. We must then look back at your father's will, to see if there is any provision in it for what should happen if Miss Cooper died unmarried and without issue.' He began rifling through the papers he'd pulled from his bag. 'I have a copy of his will here. Now then, let's remind ourselves. I am sorry I did not have chance to check this before coming here today.'

Rebecca held her breath. Surely her father would have specified that the estate revert back to her if Sarah had no heir? Mr Neville was reading slowly and silently, running his stubby finger over the lines, occasionally muttering a few words aloud, though nothing Rebecca could make any sense of.

Finally he looked up at her. 'Well then. It seems there is no provision for our current situation. I thought as much – I could not remember anything from when I read the will last, but had to be certain.'

'What does that mean for the future of the estate?' Rebecca asked.

'It leads to our third consideration. If Miss Cooper left no will, then the estate passes to her next of kin.'

Rebecca felt a cold hand clutch at her heart. 'And who is that?'

'This is where we run into difficulties. Miss Cooper's mother is dead, and no one knows for certain who her father is or was, though many have speculated as I am sure you are aware.'

Rebecca stared at him. What had people speculated? How well known was the rumour that Spencer was Sarah's father? Was that what Mr Neville was referring to? Or could it be what Sarah had hinted at on that terrible day in the cellar, the allegation Rebecca had not allowed herself to think about?

'If we can find any evidence as to who Miss Cooper's father was, then the estate would pass to him or to his heirs,' Mr Neville continued. 'If no evidence can be found, we must then try to find relatives on her mother's side.'

'I do not remember any relatives being spoken of,' Rebecca said, carefully. She did not dare allow herself to say anything more.

Mr Neville acknowledged her words with a slight nod of his head. 'In that case, if there is no will, and no living relatives can be found, then I am afraid the estate would pass to the Crown. You would, in that case, be obliged to leave.'

Rebecca slumped back in her seat. After all that had happened, she could still end up homeless. If Sarah had left a will, or even if she hadn't, Red Hill Hall might not legally pass to her. It seemed so unfair. She had been born here. Surely she had the right to continue living here? She realised with a shock that her only chance was if what Sarah had said in the cellar should turn out to be true. The thing she most wanted to forget, she now had to prove, in order to inherit the hall.

***

Mr Neville left after lunch, advising Rebecca to put all her energies into searching through Sarah's belongings in case she had left a will, or any other document that might help sort out the inheritance. She had nodded, and promised to contact him the moment she found anything.

She felt exhausted after the busy morning with the solicitor, and although she was keen to begin the search immediately, she was obliged to rest a while first. Her shoulder ached mercilessly. It was late afternoon before she felt able to begin the search. She rang for Tilly to help her.

'It is time,' she told the maid, 'to begin sorting through Miss Cooper's possessions. There are items I need to find. It is a difficult job and I would like you to help me, as I cannot make much use of my right arm.'

'Of course, miss,' said Tilly. 'Where are we to begin?'

Rebecca sighed. It would be such a big job. Sarah had moved things around such a lot in the short time she had been mistress of the house. There could be relevant papers in the study, the library, Sarah's bedroom or private sitting room, or indeed anywhere else. Including the cellars. She shuddered as she thought of the cellars. She had not been back down there since the shooting. 'Tilly, to be perfectly honest I don't really know where to begin.'

'Perhaps, miss, if I may be so bold, if you could say what it is you are searching for that might help us determine where to look. Miss Cooper did employ me to help organise some of her belongings, a few weeks ago.'

'Ah, did she? Well then, Tilly, we are looking for documents. Letters, papers. Anything written by Miss Cooper or addressed to her. Anything she might have considered private.'

'Ooh, miss, I am not sure I could look at her private things...' Tilly said, with a hand over her mouth.

'Don't be silly. Miss Cooper is dead and gone. It falls to me to sort out her affairs and I cannot do it without seeing her private documents, and I cannot sort through them myself with my bad shoulder. I am not asking you to read any of her papers – just find them and pass them to me. Can you do that? We shall begin upstairs.'

'Yes, miss. Sorry, miss.' Tilly looked close to tears but gave a quick curtsey and followed Rebecca upstairs to Sarah's small sitting room, which adjoined her bedroom – the room that had previously been Rebecca's. She'd had a large bureau moved in there after Papa had died, and Rebecca considered it was perhaps the most likely place to find important documents.

It felt very strange entering Sarah's room. As children they had spent much of their time running in and out of each other's rooms. Rebecca had known exactly what Sarah owned and where she kept everything. As they had grown up they had begun to value their privacy more, and by unspoken agreement had begun to tap on the door if either wanted access to the other's room. Of course in recent months they had kept very much apart, and Rebecca had not entered this room since Sarah had taken it over. She felt nervous. It was as though she could feel Sarah's presence there, forbidding them from entering.

It seemed Tilly could feel it too, for once they were inside she stood wringing her hands in the middle of the room. 'I'm sorry, miss, I shall try to help but it does feel so wrong.'

Tilly's reluctance made Rebecca all the more determined to push on with the job at hand. 'Come on. We shall start with the bureau in her sitting room.' She led the way through the connecting door and stood before the bureau, which was situated on one side of the fireplace. It was made of walnut and had a lid that opened out to be used as a desk, and three drawers beneath. Rebecca knew that behind the lid were several more drawers. It used to belong to Mama. She pulled on the lid but to her frustration found that it was locked. 'Oh, where might the key be?' she pondered aloud.

Tilly was fidgeting behind her. 'Miss, I believe Miss Cooper kept small valuable items in a little box in her bedside cabinet. When I helped her dress I had to make sure her brooches and rings were put in there, and I do remember seeing a key...'

'Well done, Tilly. Fetch the box, please.'

The maid scurried off and returned with a small lacquered box. Once again Rebecca recognised it as having once belonged to Mama. Inside was a jumble of costume jewellery and, as Tilly had said, a small key. It was indeed the key to the bureau. Rebecca took it out and unlocked the desk. 'Tilly, you will need to open the lid for me. My shoulder is too painful.'

Tilly stepped forward and pulled down the lid, sliding out the runners that supported the lid when used as a writing desk. Inside was a muddle of papers, untidily stacked and folded. Rebecca picked up one, and found it to be the rough draft of a letter, full of crossings out. She felt a pang of excitement. This looked promising. It would take a while to sort it all out, but it would be worth it. Who knew what she might uncover? But was there a will? Rebecca was not even sure if she wanted to find one. If there was one and it did not mention her, she would be homeless.

She realised Tilly was still standing behind her, twisting her apron in her hands. 'Tilly, I need you to look through all the other cupboards and drawers in these rooms. If there is any paperwork gather it up and bring it in here. I shall take a seat and begin sorting through it. My future, and perhaps yours too, depends on what I might find.'

Tilly's eyes widened at these last words, but she curtsied and set to the task assigned.

Rebecca began working through the papers, straightening them out, trying to put them into some sort of order before she read them all. The drawers beneath the desk held writing paper, wax, blotters, ink bottles, pens and nibs. No written documents. Still, there was enough to be getting on with for now.

She had made a neat pile of letters, some addressed to Sarah and some obviously Sarah's rough drafts, when Tilly, who was in Sarah's dressing room, let out a gasp.

Rebecca looked up. 'What is it, Tilly? Have you found something?'

'Yes, miss. I'll bring it to you.'

Tilly re-entered the sitting room holding a battered

leather-bound book, and handed it to Rebecca. She opened it and flicked through a few pages. It was a journal, with entries from this and the previous year, every page covered in Sarah's untidy scrawl. Rebecca felt a flutter of excitement mixed with trepidation. What secrets would be revealed within its pages?

CHAPTER 21

August 2015

Gemma left Anna and Jake in the bar to return to the little room she was using for her work on the archives. Her head was reeling after what Anna had told her, and she walked through the hotel in a daze.

'Hey, Gemma! Is everything OK? You look a bit shell-shocked. Can I do anything?' Don caught up with her just as she was entering the archive room.

'No, erm, I'm all right. Just had some strange news, that's all.'

'Not bad news I hope?'

'No, it's more like – interesting news, I suppose you could say.' She sat down heavily and stared straight ahead, still trying to process the news.

'Do you want to talk about it? Or should I leave you in peace? I'm guessing this has come from your friends in the bar.'

'Yes, Anna told me something… No, you don't need to leave. To be honest, I'm going to struggle to concentrate on going through the documents for a while, until I can get my head around this.' Should she confide in Don? She barely knew him, but he was so open and friendly, and she had a feeling he'd be good at giving advice. Maybe an independent observer like him was exactly what she needed right now.

'OK, so although you've just had a coffee, I think you need another one. With a shot of whiskey in it. Stay there, I'll be right back.'

He was as good as his word, and returned with two Irish coffees a few minutes later. 'Here. Now, you don't need to tell me anything if you don't want to, but I'm getting the feeling that you might need a friend to talk things through with. I'm here and I'm free, if you need me.'

'Thanks.' He was right. She did need to talk about it. She quickly outlined the history of her friendship with Nat and relationship with Ben, their brief engagement and the way Ben broke things off. 'Then, at Anna and Jake's wedding here, I saw them kissing.'

'Anna and Jake?'

'Well, they were entitled to, being just married, but no. I meant Ben and Nat.'

'A drunken mistake?'

'That's exactly what Anna says it was, and that's what I was prepared to believe, but Nat told me Ben had been the one to start it, and she'd had to push him off. And today her work colleague told me she was on holiday with Ben. But Anna says Ben's at home, moping, and hasn't seen Nat since the wedding. Apparently Ben thinks that I'd never wanted to marry him and had only said yes to him because we'd been together so long and I didn't want to hurt him.' She felt tears prick at her eyes at the memory of their break-up. It still felt raw.

'But that's not true?'

'No! I loved him. Still love him. I was devastated when he broke it off. And now Anna says *he's* devastated. I don't know what to do, or what to make of it.'

Don was grinning at her. 'Sounds like this Nat has been stirring up trouble. Some friend. Well, to me, this sounds easy to fix. Do you have your phone?'

'Yes.'

'And Ben's number is on it? You didn't delete it when you broke up?'

'No. I couldn't delete it. That seemed too final.'

'So – ring him!'

'Now?'

'Of course!'

'What do I say?' Her mind was working overtime.

'Say you bumped into Anna. Tell him what she told you. Tell him how you feel. In other words, tell him the truth.'

'What if he doesn't answer? What if he doesn't want to talk to me? What if...'

'What if it resolves the whole situation and gets you two back together again?' Don smiled, and covered her hand with his. 'It's worth taking the chance, isn't it? I know you've been hurt, but it sounds as though the whole thing was a terrible misunderstanding, stirred up by Nat. You and he just need to talk it through properly. Something you should have done ages ago, frankly.'

'I know, but I was so hurt, I couldn't bring myself to ring him or see him. Then when I thought he'd got together with Nat I just didn't want to know.'

'That's understandable. But for some reason she wanted you to think she and Ben were together, when clearly they're not. I don't know why someone who is supposed to be your best friend would do that, and I think you should talk to her about it, but that's a job for another day. For now, I would just concentrate on

Ben, and repairing your relationship with him. If that's what you want, of course?'

'God, yes. I've missed him so much.' Her heart was pounding. Could there be a chance for them again?

'So, phone him. Now. I'll be in my office, if you need me later on. The door's always open.' He picked up the remains of his Irish coffee and, with an encouraging smile, left her alone.

Gemma sipped her coffee, enjoying the feeling of fortification the spirit in it gave her. Don was right. She needed to talk to Ben, right now. She pulled out her phone and with shaking fingers, called him.

He answered quickly, his voice sounding as shaky as hers. 'Gemma?'

'Hey, Ben. So, erm, I…' She broke off, suddenly at a loss as to how to get the conversation started. What was it Don had advised? '… I, erm, bumped into Anna today. She said you were, kind of, at home, and with nothing to do, and…'

'Yeah, she's right. I guess I am a bit bored. How are you, Gemma?'

'I'm good, thanks. You?'

'Yeah. Good.' He fell silent and after a moment Gemma realised she had not yet said why she was phoning. She realised she'd have to just come straight out with it.

'The thing is, Ben, I thought you were away on holiday this week.'

'Me? No. Haven't been anywhere. Couldn't work out what your text was all about. I was going to answer it but, well, I hadn't worked out how to, yet. Wasn't ignoring it, though.'

'My text? Oh, yes, that.' She found herself blushing as she remembered the text she'd sent Ben that morning when she'd thought he was on holiday with Nat. 'Yeah, someone said you were away. With Nat.'

'What? You thought I'd gone on holiday with Nat?'

'S'what I was told.'

'Jeez. No, Gemma. I wouldn't do that. I mean, we were mates, I suppose, when I was with you. She's your best mate so of course she and I became mates, of a sort. But not so close I'd go on holiday with her.'

'Of a sort?'

'Yeah. I mean, I saw a lot of her when the three of us went out, but she's not someone I'd pick as a friend. Sorry and all, I know she's your bestie.'

'She's not, any more.' Gemma tried and failed to keep the bitterness out of her voice.

'Oh, God, sorry. What on earth happened? Shit, was this anything to do with...'

'... with you snogging her at your sister's wedding? I did see that, Ben, and it hurt. We'd only just split up, and there you were with your tongue down my best mate's throat.'

'Gem, it wasn't like that. I was drunk, and she came on to me, and, well I suppose it's her word against mine but it only lasted a few seconds and then I thought, what the hell am I doing, and pushed her away. She said she thought you'd seen us. Shit. I was going to ring you the next day. But...'

'You didn't. Ben, you broke off our engagement and then never contacted me again.'

'I'm a fool. Gem, we should talk.'

'Isn't that what we're doing now?'

'I mean, face to face. Where are you? Are you free?'

He was right. They did need to talk face to face and for a long time. She had so many questions for him. It was time to get things straight. The research could wait. 'I'm actually at Red Hill Hall hotel. That's where I bumped into Anna. I've been doing some work on the archives here.'

'I'm coming straight over. I'll be there in twenty minutes. Meet you in the bar?'

She hardly had chance to say yes before he rang off.

In a strange mixture of dazedness and elation, she realised there'd be no chance of doing any research while she waited for him to arrive. Once more the mystery of the nineteenth-century shooting would have to wait. She drank the rest of the now-lukewarm Irish coffee, and went out to the bar to wait. Anna and Jake had left, but Don saw her enter and came to join her.

'Everything OK?' he asked, for the second time that afternoon.

'I don't know yet. I rang Ben. He's coming over here so we can talk properly.'

Don smiled. 'That's great news. So, I'll leave you alone, but if there's anything you need, just say. You're welcome to stay here tonight if you want. We've some spare rooms. I won't charge you anything. Call it part payment for the research.' He winked at her and left before she could answer him.

Gemma was alone with her thoughts for the next quarter of an hour. Every time someone came through to the bar from reception she looked up to see if it was Ben. Mentally she rehearsed how she would greet him a thousand times. Would she stand up, kiss him on the cheek, hug him, stay seated, shake his hand, simply say 'hi', or what?

She was halfway through a fantasy in which he entered the bar bearing a huge bouquet of roses, fell on one knee and begged her to marry him again, when the doors of the bar burst open and a figure came flying through, skidded on the polished floor and landed in a heap at her table. She just managed to catch hold of her drink before it was knocked flying.

'Ben! Well, I must say, that was some entrance!'

'Ahem. Move along. Nothing to see here,' he said, as he picked himself up, straightened his clothing and brushed himself down.

She couldn't help but laugh. 'Are you sure you're all right?'

He rolled his eyes. 'Just bruised my dignity, is all. Erm, hi, Gemma. Can I get you a drink? If I can make it to the bar without slipping over, that is. Darned new shoes have no grip and this floor is a tad shiny. I should have worn my trainers.'

'A sparkling water, with ice and lemon, would be lovely, thanks.'

'Sure.' He tiptoed across the floor, clearly terrified of slipping over again.

Gemma felt her heart race and her insides churn as she watched him. Dear old Ben. Everything about him was so familiar and she felt so warm and comfortable with him already, despite the fact they had not spoken for months. She had forgotten just how comfortable she felt when she was with him.

He returned with the drinks, and sat on a stool opposite her. She was sitting on a small upholstered sofa by the fireplace, her favourite spot in the bar. He smiled as he passed her drink to her, and she could not help but smile back. This was the man who'd broken her heart by ending their engagement, but even so, it was Ben, and Ben was lovely, and she had a good feeling about the way this meeting was going to progress.

'So. Here we are,' he said.

'Yes.'

'We need to talk, don't we? I need to explain why I called off our engagement. Oh God, what a fool I was. I look back and wonder what on earth I was doing.'

'So, why *did* you break it off?' Gemma's memory of the night he'd finished things was blurry, despite the number of times she had run through it in her head. The problem was, nothing he'd said had made any sense. And now it seemed it made no sense to him either.

He twisted his glass – a pint of bitter – in his hands and took a sip before answering. 'Can I be totally honest?'

'Of course. We need to be honest with each other or there's no hope for us.'

'You might not like it.'

Her insides twisted. She'd thought this meeting would bring them back together, back to how they were, but perhaps not. Was there something else? Some other reason why he'd broken things off that he had not wanted or been able to tell her before? Well, whatever it was, she had to know. She steeled herself against whatever she was about to hear. 'Go on.'

'OK. It was Nat.'

'I knew it!'

'No, no. Not in the way you think. What I mean was, Nat was the one who encouraged me to break things off. No, more than that, she *told* me to end it.'

'And you just did what she said like an obedient puppy? Why?'

He took a deep breath. 'She told me you'd only agreed to marry me because you felt sorry for me. Because we'd been together a long time and it was expected we'd marry, but that actually you felt trapped and pressurised. That you were bored of me and would have ended the relationship long before but that you were just too nice a person to risk hurting me. She said

221

you'd confided in her many times, but that you would never tell me how you really felt, and that you'd made her promise not to say either, but that she couldn't stand by and let us make the biggest mistake of our lives. It was her duty to tell me, she said, to give me a chance to end things and release you, before we got too far along with the wedding plans. Imagine, she said, if you'd left me standing at the altar. Or if we'd married and then divorced within a year or two. Better to break things off sooner rather than later. So I did.' He took another gulp of his beer. 'I am guessing, from the look on your face, that everything she said was bollocks.'

'Absolute bloody bollocks,' Gemma replied. How could Nat have done this? She'd known Gemma had been genuinely over the moon about finally being engaged.

'Not even a tiny bit of truth in any of that?' Ben asked, his brown eyes doing that puppy-dog look that always made her melt.

'Not a shred.'

He reached across the table and took her hand. She felt tears prick at the corners of her eyes. 'Gemma, I am so, so sorry. Will you take me back?'

'Of course I will, you muppet,' she said, wiping away a stray tear. 'On the condition you never listen to a word Nat says, ever again.'

'I won't.'

'And you're not allowed to snog her again, either.'

'I promise I won't.' He gave a Scouts' salute, with the wrong number of fingers.

'Come here, you,' she said, patting the space on the sofa beside her. He moved over and put his arms around her. She nuzzled against his neck, feeling as though she'd come home at last.

'God, I love you, Gem,' he said, into her hair.

She smiled as tears ran down her face. Happy tears.

He pushed her away a little and looked at her, frowning. 'What I don't understand is why Nat would have sabotaged our relationship like that. You and she were always so close. What on earth happened?'

She shook her head and wiped away her tears. 'I have no idea. But it's not the only thing she's done.' She told him about the credit card purchases, and the letter to her parents.

'Bloody hell. Gem, you should go to the police. That's fraud.'

'Dad said I should, too. But I can't do that to her. I don't understand why she did it all but I need to talk to her about it first, and give her a chance to explain. I don't think we can ever be as close again, no matter what she says, but I have to give her a chance. We've got so much history together. I don't want to get her into trouble. I mean, there's no real harm done, is there? You and I are back together, the credit card company is investigating and Dad's put a stop on the cheque Mum sent her. I need to talk to her. I tried to find her this morning but she wasn't at work. Jasmine at the salon said she no longer works there. She also said Nat was on holiday. With you.'

'Ah, hence the text.'

'Yes. Nat must have lied to Jasmine.'

'She's lost it, clearly. I wonder why she's doing all this. It's as though she's holding some kind of massive grudge against you. Any idea why?'

She shook her head. 'None at all. That's why I need to see her, rather than rush off to the police or anything like that. Maybe there's been a big misunderstanding. I owe it to her to give her the chance to explain herself.'

'Like the misunderstanding between us,' Ben said, taking her hand.

'Exactly.' She smiled at him.

'If she could explain things, would you accept it, and have her back as a friend? Like you've taken me back?'

Gemma considered this. Could she forgive Nat, for undermining her relationships with Ben and her parents? It was a tough call. 'I don't know. Possibly. Probably.'

'You're a wonderful, forgiving woman, Gemma Rowling. And I love you for it. What would she have to do, I wonder, to tip you over the edge? Attempted murder?'

Gemma gave a hollow laugh. 'Don't be ridiculous. She wouldn't do that. Anyway. Enough of Nat. If we're back together, we ought to be celebrating. Off you go and buy me a bottle of champagne. I deserve it, after all you've put me through.'

He grinned. 'Whatever the lady wants, the lady shall have. But I'm driving, so can't drink much of it.'

'We can stay here tonight, if you like. Don, the manager, said there's a spare room I could use…if you'd like to share it with me?' She fluttered her eyelashes at him and smiled as he blushed profusely.

'Christ, erm, I mean, yes, of course! Wow. What a great day this has turned out to be! Right. Champagne it is, then!' He sashayed, whistling, over to the bar, slipping again but this time managing to grab hold of the bar to steady himself.

Don walked through while Ben was at the bar. Gemma beckoned him over. 'Is that spare room still on offer?'

'Of course! Does that mean you and Ben…?'

'Looks like it!' She smiled happily. 'Thanks, Don. I'll get on with the research properly tomorrow.'

'No rush. I mean, I hope you can get it done before... but no. Doesn't matter, do it in your own time. Hey, I should say congratulations! Have a great evening.' He continued on his way through the bar as Ben returned with the bottle of champagne and two glasses.

CHAPTER 22

September 1838

Rebecca gathered up all the letters and rough drafts into a pile, and laid them on top of Sarah's journal. Her heart was racing. What would she discover in these documents? They might give her an insight into Sarah's mind, and why she'd acted as she had in those last weeks of her life. She sighed. They'd been so close. She still found it hard to believe that Sarah meant to hurt her in any way. Perhaps somehow there had been a misunderstanding. But even if there was, it was too late. Nothing could bring Sarah back. She wiped away a tear that had crept unbidden into the corner of her eye. If only she could go back. Back to a time when they were children, and Sarah was her friend. When they'd loved each other as sisters. When she might have welcomed with uncomplicated joy the idea that Sarah might actually *be* her true sister.

'Miss, are you well?' asked Tilly. 'Shall I fetch a clean handkerchief?'

'It's all right, I have one.' Rebecca pulled her handkerchief out of her skirt pocket and dabbed at her eyes.

'You must miss her very much, pardon me for saying so,' Tilly said.

'Of course, I do. Don't mind me, Tilly. I'm perfectly all right. You've been very helpful, finding the key to the bureau and then the journal. You may leave me now. I shall take these documents to my own sitting room. Perhaps you could bring me some tea there shortly.'

'Yes, miss, thank you, miss.' Tilly curtseyed and left the room. Rebecca spent a few more minutes searching the drawers and cupboards of the bureau in case she'd missed anything. No, it didn't look as though she had, and none of the documents appeared at first glance to be a will. In which case she'd need to look for any evidence of Sarah's next of kin, as Mr Neville had asked. In other words, painful as it was, she needed to find proof that what Sarah had said in the cellar was true. She gathered together the documents and went to her own sitting room. It had felt too much as though she was intruding, sitting in Sarah's. The day was dull but there was plenty of light to read by if she sat beside the window, on her favourite lemon, upholstered chair. She put the letters and diary on a small side table, pulled it over beside her chair, and settled down to work through the documents.

What to read first? Her instincts told her the diary would perhaps divulge the most secrets. But what might be in the letters? She decided to start with those. There were letters addressed to Sarah, and also first drafts of Sarah's letters to others. Sarah had always been in the habit of writing a letter in rough first, then copying it out neatly. Rebecca had not realised Sarah had kept her rough drafts, but how interesting they might be!

She flicked through the letters addressed to Sarah. Some were in her father's handwriting. Some were from Charles. One or two she had sent herself, years ago. She smiled at the memory. They'd been in their mid teens, and had bemoaned the fact that neither of them ever had any correspondence to read over breakfast, as Rebecca's parents had. So they'd begun writing to each other, pretending to be foreign princesses, rich suitors or famous novelists. Rebecca still had all the letters Sarah had written during this time, but it seemed Sarah had only kept a few.

She put the letters from her father into date order. Why had her father been writing to Sarah? He did used to go away from home occasionally, but the letters he'd sent home were usually addressed to her mother, or after Mama's death, to Rebecca. Looking at the dates she realised most of the letters to Sarah were more recent – written in the last few weeks of Papa's life. He'd been at home during this time. So why had he been writing letters to Sarah? She looked next at the drafts. Some of these were to Papa. They were conveniently dated. She tucked the drafts to Papa in the pile in the right order. Now she could read this correspondence, which apparently started four months before Papa's death, in sequence.

Dear Papa, the earliest letter, a rough draft, began.

You will wonder why I am writing to you when surely I could just come down the stairs and tap on your study door, and ask for an interview. You will wonder too, I imagine, why I address you as 'Papa' rather than Mr Winton, as I have called you throughout my life to date. The truth is, dear Papa, that I have always thought of you as my father, and Rebecca as my sister. In fact now that I am grown, I would like to be able to openly acknowledge our relationships in this way. That is why I am writing to you like this – to give you time and space to think about your reply rather than responding immediately to the first thing I say, as you would have done had I knocked upon the door of your study.

Papa, the time has come, I believe, for you to treat me as equal to Rebecca. Perhaps even more than equal, for I am a little older

than her. I would like, dear Papa, a larger bedchamber – perhaps
the one next to yours? Also a private sitting room, and an allowance
at least equal to Rebecca's. And finally, though the very thought
of it pains me, we must surely think ahead to the day when you,
dear Papa, are no longer with us. I do not know what provisions
have been made for me in your will, but I should like to think my
inheritance will be appropriate to my status as your first-born child.

Regards,

Your devoted daughter,

Sarah

Rebecca put the letter down in a daze. What a cheek Sarah had, to ask for such things in that way! She recalled that Sarah had indeed moved into the larger room on the first floor just before Papa's death, although that had not proved enough, and she'd then taken Rebecca's suite. She felt a cold hand closing around her insides as she realised that Sarah's claims made in the cellar must be true. She could no longer put off thinking about it. She both wanted to read on and find the proof that would mean her future was secure, and didn't want to, so that her past beliefs might remain intact. She steeled herself and picked up the next letter in chronological sequence to read on.

My dear Sarah

I shall reply to your letter in writing, as that seems to be your
preferred method of communication. I would ask, however, that
you destroy all traces of this correspondence as soon as you have
read it, in case it should fall into the wrong hands in the future.
I have already burned your letter to me.

Sarah, I have, as you know, always treated you as though you
were my own daughter. I have given you a home, an education and
an income. You have a secure future in my house or in Rebecca's,

when she marries. You are well aware of this. I do not see how you can ask for more. The contents of my will are private. You will hear them in due course, but, God willing, not for many years yet.

Yours,

Henry Winton

Rebecca's hands were shaking as she picked up the next draft. This one was full of crossings out, and written in quite a scrawl, as though Sarah had been angry when she wrote it.

Papa, you appear to have misunderstood the meaning of my last letter. Perhaps I wasn't quite blunt enough. I shall try again.

Now that your wife is dead gone from us, there is no need to continue allowing the rumour that Spencer is my father to be believed. I understand you wanted to protect your reputation and not have your wife know that you were an adulterer, but there is nothing to be lost now by admitting the truth.

I am requesting demanding those things – a larger room, a bigger allowance, provision in your will – because I know I am entitled to them. If you continue persist in ignoring me then I shall have to make our true relationship public. I shall let the world know that you kept two women – your wife and my mother – for so many years. I shall go further, and say that you did not stop at that. There is much more I could say. I could damage destroy your reputation. And yet all I am asking for is equality with my sister. Is that really so very much to ask? I don't think so.

I shall not expect an answer immediately. Sit and ponder this a while. Consider the various scenarios that could play out, depending on what you decide. Work out which is the best one for all of us – you, me and Rebecca.

Your devoted daughter,

Sarah

The next letter was dated several days later. Papa must have taken Sarah's advice and thought things through for a while. It was very short.

Sarah,

You leave me with no choice. I shall comply with your requests, though the manner of them leaves a bitter taste in my mouth. I had high regard for you when you were younger but you have destroyed all that. Well, you will get your wishes. Thankfully Rebecca will be settled and happy with Charles de Witt, away from here and away from your malicious influence. I shall advise her not to take you with her as her companion under any circumstances. Spencer, who treated you as his own daughter throughout your life as I requested, would be devastated to learn of this side of your nature. I hope he never does.

Henry Winton

Blackmail! Rebecca put the letters down and stared into space, letting it all soak in. So Sarah had put pressure on Papa to change his will. He had been so sure Rebecca's future was certain that he'd left the Red Hill Hall estate to his blackmailer, to protect his reputation. It still seemed a bit extreme. It was one thing to give her a bigger room and a more generous allowance, but to cut his own legitimate daughter off entirely was harsh. Unless there had been other letters, of which Sarah had not written or kept a draft, between those last two? Perhaps she'd found some other way to force him to do as she wished? Whatever, she realised that she must show Mr Neville what she had found, and see if that was evidence enough that she was Sarah's next of kin. She resolved to write to him and disclose what she had found so far.

Rebecca turned next to the letters between Sarah and Charles. What would they reveal, she wondered? She steeled herself to read them. Charles's handwriting was so familiar to her. It hurt to see it again, to remember the man, his caresses and kisses, and how happy she'd been while they'd been engaged.

She sorted the letters into sequence as she had done with Papa's, and was about to start reading when there was a tap at the door, and Tilly entered without waiting to be admitted.

'Oh miss, sorry miss for disturbing you but I thought you would want to know as soon as possible, for it is terrible!' Tilly was red in the face and out of breath – she must have run up the stairs.

'What is it?'

'Oh miss, the constable is here again and there is news, and I think perhaps you ought to come and hear it direct from him and not from me, if you don't mind.' She bobbed a curtsey, and clutched at her cap, which had come loose.

'Very well. Please tell him I will see him in a few minutes. Have Spencer show him into the drawing room and offer him some refreshment.'

Tilly curtseyed again and left the room. Rebecca bundled the letters and papers together and looked around for somewhere safe to store them, away from prying eyes. Unlike Sarah she did not have a lockable bureau or box in her rooms. She had never felt the need to keep anything secret. In the end she stuffed the papers in the back of a wardrobe. Perhaps she would have Sarah's bureau moved into her room. If she was to inherit the estate after all, that is.

Downstairs, Constable Barnsworth was standing by the window in the drawing room, his hands behind his back. He bowed as she entered.

'Miss Winton, I am sorry to call on you without warning. But there has been, ahem, a development.'

'A development? In what?'

'In the case of the disappearing shooter. That is to say, the mystery surrounding who killed Miss Cooper.' The constable pulled himself up to his full height and puffed out his chest.

Rebecca felt herself repelled by his sense of self-importance, but more than that, fearful of what he had discovered. Had he found some clue that *she* was the disappearing shooter? Sometimes she thought it would surely be only a matter of time before the truth was discovered. 'Well? What has happened?'

'I have been asking around the village and estate cottages, to see if anyone knew anything or had seen someone running away on the day of the murder, or knew of someone in hiding. My first enquiries drew a blank, but I do not give up easily, Miss Winton. I made a second set of enquiries this week, to see if anyone remembered anything new.'

'And?' She tried not to sound too eager. If only he would get to the point!

'It appears one of the farmhands, who lives in a cottage on your estate, has gone missing. He lives with his sister who has reported him gone. My suspicion is that he is the person who shot Miss Cooper and yourself.'

'What is his name?'

'Jed Arthur, ma'am. He's a rough type. His sister Dorothy says he knew Miss Cooper and sometimes followed her when she went out riding on the estate.' He nodded sagely.

Rebecca stifled a gasp. She remembered the time she and Charles had seen Sarah kissing Jed Arthur. 'What on earth would have possessed him to shoot her? And shoot me as well?'

'I suppose only he would know his true motive. My guess would be that he somehow felt slighted by her. Perhaps he'd made an advance towards her. Excuse me, ma'am, I understand that is an intolerable thing to imagine – that dirty labourer having designs on your dear friend. When she rebuffed him perhaps he thought to have his revenge on her. And maybe you were just in the wrong place at the wrong time, as it were.'

Rebecca thought quickly. The constable was close to the truth about Jed's relationship with Sarah. Rebecca searched her soul. She did not want an innocent person to be accused of killing Sarah. But if Jed couldn't be found, then for now at least he made a suitable scapegoat. It would stop the authorities from looking closer to home for a perpetrator. If he was found, he'd deny it of course, and hopefully he would be able to prove it wasn't him. If necessary, she would do or say something – what, she didn't know – to help get him off the hook. She'd certainly make sure he wouldn't hang for it. But all the while he was missing he would serve her purposes nicely. Perhaps on hearing of Sarah's death he had gone away to nurse his grief. As long as he stayed away all would be well.

'Yes. That does sound possible. How terrible! Poor Sarah.'

'I must ask again – can you remember anything at all about the man who shot you? We have a description of Jed Arthur from his sister. If your memories match her description, that would lend weight to my theory.'

She shook her head. 'I am sorry, Constable. It is as I told you before – I really did not get sight of the man, and have no memory of the shooting.' Whatever happened, she needed to keep her options open in case she needed to change her story to save Jed from being hanged for murder.

He sighed. 'Never mind. Well, we now have someone to actively search for. There are notices going into local papers. He is unlikely

234

to have gone far – he would not have the means to buy a coach ticket anywhere. He might have got a lift a short distance in a farmer's cart but perhaps would not have wanted to risk being recognised or remembered. I suspect we will find him hiding in a barn somewhere within a ten-mile radius. Mark my words, Miss Winton. We'll find him and bring him to justice.'

'I do hope so,' she said. Her mind was racing. She must find Jed before the constable did. Perhaps she could warn him he was wanted for the murder, and tell him to get away, out of the county. She could give him money to do so. She wouldn't need to let on that it was in fact her who'd shot Sarah – that would be far too dangerous. She could just say that the constable thought it was Jed, but that she knew it could not have been, as Jed was a good man who'd cared for Sarah. He should take her words as a friendly warning – to get far away where the constable would not find him. And to never come back. Yes. This was her way out. But first she had to find Jed.

'I'll take my leave now, Miss Winton. My men and I have a fugitive to find.' Constable Barnsworth nodded and strode towards the door of the room.

'Good luck,' she called after him. A thought struck her as she watched him leave. Sarah's diary. What if she'd written about Jed in there? Perhaps there'd be some clue as to where he might have gone. That, and a visit to his sister, would be her best lines of enquiry.

CHAPTER 23

August 2015

Gemma ate her breakfast of smoked salmon and cream cheese on a bagel with a wide smile on her face. It wasn't just the food, although such a decadent breakfast was a real treat. It was the fact that Ben, dear funny beloved Ben, was sitting opposite her eating his full English, and they had just spent the night together in a beautiful room in Red Hill Hall. They'd spent much of the night just talking and holding each other, and the rest of it making love and making up for lost time. Gemma reckoned she'd only had about three hours' sleep but regardless, she'd never felt more invigorated and alive.

'Happy?' Ben said.

'Just a bit,' she replied, her grin widening. Her cheeks were already aching from continuous smiling and it was only nine a.m.

'What's the plan for today then? You going to show me this archive of documents? Perhaps I can help you go through it.'

'Sure, yes let's do that. But I also want to try to track down Nat again later today. I don't believe she's on holiday – that was all a lie, like everything else. Until I've confronted her with it all I don't feel as though I can truly relax. I just want it out of the way.'

'Want me to come with you?'

'No. I have to talk to her alone.' She reached a hand across the table to grasp Ben's. 'But thank you for offering. Love you.'

'Love you, too.' With his other hand he speared a piece of salmon from her plate and popped it in his mouth before she could stop him. 'Mmm. Nice.'

'You beast! That was mine.' She stole a piece of crispy bacon in retaliation.

'Oi, I was saving that piece till last!'

'Well, you shouldn't have stolen my salmon, should you?' She stuck her tongue out at him.

'When we're married, what's yours is mine, anyway.'

'Who said we're getting married?' Her heart had leapt at the words. 'You'll need to ask me again.'

'I will. Just give me time.'

Gemma smiled happily. Life was looking up. Just the confrontation with Nat to get out of the way.

***

A short while later they were back in the office Don had set aside. Gemma lifted down the box of paperwork. 'Look, there's all this to go through. I've begun sorting letters into date order but haven't read any properly yet. It'll take a while to tune into this old-fashioned handwriting.'

'Yes, very curly and swirly, isn't it?' Ben picked up a letter from the top of a pile. 'Wonder if there's any juicy gossip in them or if it's all just boring stuff.'

'I won't know until I've read them. I expect there's a mixture but I really hope some of them are from around the time of all the deaths here, and they shed some light on it all.'

'How far have you got with that research?'

'Not very. I went through the online newspaper archives but that's about all so far. There's been too much other stuff on my mind, unfortunately.'

'Sorry.' Ben put his arm round her and kissed her cheek. 'So let me read you this letter. *My dear Charles.* Ahem.' He coughed and adopted a higher pitched voice and cultured accent. '*May deah Charles.*'

Gemma laughed. 'Give it here. A man called Charles de Witt was found drowned in the well. I wonder if it's him?' She scanned the letter, and then read it aloud.

My dear Charles,

It pains me to write this letter to you but I feel as your friend I owe it to you to disclose certain facts. You have recently, as I understand it, proposed to Rebecca and she has accepted. I know that your parents, God rest their souls, had always wished for a union between our families. I know too that Rebecca's parents wished it.

But my dear Charles, you are presumably not aware that Rebecca herself has long dreaded such an event coming to pass. She has confided in me many times, hoping that you might look elsewhere for a spouse, that you would adopt a modern attitude and marry for love, and not just because this union is what was expected of you both.

Poor Rebecca. When you asked for her hand she felt as though her life was over. She told me she felt a sinking of her heart and a deadening of her spirit. It was all she could do to put on a brave, happy face, and accept you. She did this for two reasons – because she was afraid turning you down would break her father's heart, and for you. Because she is such a kind and gentle soul she did not want to let you down. You know Rebecca – you know how she always wants to please everyone, all of the time. It is one of her most endearing features but I am afraid it will be the undoing of her. Thankfully she has me at her side, and I am more able and willing to speak the truth. And that is the reason for this letter.

Charles, I suspect you proposed only because it was expected of you. Perhaps you do have some feelings for her. But those feelings are not returned. I love Rebecca with all my heart, and would not want to see her tied into a bitter, loveless marriage, which is no doubt what it would become. I beg you, Charles, release her from the engagement. Act now to avoid making a terrible, tragic mistake, which would ruin both of your lives.

I remain,

Your true and loving friend,

Sarah

'Wow!' Ben said. 'We've come across juicy gossip in the very first letter.' He took it from Gemma, read it again and frowned. 'It's kind of weird. This Sarah sounds just like Nat – she said pretty much the same thing to me when she persuaded me to break off our engagement.'

Gemma nodded. 'Hmm. I wonder if it was true or not – whether Rebecca really did like Charles or whether Sarah was just manipulating him. As Nat manipulated you.'

'To my eternal shame and regret.' He made his puppy-dog eyes at Gemma.

She gave his arm a squeeze and kissed him. She was trembling with excitement. Rebecca, Sarah, Charles – these were all the people involved in the accidents and events at Red Hill Hall in

1838. There was no date on the letter, and there were several crossings out and blots, as though perhaps it was a rough draft to be copied out later. 'I don't know. Charles died in 1838 – drowned in the well – if it is indeed the same Charles but I am guessing it is. And the names of the women involved in the shooting were Rebecca Winton and Sarah Cooper.'

'Did they both die? You were unsure last time we spoke about this.'

'I'm still unsure. The newspaper articles were contradictory. I was hoping to find evidence in amongst this lot that would confirm who died and who lived. And also confirm their relationship – they have different surnames but are described as sisters in some reports.'

'Was one married?'

'No, they were both referred to as Miss.'

'Hey, lovebirds, how's it going?' The door opened and Don entered, clutching a cup of coffee.

On impulse Gemma crossed the room to him and gave him a hug. 'It's going tremendously well. Both the research and the relationship. I can't thank you enough for facilitating both of them.'

'You are most welcome. Glad to have been able to help.' Don grinned, clearly delighted with his role in their reconciliation. 'I'll leave you to it. Shout if you need anything.'

They spent the next couple of hours going through the documents and by the end had everything sorted and numbered, and had begun reading through them. Gemma had discovered that only Sarah had died in the shooting. Rebecca had survived, and had paid a hefty doctor's bill for her treatment several months after the shooting.

'This is intriguing,' Ben said, waving another letter at Gemma. 'Listen.' He read it out.

Dear Miss Winton

Thank you for your letter of 14th inst, and the details you gave of Miss Cooper's possible parentage, which made for very interesting reading. I must admit I was most surprised to learn that Mr Winton may have been Miss Cooper's father as I had suspected someone else was, but it certainly explains why he changed his will in such a dramatic way. If your suspicions are correct then it means that, as her half-sister, you are most certainly Miss Cooper's next of kin, and therefore in the event that no will for Miss Cooper can be found and she is declared intestate, then you stand to inherit the estate. As, in my humble opinion, and if I may be so bold as to say, should have happened when your father passed away.

It remains therefore for you to continue searching Miss Cooper's and your father's papers and put to one side anything that confirms their relationship. I will inspect all such papers when I return to Dorset in a fortnight's time.

Until then, I remain,

Your obedient servant,

Nathaniel Neville (Solicitor)

Ben finished reading and Gemma stared at him. 'So if I understand this correctly, it sounds as though Rebecca and Sarah may have been half-sisters. Interesting.'

Ben was frowning. 'What's all that about the father's will being changed dramatically?'

'I don't know. But I do know that the National Archive keeps copies of wills, and you can download them for a fee from their website. And I will do exactly that as soon as I am back home with my laptop. Or at the museum.' She picked up her notebook and wrote herself a note to search for Henry Winton's will.

'I can see why you're so hooked on all this,' Ben said. 'I can feel myself getting sucked in as well. But it's probably lunchtime. Here, or somewhere else? My treat.'

She shook her head. 'Thanks, love, but I'll just grab a sandwich. I'm then going in search of Nat this afternoon. How about we get together this evening? Come round to my flat and I'll cook you a dinner?' With a pang she remembered the last dinner she'd cooked for Ben, the one they'd never eaten, as he'd come round to break off their engagement. Nat's doing. She had to find her and ask her *why*.

***

Gemma spent the afternoon searching for Nat. She was not at her flat. She did not want to ring or text her – Gemma's idea was to surprise her face to face. She wanted to see Nat's immediate reaction and not give her any time to prepare herself for a meeting.

As a last resort, she decided to drive to Nat's mother's flat, on the edge of town. She knew Nat rarely saw her mother – an alcoholic who'd thrown her daughter out when Nat was just sixteen. But perhaps she would know where Nat was. Gemma didn't believe she was really in Tenerife. Not if she'd lost her job and was so short of money that she was trying to extort some out of Gemma's parents.

Nat's mother's flat was in a dingy sixties block. The lift wasn't working so Gemma climbed the three flights of stairs. Mrs Heller's glass front door was boarded up, and several bin bags were stacked under her kitchen window. Gemma took a deep breath and rang the doorbell. She hadn't seen Nat's mother for several years. When

Nat was growing up they'd lived in a terraced house near the centre of town. It had been small but much nicer than this place, which was clearly suffering from years of neglect.

Gemma barely recognised Nat's mother when she opened the door. Her hair was stringy and unwashed, her face gaunt and lined.

'What do you want?' she asked, her voice rough from years of smoking.

'Hello, Mrs Heller. Do you remember me? I'm Gemma Rowling, a, erm, friend of Natalie's.' It hurt to say the word 'friend'.

'I remember you. The posh kid. What have you come here for?'

'I'm looking for Nat. I really need to talk to her about something.'

'Why don't you ring her?' Mrs Heller was standing in the doorway, her arms folded. Beyond her, Gemma glimpsed a movement as though someone was lurking in the hallway, listening. Could it be Nat?

'I need to see her face to face. It's important. Do you know where she might be?'

'Her home? Her work? I don't keep tabs on her.'

'I've looked everywhere. Please, Mrs Heller, if you have any ideas...'

Suddenly Nat's mother stood aside. 'For fuck's sake, I can't be bothered with these silly games. She's here. Come in and talk to her. I'm off out for some fags.'

Behind her, Nat was standing with her hand over her mouth. 'Mum, I told you...' she began, but Mrs Heller had grabbed her purse from a small table just inside the flat and pushed past Gemma towards the stairs.

Gemma went inside. The flat smelt of rotting vegetables and there was thick dust on every surface. Nat had turned her back and walked down the hallway into the living room, so Gemma followed her. There was a good view over Bridhampton. Gemma could make out the town hall clock tower and beside it, the museum.

'What do you want?' Nat said, her words echoing her mother's.

'I think you can probably guess, can't you? Why, Nat? That letter to my parents, what you said to Ben to make him break up with me, and the stuff you bought and charged to my credit card. I mean, I could go to the police with that last one. But I thought I'd give you a chance to explain yourself first.'

'I don't need to explain myself to you. You deserve it all.' Nat turned away from Gemma to stare out of the grubby window.

'I deserve it? How? Why? Come on, Nat. We were so close for so long. You owe me an explanation.' Please, Nat, Gemma thought. Give me an explanation, a reason to forgive you. She wanted to keep Nat in her life, but whether she could or not all depended on what Nat said next.

Nat stood in silence, her back to Gemma, for a minute. When she spoke again her voice was tight as though she was trying to control her tears. 'You have always had it so easy, Gemma. You have no fucking idea what it's like to live in the real world. Nothing bad has ever happened to you, has it? No. You sailed through school, teacher's pet, everybody's darling. Your parents had your back at every step of the way. You went off to university then came home to your dream job in your home town. Then you found a lovely bloke who adored you. I wanted all that, too. I could have gone to college, if I'd had even just a tiny bit of support and encouragement from my useless mother. I wanted to be a nurse, not a fucking manicurist. And I'd love to have found a genuinely good man like Ben. You had no idea how lucky you were.'

'I did, Nat, I *did* know how lucky I was with Ben!'

'No, you really didn't. You have never had to fight for anything, Gemma. It's all just landed on your lap.' Nat spat the last words out and spun round to face Gemma. Her eyes were brimming with angry tears.

'So, what, you thought you'd undermine everything I had? I was so happy when Ben proposed, and it broke my heart when he ended it. That's what you wanted, is it, my heart to be broken?'

'Why not? Mine has been on so many occasions. Remember Mike, who dumped me two weeks after asking me to move in with him? Chucked all my clothes out on the street, didn't he, and changed the locks, while I was at work at that shitty bar job I used to have. Then there was Alex, who strung me along for three months before telling me about his wife and four kids. And Simon, gorgeous, handsome Simon, who I thought I was totally in love with, until he sent me a text saying, 'Bye, thanks for the shags, see you around,' and then disappeared off the face of the earth. Oh yes, I've had my heart broken often enough. About time you grew up and found out what it was like. I suppose Ben told you, then, that it was me who warned him off? I wasn't lying though – I do believe your marriage wouldn't have lasted. I've done you both a big favour.'

It was on the tip of Gemma's tongue to tell Nat that she and Ben were reconciled but she decided against it. Who knew what Nat would do next if she thought she'd failed in splitting them up. 'What about that evil letter to my parents? That's fraud. Dad's stopped the cheque.'

'Your parents have always bailed you out, haven't they? They paid your university fees. They loaned you the deposit for your flat. I've never been able to afford anything more than rubbishy rented bedsits. Your parents have got more than enough. Your mum told me once I was like a second daughter to them. So why shouldn't I have some of their money?'

'Jesus, Nat. If you needed money and you'd asked them for a loan they'd probably have said yes. But lying to them about me like that, trying to make them doubt me... It's disgusting.'

'I've been doubted by my own parents all my life. I was always just a hindrance to Mum – something that cost money that could have been spent on booze. Hardly know my Dad. He got out while he could, sensible man, and went as far away as possible. I'd join him in Australia if I could.' Nat sniffed and wiped her forearm across her nose.

'Why don't you?' Gemma asked.

'You don't get it, do you? I've lost my job and can't pay the rent on my flat so I've had to move into this dump. I can't afford a trip to Australia. I know *you* could. Oh, you'd just stick it on your credit card and pay it off with your next pay cheque. Or ask Mummy and Daddy to fund you. I can't even *get* a credit card.'

Gemma felt a pang of sadness for Nat. Things must be bad if she'd had to move in with her mother. And yes, she had to agree that life had been easier for her than for Nat. But it was no excuse for the way Nat had behaved. 'So you thought you'd use my credit card? That dress you wore to Anna and Jake's wedding?'

'What do you want me to say? I'm not admitting to it. I'll deny it. You can't prove it.'

'My card was used in *La Belle Femme* and they'll have the transaction details showing that dress was bought, presumably by phone or via their website. And there are photos of you wearing it. There's proof enough, if I decide to go to the police. I could also show them the letter you sent Mum and Dad. You'd be charged with fraud.'

'Yeah, but you won't do it, will you, Gemma? It'd all be too unpleasant, and you don't like unpleasantness. You like everything to stay rosy in your little world. Nothing nasty can happen. I've done you a favour. I've helped you grow up a little and see what life's like for the rest of us. Call it a valuable life lesson. You should be thankful. And you've not lost anything. Except Ben, who you didn't deserve anyway. He'll be happier without you.'

Gemma had heard enough. She'd given Nat her chance. It was obvious she was not going to apologise at all. She needed to go away, discuss everything with Ben and decide what to do next. She turned away. 'Keep out of my life from now on, please, Nat. You've done enough damage. I'll see myself out.'

'Yeah. Fuck off back to your boring, cosy little existence,' Nat called after her.

***

It was only when Gemma was safely back in her car that she burst into huge, sobbing, convulsing tears. She hated Nat for what she'd done. But somehow, despite it all, she still loved her too. She'd lost her – she could see that now. There was no way back from this. Nat's jealousy of what Gemma had seemed to have consumed her. She was no longer the fun, supportive friend she used to be. It was a full ten minutes before Gemma could compose herself enough to drive home. Thank goodness Ben would be round in a couple of hours. She had never needed him more.

CHAPTER 24

September 1838

As soon as Constable Barnsworth had left, Rebecca rushed straight upstairs to her room, to continue reading Sarah's letters and diary. She was tired, and her shoulder ached. She knew she should rest but having learned that Sarah had been blackmailing Papa by threatening to reveal that he was her father, Rebecca was desperate to know what other secrets might be uncovered. She also needed to write to Mr Neville, disclosing what she had found so far. He would keep the confidence, she knew. But it could mean she would inherit Red Hill Hall and her future would be secure. Assuming no will of Sarah's was found.

Rebecca took out Sarah's diary and settled herself in the chair by the window. The evenings were beginning to draw in but there would be another couple of hours of daylight before dinner and she intended to make full use of them.

The journal began two years earlier. Rebecca skimmed through those first entries. They recounted days out riding across the estate, mornings trapped inside when it was raining, playing games of Patience, afternoons spent walking the grounds with Rebecca. She smiled at the memories. Those had been good days

– when both Mama and Papa were alive and she and Sarah were best friends without a care in the world. But as the journal entries progressed Rebecca began to notice a change in tone. Instead of the excited, girlish earlier scribblings, the language became more measured, more introspective and reflective. A bitter tone crept in. *Why did Mama have to die?* Sarah had written. *If she had still been here, perhaps she could have prevailed upon Papa to treat me as an equal to R. Mama would not have wanted me to have a future merely as R's companion. She would have insisted that I be launched into society at the same time as R, and have equal chance at finding a husband. I miss Mama.*

Rebecca turned a few pages more, to the entries from just over a year ago. *It is not fair. R has both a mother, and a father who acknowledges her. I have no one. I cannot bring Mama back, but perhaps I can even things up in some other way.*

She gasped. This had been written just a couple of weeks before Mama's lethal fall down the stairs. A memory surfaced – Sarah, at the top of the stairs while Mama lay crumpled and broken at the foot. Her expression – it had struck her at the time but then she had forgotten it as she fussed around her poor mother's lifeless body – had been one of triumph. No! Had Sarah... could she have... pushed Mama down the stairs? Just to 'even things up' as she'd written?

But the next entry, written the day after Mama's death, was smudged as though tears had fallen on it. In it, Sarah lamented their loss, expressed profound sadness, and bemoaned the tragedy that had fallen on their household. It sounded genuine. Rebecca wondered if she'd ever know for sure. She wondered too if she really wanted to know. Sarah had shot at her – that was one thing – but to know for certain she'd had a hand in Mama's death was unbearable.

She read on, flicking over a few pages past those dark days of last summer and through to spring of 1838, and the heady days of her engagement to Charles. What had Sarah written about that, she wondered?

Terrible day. C has proposed to R. She's accepted, and is skipping around the house with the stupidest expression on her face. I want to smack it off her. Instead I have to pretend to be as delighted as Papa is. All those times I went riding with C, trying to make him see which of us was better suited to him as his life's partner – all for nothing. He followed his dead parents' wishes and picked R. He is obviously weaker than I realised. But weakness is good, and I can turn it to my advantage, if I am clever enough. And I am clever. Mama always told me I could do anything if I set my mind to it. So I shall set my mind to this. R shall not have him. I shall turn him away from her and towards me. She has so much – she shall not have him as well.

Rebecca felt sick. She remembered Sarah's careful expressions of delight when she'd told her Charles had proposed. Her reaction had been reserved but polite, and she'd hoped at the time it was genuine. And yet it was entirely put on. This journal entry had been written on the very day of the proposal, and was full of so much bitterness and – yes, and hate. Rebecca hesitated to use the word but hate was oozing out of Sarah's written words, in spades.

She took a deep breath, and turned the page.

Despite writing to C the engagement continues. I must find a way to meet him in person. Perhaps if I tell him face to face what I have already written, he will believe it more.

What had been in that letter? Rebecca wondered. She read the next entry.

I am exhausted this evening. I spent hours out riding today,

trotting back and forth across the fields in the hope I might 'acciden-
tally' bump into C. Finally it happened. We rode for ages together,
and I steered the conversation skilfully around to his engagement.
I told him R didn't love him; that she had only agreed to the engage-
ment out of a sense of duty; that theirs would be a bitter, unhappy
marriage and the best thing he could do would be to break things
off as soon as possible. I impressed upon him that he was a free,
adult man, who did not need to follow his parents' wishes. What
they would wish most for him was for him to marry a woman who
loved him and with whom he could be happy and content for ever.
They would not want him to shackle himself to a woman who would
make him miserable in time. I told him Papa would understand and
would not hold him to any obligation; especially if the engagement
was terminated swiftly before any wedding preparations were made.

He owed it to her, I said. If he cared for her he would release
her rather than force her to go ahead. I explained that she would
protest, she would say she loved him and that she did truly want
him, but that she had told me privately that she was devastated to
find herself in such a difficult position. I made him swear not to tell
her I had told him that last part, as she had told me in confidence.

He believed me. Every word of it. We came back to the Hall after
the long ride, and he saw her briefly but to my disappointment said
nothing of any importance to her. I only hope and pray that he felt
the need to sleep on it, to steel himself to do it, to decide on the best
way to break the news. He is to come again tomorrow.

Rebecca snapped the journal shut and threw it across the
room. She did not need to read the next entry. She did not need
to read Sarah's joyful crowing that she'd got what she wanted.
She'd hinted that what she really wanted was Charles, and
although she'd managed to manipulate him into breaking off his

engagement, she hadn't managed to turn him towards her before he died. Had he thrown himself into the well heartbroken because he believed she, Rebecca, didn't want him? Or, worse, had Sarah had something to do with Charles's death? Perhaps he'd spurned her, and she could not take his refusal? If she had actually pushed Mama down the stairs, it would not be beyond imagination that she'd done the same to Charles. Had Sarah been evil through and through – a cold-hearted murderer? If so, then her own killing of Sarah may have saved other lives…

She sat motionless for perhaps half an hour, contemplating what she had read. It was enough for now. She had seen that Sarah had turned against her, manipulated Charles into breaking off the engagement and her father into changing his will. Sarah had clearly wanted to destroy her. Rebecca straightened her spine. Sarah had not succeeded. When the critical moment came, it was Rebecca's shot that was true.

***

The following day dawned bright and clear, and she woke feeling energetic and determined to resolve some of the mysteries. Her shoulder felt better, so after breakfast she put on her cape and informed Spencer that she was going out for a walk in the estate.

'Should you, Miss Winton? Are you well enough?' he asked, his brow furrowed with worry.

'I am perfectly well, thank you, and I think it will do me good. I have not left the house since before the, erm, accident.'

'Would you like someone with you? A groom, or Tilly perhaps, just in case you need help?'

She considered, but declined. She had resolved to visit Jed

Arthur's sister, and try to find out more about his disappearance. It would not do for Tilly or another servant to hear anything Dorothy Arthur had to say. 'I shall go alone, Spencer. Thank you for your concern. I shall be back in time for luncheon.'

He nodded, and held open the grand front door for her. She left the house and began walking up the long driveway. The Arthurs' cottage was, she knew, somewhere over to the east of the estate, beyond the copse. It was a warm day and she soon began to regret wearing the cloak. She pulled it off and draped it over her good arm.

The walk was further than she'd thought, and by the time she reached the little row of farm workers' cottages she was exhausted and her shoulder was aching once more. Still, she'd be able to sit down in Dorothy's cottage and hopefully that would revive her enough for the walk back. She tapped on the door of the end cottage.

The woman who answered was tall and thin with a face that should have been pretty but her pinched, tired expression made her look gaunt and older than her years. Rebecca recognised her from church. 'Dorothy Arthur?'

'Yes, that's me. Oh, it's Miss Winton, ain't it?' The woman bobbed an ungainly curtsey. 'Do you want to come in?'

'I would like to sit and rest, if you don't mind.' Rebecca followed her into a small but clean cottage. The door opened directly into the kitchen, which doubled as a living room. There was one bedroom to the right, and a set of narrow steps led to a loft in which she supposed was another bedroom. Rebecca pulled a bentwood chair out from under a scrubbed pine table and sat down, while Dorothy fussed around putting a kettle on the hearth to make tea.

'I hope you don't mind me calling on you like this,' Rebecca said.

Now that she was here she wasn't sure quite how to begin the conversation. She wished she'd rehearsed it a little in her head beforehand. 'I heard only yesterday that your brother was missing, and I wanted to check you were all right, and whether there was anything I could do for you.'

Dorothy forced a smile. 'You're very kind, miss. It is hard without him. I fear for what has happened to him. It is not like him to go away like this.'

'No, I imagine not,' Rebecca said.

'I heard tell the constable thinks he might have… could have been the one who…' Dorothy put her hand over her mouth and shook her head.

'Been the one who shot Miss Cooper and me?' Rebecca asked, gently.

Dorothy simply nodded, and sat down quickly on the chair opposite Rebecca's, her hand still over her mouth.

'And you don't think he did?'

'No! No, miss. He never did it. I know it. He never would hurt anyone, let alone Miss Cooper. He loved her, oh!' Again she clamped her hand across her mouth as though to stuff the words back inside.

'Loved her?'

'I shouldn't have said it. But he did! He worshipped her. She came here often on her horse or walking, and he'd go out and meet her and they'd go off together for hours. I thought it strange, her being a lady up at the big house and him being but a labourer, but he told me love knew no barriers – that's what he said to me, love knows no barriers. I saved that in my head. Beautiful words.'

'They are beautiful words, it's true.' Rebecca pondered. Jed had clearly been struck with Sarah, but had his feelings been returned? And where was he now? 'Dorothy, I believe you are right – Jed would not have harmed Miss Cooper if he cared for her so much. But where is he? It is so strange that he should disappear immediately after the shooting.'

'He didn't disappear after it. He disappeared before. I had not seen him for some weeks before.'

'Oh, I misunderstood. The constable implied he had gone missing just after the shooting. I thought if he cared for Miss Cooper as you say he did, perhaps he went away in grief. Are you quite sure about this?'

Dorothy nodded emphatically. 'He was here on my birthday. And the day after that he went out to meet Miss Cooper and never came back. I looked everywhere – called at every cottage on the estate and in the village, came up to the hall to ask the grooms, asked the landlord at the inn to keep an eye out and let me know if Jed went there at all. But no one saw him that week, nor the next, nor any day since. He's been spirited away. I was trying to pluck up the courage to come to the hall and ask Miss Cooper if she knew anything, but then the shooting happened.'

'Goodness. Well, that rather changes things. But Dorothy, do you really have no idea where he might be? It's surely not in his character to just go away without telling you?'

'He's never done it before. I'm running out of money, too. Without his wages coming in I don't know how I'm going to cope. Rent's due, as well.' Dorothy looked down at her hands as she said this, as though she was embarrassed to be caught asking for charity.

'I shall speak to the estate manager. You will not have to pay rent until Jed returns. And, here, take this.' Rebecca fumbled in her skirt pockets and pulled out a purse. She tipped the contents onto the table and pushed the coins over to Dorothy.

'Oh, miss, no, I didn't mean...'

'Yes you did, and don't worry, I am happy to help. I only wish your brother could be found safe and well.' Although, Rebecca couldn't help but think, if he stayed away it would help keep suspicion diverted away from herself. As long as the constable didn't hear that Jed had gone missing long *before* the shooting.

'Thank you, miss. You are very kind.' Dorothy picked up the coins and dropped them into a small pot that stood on the mantelpiece.

Rebecca stood to leave. 'I shall send a basket of provisions over to you later. If you have any more thoughts about where Jed might have gone, or if he comes back or contacts you at all, would you please let me know first?'

'Yes, miss. Of course, miss.' Dorothy bobbed one of her ungainly curtseys and rushed to open the door to let her out. 'Thank you for calling, miss. I appreciate your kindnesses. I shouldn't say it, but you are far nicer than Miss Cooper. She never once said a word to me, in all the times she came by. Oh! I shouldn't speak ill of the dead, should I? My mouth runs away with me at times. Ma always said I didn't know when to keep quiet.'

Rebecca nodded at her and left the cottage. She needed to mull over what she had heard. And she needed to revisit Sarah's diaries. She must have written something about Jed in them, if Dorothy was to be believed about how often they'd met up. What had Sarah been up to? And why had Jed so suddenly disappeared? Rather than solve any mysteries, the visit to the cottage had piled more mysteries on top. Rebecca felt as though her head was spinning with the effort of trying to work it all out.

CHAPTER 25

August 2015

How could her week off be over already? was Gemma's first thought as she flicked off the alarm on Monday morning. Her second thought was how wonderful it was to wake up with Ben beside her. She smiled, stretched and turned over to cuddle up to him for a few more minutes.

'Morning, love,' he said. 'Sleep well?'

'Like a log. In fact I wonder how I ever slept when you weren't here.'

Since the night in Red Hill Hall hotel, they had spent hardly any time apart. Gemma had been revelling in Ben's company. The research at the hall had been put on hold, with Don's blessing, while they spent the rest of their week off going for walks and picnics, hiking the undulating cliffs or strolling along the broad beaches of the Jurassic coast. Ben had collected a few small ammonites, which were now adorning her mantelpiece, much to her exasperation. Could she never get away from fossils?

The rest of the week had felt like a honeymoon as they rebuilt their relationship. Even the weather had vastly improved, as if in support of them. Sadly, today they both had to return to work.

What a let-down. But what an amazing few days it had been! Before rising she allowed herself a few minutes thinking back over all that had happened. She was certainly in a different, and better place in her life at the end of the week than she had been at the beginning.

Except for the problem with Nat, which still felt unresolved, despite the visit to her mum's flat a few days before.

∗∗

The museum looked just the same as it had before her holiday. Gemma found this vaguely surprising. Her life had changed so much in the week that it seemed everything else should have altered as well. But there was Roger in a salmon-pink jumper, and there was Christine manning the entrance desk, and there were the tourists mooching around the displays wearing cheap pac-a-macs and flip-flops. It was a wet day so the museum was likely to be busy.

'You had the best of the weather last week. The second half of the week, anyway,' Roger said to her, as she settled down to work. 'Had a good holiday? I mean, given your circumstances it wouldn't have been brilliant but I hope it was relaxing at least.'

Gemma grinned at him. 'It *was* brilliant. I'm back with Ben, and we're very happy.'

'Oh! Yes. Erm, that's good news. Well done. Ahem.' Roger blushed furiously and left the room.

Gemma smiled to herself. He needed to know she was no longer available and there was no way she could have broken the news gently to him. If she'd been subtle he probably wouldn't have realised what she was saying. Better this way – be direct and clear. He'd be all right about it by lunchtime. She fired up her laptop.

Cataloguing was going to have to wait till this afternoon. She had a long list of things to check up on about Red Hill Hall and its occupants first, using the museum's subscription to Ancestry and other websites.

She started on the National Archive's site. After ten minutes searching she found the will of Henry Winton, of Red Hill Hall, who'd died in 1838. Bingo! That letter from the solicitor Nathaniel Neville to Rebecca Winton, which mentioned a sudden change in Rebecca's father's will, had intrigued her. Now at last she could find out more about it. She paid the download fee using her own debit card, and printed the will.

At first glance it was unintelligible. As with the letters, it would be a case of getting used to the handwritten, curly script. The will was just three sides of A4 so shouldn't take too long to transcribe. She'd also found Henry Winton's death certificate. He'd died of heart failure. Interestingly, the date on his death certificate was less than a fortnight after the date he'd signed his will. She began working on the will immediately, and by lunchtime had copied out the whole thing and made separate notes of the most pertinent points.

She shook her head in astonishment. So Mr Winton had left his entire estate to Sarah Cooper, his illegitimate daughter according to that letter they'd found from the solicitor, and had completely passed over his legitimate daughter Rebecca! How unfair. Perhaps Rebecca had done something unforgiveable to make him disinherit her like this. Even if he'd thought she would be marrying into a larger estate, it was an odd move for the time to name an illegitimate child as his heir. A thought occurred to Gemma. Perhaps Sarah had somehow manipulated him into naming her as his heir? She recalled the letter from Sarah to Charles de Witt, persuading him to break off the engagement. If she'd manipulated him in that way, maybe she'd done the same to Rebecca's father? Once again, the similarities between Nat and herself, and Sarah and Rebecca struck her. Nat had caused Gemma's engagement to Ben to end, and had tried to defraud her parents' out of some money. Sarah had tried to end Rebecca's engagement to Charles de Witt, and had somehow got herself named in the will, taking Rebecca's inheritance.

Well, that was one item on her list – Mr Winton's will. The next item – checking who lived in the hall at the time of the censuses, would have to wait until after lunch. She was due to meet Ben. She picked up her jacket and handbag and closed her laptop lid.

Roger was at the museum entrance. 'Just off out for lunch,' she told him.

'Yes, erm, of course. See you later,' he said.

He looked distracted and dreamy, and she followed the line of his gaze. There was a red-haired woman on her own, peering intently at a display of medieval weaponry Roger had put together a couple of weeks earlier. She looked to be in her mid thirties and had a studious air about her. As Gemma watched, Roger adjusted his tie and headed over to the woman. He said something to her and she straightened up and smiled warmly at him before answering.

Gemma grinned. Hopefully she had just witnessed the start of a romance. Roger deserved to find someone suited to him. She pushed open the door of the museum and went out into the street. The earlier rain had stopped, and it was a fine day, cool and fresh after the rain. She put on her sunglasses and walked up towards the sports centre to meet Ben.

They had lunch sitting outside a coffee shop halfway between the museum and the sports centre. Gemma told Ben about the will she'd found.

'Wow! Rebecca must have been devastated. So her engagement was broken off, then her fiancé died and her father died, and then she found herself disinherited in favour of her half-sister? So many blows all at once. Poor girl.' Ben shook his head, sadly. 'Wonder what happened to her?'

'That's what I'm hoping to find out next,' Gemma said. 'I'll try to trace her in the 1841 census. I don't know whether she stayed at the hall.'

'I'd guess she did – that letter to the solicitor implied she would have inherited the hall when Sarah died in that shooting.'

'Yes, although after so much tragedy there perhaps she didn't want to stay.'

'But if it was her ancestral home, belonging to her family for centuries, she'd have got over that, surely. She'd have kept it on even if she decided to spend most of her time somewhere else, in London or whatever. Did she ever marry?'

Gemma smiled. 'Something else I've got to search for this afternoon. If she did end up inheriting the hall she'd have been quite a catch so I imagine she did. What a shame Charles died – with Sarah out of the picture perhaps they could have made it up. Like we did.'

'There isn't always a happy ending, Gem,' Ben said.

'Poor Rebecca. I'm becoming fond of her, somehow,' Gemma replied.

'That's because you identify with her. She was treated badly by Sarah, just as you have been by Nat.'

Gemma nodded. 'Yes. And you know, the more I think about it all the more I can't wait to get on with the research. I can do a bit more online this afternoon although I'm going to have to make a start on another box of fossils before Roger gets fed up with me.

The cataloguing is taking ages. There are still at least a hundred boxes to go. Anyway, I've got Wednesday afternoon off, and I'll go back to Red Hill Hall then and try to go through more of the archive. Maybe Don will let me bring some of the papers home.'

'You won't get much done with me around,' Ben said, winking at her.

'You can be doing the cooking or the housework or something, while I work,' she replied. She sighed and smiled. 'Then life would be truly perfect.'

Ben laughed. 'Dream on, sweetheart, dream on.'

***

That afternoon back at the museum, Gemma fetched a box from the archive and began unpacking, strewing its contents (fossils, of course, and some rusty Iron Age spearheads) across the table. She opened her cataloguing spreadsheet so she could quickly switch back to it if Roger came in, and then logged into the museum's Ancestry account. Firstly she went to the 1841 census and searched for Red Hill Hall, to find its occupants. It took a while to work out how to find the records by place rather than by name but eventually she homed in on the census returns for the hall and its estate. There were several names listed – obviously some were live-in servants, or stables staff living in the attached cottages. She recognised the names of some from Henry Winton's will – George Spencer the butler, Martha Mitchell the cook. No mention of Rebecca Winton. Perhaps she had married?

She then searched for marriage records for Rebecca Winton, between 1838 and 1841. Luckily for her, compulsory registration of marriages had begun in 1837. There were several likely records – it was a common enough name. One of them leapt out at her – the groom's name was Charles de Witt.

Charles de Witt? But that was the name of the man whose body had been pulled from a well in 1838, according to several newspaper reports. How could he be living at Red Hill Hall? Unless it was a different Charles de Witt. But surely that wasn't a very common name? No, it had to be the same one. The newspapers must have made a mistake. She reread the reports she'd found and downloaded, of the body found in the well. It had definitely been identified as being Charles. There was no mention of there being any doubt about the man's identity, although one report said the body was partly decomposed having been in the water for a couple of weeks. Perhaps they had got it wrong then, and Charles had not been drowned at all? She realised she would need to trawl through the newspaper archives again, searching for later mentions of the story. Surely there would be something that said that Charles de Witt had not drowned, and had been found alive and well, and then some further news as to who the drowned man actually was?

The more she tried to resolve the mysteries of Red Hill Hall, the more mysteries seemed to appear. It was like peeling the layers from an onion. There was always another layer beneath. When would she get to the heart of it?

She looked again at the marriage registration entry. Charles de Witt and Rebecca Winton, the marriage registered in Dorset. It looked as though there had been a happy ending for Rebecca, after all.

But who had killed Sarah, and who was the man found drowned in the well? Why had the authorities identified him as Charles de Witt?

CHAPTER 26

September 1838

Rebecca was exhausted after her walk to Dorothy Arthur's cottage. She'd done too much, too soon. Her shoulder ached dreadfully and she was forced to spend the next couple of days resting. But even with only one usable arm it was still possible to read documents, so she had Tilly bring the bundle of Sarah's books and papers to her in bed.

'Don't tire yourself out, miss. Let me plump up the pillows for you.' Rebecca lay back and let Tilly fuss around until she was satisfied.

'Thank you. Tie back the curtains, would you, to let as much light in as possible.'

Once the maid had gone, Rebecca picked up Sarah's journal. She turned to the pages she had been reading before, where Sarah had written of how she had talked Charles into breaking off the engagement. Poor, dear Charles. If only she could go back to that day, convince him that Sarah was wrong and that she did love him, and then somehow keep him safe and away from the well! Why did he have to die? If he was here now she could go to him and show him the journal, and tell him she did love him with all her heart. There might have been a second chance for them.

She sighed. It was impossible to go back through time. But for her own satisfaction, she must discover the full truth. She began to read.

It is done! C has broken off his engagement to R! So that is the first part of my plan accomplished. But I have a way to go yet, before I have everything I want, nay, that I deserve. And my growing suspicion that I may be with child of course will make everything more difficult. It will mean I need to speed up my plans.

With child? Sarah? Rebecca put down the journal and stared across the room in shock. Could it be true? If so, whose was the child? It meant – oh, she could hardly bear to bring herself to think the words – that she had not only killed Sarah but also her unborn child. Her own niece or nephew. She felt a wave of nausea at the thought of that tiny, unformed, innocent life that was lost through her own actions.

She forced herself to pick up the journal and read on.

I shall not tell Jed. He shall not know that the child is his. If he should ever come forward to claim it, I shall deny everything, and who would believe his word – an uneducated, rough farm labourer – over mine? I am an educated lady. I am a person of standing, who commands respect.

But the child will have to be claimed by someone. I must waste no time in ensnaring Charles. He likes me; I know he does. He always did. I just need to turn that 'like' into 'love', or at least a moment of 'lust'.

I have realised I can use my pregnancy in other ways as well. If Papa won't acknowledge that I am his daughter and threatening to make that fact public is not enough to make him bow to my will, I shall try another tactic. What would society think if it were to be known that Papa had seduced his young ward? The daughter of his one-time housekeeper, to whom he had very charitably given a home after her mother died? What if it became known that he had abused her, for years perhaps, and now she was pregnant by him? Even though he would of course deny it and claim there's no proof, there would be my expanding waistline as evidence, and the mud, as they say, would stick. It is highly distasteful to me, but needs must, and I shall get my way! I shall pen another letter to Papa right away. One he won't be able to shrug off. He will no doubt burn it but he will not be able to ignore it.

This time there was no holding back the wave of nausea that engulfed Rebecca. She leaned over the side of the bed and vomited. The threat to tell the world of his illegitimate daughter had not worked, so Sarah had applied more pressure, threatening to accuse him of making her pregnant? And if she'd used the two threats together, that would mean incest. No wonder Papa had succumbed and altered his will in her favour. Rebecca thought too that the strain of dealing with Sarah's blackmail attempts may have hastened his death. His heart had been weak for years. This kind of stress could certainly have had a detrimental effect on him.

She wiped her mouth on the back of her hand, pushed the journal out of sight under her covers and reluctantly tugged on the bell-pull. Tilly arrived a minute later.

'Yes, miss? Oh!' She gasped in shock and instantly began clearing up the mess.

'I am so sorry, Tilly. I don't know what came over me.'

'You are not well, miss. You look terribly pale. Should I send for the doctor?'

'No need. I shall be all right when I have rested. Perhaps you could bring me some light refreshments to help settle my stomach.'

'Yes, miss. I shall go straight away to see Cook.'

Rebecca was left alone with her thoughts. The affair with Jed Arthur had been real, and he had fathered a child on Sarah. Sarah had used the pregnancy to blackmail Papa into changing his will. She'd also planned to seduce Charles and then presumably pass the baby off as his, but he had died before she had chance to put this plan into place.

Perhaps she *had* tried to seduce Charles, and he had spurned her, and that was why she had pushed him into the well?

CHAPTER 27

August 2015

Wednesday afternoon took for ever to come around but at last it was time to go back to Red Hill Hall for another look at the archive. Gemma realised that had she not spent most of her holiday week with Ben she would have had the chance to read through much of it by now. But she didn't in any way regret the days they'd spent repairing their relationship.

So it was with a happy heart that she packed up on Wednesday lunchtime and headed out of the museum and off towards the hall. The sun was shining and she sang along to the radio for the whole journey.

'You're on good form today,' Don said, as she skipped through the entrance hall. 'Things are going well with Ben, then?'

'Yes, and I've also managed to find out some more about the events that happened here,' she replied. 'But let me get a bit further and pull it all together before I tell you about it.' She grinned at his crestfallen expression.

'You get me all excited and then let me down,' he said, pulling down the corners of his mouth. 'But whatever you think best.

I can't wait to hear all about it. Well, I won't keep you chatting any longer.'

She made her way to the old butler's pantry and got straight to work, pulling out the boxes of papers. The preparation work she'd already done – putting letters into date order etc. – paid off and she was able to continue reading through, jotting down the most interesting points. They should all be scanned, transcribed and stored digitally, but for now it was enough to read through and make notes. She marked each document with a reference code written in soft pencil as she progressed. She concentrated mostly on the documents relating to 1838 – that was when most of the major events had happened at the hall. The rest of its history could wait a little longer to be discovered.

One document was a journal of some sort. It spanned the years from 1835 to mid 1838 where it ended abruptly. It was written in a scrawly copperplate, which Gemma recognised from some of the letters she'd already read – the one from Sarah Cooper to Charles de Witt, advising him to break off his engagement. Could this be Sarah's journal? If so, she must have kept it right up until the time she died. Gemma flicked to the last entry – it was dated 3rd August 1838. She checked her notes – the newspaper reports of the shooting were from various dates in the first week of August 1838.

She should, she knew, read the diary in sequence. But instead she began by reading the final entry. It might even have been written on the day Sarah died, or the day before.

The Constable is convinced the body they pulled from the well is C, for it was wearing one of C's jackets. I insisted on viewing the body, and reacted as they would expect a lady to react, and confirmed it was indeed him. I would not let R go near in case she contradicted my identification. It was decomposed enough to make recognition difficult – hard to think this was once a man of flesh and blood – but the jacket and my confirmation were enough to satisfy them.

I look back on my diary entries for these last months and realise how far I have come and yet it is not over yet, and not everything has worked out according to plan. I am now mistress of Red Hill Hall as I wanted. Papa did me the favour of dying naturally, conveniently just after writing his will naming me as his heir. I shall cast Rebecca out as soon as I can do so without it appearing vindictive. One has to consider one's reputation, when one is a lady!

C remains the problem that cannot be resolved. It suits my purposes for now for the Constable to think it was he who drowned. But I had wanted him to be engaged to me by now. I wanted us to have become bound to each other physically. In another week or two I would have told him of my condition and he would have been happy to accept his future role as the father of my child.

I don't know whether to write this next part. No one will find this book – I keep it under lock and key, and the key well hidden. Lord knows there are enough incriminating secrets within it. Even so, this is hard to write. But writing in here helps set my thoughts in order and helps me find ways to achieve what I want. So I shall continue.

I fear that R will be in my way. Even if I send her away from Red Hill Hall, she will always be tied to this place of her birth. People will ask about her. People will assume we are still the closest of friends as we used to be – as she thought we were. I acted the part too well for so many years. I loved her once, when I was younger, and before I was able to see clearly the differences in our situations in life.

I fear that she will begin to guess at my part in her misfortunes.

She might take it into her head to hurt me in some way. To repay me. She is not as clever as I am – she would not be able to concoct any kind of plan to destroy me. But what if she took a more direct route, and tried to harm me physically?

I have decided to take steps to protect myself against her. She is a gentle soul but I do not trust her. Perhaps I have pushed her too far, and like a tightly coiled spring she will snap and lash out at me. I must be ready for this, and strike before I am struck.

Gemma turned the page but there was no more. That was the last entry written. What a piece of work Sarah had been! It was clear that she knew the body in the well was not Charles, and if she knew it wasn't Charles that implied she knew who the body actually was. But she hadn't written it in her book! Damn you, Sarah Cooper, Gemma thought. You've revealed so much else but why not that?

The pregnancy was a surprise. Gemma had not expected that. It must have been in the early stages as it sounded like Sarah was keeping it hidden for the time being. Perhaps no one had known about it when she died.

And that last part. Gemma read through the final paragraphs again. Sarah scared of what Rebecca might do to her? What did she mean? Gemma jotted down a few notes, then went back to the start of 1838 in the journal and read through in order.

By the time she had finished, she felt she had a good idea of the kind of person Sarah Cooper had been. She was shocked and horrified by the lengths Sarah had been prepared to go to, to achieve her goals. Her own problems with Nat paled into insignificance in comparison.

***

'How's it going?' Don asked, as he entered with a cup of tea and a biscuit for her halfway through the afternoon.

'This stuff is better than a soap opera,' Gemma said, tapping the journal. 'The girl who died in the shooting, well she has turned out to be a right bitch.' She outlined the things Sarah had done, in her efforts to get what she wanted.

'Wow. You're right, she was not a nice person at all.' Don shook his head.

'Someone must have loved her once. Her mother, at least, when she was a child,' Gemma said. What had made Sarah become so vindictive? What had made her hate Rebecca so much she had set out to destroy her?

'Ah yes, a mother is usually blind to her offspring's faults. What happened to her mother anyway?'

'I don't know. I imagine she died when Sarah was young, and Sarah was brought up at the hall as a companion to Rebecca.'

'And because she was actually Rebecca's half-sister anyway,' Don added.

'Indeed. So I suppose Henry Winton felt obliged to do right by her. And then she repaid him by such revolting blackmail to make him change his will!'

'Revolting is right. She was prepared to tell the world her father had committed incest, raped her and made her pregnant.' Don shook his head in disgust. 'What kind of person would do that? I'm so glad *she's* not anyone's ancestor. Imagine discovering someone like her in your family tree? I suppose I'm the last person to understand women, but she really takes the biscuit. Well, I'll leave you with your tea to see if there's any more juicy gossip about those people to uncover.'

'Thanks.' As he left she briefly wondered why he'd think he

was the last person to understand women. He'd always seemed very in tune with her – ever since he'd advised her to call and make things up with Ben she'd felt she could talk to him in the way she would to a girlfriend. She picked up a bundle of letters in an unfamiliar hand and began reading them. Some she skimmed through and others she read more closely, especially when she realised who had written them. One short note, in particular, dated 1840, made her gasp.

My dear Rebecca,

I am missing you so much, but I shall be back at Carlstone Hall with you within the week. I had not appreciated it was the anniversary of Sarah's death or of course I would not have fixed my business trip for this month. I would have stayed at your side.

My darling, do not pay any heed to what people are saying. They do not know the whole story. They can never know the whole story. I know, and I understand, and I believe that you did the only thing you could have, in the circumstances. Anyone who spreads gossip shall not be invited to the Hall.

Give the little one a kiss from Papa, and stay strong. I shall soon be with you.

Your adoring husband,

Charles

Gemma reread the letter several times and made some notes. Carlstone Hall. She jotted down a note to search the census records there. It was all becoming clear to her now. She couldn't wait to tell Ben everything she'd found out, and on impulse texted him to suggest they met in the Men At Arms for a pub dinner, as soon as he finished work. His answer, 'Sure! Great idea!' was back within seconds.

The rest of the afternoon passed quickly as she read through more letters, jotted down notes and let the whole story clarify in her mind. At last it was six o'clock and time to pack up and go to meet Ben. She put the documents back in their boxes, stowed the boxes in a cupboard and left the hotel, waving cheerily to Don on the way out. 'I'll be back at the weekend, Don.'

Ben arrived at the Men At Arms at the same time she did, and they ordered a bottle of wine and a sharing platter for two. Gemma barely allowed him to sit down before she started recounting the contents of Sarah's diary.

'So what's the timeline here?' Ben said, when she'd told him everything. 'Mrs Winton falls down the stairs. Possibly pushed by Sarah.'

'Yes, then Rebecca gets engaged to Charles de Witt. But Sarah persuades him to break it off.'

'Bitch.'

'Indeed. But he does, believing what she said about Rebecca only having agreed to keep her father happy.' Gemma took a sip of her wine. 'Then Sarah finds she's pregnant by some bloke called Jed.'

'Or possibly she knew she was before sabotaging the engagement? Because she wanted Charles for herself, as a father for her child.'

'Possibly. Either way, she then began blackmailing Mr Winton. First threatening to reveal that she was his illegitimate daughter, then saying that she would tell the world he had abused her and made her pregnant.'

'*Was* she his daughter?'

'Can't be sure, but it would explain why he'd given her a home. What a way to repay him, though.'

Ben nodded. 'Like I said, what a bitch.'

'So Mr Winton gave in to her blackmail and changed his will.

He thought that Rebecca was going to marry Charles and would therefore be provided for and have a home at Carlstone Hall. So presumably he didn't know about the end of the engagement. Whatever – he died very soon after making his new will.'

Ben frowned. 'That's suspicious that he died so soon after changing his will. Did Sarah have a hand in it?'

Gemma shook her head. 'The death certificate said he died of heart failure. But perhaps Sarah's actions made his condition worse.'

'Then after he died and Sarah had inherited the estate, a body gets pulled from the well and everyone assumes it is Charles.'

'Yes, and Sarah herself helped identify the body. She knew it wasn't Charles, though.'

Ben topped up both their glasses. 'Gosh, we're getting through this bottle quickly. Why did she want people to think it was Charles? And where was Charles anyway?'

'I haven't answered those two questions yet. I am guessing Sarah knew who the body really was. And Charles must have gone away for some reason. Presumably Sarah knew this so she knew it was safe to let on the body was his. But sooner or later it'd have become known that he was still alive. Anyway, whatever her reasons were, not long afterwards the two girls were shot with those duelling pistols.'

Ben nodded. 'And no one ever found out who shot them.'

'But Sarah wrote in her diary the day before that she felt scared she'd pushed Rebecca too far, and that she might turn against her and try to hurt her. So Sarah wanted to be ready to defend herself.' Gemma's eyes were shining. 'Ben, I think Rebecca shot Sarah.'

'Who shot Rebecca then?'

'Sarah.' Gemma took a large gulp of her wine. 'I reckon they had a duel.'

'A duel!'

'Yep. They were duelling pistols, after all.'

'But women didn't duel! And anyway, duels happen outside, and each duellist would have a second who would load and prime their weapon. Weren't they found in the cellars?'

'Yes, they were. I don't think it was a proper, organised, pistols-at-dawn type of duel. Ladies wouldn't have done such a thing. But I reckon they had a pistol each and shot each other at the same time. One of the newspaper reports said that the butler heard the two shots almost simultaneously, and that it was assumed the murderer had held a pistol in each hand. But what if the girls shot at each other?' Gemma looked at Ben triumphantly.

'If you're right, why did no one suspect that at the time?'

'Because it was assumed firstly that the girls loved each other and secondly that young ladies would not know how to load and fire pistols.'

'How did they know?'

Gemma punched him playfully. 'Come on! I've come up with a plausible theory and you're just trying to find holes in it. I have no idea how they knew but maybe someone showed them. Maybe the pistols were already loaded. Whatever. But what do you think?'

'It's possible, I suppose.' Ben looked serious.

'What's the matter?'

He frowned again. 'You don't think, God, I know it's stupid, but I keep thinking of the parallels between Rebecca and Sarah, and you and Nat. What if, I mean, might Nat try to hurt you? Physically, I mean. She's done enough damage in other ways, but what if she tried to injure you somehow?'

Gemma laughed. 'Nat hates me for some reason, and has been

a bitch lately, but she wouldn't try to kill me. You are definitely being ridiculous now.'

'Jeez, I hope so. But, humour me, be careful, all right? Don't go near her again. She's unhinged.'

'She's acted strangely but she's not dangerous, Ben. She's not in the same league as Sarah.' Gemma patted his knee in what she hoped was a reassuring way. But he'd worried her. She gulped back the rest of her wine and changed the subject.

***

The rest of the evening passed in a companionable blur of good food, wine and laughter. All too soon it was closing time.

'Coming back to mine again?' Gemma asked, linking arms with Ben as they left the pub.

'If you'll have me,' Ben replied.

'Oh yes, I'll have you.' She laughed. 'You know, we should really think about moving in together properly.'

'Yes, we should. Fancy going house-hunting at the weekend? Neither of our flats is really big enough for two but if we sold them and pooled resources we could probably get a pretty nice semi...'

Gemma grinned. He'd never before talked about buying a house together, even when they'd been engaged. 'Sounds like a great idea. But for now you'll have to put up with my tiny place.'

'Cosy. Bijou. Those are better words than tiny. And here we are.'

They climbed the steps and went into the shared hallway of Gemma's building.

'Can you smell gas?' Ben said.

'Hmm, yes, a bit,' Gemma replied, heading up the stairs to her flat's front door. The smell of gas became stronger as she reached her floor. She turned the key in the lock and pushed open the door. The stink of gas was almost overpowering as she reached out automatically to flick on a light.

CHAPTER 28

September 1838

Rebecca was at breakfast when the letter arrived. The handwriting of the address looked familiar, but it couldn't be. She broke open the seal with her paperknife and began reading the contents. What she read made her drop her coffee cup, which smashed on her plate, splashing coffee across the table and her gown. She gasped, her hand at her mouth.

Spencer rushed into the room at the sound of the breaking crockery. 'What is it, Miss Winton? Is everything all right? Can I help in any way?'

Rebecca could only stare at him and wave the letter. She could form no words. He crossed the room and took the letter from her. 'Should I read it aloud, Miss Winton?'

She managed to nod, and watched as he first scanned the letter, his eyes widening, and then read it out in a voice shaking with emotion.

My dear Rebecca

News has only just reached me of the death of poor Sarah. What a truly terrible, tragic event. I can only imagine how you must feel to lose someone so close to you. I wish I could have been near at hand and able to assist, perhaps, as you dealt with such a blow, coming so soon after your dear father's demise. But as you know, I was called away suddenly on business in London, and that business then required that I make a trip to first Paris and then Marseilles, Naples and Rome. Thankfully all is now resolved and I have at last been able to return to my London residence, where I first heard the news.

Dearest Rebecca, although we parted on a sad note I hope that you still think of me as a friend. I am planning to return to Dorset within a day or two, and hope that you will receive me still at Red Hill Hall and that perhaps I can be of some comfort to you at this difficult time.

I need too, to discuss with you another matter – it has come to my attention that there were reports of my own death having occurred at Red Hill Hall a month or so back. I don't understand how those rumours began but clearly I wish to quash them.

Therefore, may I ask you to please write to me by return at the address above, and let me know whether you would be happy to receive me at Red Hill Hall, or if I should make some other arrangements. I need to come to Dorset to prove to the Magistrate and the Constable that I am indeed alive and well, but if you do not wish to see me I shall fully understand. After all you have been through the last thing I want is to cause you any further distress.

With deepest sympathy and fond regard,

Charles

Spencer handed back the letter in silence. Rebecca opened her mouth to try to say something but once more the words would not come. Charles was alive! Whoever the body was in the well, it was not Charles. She could not take it in.

'Miss Winton, let me fetch you some water. You look pale. It is a shock, indeed, but a pleasant one, to find Mr de Witt is alive and well after all. I can fetch your writing implements as well, if you are ready and able to send a reply to him? Or would you rather wait to do that later?'

Rebecca looked up in confusion at Spencer. All those words he was saying and yet none of them were going in. Charles was alive! It was all she could think about. But Spencer was expecting a reply. She nodded, and it seemed to satisfy him for he bustled off, leaving her alone. She picked up the letter and read it through again to make sure she had understood its message. Yes, she had. Charles was alive!

Spencer was back within minutes with water for her – which she did not want – a pen and a sheet of notepaper. She scribbled a note quickly – of course Charles was welcome and she looked forward to seeing him. If he only knew how much she looked forward to it! Spencer was dispatched immediately to send the letter, and Rebecca spent the rest of the day calculating when Charles might arrive.

***

It was after lunch the following day, a dark and rainy day, when Rebecca was disturbed from her reading (although if truth be told, she had read the same page of Cowper's verse a dozen times and still could not have said what it was about) by a commotion in the hallway. She rushed out of the drawing room to find Charles, removing a sodden cloak, and answering excited questions from Tilly and another maid, while Spencer tried to calm the girls.

'Yes, as you can see, I am not dead. No, it was not me in the well, although I am currently wet enough for you to believe I am drowned. No, I have been away. Abroad. On business, and what that was is none of yours, Tilly!'

'Now, now, Tilly and Mary. Off you go back to your chores. Tilly, hang Mr de Witt's cloak before the range in the kitchen so it has a chance to dry. Ah, Miss Winton. I was about to show Mr de Witt in to you...' Spencer had a sparkle in his eye and was doing a poor job at suppressing a smile. Rebecca felt her heart jump. After so much tragedy, here at last was some good news for Red Hill Hall! As she approached Charles, her hand outstretched to shake his, she wondered whether there might be a tiny chance they could rekindle their relationship in time.

'Miss Winton. I am so very glad to see you again.' Charles bowed formally and then took her hand and kissed it. The warmth of his lips sent a shiver coursing through her.

'And I am delighted to see you again,' she replied, as she led the way into the drawing room. She took a seat near the fire, which had been lit to take the chill off the day despite it only being September.

Charles sat opposite her. 'We have much to talk about. I am glad you allowed me to call today. I confess – I am hoping we might be able to put the past behind us and perhaps start again as friends.'

Rebecca flinched internally at those words 'as friends' at the end of his speech – did he mean that he did not want their relationship to be any deeper? Well, it was a start, and perhaps in time they might grow closer once more. She nodded and smiled at him. 'Yes, I hope so too. So tell me. After you spoke with me that day when you broke off our engagement, you did not come back to the hall. We saw you only once more, at Papa's funeral. And then we heard nothing more from you. Where did you go? A few weeks later, there was the grisly discovery of the body in the well.'

'As I said in my letter, I was called away on business. It is true I did not return to the hall, but I did see Miss Cooper a couple of times, whilst out riding. I think she may have intentionally ridden where she knew I might be. Our encounters were too frequent to be entirely accidental. The last time I saw her was just the day before I went away. I had received news that meant I would need to leave for London on the early coach, and was having one last gallop across the fields to clear my mind, knowing it would be the last chance I'd have. I came across Miss Cooper that day. We rode a short way together, and I told her I was leaving in the morning, and asked her to pass the message on to you. I did not want you to think I was snubbing you by staying away.'

'She did not pass on the message.'

'It seems not. And from London I had to travel to the Continent. I wrote to you, once, from London to say I would be away for some time.'

'I never received that letter.' Sarah must have intercepted it, Rebecca realised.

Charles looked at her. 'Because I had no reply, I did not dare to write again. I thought your lack of response was your way of telling me you wanted no further contact. The trip to France and Italy, while it is true it was partly for business, if I am to be entirely honest it was also designed to put you out of my mind. I had no news from home while I travelled, for I did not stay in any one place long enough to receive letters. It was only when I returned to London that I found out about Miss Cooper's death, your own injury, and the rumours of my own death. I wrote to you immediately.'

'I am so glad you did,' Rebecca replied softly.

'So now, please, tell me of the events here after I went away.

From your father's funeral onwards.' Charles leaned forward expectantly.

'Very well. I need to start by telling you about the contents of Papa's will,' she began.

'His will? Surely there were no surprises in it?' Charles stared at her.

'On the contrary – it was quite a shock. He had assumed, you see, that I would marry you and would be well provided for by your own fortune. He therefore left Red Hill Hall to Sarah.'

'What?'

She pressed her lips together and nodded. 'Yes, Sarah inherited everything.'

'Why on earth? I mean, I would have expected him to provide for her in some way, perhaps a legacy or an annuity from the estate, but you were his only surviving relative, and should have inherited the hall, regardless of your matrimonial state.' Charles shook his head in disbelief.

Rebecca thought for a moment. Should she tell him now about the letters she'd seen? He still, as far as she knew, thought Sarah had been a sweet, innocent girl. He had cared for her. Telling him about the letters, and the other secrets she'd uncovered in the diary, would shatter his illusions about her for good. But maybe that was not a bad thing. 'Charles, prepare yourself for you may find this next part distasteful. I have discovered that Sarah was blackmailing my father. I believe she manipulated him into changing his will in her favour.'

'What? How? And how did you find out?' Charles's eyes were wide.

'Do you mind if I don't go into the details just yet? But the evidence is substantial. I'm sorry, Charles. I know you liked her.'

'I appreciated her company when I was riding. That is all.'

Rebecca raised her eyebrows slightly. He seemed to want to distance himself from Sarah now. 'To continue, then – Sarah became mistress of the house. She informed me she wanted me to move out and find some other accommodation. I had no idea what I would do or where I would go, but she reluctantly agreed to give me some time to organise things. And then the body was found in the well.'

'How was it discovered?' If Charles sat any nearer the edge of his seat he would topple off and onto the floor, Rebecca thought.

'The well is not often used nowadays, but sometimes water is brought from it to replenish water troughs for the animals in a dry spell. The water came up bad, and a man was lowered on a rope to investigate. It was assumed an animal must have fallen in. He found the corpse and it was then pulled up and brought to the stables here.'

'Why was it assumed to be me? I don't understand!'

'The body was partly decomposed and, I'm told, unrecognisable. But it was wearing your jacket – a dark green riding coat. I did not look closely, but Sarah did and it was she who confirmed the body was you. He, whoever he is, has been buried at the edge of the churchyard. Sarah paid for the funeral.'

'I don't understand. How could he have been wearing my coat? Oh!' Charles clapped his forehead. 'I left a jacket here once – it had become muddied after a fall from my horse when riding with Sarah. Many months ago. Spencer said he'd have it cleaned and returned to me, but then I forgot all about it, and never retrieved it. Somehow the dead man must have got hold of it.'

Rebecca stared at him. 'It was Sarah who recognised your coat. I wonder if perhaps she passed it on to the dead man...'

'But who was he?' Charles stood and paced around the room. 'If he's local then surely someone would have reported him missing...'

'There is someone who has been reported missing,' Rebecca said, slowly.

'Could that be the man in the well?'

She nodded. 'Yes, I think it could be. Sarah knew the missing man – his name was Jed Arthur. He lived in a cottage on the estate. She may have given him the jacket.' She did not want to tell him just how well Sarah had known Jed.

'But then, surely, she'd have identified the corpse as this other man, rather than me? Unless for some reason she wanted people to think it was me and not him? It's all very strange. But you have not finished telling me of all the events. I realise it must be very painful for you to recall, but please tell me how Miss Cooper's death came about.'

Rebecca took her time answering. This was it. Should she tell him the full truth? Would he understand? Or would he report her to the authorities as a murderer? The burden of carrying the secret and not being able to talk to anyone about it was overwhelming at times. If only she could confide in Charles! But she dared not risk it.

She told him the same story she had told the constable. That she'd caught a glimpse of a man with the two pistols but had not seen his face. That she struggled to remember very much of what happened.

Charles's expression was one of deep concern and compassion as she spoke. He was accepting her words as the truth. And why shouldn't he? She had never given him any reason to doubt her.

'So the constable is still looking for the murderer?'

Rebecca flinched at the last word. What would he think if he realised he was talking to Sarah's killer? 'When Jed Arthur was reported missing, the constable assumed that he'd carried out the shooting and then run away and gone into hiding. They're still searching for him.'

'But now we suspect the body in the well was this Jed Arthur. So he could not have been the gunman, because he was found in the well before the shooting occurred.' Charles frowned, and stopped pacing, standing before her.

'No. It cannot have been Jed.' Rebecca said quietly.

He was quiet for a moment, as though reflecting on what he had heard. Then he stood abruptly, as though he had come to some decision. 'I must leave you now, Miss Winton. I must meet with the magistrate and the constable, and prove that I am still alive and therefore not the man in the well. With your permission I will suggest they follow up the idea that it might be Jed Arthur. That means they will now be looking for someone else for the shooting.' He looked carefully at her. 'I hope that doesn't cause you any problems.'

'Not at all. They must investigate fully,' she said.

Charles looked at her quizzically. 'Perhaps we shall never know who it was.'

She smiled. 'Perhaps not.'

He stood to leave, but she laid a restraining hand on his arm. 'One last thing. Please, can you tell me truthfully why you broke off our engagement?'

He sat down again, this time at her side. 'I was so sorry for you that day. It was a terrible thing for me to do. I cannot tell you how awful I felt when I left you. But I thought I had done the right thing. I – I was given to understand that you had only accepted

287

me out of a sense of duty, and that secretly you were devastated by the idea of marrying me.' He stopped speaking, looked down at his hands and sighed. 'You want the truth, and you deserve it. It was Miss Cooper. She told me you did not want me, and that the best thing for both of us would be if I called it off, sooner rather than later. She was your best friend, your adopted sister, and I believed that she knew your heart and was acting in your best interests. I am so sorry.' He took her hand. 'Miss Winton, Rebecca, I would like to know – I need to know – whether Miss Cooper was telling me the truth. *Did* you only accept me out of a sense of duty?'

Rebecca shook her head. 'No. Not at all. I accepted you because I wanted nothing more than to be married to you. I was never happier than during that brief period when we were engaged.'

He smiled. 'Then there is hope for us yet, dear Rebecca.'

CHAPTER 29

August 2015

'Don't touch that!' Ben screamed, knocking Gemma's hand away from the light switch. 'The flat is full of gas. Go outside and call the gas company. I'll get the windows open and turn the gas off at the mains. Go!'

Gemma hesitated, wondering whether it was safe for Ben to go into the flat, but he'd already gone in and she could hear him rummaging in the hall cupboard where the gas meter and shut-off valve were. She hurried downstairs, pulling out her phone. What was the number you called to report a gas leak? She had no idea so pressed 999 instead and reported the problem. The operator confirmed the message would be passed on, and asked if anyone was in the building.

'My boyfriend. And my neighbour in the downstairs flat.' Gemma felt herself growing panicky.

'Get them out of the building if you can,' the operator advised.

'Ben! Get out!' Gemma shouted up the stairs, while simultaneously banging on her downstairs' neighbour's door. 'Alan! You need to get out – there's been a gas leak in my flat!'

The door opened and her elderly neighbour Alan appeared, in his dressing gown and slippers.

'Alan, come outside, now. There's been a gas leak upstairs. I've called the emergency services.' She took his arm and led him out.

'Oh dear, oh dear,' Alan muttered, as they made their way outside. 'What a thing to happen.' Thankfully Ben came running down the stairs as well, and they all left the building and went up the street a little way.

'I opened all the windows,' Ben said. 'And turned off the gas at the mains. It should clear quickly. Wonder what caused it?'

'Funny. Your friend said nothing about a smell of gas when she was here earlier. I have no sense of smell, so I didn't pick it up. Thank you for rescuing me, Gemma,' said Alan. He looked a little shaky.

'Here, sit on this garden wall,' she said, helping him onto it. 'I can hear sirens. The police will be here soon. What friend?'

'A young woman. She was ringing your doorbell as I came home. I told her you weren't in and I think she then went away.' Alan sighed and wiped a hand across his forehead. 'Good job it isn't raining, what with us sitting out here, eh?'

'There's the police. I'll fill them in on what's happened,' Ben said. He went over to the police car, which had pulled up outside, and spoke to them. A few minutes later the gas emergency van arrived. The gasman went inside.

'We'll be able to go back indoors soon, Alan,' said Gemma, patting the old man gently on the shoulder. A few other neighbours had come out to see what was going on, and one brought out mugs of tea. Ben came back over to them and they sipped tea while waiting to be allowed back inside.

Eventually the gas engineer came out, and had a word with

the police, who then left. He then crossed the road to speak to Gemma and Ben.

'It's safe to go back inside. The gas has dispersed. It looks like someone left the gas hob on, and the safety cut-out valve is stuck. Clogged up with grease. You should get that fixed, and be more careful – don't leave the gas on and clean up any grease you spill before it can cause a problem.' He glared at them sternly. 'That safety valve is there for a reason, you know. It can't do its job if you let it get gummed up like that. Anyway, I'll be off, now.' He nodded, and went back to his van.

Gemma looked at Ben. 'I did not leave the hob on. I know I did not leave the hob on. I always check it when I leave the house. You know I do.'

'OK. Don't think it was me, either. I didn't use it this morning. Come on, Alan, you can go back inside now. Are you going to be all right?' Ben said.

'Yes, I'm fine. Bit of excitement, eh?' He gave a mock salute, trotted across the road and went back inside.

Gemma returned the tea mugs to the neighbour who'd brought them out, and then joined Ben in the street. 'How on earth did that gas get left on? Darn it, Alan's pulled the door shut behind him. I haven't got my key. I dropped my handbag upstairs.'

'You've got a key safe, haven't you?' Ben said.

Gemma rolled her eyes. 'So I have. Doh.' It was to the left of the communal front door. She opened the shutter that covered the key safe's combination lock. 'That's funny.'

'What?'

'Call me OCD but I always leave the combination set at all 9s if ever I use this key. But look, it's all random. Actually, two of the numbers are the right ones. Someone's used this key.'

'Who knows the combination?'

'Me, Mum and Dad, you.'

'Is that all?'

'And Nat. I told her it so she could let herself in to water my plants while we were on holiday last summer.'

'Alan said a young woman called round earlier. You don't think...'

Gemma stared at Ben. 'What are you suggesting?'

'Let's go inside. We need something stronger than tea.'

Upstairs, Gemma poured them both a glass of wine. Ben was peering at the hob. 'Your hob's pretty new, isn't it? Yet there's thick grease on that shut-off valve.' He poked at it, then sniffed the grease on his finger. 'Smells more like engine grease. Not something you'd have been cooking with.'

'What? Do you think someone came in here and deliberately gummed up the valve and turned the gas on?' Gemma stared at him.

'I think it's quite possible. And if so, I think that person would have been Nat.'

'Jesus.' Gemma sat down heavily. 'But why?'

'Gemma, look. She tried and nearly succeeded in destroying our relationship. She stole your identity and made those credit card purchases. She tried to extort money from your parents. For some reason she's out to hurt you.'

'But she wouldn't do this – I mean, if you hadn't stopped me flicking the light switch, there could have been an explosion. We could *both* have been killed.' She took a huge gulp of wine, then put her glass down. Her hand was shaking. Surely Nat wouldn't have wanted to physically harm them?

Ben took hold of both her hands and looked her in the eye.

'Maybe that's what she intended. Gem, I think we need to go to the police with this. I know you didn't want to before, but now, surely…?'

She shook her head. 'No, we can't do that. We don't have any evidence it was her.'

'We do! Alan saw her, and then we know someone used the key from the key safe. She's the only person who knew the combination.'

Gemma pulled her hands away from his and took another gulp of her wine. 'There's no concrete evidence she is the one who opened the key safe. I know someone did because I always leave the combination on all 9s but that wouldn't be strong enough for the police, believe me. And although Alan saw her he thought she'd rung the doorbell and then left. The valve could have accidentally got stuck. It's not definite sabotage. No. We can't go to the police.'

'Something has to be done to stop her doing all this to you.' Ben's voice was cold. 'Why are you protecting her, despite all she's done? I don't understand it.'

'She was my best friend for so long. We were like that.' Gemma held up her crossed fingers. 'I mean, there's something special about best friends, isn't there? Maybe it's different for blokes, but a best girlfriend, well, they're always there for you. They'll do anything for you, and you would for them. And that was us – Nat and me. In some ways, when I think of all we've shared together over the years, I've been closer to Nat than anyone. Including you, love.' She shook her head sadly. 'I just can't believe she really wants to hurt me.'

'She has already hurt you, Gem. More than once. Christ, I don't want to risk losing you to that madwoman!' Ben sat beside her and held her tight.

'You won't lose me. This – I don't know – this is all some kind of horrible mistake. If she did come in here tonight she can't have left the gas on intentionally. I just don't believe that.'

'Grease on the safety valve?' Ben raised his eyebrows at her.

'Could have been there since I bought it? Hob's only two years old.'

'Rubbish. The manufacturers wouldn't send it out in that condition. Someone's tampered with it. And be honest, you know she did. It must be her. There's no other explanation.'

Gemma felt the tears, long held back, well up and spill over. 'I want there to be another explanation, Ben! I can't believe she'd do that. I just don't want to believe it. We were at school together. We used to pool our lunch box contents. She'd eat my ham sandwiches and I'd eat her cheese-strings. We went on our first dates together – aged fourteen – us and Billy McIntosh and Charlie Wossname. We went to the cinema. The boys wanted to see the *Star Wars* film again but we refused and all ended up seeing *Toy Story 2*. We've done so much together over the years. She wouldn't try to kill me. She wouldn't, Ben!'

He held her as she sobbed on his shoulder. 'Shh, love. It's all right. Listen, I'll stay with you until all this is sorted out, one way or the other. I'm not leaving you.'

'You've been here permanently since last Wednesday anyway,' she sniffed.

'I know. Gem, I love you. I don't ever want to leave you.'

'I'm not even going to let you leave me.' She held him tighter. He felt warm and solid, and she felt safe in his arms. But what could she do about Nat? He was right – she knew it. The gas leak was Nat's doing. For whatever reason, Nat was trying to destroy her. Gemma knew she would have to confront her again. But after an attack like this, which could have killed not only herself but also Ben, could there really be a chance to resolve things by simply talking it through? It didn't seem very likely. She needed to come up with some more drastic solution.

'Come on, love. Finish your drink and let's get to bed. It's late and we've both got work tomorrow.' Ben's gentle voice of calm broke into her thoughts. She drained her glass and followed him into the bedroom, knowing full well that sleep would be a long way off.

***

She woke up with the dawn, the birds outside her open window heralding the start of a bright, warm day. She was curled in Ben's arms, and nuzzled happily against his shoulder while still in that delicious state of part sleep, part wakefulness.

And then she remembered the events of the previous night, and her decision, reached at some point in the darkest part of the night, after she'd lain awake and restless for hours. She ran through her plan in her mind. Yes, it would work. She felt a kinship with Rebecca Winton whose best friend and half-sister had tried to destroy her – undermining her relationship with her fiancé and turning her father against her so that he changed his will. Rebecca too had felt threatened, and if Gemma's theory was right, had then turned against Sarah and shot her. Rebecca must have realised that she could not carry on with Sarah in her life, and had taken steps to remove her.

The long insomniac hours while Ben snored gently at her side had convinced Gemma that she too could not continue with Nat in her life. Who knew what Nat would do next? She would be forever looking over her shoulder all the while Nat was around. She would be living in fear, for Ben as well as for herself. And that was no way to be.

She had to get rid of Nat. There was no other answer.

CHAPTER 30

July 1839

A few weeks after Charles's return from the dead, as Rebecca often thought of it, he asked her once more to marry him. She accepted readily. Without Sarah to undermine things this time she was confident everything would work out.

And indeed, a month later they were married, at the little church in the village. Everyone turned out to see the happy couple. Another month after that they moved to Charles's ancestral home – Carlstone Hall in Leicestershire, which had been renovated ready to receive its new mistress.

Rebecca had not been sad to leave Red Hill Hall. Although it had been her childhood home, and the only home she had ever known, there were far too many distressing memories associated with it now. And, she realised, it would be no bad thing to move away from Constable Barnsworth in case he ever took it into his head to re-investigate Sarah's death. The magistrate had ruled that the case should remain classified as open and unsolved.

Not so with the case of the body in the well. Dorothy Arthur had been called upon to look at the clothing retrieved from the well. She identified it as having belonged to her brother – including the jacket, which Dorothy said had been a present to him from Miss Cooper – which satisfied the constable and magistrate that the body was that of Jed Arthur. A new gravestone with the correct name upon it was commissioned and paid for by Charles. A second inquest was held and a verdict of accidental death returned – it was assumed that Jed had somehow overbalanced near the well and tumbled in.

Rebecca wasn't so sure. She had reread Sarah's diary. She suspected Sarah may have pushed Jed into the well to get rid of him, so that he could never come forward and claim her child as his own. He had presumably outlived his usefulness. Though how Sarah had planned to have a baby by herself, unmarried, was a mystery. Rebecca could not conceive of a way Sarah could have managed this, without completely losing her standing in society, mistress of Red Hill Hall or not. She must have assumed that somehow or other she would get her claws into Charles and become a respectable married woman.

Well, it was all in the past now, Rebecca thought. Sarah was gone, as was her unborn child and the child's father. It was time for a fresh start for herself and Charles, in Carlstone Hall, in a county where she was not known.

Rebecca strolled through the gardens of Carlstone Hall, her hand protectively across her midriff. It was a perfect summer's day, the type where the breeze felt like a lover's caress, floral scents and birdsong filled the air. The events of the previous summer at Red Hill Hall seemed a distant, bad dream. Life was so much better now. Her marriage to Charles was a success – they were deeply in love and spent as much time as possible together, when Charles's business commitments allowed it. He had employed an estate manager at Red Hill Hall and visited just twice a year to go over accounts. Another estate manager was employed at Carlstone Hall, but even so, Charles had other business interests in London and Paris. He was away now – at Red Hill Hall, spending a few days in Dorset to check on the estate management and authorise any necessary expenditure. Rebecca was counting the days – no, the hours now, for he was due back today – until he was due to return.

She had felt the baby quicken that morning, and couldn't wait to tell him of her pregnancy, see his delight at the prospect of becoming a father. He would put his hand on her belly and perhaps feel the baby move too. It was miraculous, this life starting inside her. Just as she had started a new life for herself with Charles, so they had managed to create another. With a child, the product of their love, life would be complete and perfect. Nothing could spoil it.

'Rebecca? Ah, there you are.'

She looked up towards the house to see Charles striding across the lawns towards her. He was back already, sooner than she had expected.

'Charles, my love! How was your trip? I am so excited to see you again. Wait till I tell you…'

He held up a hand to stop her. 'Shh, please. I must speak with you.'

'Of course! But first hold me and say you are glad to be with me again!' She reached for him but he turned away and took a step back, his face twisted into an expression of confusion.

'Please sit, Rebecca, and let me speak.' He indicated a bench, set beneath a trellis arch of roses, and she perched herself upon it. He remained standing.

'What is it, Charles? What has happened?'

He coughed, and sighed deeply before replying. 'This is going to be difficult for us both. But I must speak. I always hoped that our relationship would be one of openness and honesty, and that neither of us would keep secrets from the other. It pains me to find this is not the case. Rebecca, you have not told me everything about the events of last summer, have you?'

'I – I have told you the truth,' she said, but she could hear the falter in her own voice. What had he discovered? And how?

'You have not told me everything. Rebecca, I was searching for some missing estate receipts, from last year. One of the servants suggested you had kept some papers in a bureau in your old rooms, so I went to look there. Perhaps it was wrong of me to go through your private papers, but I thought you had brought everything you wanted here, and that anything left in Dorset was connected to the estate. So I searched your bureau. I did not find what I was looking for, but I did find some very enlightening papers. Not yours, but Sarah's.'

He paused and stared at her, as though giving her one last chance to admit the truth. She gazed back at him, her mouth slightly open as her mind raced. So he had read Sarah's letters and diary. He would know the truth of her treachery then. But there was nothing in those papers that could prove who shot Sarah, was there?

He shook his head sadly. 'I see you still don't wish to confess. Rebecca, it was no surprise to me to discover the extent of Sarah's deceit. I was saddened to learn that she had been with child when she died, and that the father was the poor man who drowned in the well. How he came to be there I can only conjecture. I cannot bring myself to think it could have been Sarah's doing, despite what I learned about the way she manipulated both your father and me.'

He sighed before continuing, his voice quiet and sad. 'It was the last entry in Sarah's diary that shocked me. The one in which she admitted feeling threatened by you. You may have had just cause to hate her, after all that she had done, but you did not have the right to...'

'To what?' she whispered, as his words trailed away.

'Did you? Do you admit it? You shot her?'

'I was shot too,' she said, touching her shoulder, which still troubled her at times.

He gazed at her, his eyes wide and troubled. 'Tell me, Rebecca, tell me what really happened that day. I know not whether I will be able to accept it, but I do know I cannot accept you hiding the truth from me. I require complete honesty in our relationship, at all times.'

She realised he meant it and that she could lose him, if she did not confess. She might lose him still, once he knew the truth, but she had to take that risk. Besides, the burden of keeping the secret had been almost too much to bear. She resolved to tell him everything, and let the future take its course. Her only worry now was for her own unborn child. If she told him, and his sense of justice forced him to report what he knew to the authorities, she would be tried and if found guilty, she could hang. Her child would die with her. Or would they wait until she had given birth before hanging her?

Perhaps Charles would keep quiet, and simply share the secret with her. That was her only hope. She drew a deep breath.

'Very well. I will tell you everything. But first, you must understand that I too felt threatened. Sarah had robbed me of my fiancé and my inheritance. I had lost both my parents – I suspected she might even have had something to do with Mama's death.

I thought you were dead, and my mind ran riot, thinking perhaps she had pushed you into the well. And I *do* think her capable of having killed Jed. I don't understand her motives, but I am certain she caused him to fall into that well.'

'All right, so you each felt threatened by the other. What happened?'

She told him the events of that awful day. How she had gone to the cellar in search of the pistols, with no intent to hurt Sarah but just to feel she could defend herself if necessary. How she had discovered one pistol missing, and guessed Sarah had taken it. How she had remembered Spencer showing them how to load and prime the weapons, long ago when they were children. She told him of her shaking legs and sweating palms as she loaded the pistol. How she'd hidden it in her skirt pocket, just before Sarah appeared in the cellar. Their row, the accusations, and then the terrible moment when Sarah pulled out her pistol, and the two found themselves at the point of no return.

Her voice faltered and the tears streamed as she recounted how she had focused on Sarah's finger, waiting to see if it squeezed the trigger. She had not wanted to fire her weapon. She had wanted, somehow, for Sarah to back down, lower her pistol, then she too would have, and then they would have come to some agreement, some way in which they could move forward and forget it all. But that had not happened, and Sarah's finger had moved on the trigger, and Rebecca had had no choice. How she had felt the searing, agonising pain in her shoulder at the same moment she had squeezed her own trigger. The noise, the smell, the smoke, the agony.

She paused a moment, watching his face. He was silent, white, shocked, shaking his head. She debated telling him how in that moment, when she thought they were both going to die, she forgave Sarah everything. No, that moment, that feeling of pure love mingled with bitter agony was hers and hers alone.

'I passed out, I think. Spencer found us. You know the rest of the story.'

'You lied to the constable about the man in the cellar.' It was a statement, not a question.

'I made it clear I had not definitely seen anyone. But yes, when it was suggested a man had broken in via the steps from the garden, I did allow them to think I'd glimpsed someone, and that person had shot us both. Charles, if the truth comes out I shall be tried and hanged! Please, don't let that happen!'

His face was contorted, as though he was battling with conflicting emotions. 'I abhor violence. To be married to a – a killer, for that is what you are – can I live with that? I don't yet know if I can accept it. I loved you, Rebecca, with all my heart. I still do – but I cannot imagine lying by your side at night knowing as I now do, that Sarah's death was by your hand.'

'Charles, she would have killed me…'

'We don't know that. She shot at you, but at your shoulder. Perhaps she only meant to injure you, not kill you. Perhaps she only meant to scare you, and fire over your shoulder, but you moved and she hit you. We will never know.'

'I know! I was there! She meant to kill me. Her aim was poor, or perhaps I did move so that she only hit my shoulder and not my heart. It was her or me. I shot in self-defence. Charles, you have to believe me! I cannot stand it if you don't!'

'I believe you, but even so, it is hard to stomach.' He sighed, and his shoulders sagged. 'Perhaps… perhaps you should put yourself forward, and tell the truth. At trial, the judge will take your plea of self-defence into account. You would escape hanging, I am sure.'

'But I would have to go to prison!' Rebecca was not sure which fate scared her more. She had heard terrible things about women's prisons. Even though she would be able to afford to pay for better food, a private cell and small comforts, the idea of being incarcerated with all manner of criminals appalled her. She was not brave enough to survive that. It would be better to hang. Not for the first time she found herself wondering if it would have been better if she had died in the shooting, too.

'You would, yes, but not for life,' Charles replied. 'Oh God, Rebecca. I know what is the right and proper thing to do but...' He tailed off and shook his head. His voice was unsteady and he would not look at her.

There was one chance to change his mind, and persuade him to keep the secret. One last chance. This was not how she had wanted to tell him, but she had no choice.

'Charles, please, there is something else you need to know,' she began.

He turned to stare at her. 'More secrets you have kept from me?'

'I kept this one only until I was sure. Charles, you are to become a father. I am with child. About four months, now. I had planned to tell you as soon as you came back from your trip. I felt the baby move this morning, for the first time. Our child, Charles.' Tears were streaming down her face. The happy, perfect future she had imagined just an hour or so ago lay scattered around her like fallen blossom. Gone, unless he realised how much he too could lose, if he insisted on her owning up to her crime. Unless he buried his sense of justice and became complicit in keeping her secret. She had thrown herself on his mercy by confessing to him. But she'd had no choice.

The blood drained from his face. He sat down heavily on the bench next to her, close, but not touching. A blown rose shed its petals onto his thigh. He brushed them off and leaned over, his face in his hands. She kept quiet, allowing him time for the news to sink in, for the implications to work their way through his thoughts.

'I had longed for this, Rebecca. I had hoped it would happen early in our marriage. But now – I don't know. I don't know how I feel. I wanted a child more than anything. I wanted us, together, with a growing brood at our feet. But I value truth and honesty above all things, which is why I wanted you to confess to shooting Sarah, and let justice take its course.' He shook his head sadly. 'But how can you confess now that you are going to be a mother?'

She kept quiet. There was nothing more she could say. Her fate was entirely in his hands.

At last he stood up, and turned to face her. 'I need time to think, Rebecca. I was so sure I knew what was the right and honourable thing to do. I need – to go. Do not follow me. I need time, and space.' At this he turned and strode away across the lawn, leaving Rebecca staring at his retreating back, the tears streaming down her face.

She remembered how he'd said part of his reason for travelling on the Continent after their first engagement had ended was because he wanted to get away from it all, to forget. Was this his way of dealing with problems – to turn tail and run away? There were five months until the baby was due. How long would he be gone for, and what would be his decision on his return? Would he even write letters to the authorities while he was away, telling them what she'd said, so that one day there would be a knock at the door and she would be arrested and taken away to await trial?

Rebecca felt herself rooted to the bench. She could not move. Damn Charles's sense of righteousness! Damn his belief that justice must be done! She had acted in self-defence. Sarah would have killed her.

And for all that, she missed Sarah terribly. They had been so close. As a child she had wanted Sarah to be her sister. Now she knew that her wish had come true – Sarah had been her half-sister. Her half-sister whom she had murdered, along with her unborn child. Had she not been punished enough already, carrying this terrible secret within her? She bent over, her face in her hands and gave in to the sobs that wracked her body.

***

'Rebecca?'

She looked up, and found Charles standing over her. She pushed away the tears, not sure for how long she had been sitting there crying.

'I did not even reach the door of the house before making my decision, Rebecca.' He sat down beside her and reached for her hands. 'You did no wrong. You had no choice. The outcome was regrettable but the alternative – that Sarah might have killed you – far worse. You rid the world of a blackmailer and cold-blooded murderer. I think you are right, and that Sarah may have killed Jed Arthur and possibly even your mother.' He took a deep breath. 'I will not divulge your secret, Rebecca, and neither will I force or encourage you to do so. It is our shared secret now. We started over once before. Can we do it again? I want you, Rebecca, and our baby, and the happy family life we had dreamed of. Can you forgive my behaviour today? I was in shock…'

'Of course I forgive you that! It was entirely understandable,' she said, raising his hands to her lips to kiss.

'Then we are reunited. I ask for one promise, only.'

'What is that, my love?'

'That we never speak of this matter again. I want the secret to go to the grave with us.'

She smiled with relief. She was saved, and so was her child. 'Agreed.' And then she leaned in to kiss him, long and deep, as the baby shuffled around inside her.

CHAPTER 31

August 2015

Gemma reached out and turned off the alarm. Ben rolled over and smiled at her. 'Morning, gorgeous. Sleep OK?'

'Not really. Too much on my mind. I've been thinking, Ben. Finally reached a decision.'

'You have? Funnily enough, I was thinking too, and have also come to a conclusion.' He grinned at her and pulled her close for a kiss.

'Go on then. You first,' she said. Had he been thinking what to do about Nat as well? From what she'd seen he'd gone straight to sleep last night and hadn't moved, while she'd tossed and turned for hours.

He grinned again and slipped out of bed and onto the floor, where he knelt beside the bed and reached for her hand. 'Gem, this may not be the most romantic way to do it, but I can't hold out any longer. I want us back the way we were before – no – moving forward from there. Gem, darling, will you marry me?'

She laughed, and for a moment he looked heartbroken. Realising how her laughter could be misconstrued she pulled him back into bed. 'Course I'll marry you, you silly thing! I assumed that was a given, once we'd got back together again. I mean, I know I hadn't put the ring back on but you didn't really need to ask.'

'Phew! Thought for a moment there you were going to say no way! Wear the ring I gave you, please. And this time nothing's going to push us apart. *Nothing.*' He wrapped his arms around her and she snuggled into his shoulder.

'I think we're closer now than ever,' she said.

'Mmm, you could be right.' Ben pulled her even tighter. 'Your turn, then. What's your big decision? To love and cherish me for ever and ever?'

'Not exactly, although…'

'What? You're not going to love me for ever?' Ben pulled a sad face.

'Course I am, you wally! But that's not what my decision last night was. It was about how to deal with the Nat problem.'

'Ah. Yes, that.' He rolled away and propped himself up on one elbow. 'So? Are you going to the police?'

She shook her head. 'No. I just don't think there's strong enough evidence. And I can't face a court case and everything, while we are trying to plan a wedding. Besides, she'd still be around, and might try something else to hurt us.'

'You could get a restraining order. She'd be arrested if she came anywhere near.'

'She nearly killed us last night, without being anywhere near us.'

'Good point.' He frowned. 'What, then, if not the police?'

She took a deep breath. 'Ben, I have to be rid of her. All the while she's still here she could hurt us. I've got to get rid of her.'

He stared, wide-eyed. 'Gem, what are you saying? You can't… I mean… You don't mean it, surely?'

'I can, and I do. She's got to go. And I know how I can do it.' Gemma threw back the duvet and got up, going straight to the bathroom before Ben tried to talk her out of it. It was a radical step to take, but she had to do it. As so often the previous night, thoughts of Rebecca and Sarah came to her mind. Sarah had ruined Rebecca's life, and Rebecca hadn't hesitated in doing away with Sarah, and it had worked. The parallels were too strong to ignore. It was as though she'd discovered the truth about Red Hill Hall for a reason – to help her work out how to resolve the problem of Nat.

By the time she'd finished showering she'd formulated her plan in detail. She knew she had to put it into action immediately, before she lost her nerve. She tugged on some clothes and rummaged in her jewellery box for her engagement ring, which she slipped on. She threw Ben a hasty kiss. 'See you later, love you.'

'Jeez, what's the hurry, Gem? We just got engaged; can't we have breakfast together?'

'Gotta rush. Stuff to do before work. Sorry,' she said, charging out of the door. 'We'll celebrate this evening – come to the museum at six, OK?'

'Sure, will do. Don't do anything stupid, will you?' she heard him call after her.

As she hurtled down the stairs and out of the front door she pulled out her phone and called Roger. 'Roger? Hey, it's me. Listen, I'm going to be a tiny bit late today. There's something I have to do. Sorry, I know. I'll make up the time. I wouldn't normally do this – you know that – but this is urgent. No, I'm all right. More than all right. Ben and I have got engaged again. Yeah, I know! Brilliant, isn't it? OK, see you soon. Cheers, bye.'

There was something she needed to buy before going to work.

Surprisingly, it didn't take as long as she'd anticipated. With her purchase tucked safely in her handbag she arrived at the museum only twenty minutes late, to quizzical looks from Roger. She spent the morning cataloguing, but also managed to track down Rebecca and Charles de Witt at Carlstone Hall on the 1841 and 1851 censuses. She smiled as she made a few notes about her latest findings. Rebecca's story had a happy ending, despite what had happened in the cellars of Red Hill Hall. Would her own story end happily as well? There was a chance it would, if she could pull off her plan.

She looked at the clock. It would be tight to achieve all that she needed to in her lunch hour but if she was late back she'd just have to make yet more excuses to Roger. It wasn't as though she made a habit of being late. She'd only have to do this once, then Nat would be gone for good. On the dot of twelve she grabbed her bag, jumped in her car and headed over to Nat's mother's flat. She just had to hope Nat was in. Ideally without her mother being there; if not, she'd have to find some way to get Nat alone.

But it was Nat's mother who opened the door. 'She ain't here. She won't want to see you, neither. Piss off.'

Gemma rammed her foot in the door before it was slammed in her face. 'Where is she? Tell me, Mrs Heller, then I'll leave you alone.'

'Gone for a job interview, ain't she? As a barmaid. Bet she won't get the job though. Up at that big place – hotel I think it is. Red Hall, or somefink.'

'Red Hill Hall? Right. Thanks.' Gemma spun on her heel and left, running along the walkway, down the stairs of the block of flats, and out to her car.

Fifteen minutes later she pulled into the car park of Red

Hill Hall, switched off the engine and took a deep breath. This was it. Now she just had to find Nat and confront her. Just as Rebecca had confronted Sarah. Their showdown had been in the cellars. This time it would be different, although if things went the way Gemma had planned, the outcome would be much the same and Nat would be gone for good.

If the interview was for a position working in the bar, she could reasonably assume that's where the interview would take place. She went through, and sure enough there were a few people in smart clothes sitting at a table with no drinks, looking nervous. Nat was amongst them. She was wearing ripped jeans and her hair was unwashed. Not the kind of look Don would be after for his classy hotel, Gemma thought. She caught Nat's eye and was pleased to see the colour drain from her face.

'We need to talk. Now.' She nodded towards the entrance.

'I'm waiting for a job interview,' Nat said, her voice whiny.

'You won't get it. I know the manager here.' Gemma stood back and waited for Nat to stand up.

Eventually with a dramatic sigh and roll of her eyes, Nat stood and followed Gemma out to the grounds of the hall. Gemma led her around the back to the old kitchen garden, which was secluded and not overlooked. Set into the wall of the hall was the old door, now almost completely hidden by overgrown vegetation, which led down to the cellar. It seemed a fitting place for what had to happen – just yards away from Rebecca and Sarah's showdown.

'What the fuck do you want, Gemma?' Nat spat.

'I think you know. You were at my flat last night. You tampered with the gas cooker and turned it on. I could have been killed.'

'What? I did no such thing. You've no proof,' Nat said, but her eyes dropped to the floor, and her heightening colour betrayed her.

'My downstairs neighbour saw you. You know the code to my key safe and I could tell someone had used it.'

'I rang the bell and when there was no answer I left. Sorry you had a gas leak. Could have been nasty.' Nat smirked. 'Shame it wasn't.'

'What have you got against me, Nat? All the things you've done, starting with turning Ben against me. I could go to the police!'

'What, and tell them your boyfriend dumped you and you blame me? Ha. Like they'd be interested.'

'You fraudulently used my credit card. You extorted money from my parents. You entered my flat and tried to cause a gas explosion. I have enough evidence. You'd be convicted of attempted murder and go to prison for a very long time.'

Nat laughed. 'No, you don't have enough evidence. You have nothing.'

Gemma sighed. 'Nat, just tell me why? We were friends, we did everything together and then suddenly you turn against me and try to destroy me. I don't understand. And I need to, before... before I...'

'Before you what? Try to destroy me in return? I'd like to see you try. Ha. You're weak, Gemma Rowling. Too nice to be able to hurt anyone or do anything decisive.'

Gemma pressed her lips together. Just you wait, Natalie Heller, she thought. If only the door to the cellar could be opened. She could just shove Nat down there and leave her to rot. If Don hadn't planned to renovate the cellars, Nat would never be found.

Nat smirked at her. 'But you want to know why I did all this? Isn't it obvious?'

'Tell me. Explain everything. Give me a reason not to fucking kill you!' Gemma felt her blood boiling. In her pocket she closed her fingers around the one thing she had that could remove Nat from her life for good.

'Kill me? Now you're being a bit melodramatic. Gemma, you're right, we were friends once, and it was good. But then I gradually realised that it was an uneven kind of friendship. You had everything – I had nothing. You couldn't see that, and it made me mad. You have your kind, supportive parents, whereas I have an alcoholic mother who hates me and a father who's pissed off to the other side of the world. You have your amazing job, which you love, with your eccentric but lovable boss. I have – no, *had* – a shit job I hate with a bitch of a boss. You have your pretty little flat, rising in value, with an easily affordable mortgage, and I have – *had* – a grotty rented place with mould in the bathroom. Then I got chucked out of that.' Nat took a deep shuddering breath. 'To top it all, you had a lovely fiancé and the prospect of a dream wedding ahead, and a cottage with roses round the door and a clutch of cute children. I have no prospects ahead of me. You had it all.'

'You were jealous?' Was that really all that was behind it? But then, jealousy could be a powerful force. Sarah had tried to destroy Rebecca's life due to jealousy as well.

Nat rolled her eyes. 'That makes it sound as though we're kids, and you've got the better Barbie doll. It's a bit more than that. You have everything. You probably felt sorry for me – poor little Nat with her shit life. Let's take her out, once in a while, show her how good life can be if you're one of the lucky ones. You rubbed my nose in it, all the time. Look what I've got, more than you, Nat, but I'll condescend to share just a tiny bit with you. Not too much, just enough so you can see what you could have had, who you could have been. Well screw you, Gemma Rowling. I just tried to take away a bit of your luck, to even out the cosmos a bit. Show you what life's like when luck is not on your side. That's all.' She folded her arms and glared defiantly at Gemma.

Had she done that? Had she been condescending? Rubbed Nat's nose in her own good fortune? Gemma's mind frantically went back over the years, looking for evidence. No. She hadn't. They'd been equals. They'd shared everything. They'd been *friends*, Goddammit!

She glared back at Nat. 'You went too far, messing with my gas cooker. Ben was with me and you could have killed us both if there'd been an explosion.'

Nat's eyes widened and she gasped. 'Ben was with you?'

Gemma nodded, and flashed her left hand at Nat. 'We're back together. He proposed again this morning, and *this* time you won't get in our way.'

'He could have been mine. If I'd met him first. It was only luck that he met you first and asked you out, not me.'

Gemma shook her head. 'You're deluded, Nat.'

'Can't believe that he's gone back to you. He could have been hurt. I wouldn't have wanted to hurt *him*.' Tears were streaming down Nat's face. Good, Gemma thought. She's finally beginning to realise what she's done.

'I'm not going to let you hurt either of us again,' she said quietly. 'I want you out of my life, for good.'

'How are you going to do that? Police won't listen to you, and you know it, for all your threats. Your so-called evidence won't stack up. I'll have explanations for everything. And you're too soft to try to hurt me.'

'There are other ways.' This was it. The moment from which there'd be no return. Gemma took her hand out of her pocket, pulling out her purchase from that morning that she'd been clutching while they talked. Nat frowned in confusion as she passed it to her. 'Here. Take this.'

Nat opened her mouth as if to speak, but took the envelope and opened it. Her eyes widened as she saw the contents. 'What's this? I don't understand…'

'It's what it looks like. A plane ticket, in your name, to Sydney, Australia. That's where your dad lives, isn't it?'

'It's one way,' Nat whispered.

'Yes. You go, stay with your dad till you get yourself established. Find a job. Your dad's Australian so you can get Australian citizenship easily enough. You make yourself a new life out there. You never come back here or contact me or Ben again. Never.' Gemma held Nat's gaze. 'This is your chance, Nat. You always said you'd move to Australia if you could afford to go. Now you can go. I'll even pay off your fucking debts as well. I just want you gone, out of my life for good.'

'What if I don't go?' Nat's voice was shaky.

'Then I definitely go to the police. Your fingerprints will be all over the flat and the key safe. Along with my neighbour's evidence, the letter you wrote to my parents and the credit card bill, it'll be enough. Take the flight. It's booked for tomorrow so you've just got time to contact your dad and pack.'

Nat was silent, her gaze alternating between Gemma and the ticket. Gemma watched her carefully.

'You'll pay off my debts as well?'

'If it'll get rid of you, yes.'

'Looks like I haven't much choice, then. I'd better go and pack. I'll post you the details of my debts.' Nat turned away, then said, over her shoulder: 'I didn't intend to hurt you. The gas thing,

316

I mean. It was… stupid.' Then she strode off across the gardens towards the car park, her head held high, the ticket in her hand.

Gemma watched her go. She hadn't expected any thanks for the tickets, and those last, unexpected words were the nearest she'd get to an apology. She committed the sight of Nat walking away from her, denim jacket flapping open in the summer breeze, a hand pushing her hair away from her face, to memory.

Just before Nat reached the car park she turned and stood for a moment, gazing back towards Gemma, as though she'd wanted one last look at her friend. Gemma watched, blinking back tears, as Nat raised a hand in a gesture that could have meant goodbye, or thank you, or perhaps even sorry.

It would be the last time she saw her oldest friend; Gemma knew that. She wiped away a tear with the back of her hand. This was what she wanted – no more Nat. But she'd given her a chance to start again. It was up to Nat, now.

***

When Nat was out of sight Gemma went around the hall and back into the bar. She needed a few minutes, and possibly a stiff drink, before going back to work. There were still a few interviewees waiting their turn, but not as many. As she ordered a small white wine, Don entered the bar, shaking the hand of the last person he'd interviewed.

'Gemma! What brings you here? Not after a job, are you?'

She laughed. 'Already got two, thanks. I was, erm, meeting someone. But hey, now I've bumped into you, fancy coming into town for a drink with Ben and me this evening? At the Men At Arms. We're celebrating.'

'Sure, I'd love to. But, erm, my other half's arriving later this afternoon.'

It was news to Gemma that he had a partner. 'No worries, bring her as well if you want.'

'Ahem. Him. Not her. Peter's been contracting in the States for the last six months, but he comes back today.' Don looked excited and nervous. Gemma supposed it was a long time to be apart.

'Ah, right. Well, I guess he's not going to want to go out on his first night back. Don't worry – we can catch up another time.'

'No, he'd like to come, I'm sure, if you don't mind. And anyway, I'd love you to tell him all about your research about this place. I kind of bought it for him, in a way...'

'How romantic, you old softie!' She laughed and he blushed.

'See you later then. About seven?'

'Great!' She gave him a thumbs up and left him to his interviewing, taking her drink to a small table outside, on a terrace overlooking the parkland. She smiled to herself. It had been difficult, but the showdown with Nat had gone the way she wanted it to. Nat would take that flight to Sydney and be out of her life very soon. Had Rebecca sat here on the same terrace, after disposing of Sarah? Had she felt euphoric, or regretful? Or terrified she'd be found out? Thank goodness there had been a better way to be shot of Nat!

***

Thirty minutes later she was back at the museum. She checked her watch. Just five minutes over her allotted lunch hour. 'Sorry, Roger. I'll make it up.'

'No problem, Gemma,' he replied.

She smiled. 'Will you come for a drink with me and Ben this evening? At the Men At Arms, to celebrate our re-engagement?'

To her astonishment he blushed. 'Erm, yes. I would like that. But would you mind if I, erm, if I brought someone else along as well?'

'Not at all! The more the merrier, I say. Who is it?'

'Erm, a lady friend. Called Bryony.' He was red to his hairline now.

'A date?' She hoped so. Another new person to meet this evening!

'Erm, I suppose so. Right then, Men At Arms this evening. Back to work, now. Ahem.' He straightened his tie, which hadn't needed straightening, and left her to her work. Her first task was to call Ben.

'Nat has decided to emigrate. She leaves tomorrow. For Australia,' she said.

'Blimey! That was a bit sudden. Was that your doing?' he replied.

'Shall we say, I persuaded her to go?'

'Persuaded? I dread to think how… but you don't need to tell me if you don't want to. Well, that's a result. Still think we should have gone to the police.'

'We don't need to, now. We can put it all behind us.'

She spent the afternoon typing up a display board to go alongside the ruby pistols in a new exhibit, as per her proposal to Roger. Time passed quickly and soon it was time to shut down her laptop. Roger closed the museum and as they left, Ben was waiting outside. So was another woman – a studious looking redhead in a lacy cardigan. Roger blushed furiously and introduced her as Bryony. Gemma felt sure she'd seen her somewhere before – yes, she'd come to the museum and asked Roger about the exhibits. That must have been the start of the romance. There was someone for everyone, out there. Gemma surprised herself by finding herself hoping Nat would find some Australian hunk – a gentle giant, perhaps, tanned and muscled, someone who would adore Nat and help ground her.

Anna and Jake arrived at the pub soon after, invited by Ben. And Don wasn't far behind, accompanied by a tall, fair-haired man who was every bit as good-looking as Don himself. Don introduced him as Peter, and Gemma introduced everyone else, while Ben went to the bar and bought a couple of bottles of champagne.

'We're celebrating,' she said to everyone. 'Ben and I got engaged again. And this time it'll last.'

'Woohoo, I'm so pleased!' said Anna, reaching over the table to give Gemma a hug and a kiss. 'We'll get to be sisters after all! So my stupid little brother came to his senses. Thank goodness for that!'

'Great news, Gemma!' said Don. 'I hope it means you'll still have time to write up the history of Red Hill Hall, though. I mean, you began it as a way to take your mind off things, but now you've a wedding to plan…'

Gemma laughed. 'Don't worry. I'll keep going, of course I will. It's far too fascinating to put aside.'

'I need that history,' Don continued, with a sideways glance at Peter. 'You see, you're not the only one getting married. Peter and I plan to, soon. At Red Hill Hall, of course.'

'I asked him to find a suitable wedding venue for us while I was away,' Peter said. 'Didn't mean for him to buy one outright. Hiring is good enough for most people!'

'I liked it so much I bought the company,' drawled Don in a parody of the old Remington adverts. 'But there's another reason I bought Red Hill Hall and not any of the other hotels that were up for sale.'

'Go on,' said Gemma. She had always thought there was some deeper reason why Don was so keen to know the hall's history.

'Peter's researched his family tree,' Don said. 'I should tell you – his surname is de Witt.'

Gemma gasped. So did Ben. Bryony, Anna and Jake looked confused, and Roger frowned as though trying to recall the details of Gemma's research.

Peter grinned. 'I've gone as far back as the early 1800s, and I know my four-greats grandmother was born at Red Hill Hall.'

'You must be descended from Rebecca and Charles, then?' Gemma couldn't believe it. Here was a living, breathing descendant of the people she'd spent the last few weeks researching.

'Yep, I certainly am!'

'OK, enough, enough,' said Anna, holding up her hands. 'Sorry to be rude, but what on earth are you all talking about? Who are Rebecca and Charles? And what's it all got to do with Gemma and Red Hill Hall?'

Gemma laughed, and told them the story, from finding the ruby pistols in the museum storeroom right through to what she'd found out by reading through the letters and Sarah's diary.

'Did you ever find out who shot those girls?' Roger asked.

'Sort of. I have a theory.' This was slightly awkward, now that she was sitting opposite Rebecca's descendent. How do you break the news to someone that their ancestor probably killed someone? But Peter, Don and the rest of them were waiting expectantly, so she had to tell them what she'd worked out to be the only possible explanation, playing up the idea that Rebecca almost certainly shot at Sarah in self-defence.

'Wow. What a story. I like that my ancestor stood up for herself in the end. If she hadn't, I wouldn't be here now,' Peter said.

'And the latest news is that I tracked down Rebecca and Charles in a couple of censuses. They were living at Carlstone Hall in Leicestershire by then. I expect too many bad things had happened at Red Hill Hall for them to want to stay there.'

'Good that they had a happy ending, after all that went on,' Anna said.

'Yes. They had five children, in all, including two sons – Peter must be descended from one of them. But their first child was a girl, and you know what? They called her Sarah.'

'Aw! As though Rebecca had somehow forgiven Sarah for everything she'd done,' said Don. 'And if you're right about the shooting, perhaps it showed she regretted it.'

'Perhaps. I guess we'll never know,' Gemma said. 'But I like to think she was happy, in the end, even if she did mourn the loss of her sister.' She picked up her glass. 'Well, here's to happy endings. Cheers!' She caught Ben's eye. He was the only one who knew she was not just talking about Rebecca's happy ending.

She looked around the table at her friends. All there except Nat. She pulled out her phone and on an impulse, sent Nat a brief text. 'Enjoy your flight. Best wishes. Miss you xx.'

And then she deleted Nat's contact details from her phone.

ACKNOWLEDGEMENTS

My thanks are due as always to my editor Victoria Oundjian and everyone else at Carina, for their advice, support, superb editing and wonderful cover designs.

Thanks also to my writing buddies – the other Carina authors, the Write Women and my friends in the Romantic Novelists Association. Writing is a lonely activity, and the online chats and occasional meet-ups are what keep me going.

My sons, once again, helped me out with this book. Fionn McGurl gave me valuable feedback as my beta-reader, and Connor McGurl acted as a sounding-board and helped me work out some tricky plot twists. My heartfelt thanks to both of them.

Thanks to Della Galton, whose writing classes I attended for many years. This novel grew from a prologue I wrote for one of her end-of-term competitions.

And finally, thanks to my husband Ignatius McGurl who was so enthusiastic about that prologue that it spurred me on to complete the entire novel.

Dear Reader,

Thank you so much for taking the time to read this book – we hope you enjoyed it! If you did, we'd be so appreciative if you left a review.

Here at HQ Digital we are dedicated to publishing fiction that will keep you turning the pages into the early hours. We publish a variety of genres, from heartwarming romance, to thrilling crime and sweeping historical fiction.

To find out more about our books, enter competitions and discover exclusive content, please join our community of readers by following us at:

@HQDigitalUK

facebook.com/HQDigitalUK

Are you a budding writer? We're also looking for authors to join the HQ Digital family! Please submit your manuscript to:

HQDigital@harpercollins.co.uk.

Hope to hear from you soon!

If you loved *The Daughters of Red Hill Hall*, turn the page for an exclusive extract from Kathleen McGurl's *The Pearl Locket*.

CHAPTER ONE

July – August 2014

'So, this is it,' Ali said, gazing up at the house. 'It's smaller than I remember. But I was just a child when I was last here.' She had only vague memories of being here before – muddled images of an imposing, double fronted art-deco-style house, with bay windows, a large garden and, best of all, the beach just a couple of minutes' walk away. It had been her spinster great-aunt's house, and the childless Betty had left it to Ali in her will.

'Smaller?' said her husband, Pete. 'It's huge! Well, compared with everywhere else we've ever lived.'

Ali nodded. She couldn't argue with that. But the size didn't matter, as she was going to put the house on the market immediately. They had no intention of living in it. 'I suppose we should have a look round inside, now that we're here.'

'Well, that *was* the point of the visit,' Pete said, smiling. He took Ali's hand and led her to the front door. She was grateful for the gesture of support. It was strange being here. Although the house now belonged to her, it didn't feel like it did. She'd never owned a house before; they'd always rented. She felt like an intruder. The front door was stiff – Betty had spent the last couple of years of her life in a nursing home, and apparently very few people had entered the house in that time. A pile of junk mail lay on the doormat. Ali gathered it up and placed it on a dusty sideboard in the hallway. She glanced around.

'What a state. I guess we'll have to clear everything out before we can sell it. What'll we do with all the furniture? I suppose we might want to keep a few pieces but not much.' She opened a drawer in the sideboard. It was full of pens, coins, elastic bands, buttons, old receipts and other odds and ends. 'And we'll have to sort all the contents out as well. Gran might want to keep a few things. It's going to be a huge job.'

Pete had peeked into a room on the left – the sitting room as far as Ali recalled – and was now crossing to the room on the right, the dining room. He turned back to Ali with shining eyes. 'Fantastic rooms, those two. Great proportions. They'd look amazing if they were done up. Come and see the kitchen.' He pulled her to the back of the house where they entered a large but very dated kitchen. Probably last fitted out some time back in the sixties, Ali thought, wrinkling her nose at the musty, unlived-in smell. 'Imagine it, Ali, with a run of units along that wall, an island there, an American-style fridge-freezer there, granite worktops and Shaker-style cupboard doors. This house could really be something special.'

It could; she could see that. Someone else with money and the time and energy for an awful lot of DIY would have a lot of fun with this house. She just wanted her hands on the money they'd get from selling it. With Pete's redundancy money fast running out and their landlord about to put up the rent, they could certainly do with it. She was already working full time, and as yet Pete had had no luck finding another job since Harrison's had laid him off.

'Let's go upstairs,' Pete said, again reaching for her hand. She followed him up. The stairs turned on a half landing, a grand newel post supporting the oak-panelled banisters. There was a cold draught as they turned the corner. Ali shivered. 'There's a crack in that window,' Pete said, nodding at the bowed and leaded window on the half landing.

Upstairs were four double bedrooms, a box room and a bathroom. As a child Ali had never been up here. She'd only ever paid a few duty visits to her great-aunt, with her father, so many years ago.

As they gazed out of the front bedroom window, from where you could just about get a glimpse of the sea, Pete turned to Ali. 'What if,' he said, with a glint in his eye, 'we didn't sell up? What if we cleared it out, then moved in?'

'Pete, it's in a horrible state! And we need the money from the sale. You know we do.'

'We could use the rest of my redundancy money to do it up. And if we didn't have to pay rent, we could easily live off your salary for a while. Think about it, Ali! If this place was modernised and redecorated, it'd be worth twice as much. Then we could sell it, if we still needed the money, and buy somewhere smaller. But with luck I'd get a job then, and we could just stay here.'

Ali opened and closed her mouth a few times. So many thoughts were racing around her head she didn't know which one to articulate first. 'But, Pete, the risk! What if the property market goes downhill and we can't sell it? What if we run out of money before we've finished doing it? What if you get offered a job but it's away from here and we need to move to another town?'

Pete smiled at her and shook his head. 'Don't just look at the negatives. There are loads of positives. The kids would love this house. Ryan could kick a football around in that garden. And look how close we are to the beach – Kelly would adore that! But at least you didn't say no. Does that mean you'll consider it?'

Ali sat down on the bed. It had a pink candlewick bedspread neatly placed across it. A puff of dust rose up around her and she flapped it away. 'The safe option is to sell. Some property developer would probably snap it up quickly, at the right price. And then we could buy a smaller, cheaper house, perhaps a little further from the sea. We'd be rent and mortgage free, and wouldn't have a big mess of a house to do up. And we'd have a big pot of money in the bank to add to what's left of your redundancy. Then you could concentrate on finding another job.'

'You're right.' Pete sat down beside her and put an arm around her shoulder. Ali was surprised he was giving in so quickly. Usually once he had an idea in his head he'd keep at it, trying endless different angles, until she either gave in and agreed or threatened to cut up his prize Munster Rugby shirt signed by the entire team of 2008 if he mentioned it even one more time. 'That would indeed be the safe option. And the boring option. Ali, you only live once! This would be a fabulous house to live in, even if it's only for a year or two while we do it up. And we could make a fortune on it. If we sell it as it is, we'd barely have enough to buy another place big enough for the four of us. There'd certainly be none left over. But if we do it up and *then* sell it, we could buy a smaller place and have stacks of money spare for holidays or cars or a new handbag for you or whatever you'd want. Or –' he looked sideways at her '– to help finance the kids through university.'

Ali smiled wryly. He always knew which buttons to press. The thought that they might not be able to help first Kelly and then Ryan with their university living expenses had always tormented her, especially since Pete had been made redundant. They'd never had enough to be able to put some by for that purpose, but she was determined that the kids would go to university if they wanted to. Even if she had to ask her parents, who'd retired to Spain, for financial help. Great-aunt Betty's will had meant they'd be financially secure, buying a house and living off Ali's salary until Pete found a job. But now, this plan meant that in a year or two there could be a lot more money on top. Did they dare take the risk? Another thought struck her. 'But Pete, who'd do the work? This house would need so much doing and we'd be living in a building site for months.'

'I'd do it. Except for the electrics – I'd get a professional in for that. But I'm quite handy, you know. And we could go room by room, so some of it is liveable while we do up other rooms. I'd do some of it, the really disruptive stuff like the kitchen, before we move in. We've got to give a month's notice to the landlord anyway. And as probate's complete and this house is yours already, there's no reason I can't start tomorrow. If you agree, of course. It's your house...'

He was giving her that puppy-dog look, the one that always made her melt. Ali still had misgivings about the project but there was some sense in what he said, and maybe it would work out. 'I suppose – it's not as if the decision is irreversible – we could give it a go. We could always put it on the market later if things changed or the work was too hard for you.'

Pete flung his arms around her and kissed her. 'I love you, Mrs Bradshaw! The work won't be too hard for me; I'm a man not a mouse! Right then, I'll get started today. First things first, I'll need to hire a skip. Can you go through and mark all the things you want to keep? Wow, the kids are going to be so excited when they hear we're moving in!'

***

'I can't believe how unlucky we are with the weather today,' shouted Ali to Pete, over the noise of the lashing rain, raging wind and swearing removal men. She pushed a strand of wet hair out of her eyes and stood aside to let two men past her into the house, carrying sodden boxes. Of all the days to get a huge summer storm, why did it have to happen on their moving day? It was just a month after they'd visited the house for the first time.

Things had started well that morning. The van had arrived on time and everything was loaded into it within four hours. The keys had been handed back to the landlord. Both the family and the removal men had gone for lunch then met outside number nine at three p.m. to unload. But as soon as the van had pulled up outside it had begun to rain, and now it was coming down in sheets.

'Bugger!' The sound of smashing glass and swearing sent Ali running out to the back of the van. One of the removal men was standing amid a pile of broken wine bottles, with a wet bottomless cardboard box in his hands.

'Er, sorry love, the box got wet and the bottom just gave way. Saved one. Look.' The man held out one bottle, which had stayed in the box. Ali took it and sighed. There goes our wine cellar, she thought. At least there was one left intact to celebrate their move later this evening.

'Don't worry; it wasn't your fault. I'll find a broom and clear this lot up.' She went inside in search of the cleaning equipment. Maybe it was still on the van, but she thought she'd seen someone come in with an armful of mops and buckets earlier.

Inside, Pete was shifting boxes around in the newly fitted

kitchen to make way for those yet to be unloaded from the van. 'Who'd have thought we had this much stuff?' he said. 'The rented house was half the size of this one, but I'm wondering where on earth we're going to put everything.'

'It'll be OK when we unpack. Seen the broom?'

'Downstairs loo.'

'What's it doing in there?'

'Removal bloke thought it was an under-stairs cupboard and just dumped it and a pile of other stuff in there. We'll sort it later, I thought.'

Ali shrugged and went to collect the broom. Passing the bottom of the stairs she came across seventeen-year-old Kelly, who was sitting on the third step, phone in hand, composing a text.

'Kelly, love, you'll be in the way there. Can't you go up and start organising your bedroom?'

'Yeah, Mum. Will do. Just updating Matt on progress. Is it cool if he comes round tomorrow? He said he'd help sort out my new room.'

Ali nodded. She liked her daughter's boyfriend. He was a pleasant, steady lad and a good influence on Kelly. 'Of course he can come. But you'll have to do some of the sorting out tonight, or you'll be sleeping amongst piles of boxes.'

Two men pushed past carrying a chest of drawers destined for thirteen-year-old Ryan's room. Ali grimaced as she saw how the rain had caused the veneer to lift off around the front edge. Well, it was only a cheap thing. They'd probably have to buy some better furniture more in keeping with the house. She turned back to Kelly. 'Come on. Out of the way. Go up and make a start.'

Kelly stood up and slipped her phone into her jeans pocket. 'OK. It's such a nightmare up there, though. I don't know where to start.'

'You and me both, love,' Ali said. It was exciting moving into a house they owned, but daunting as well. And she still had occasional misgivings about whether it had been the right thing to do. She shooed the thoughts out of her mind and went back outside into the rain with the broom.

***

Eventually, after hours of chaos, the removal men left, and the family were sitting in the living room on a jumble of sofas, chairs and boxes, eating take-away pizza. Ali had managed to find the box containing the wine glasses, and was opening the only unbroken bottle of wine.

'Can I have some, Mum?' Kelly asked.

'Why not? We're celebrating,' Ali said, smiling, as she poured out three glasses.

Ryan made a face. 'Ugh, wine's disgusting.'

'None for you, anyway,' said Pete. 'You stick to your lemonade.'

'Well, cheers, family,' said Ali, raising her glass. 'Here's to our new home. I hope we're going to be really happy here. It's twice the size of our old house, close to the beach, nearer Ryan's school, nearer the station for Kelly to get to college, and renovating it will give your dad something to do until he finds a new job. Everyone's a winner!'

'Cheers!' said Pete, clinking his glass against the others. 'Which room shall I decorate next?'

'Sitting room,' said Ali. 'So we have somewhere nice to bring guests into. I can't bear this worn out, stained carpet.'

'Mine,' said Ryan. 'I love how big my room is but I hate that flowery wallpaper.'

'Well my wallpaper is already peeling off, around the sink in the corner,' said Kelly. 'Also I'll be moving out in another year and a half when I go to uni. So it makes sense to do mine first so I get a chance to enjoy it.'

Pete laughed. 'Looks like I'm going to be a busy boy, doesn't it? Well, you can all chip in and help me get it all done.'

Ali smiled. She wouldn't be chipping in to help. She was the breadwinner in the family at the moment, and the chief cook. It would be exciting as Pete worked his way through the house, renovating each room. He'd done a great job on the kitchen, though it wasn't completely finished yet. He'd also managed to get an electrician to do most of the rewiring before they moved in, but they needed a new central heating system and a new bathroom as well as all the general decorating. They'd done the figures and it looked as though the remains of the redundancy money would just about cover the work. It'd be tight, but if they budgeted carefully, and if Pete got a new job quickly after the work on the house was done, they'd manage.

After everyone had finished their pizzas and the boxes had been put out in the recycling bin, Kelly and Ryan went upstairs to sort out their rooms or – more likely, Ali thought – text their mates. She and Pete stayed in the living room, finishing the bottle of wine. Pete was on the sofa in the middle of the room, and Ali went to join him, curling up beside him. Outside the rain was still lashing down.

'Once we're sorted, we'll have to get that chimney swept so we can have a real fire in the winter,' Pete said.

'Mmm, that'd be nice,' Ali replied. She could picture the room, decorated, with new curtains and a blazing fire in the grate. It was a big room but well proportioned and she was sure she could make it look cosy. 'The kids seem happy with the move. I'm glad about that. You never quite know how they'll react.'

'What's not to like, here? It's not as though we've taken them away from their friends or schools or anything. And with the beach just down the end of the road, they'll have a fabulous time all summer. You'll be forever sweeping up sand and washing beach towels, I bet.'

Ali laughed. 'They can sweep up their own sand. Anyway, tomorrow shall we call on our new neighbours and introduce ourselves?'

'Good idea.' Pete kissed the top of her head. 'And when do you want to bring your gran round? It'll be quite a surprise for her that we've moved here, after you'd told her we were going to sell it.'

'Next weekend, I think, once we've got everything straightened out. I think she'll be delighted we've moved in and are bringing the house back to life again. It's been empty so long. This is where she grew up, of course.'

'She must have such happy memories of living here,' Pete said. 'Shame Margaret didn't get on with Betty in her later years.'

'I'm not sure she ever got on very well with her,' Ali replied.

CHAPTER TWO

January 1944

There was no jam for tea. No cake, either. Just plain bread and margarine, and one rich tea biscuit each. Joan craved something sweet, anything sweet. She poured herself a cup of tea, dipped her teaspoon in the sugar bowl and tried to heap it up as much as possible without being noticed.

'Put that sugar back at once! No more than a quarter teaspoon per cup of tea. You know the family rules.' Father glared at her from the other end of the table. Joan shook the spoon so that most of the sugar fell back into the bowl, and meekly stirred in the remaining quarter. She tasted her tea and grimaced. Her sister Mags, who was sitting next to her, winked in sympathy, and whispered, 'You're sweet enough already.' They were sitting in the dining room, the second-best lace tablecloth spread over the table. War or no war, Father insisted on sticking to traditions and doing things 'properly', as he put it. They were firmly in the middle class, and he refused to let standards slip. Joan thought it all a complete waste of time and effort. Why couldn't they just eat their tea at the kitchen table? So much less fuss and work!

'Mother, when do you think rationing will end?' she asked. Her mother smiled weakly and looked at Father. Just like Mother. She wouldn't dare answer a question like that herself. She would always defer to the head of the household. That was why Joan had directed the question to her mother – just to stir things up a bit.

'Not until this war's over. We all have to put up with it until then, so stop making such a fuss. You're not a baby any more.' Father gave her a stern look, and tapped the side of his cup with his teaspoon. Joan sighed as her mother immediately leapt into action, pouring her husband a second cup of tea. Why was she such a doormat? If Joan ever married she liked to think she and her husband would be on a much more equal footing than her parents were.

'Would you like more bread and margarine, Father?' asked her other sister Elizabeth, pushing the serving plate towards his end of the table.

'Thank you, Betty,' he said. Stuck up Elizabeth, sucking up to Father as always, thought Joan. Another doormat. Well, it was now or never. She knew what the answer would be, but she had to ask anyway. Nothing ventured, nothing gained, as Mags would say.

'Father, may I ask a question?'

'Not if it's anything more about rationing, child.'

'No, it's something else. The thing is, there is a dance on at the Pavilion tomorrow evening, to celebrate the New Year, and I would rather like to go.'

Father put down his teacup and stared at her over the top of his horn-rimmed spectacles. Joan forced herself to keep her eyes on his. If she looked away she'd lose her nerve.

'You? But you're far too young to be attending dances. You're only sixteen.'

'I had my birthday yesterday. I'm seventeen, Father.'

'Don't contradict me! You're too young. I forbid you to go.'

'But Father, Elizabeth and Margaret went to their first dances when they were seventeen.'

'Are you arguing with me? I've said no, and that's that.'

'Mother, Mags is going and she said she'd look after me. Please, may I?' What was the point? Her mother just shook her head gently and looked again at Father. Of course she would never go against anything he said.

'Mother agrees with me. You are not to go. And Margaret, you will be home by ten o'clock. There's an end to it.' He picked up his newspaper and flicked it open, signifying that the topic was closed.

'Please may I leave the table?' Joan asked. Not waiting for an answer, she pushed her chair back and began gathering up plates and cups for washing up. Mags quickly joined her, and the two girls took the dirty crockery through to the kitchen.

'It's so unfair. *Why* can't I go? He's always stricter with me than he ever was with you or Betty.' Joan turned the tap on full blast, spraying water everywhere.

'Watch out, you're making me wet!' yelped Mags, as she jumped out of the way, brushing droplets off her skirt and blouse. Joan turned off the tap and clattered some plates into the sink. 'And now you're going to chip those plates. Let me do it. You're too cross.'

Joan stood aside and let Mags take her place. Mags was right; she was cross.

'Elizabeth's not going, is she?' she asked.

'No. She's going to the cinema to see some worthy French

subtitled film. So I'm going to the dance on my own. But Mary and Noreen will be there, and some of the other girls from the WVS, so I won't be alone.'

Joan picked a plate from the draining board and began wiping it roughly with a tea towel. She liked Mary and Noreen. It would be such fun attending a proper, grown-up dance with them and Mags.

'I wish I could go. I feel like Cinderella, having to stay home while my sisters go out and enjoy themselves.'

Mags flicked soapsuds at her. 'Are you calling me an ugly sister, Joanie?'

'No.' Joan giggled. 'Betty's the ugly one.'

'Just think,' said Mags, 'if there was any way you could come to the dance, you might just meet your own Prince Charming.'

Both girls giggled uncontrollably at this, until Mother appeared at the kitchen door and told them to shush. They were annoying Father.

***

Washing up completed, they went upstairs to Joan's bedroom. It was only four-thirty but already dark, and time to close the blackout curtains. Although their coastal town hadn't suffered many air raids, unlike London, it had still had its fair share. Besides, Joan knew Father would be angry if they didn't draw the blackout blinds before putting on any lights. And she'd annoyed him enough already for one day.

'Mags,' she said, as they flopped down onto Joan's bed, 'do you think I could sneak out and go to the dance? Without the parents finding out?'

'How on earth could you do that? Father would expect you to be downstairs after supper, to listen to the news on the wireless.'

'What if he thought I was out but somewhere else? Maybe, I don't know, volunteering at the WVS? The soup kitchen's open tomorrow night isn't it? I could say I'm working there…'

'Ooh, Joanie, there's an idea! But what if he checked up on you?'

'He wouldn't check. Well, at most he might ask Noreen or Mary. Do you think they would cover for me?' Lie for me, Joan thought. It was probably a bit much to ask, but she knew the other girls sympathised with her and Mags over their draconian father.

'I'm sure they would. You know, I think that's a plan! I'll see Noreen this evening anyway – I'm doing a shift at the soup kitchen from six till eight. I'll get her to put your name down on the rota. You were about to start volunteering anyway, weren't you? He agreed to you doing it after Christmas, and we're already into the New Year. Won't he be suspicious though – first you ask if you can go to the dance, then when he says no, you announce you're starting at the WVS?'

'I'll mention the WVS tomorrow at teatime. He'll have forgotten I asked about the dance by then. You know he never takes any real interest in what you or I do. Not like Elizabeth. He'll be asking her about every detail of the film she's going to.' Joan clapped her hands with excitement. 'Now then, what shall I wear?'

'Well, you can't pretend you're going to the WVS if you're in a party frock,' Mags pointed out. 'Unless you put your coat on over it, and don't let him see what you've got on underneath. And no lipstick, until you've left the house. Tell you what, I'll ask Noreen if we can meet up at her house and you could get ready there.'

'Perfect! And shall I wear my blue frock? It's my newest.'

'You look lovely in that one. I'll help you do your hair at Noreen's,' said Mags.

Joan hugged her. 'You're definitely not an ugly sister. More like a Fairy Godmother, saying, "Joanie, you *shall* go to the ball!" '

'But I wouldn't recommend wearing glass slippers. It's a long walk home.'

Both girls dissolved into giggles at this, and continued laughing until Elizabeth came into the room.

'What's so funny? Father's really cross at you both again. He says if you can't stop your silly giggling you'll have no supper. And it's rabbit stew with dumplings tonight. I made it.'

'All right, we'll stop laughing. No fun allowed in this house. We should have remembered,' said Mags. Joan stifled more giggles.

'What was so funny anyway?' asked Elizabeth again. 'You two always leave me out of things. It's not fair.'

'It's only silly little girl jokes,' Joan said. 'You're too grown-up to find them funny. Mags has almost grown out of them, too.'

'Hmm, well. I'll leave you to it, then. But don't annoy Father any further. That would be my grown-up advice.' Elizabeth turned on her heel and left the room.

'I hate rabbit stew,' said Mags.

Joan had to stuff a pillow in her mouth to stop herself guffawing aloud at that comment. She felt so happy. She was going to the dance, and no one could stop her!

Everything went according to plan. At teatime on the day of the dance Joan announced Noreen had put her on the WVS soup kitchen rota, and that she would be starting that evening. Father just grunted in reply from behind his newspaper. Mother opened her mouth as if to make some comment, but after a glance at Father presumably thought better of it. Elizabeth appeared not to have heard, and chattered happily about the film she was going to see with her friend from work.

After supper, Mags and Joan washed up quickly then ran upstairs to get ready. They left the house separately, and reconvened at the corner of the street before going together to Noreen's, and then on to the Pavilion. Joan was buzzing with excitement. Every time they saw someone else heading the same way she couldn't help herself asking the older girls whether they knew the person, whether they were going to the dance as well.

It was a long cold walk along the seafront to the Pavilion and Joan giggled to herself as she found herself being thankful she hadn't worn glass slippers. At last they arrived and went quickly inside out of the biting wind. Joan gazed around in awe as she handed her coat to the cloakroom attendant. There may be a war on but the Pavilion was glittering. The Christmas decorations were still up, as it was not yet Twelfth Night. Tinsel and baubles hung from the ceiling, and boughs of holly garlanded the hall above head height. Joan followed Mags to the bar and bought herself a lemonade. Young men in various uniforms stood in groups, trying to catch the eye of any girl who passed.

Mags and Noreen found their friend Mary, who immediately began to regale them with a long, funny story about her last WVS shift. Joan listened at first, but soon found her attention wandering. The band had started up – a ten-piece swing band playing Glenn Miller's hits. She couldn't help but jiggle around to the music; she was most definitely 'in the mood'. There was a group of Canadian airmen standing across the room, their loud voices and raucous laughter at times almost drowning out the music. All of them were tall and handsome. One, especially, was very good-looking – with sandy hair, broad shoulders and a mischievous look in his eyes. Joan wondered whether she would manage to catch the eye of any of them. She supposed not. After all she was probably too young, and not pretty enough for them. But just imagine, if one of them asked her to dance, how exciting that would be!

As couples began to take to the dance floor, Joan noticed a shy-looking young man in civilian clothing watching her. He had dark, floppy hair and wore a pair of spectacles that had one broken arm, held together by tape. His jacket looked worn but clean. He raised his glass in her direction, but Joan gave him a small, non-committal smile. He was no Prince Charming, though he had a kind and gentle look about his eyes.

'Hey, beautiful, why are you standing on your own?'

Joan turned to find the sandy-haired Canadian airman beside her. This was more like it! She felt her tummy flip over as she smiled encouragingly at him. 'I was just waiting for the right person to come and sweep me off my feet,' she replied.

'And here I am,' the airman said, winking at her. He took her glass out of her hand and put it on a nearby table, then scooped her into his arms and whirled her onto the dance floor. Joan laughed and gasped, trying desperately to keep up with his lightning-fast dance steps. She couldn't believe this was happening – she was dancing with the best-looking man in the room!

'What's your name?' he asked her.

'Joan. What's yours?'

'Ah, Joan, Joan you'll make me moan,' he said, grinning. 'I'm Freddie, and always at the ready.'

She giggled, and he pulled her in tighter. She saw Mags, Noreen and Mary dancing with a group of soldiers. Mags caught her eye and raised an eyebrow. She looked as though she disapproved of Joan's dance partner. Well, it wasn't up to her, was it? Joan was enjoying herself. Freddie was handsome and funny, and seemed to really like her. She was determined to make the most of her evening out.

The music ended, and Freddie let her go. 'I'll get you some refreshments,' he said. 'Don't go away.'

A moment later he was back with an iced drink for her. She sipped it gratefully. 'What is this?'

'G and T,' he said. 'Mostly T though, so don't worry. I'm not trying to get you drunk.'

Joan had never had an alcoholic drink before. It was quite pleasant, she thought. She gulped it down.

'Nice, eh? Here, have mine as well.' Freddie handed her his own glass.

'Let's dance some more,' Joan said. 'It's such fun!'

'I've a better idea,' he said. 'We'll dance again later but for now let's find somewhere quiet where we can sit and get to know each other better. Finish that drink quickly. I know where we can go.' He took her hand and pulled her towards the cloakrooms. Joan giggled as she knocked back her drink and followed him. He pushed open a door that led into a narrow corridor with other doors leading off.

'Where are we?' she asked.

'Backstage of the theatre. There's nothing playing tonight. Come on, in here.' He opened a door and pulled her into a dressing room, flicking on the light switch. 'That's better. We can properly get to know each other now. Come here, beautiful.'

Joan looked around her at the tatty room, with its smells of greasepaint and powder. There was a worn sofa against one wall, opposite a dressing table. Freddie sat on the sofa and pulled her gently down beside him. He put an arm around her shoulders, and with his other hand, stroked her cheek.

'There, now. This is cosy, isn't it?' he said. He leaned towards her and kissed her gently.

She was being kissed! Her first time, and by such a handsome fellow! But what would Mags say? Was she being too forward? She tentatively kissed him back, and he must have taken this as encouragement because his kiss became more urgent, and his hand slid down from her face, over her neck and shoulder, and onto her breast. Suddenly he thrust her roughly back on the sofa and lay on top of her, kissing her harshly.

No, this wasn't what she wanted! She turned her head away and tried to push him off, but he was too heavy and strong.

'Stop it, Freddie, oh please stop it. Can't we go back and dance now?'

'Aw, sweetheart, I only want a kiss. That's not too much to ask, is it? My leave finishes tomorrow then I'm back to the war. You wouldn't deny a poor airman his last bit of fun, would you? Not when he's putting his life on the line for you?' He kissed her again, his mouth hard against hers, his tongue forcing its way into her mouth.

'Stop it! I shall scream!'

'Aw, no you won't. Just relax; enjoy it,' he said. 'I'm not going to hurt you.'

But he was hurting her. He was lying on top of her, his elbow digging into her ribs and his stubble scratching her cheeks as he continued to kiss her.

'Get off her, you thug! Get off! Off!' It was the boy with the broken glasses, his hair flopping over his eyes as he burst through the door, hauled Freddie off her, and landed a punch on his nose.

'Ow, you little shit. What did you do that for? Me and my girl were just getting comfortable.' Freddie clutched at his bleeding nose and spat on the floor.

'She didn't look very comfortable to me. Get out, and leave her alone.'

'Oh yeah? Who's going to make me?'

'I am. Now get out before I hit you again!' The boy squared up to Freddie. He was a little taller, but not as well built. Nevertheless there must have been something in his eyes that made Freddie think the better of taking him on, for he spat again and took a step towards the door.

'She's nothing but a tease. Maybe you'll get more out of her, mate,' he said, as he slammed the door behind him.

'Are you all right?' said the boy, extending a hand to pull Joan up from the sofa.

She nodded, stood and straightened her clothing. 'Thank you. I shouldn't have come with him.'

'I saw him pull you out of the dance hall and thought you might be in trouble. Are you sure you're all right? Can I get your friend for you?'

Mags. How would she tell her how stupid she'd been? She wouldn't. Not unless she had to. If Mags hadn't seen her leave with Freddie maybe she could get away with not saying anything.

'She's my sister. But it's all right. You've been very kind. I'll freshen up now and then go back to the dance hall. I hope that airman has gone home.'

The boy nodded. 'I hope so, too. But I'll keep an eye out, just in case.' He held the door open for her and followed her back along the corridor towards the cloakrooms. Joan ducked into the ladies room, and when she came out, he was no longer around. She felt a pang of guilt – he'd rescued her but she hadn't even asked him his name.

Want to read on? Order now!